States of Emergency

A NOVEL

Chris Knapp

THE UNNAMED PRESS
LOS ANGELES, CA

AN UNNAMED PRESS BOOK

Copyright © 2024 by Chris Knapp

Published in North America by the Unnamed Press.

www.unnamedpress.com

Unnamed Press, and the colophon, are registered trademarks of Unnamed Media LLC.

Hardcover ISBN: 978-1-961884-04-5
EBook ISBN: 978-1-961884-05-2
LCCN: 2023947199

Cover photograph by Matteus Silva, provided by Unsplash
Designed and Typeset by Jaya Nicely

Manufactured in the United States of America

Distributed by Publishers Group West

First Edition

for Lola

States of Emergency

Part 1

Summer and Fall 2015

1
Heatwave

As word spread around the city that temperatures would soon reach a hundred degrees and stay that way for most of the week, my wife and I began to fret about how the heat would affect the outcome of a medical procedure we'd undertaken precisely a week before the heat was to begin. There were no air conditioners in Paris, none that we knew of, and certainly not in our apartment, on the top floor of a building held up by wooden beams, where even moderately warm days were intolerable, and where we felt particularly exposed to the exceptional heat in store. Buildings in sepulchral, Haussmannian districts like the seventh and the sixteenth arrondissements were encased in thick layers of calcite, quarried in centuries past from the cool and dank stratum of limestone beneath the city itself, and these walls would insulate the people who lived within them from the air outside. Because as many as fifteen thousand people had died in France during a heatwave twelve years before, senior citizens nationwide would be receiving phone calls from the government daily, to make sure they were alive. The rest of Paris would be left to see to its own well-being, however we might. Ella assumed a stance of exasperation when I began to ask strangers around the city—with my pen poised over a notepad like a reporter, which she could have but didn't point out I definitively was not—how they planned to cope. At Nation, at Luxembourg and Tuileries, laborers from every corner of the world stretched out in shady patches of grass to nap. West African prostitutes on rue Saint-Denis asked respectable passersby to buy them cans of beer, a loopy, ironical provocation to pass the time. At our bus stop, an old woman I recognized was cracking a cold pack, to be worn, she explained, grinning slyly, beneath her hijab on the back of her neck. The Vietnamese bistro, which was hardly ever open anyway, remained shuttered through lunch and dinner, and Estelle and her husband were nowhere to be found. At the grocery store, the line backed up into the aisles as a group of prepubescent boys presented, spread out in their palms for the clerk to count, the change they'd collected for a six-pack of ice cream sandwiches, to be distributed outside by an exceptionally large, doughy boy of twelve or thirteen, who kept pausing to wipe sweat from behind his enormous ears. Even trying to formulate the question, Ella observed—whether the heat would affect the procedure—so it wouldn't sound stupid to a medical professional, made her feel helpless and small. That neither of us was in a position to know whether the heat would affect the procedure, I said, could be taken as evidence that we were unfit to benefit from the procedure's intended result, which is to say, unfit to have and ostensibly care for a child. Ella laughed: You stupid, she said.

We hadn't been sleeping well, and in the cool morning, with our eyes burning from fatigue, we held each other as through the open windows evidence reached us of the earliest stages of the city's coming to life—the slightly chemical smell of the industrial bakery and the slightly carnal smell of the sanitation truck, the safety noise from the forklift in the warehouse across the street, the heavy-duty rattle of pallets being loaded in and out of box trucks, our own front gate swinging open and slamming shut, the rush of water in the walls as toilets downstairs began to flush, the morning songs of birds and the shadows of birds in flight, the lifting of the curtains in the stirring breeze, and, of course, the gradual appearance of the sun in the shafts of dust that hung in the air around us—and it was a strange experience, we agreed, to feel that the limits of self were expanded in the mere anticipation of intemperate weather, of extenuating circumstances, of heat, in a word, heat and light; our sudden feeling, that is to say, that we belonged to the world outside, but at the same time, our place was here, with unbrushed teeth. You stupid, Ella said, which was shorthand for delight, because it was true that our wish to have a child had nothing to do with the way we lived our life.

Since the day of the procedure, Alexis Tsipras had thrown the entire continent into turmoil by announcing that the question of whether to accept the humiliating bailout terms presented by the European Council, the European Central Bank, and the International Monetary Fund—three discrete and outlandishly complex bureaucracies that the news media referred to collectively in Russian—would be settled by the people of Greece themselves in a few days' time. It was in fact the very moment of this announcement that Ella and I rode the train from the lab on rue Drouot to Docteur Risteau's offices at Saint-Paul with a cardboard tube that contained a glass tube the technician had advised us not to unsettle in the least way, to imagine as containing a volatile chemical agent that might at any moment combust, an image that had caused to appear on Ella's grave face a mischievous, heartbreaking grin, as if it were a rule she herself observed fastidiously never to describe sperm this way. The technician, a round, duckfooted man in his forties, had shaken our hands and wished us the best of luck; and moments later, on rue Drouot, walking past the philately shops, we'd amused ourselves by wondering whether these best wishes pertained to delivering my centrifuged sperm across the city, which he had explicitly described as a perilous undertaking, or to conceiving a child and starting a family and having a happy life, the peril of which was implicit. It was a relief to hear Ella laugh. On the train, she took over responsibility for the tube's safe passage, and held it with exaggerated care, describing in English various scenarios in which its contents could be used to cause a public disturbance. There's a power to it, she mused, walking around with all this sperm—though of course, she said, I guess you already know that. In all likelihood, I said, a lot of these nice people minding their business on the metro understood English perfectly well; it was possible that my sperm was already causing a public disturbance, because we were discussing it so loudly and in such vivid terms. Sitting across from her, our knees touching as the train swayed in the tunnel, I watched her face, which grew brighter and brighter as she filled her head with lighthearted thoughts, in order to distract herself from a mounting sense of panic that had become a general fact of life and that the procedure would renew. At length we fell silent, and her features settled from brightness into something else—into blankness, as if within herself she were conducting a calm and orderly evacuation, a drill I'd seen her practice often in the course of our marriage, and one that on this occasion became oddly connected in my mind to the announcement of the Greek vote on the Troika bailout package, which I was just then reading about on my phone, and which I came to understand only vaguely, as a further milestone in the long dissolution of human society, in the days following the procedure, during which Ella remained beyond reach, so that I wasn't exactly sure what she meant nearly a week later, on that cool morning before the heat set in, when, having called me stupid, she observed with her peculiar morning frankness that it had not always been the case that she experienced hope as dread.

■

The heat was forecasted to last seven days and to break on the first day of Ella's new cycle—the day we'd learn whether the procedure had worked or whether we'd be disappointed once again. We had spent long hours discussing contingencies for both outcomes, either of which would be complicated by the fact that at the end of the month of July we'd be moving to Charlottesville, Virginia, where I'd been offered a place in the creative writing program, with funding generous enough to cover a modest existence for us both, but with health insurance that covered only me, meaning that if she did become pregnant, we'd have to either find money for a policy that covered prenatal care, or find a way to qualify her for Medicaid, and that if she didn't become pregnant, we'd have to either put the entire process on hold for two years, until I graduated and we could move back to Paris, or organize further attempts around visits we'd make back to Paris as often as we could. Further complicating matters was the fact that our present attempt at intracervical insemination was the last the French government would pay for, and if it failed, according to Docteur Risteau, Ella might have to undergo an exploratory surgery to find out what, if anything, was wrong before the government would sign off on in vitro.

All these questions remained unresolved as the heatwave began.

There was a hushed busyness in the streets that morning, as if a long-awaited invasion might begin at any time. At Place de la Réunion, I found the boy with the enormous sweaty ears washing the tires of some-one's car, possibly to earn money for more ice cream sandwiches. In the course of a trip on the metro I'd heard the Peruvian folk tune El cóndor pasa three different times: on a zither at Saint-Lazare, on a xylophone at Châtelet, and on a nylon-stringed guitar at Nation, where I once again saw the boy with the sweaty ears, with the casual world-weariness of a much older man, toss a coin into the musician's hat as he walked past, a coincidence on top of coincidence that gave focus to the weird, childish excitement that had taken hold of me, with respect to the heat.

The Lidl by the metro station was advertising Perrier at half price, and because the line wasn't too long, I stopped and bought two cases, carrying them home on my shoulders as if I'd killed them myself. Ella put two bottles in the freezer and by the time they were cold enough to drink it was hot enough outside to strip down to our shorts. French radio murmured from Ella's computer. For a moment she fanned herself with a flattened Special K box, before deciding it was beside the point. To preserve the cooler morning air, we shuttered the skylights and covered the windows with cheap fleece blankets we'd collected over the years from Ikea and Icelandair, and in the half-dark apartment, Ella's face was lit by the glow of her laptop screen, which somehow contributed to the uncanny feeling that I was in a dream. A video on YouTube featured nine minutes of a failed attempt at in vitro fertilization, magnified ten thousand times, a nightmarish spectacle that for months I'd often found Ella watching intently, at any time of day or night, and that I could tell she was watching now by the peculiar intensity of her expression, as if it demonstrated some mistake she might learn to avoid.

The sounds of the city grew fewer, and fainter, and further between.

■

That first night, as the heat crept into the city, whatever subconscious faculty it is that keeps track of passing time broke down in both our brains, the way it will under the influence of certain drugs, so that I kept losing track of the hour or the day of the week, or found, after becoming lost in thought for what seemed like ages, that only minutes had elapsed. And likewise, the way your own name becomes strange when you repeat it aloud, I found that as I turned over in my mind the facts of my life, I felt an uncanny dissociation from the person I'd always imagined myself to be.

As the temperature continued to climb, and as our feeling of being trapped in our bodies increased, I began to understand what it was about the miserable week ahead of us that I was somehow looking forward to: that with the effort to escape our bodies, the usual considerations of daily life would fall away, and that in a way I couldn't explain, the entire experience would restore something we hadn't realized we'd lost. Heat was subjective, I kept saying, which Ella pointed out was false: Time is subjective, she said, beauty is subjective; our bodies experience heat within precise limits, it's a matter of regulation. We were, at that moment, dragging the mattress down the stairs to install on the living room floor, there was no question of sleeping on the mezzanine level, where hot air gathered in a dense cloud. On Ella's computer, France Inter continued, and for a moment I stopped what I was doing, having found myself suddenly following not only the general drift of the discussion but every word—a rare, thrilling experience of comprehension for me, something like leaping aboard a train just as the doors slide shut. Ella paused as well, and we stood listening soberly as men's voices hashed out the fate of Greece, the ethics of austerity, the chimerical notion of supranational consensus in a union founded for the purpose of trading steel and coal, and the uncertain wisdom of entrusting to the democratic process such a complex and technical decision, which so little of the population could be expected to understand. By this time it seemed safe to open the windows; beyond the permanent dusk we'd created in our apartment was the actual dusk of the world outside, an effect, it somehow made me uneasy to remember, of the planet's continued turning. For the EU to agree to restructure Greece's debt, Ella explained once I'd lost the thread and we'd resumed wrestling with the sheets, would be to admit that hundreds of billions of euros in existing loans, none of which should ever have been approved in the first place, were now beyond recovering. But meanwhile, for the Greek government to accept the Troika's terms would be to lead the nation into protracted fiscal ruin. The self-righteous tone Troika officials had taken, Ella said, switching to French now, reinforced the grotesque principle that to borrow money recklessly, whether out of optimism or desperation, was a greater sin than to lend money recklessly, irrespective of the risk incurred. Apostolos, our downstairs neighbor, had flown back to Athens just that week—hoping to accomplish what it was difficult to say, because banks were closed until further notice, and withdrawals at ATMs were limited to sixty euros per day. We lay on the newly made bed, staring up at the blank wall that faced the couch, and as we lapsed into silence, I realized that she was fuming, and that the formulation of these thoughts was an aspect of the mounting psychic pain of waiting to find out whether she was pregnant. Meantime, she went on a while later, as if no time had passed, Syrians are walking across Turkey and paddling out to Kos or across the water to Greece's Aegean shore, where the resources and infrastructure to accommodate them simply don't exist—for which privilege, she added, they pay smugglers two thousand euros per person—a sum, I remarked in awe, before I could stop myself, that would cover the minimum payments on our credit cards for nearly three months.

We were in our third year of marriage, and second year of trying, when the decision to consult a fertility specialist became unavoidable. Because to afford such in New York we'd have needed to sell the resulting firstborn anyway, we moved not only to Paris, Ella's hometown, but into a studio across the hall from the apartment where she'd grown up, and where her mother lived still, though she'd taken the occasion of the heatwave to visit friends on the coast.

It was true that a long time had passed since the first phase of our attempts to conceive, which really entailed nothing more than a gradual suspension of our attempts not to conceive: we were still living in Brooklyn when, a year or so into our marriage, Ella stopped taking her birth control, an organic development that felt like a deliberate assertion of our adulthood, our feeling of a new invincibility, a sense we shared that together we could handle whatever came our way. There followed in our intimate life a period characterized by the method of withdrawal, an exhilarating approach to birth control we'd both from a young age been taught to distrust, and then when the withdrawal method proved too effective, the rhythm method briefly entered our thinking: Ella installed an app called Cyclr on her phone, only for it to fall into disuse after just a few months, when we abandoned the pretense of avoiding the middle of her cycle and surrendered to the whims of fate. Meanwhile, during this process of gradual contraceptive de-escalation, we grew closer with every month that passed, as the stakes of our shared life rose. I had finally, I told myself, put away childish things, and was ready to become what my father referred to as a man. In an idle and half-ironic way, as our second anniversary approached, we began to toy with baby names, especially at night, when having practiced the non–rhythm method in concert with the non–withdrawal method we lay awake in distress over other areas of our life, such as the financial area, which was going to pieces because I'd quit a job as a bartender where I'd made cash hand over fist because I'd promised myself to do so when I'd finished the novel I'd been working on for years, which now that it was complete even I didn't want to read—in the dark, we began to toy with baby names, though it turned out to be difficult to think of any that didn't already belong to people we despised, or to the pets of family friends. Ella's period, which in the earliest phase of our trying to conceive—the phase of not trying not to conceive—always arrived as a mild relief, now arrived as a mild disappointment, and then as a source of low-frequency despair. To boost our spirits, we tried to envision what a baby we made together might look like: Would she—we both hoped for a baby girl—have my beakish nose, Ella's round cheeks? Was it possible she'd have my blue eyes, and safe to assume she'd get Ella's tight curls? My parents were both as Anglo-Saxon as could be, while Ella's mother was Martiniquaise, and her father was descended from Sephardic Jews expulsed from Spain; what sort of granddaughter, we wondered, would this combination of four people produce? We reinstalled Cyclr on Ella's phone and put it to the precise opposite of its intended use, whereupon there began a phase of desperation that mounted month by month, until the sight of a pregnant woman, news of a pregnancy on social media, the use of certain words in either French or English had the power to reduce Ella to fits of weeping so convulsive they seemed to demand medical attention. Was there anything, I would say when these fits occurred, that I could do to help? Get me a straitjacket, she would sob. Swaddle me and make me calm.

■

Running the dishwasher was a mistake we would not repeat. The cloud of steam it released condensed on my skin and immediately became indistinct from my own sweat. Through an open skylight, we could hear neighborhood teenagers marching up the Petite Ceinture, an abandoned train line directly behind our building; we could hear their footsteps on the loose stone ballast, headed toward the tunnel up the tracks, a cool place to do whatever they did for fun; to hear them better, I made delicate work of returning our plates and bowls and glasses to their shelves, reflecting upon the anticipation their voices contained, these teenagers, the faith in possibility, the sense that the heat was only another aspect of their need of each other's bodies; and the thought that Ella had been one of these kids, had made trouble on these same tracks—all of this pleased me to no end. Feeling playful, overcome by affection that was both specific to her and general to the world, I broke another long period of silence by asking what she thought it meant about the type of adult we'd become that we used so many more spoons than forks or knives. She didn't laugh, but rather kissed me between my shoulder blades, and then asked me what we should eat, as if the taste of my sweat had stirred her hunger. Turning on the oven, or even the stove, or even the microwave, was out of the question; when it was finally fully dark outside, close to eleven, we ate a bowl of frozen raspberries apiece, sitting cross-legged on the mattress, engaged in the earnest nightly ritual of deciding what we'd watch on the projector, which although it generated a lot of heat we agreed we couldn't do without. It was practically ritual that two movies we started and abandoned hinged on untimely pregnancies, and that a third involved an illegal abortion. Ella knitted her eyebrows but remained steady as we began a fourth, in which no children had been born anywhere on the planet for eighteen years. I said to Ella that it was difficult to square the world that was being depicted—in which global order had collapsed and militarized police corralled asylum seekers into chain-link cages—with the problem of underpopulation. This looked like a world, I said, with *too many* humans, not too few. We were both by this time completely nude, and with a bottle she'd bought for the purpose, she occasionally sprayed a fine mist into the air above us, which hung for a moment in the projected light before it fell over our skin. If everyone stopped having babies, I said, you'd expect society to become more manageable rather than less. Ella replied with a shrug, and said maybe I had it the wrong way around, meaning, I think now, that in the moral logic of the film, universal infertility was not the cause of dystopian collapse but rather one of its effects: symptom of the death of hope. At any rate, by the time it became the hero's business to escort the world's only known pregnant woman to safety, Ella was fast asleep, and not until the movie was in its harrowing climax did she wake: a six-minute shot set in a bombed-out refugee camp, tracking a sprawling gun battle, the emotional stakes of which were defined by the distant sound of a baby's crying. She blinked awake, Ella, in the blue light, nodding slightly, as if the events onscreen confirmed some problem of a dream. The apartment had not yet perceptibly begun to cool. I watched her chest rise and fall. I remember feeling, as we continued watching, that my own experience of the rest of the movie was a function of what I imagined her experience of the rest of the movie to be, in the confusion of half sleep, in the confusion of half darkness, of misfired synapses, private anguish. The film ended, and the title card appeared: *Children of Men*. As the credits played she killed the sound and began very lucidly to speak.

I need you to understand, she said evenly, it's not something I ever consciously wanted, but it's something my body suddenly knows. What I feel is a physical emptiness, a kind of phantom limb.

The kids were tromping out of the tunnel now and back up the tracks toward home. Some of them were singing. The projected light of the film caught the apartment's fan-tossed dust, and the sweat at Ella's temples and along her sternum, and of course her dark brown eyes.

I know that your life has had its deferrals and frustrated expectations, she went on. But I need you to understand that you don't know how this feels.

■

In that first day or so, it was still possible to think of perspiration as something that could be helped. We took cold showers, stood at the open fridge, froze bowls of water and set them before the fan. Until the early hours of the morning, we watched stylish works of French and Japanese and Czech surrealism, movies that, as Ella put it, blurred boundaries, muddied the notion of a discrete and coherent self. If we didn't move when these movies ended, the projector would power down after fifteen minutes, and because Ella's computer was set to play a slideshow of her photos after five, inside a ten-minute window we got a random little tour of our life: visits to beaches, our niece's birthday, one or the other of us in a wig or a funny hat. A lot of them were photos I'd texted her of labels from the grocery store, where I often found myself staring at an entire wall of yogurt or quinoa or laundry soap without any idea which one to buy. There were many photos of Ella in dressing room mirrors, wearing clothes she didn't buy. A screen grab from *Turner & Hooch*, which I'd sent in gratitude: *T. Hanks!* It was the dead of night, and we'd just finished watching Věra Chytilová's *Daisies*— a trippy antecedent to *Broad City*—when a photo appeared featuring the graffiti on the door to our apartment: the French word for a biracial woman spray-painted in various sizes and colors, all overlapping, dozens of times, the way schoolkids scrawl the names of crushes on their binders. The white director who'd once lived in our apartment had named his first feature film Métisse, in celebration of the release of which he'd written its title all over what had then been the door to his home, an incident my wife, who was eight years old at the time and lived next door, remembered by the fumes that filled the stairwell and by the mild fuss it caused among the building's other residents, many of whom had lent their names to minor characters or appeared as extras, and all of whom had been fond of the director's wife, who happened to be my own wife's cousin, starring as a young woman newly pregnant with a child who would be, depending on which of her lovers was the father, either three-quarters black or three-quarters white—and this character, the pregnant métisse of the title, bore the first name of the director's wife's eight-year-old first cousin: bore, in short, my own wife's first name. All of which confusion I think now must have been on Ella's mind during the few seconds the photo was projected on our wall, because it was apropos of nothing else I could see that she asked abstractedly whether it were possible that our own daughter would be darker-skinned than she herself was and, if so, whether her life in certain ways would not be easier; would it not be easier, that is, if our daughter were to bear the outward traces of the history that was in her blood? I was prepared to say only that the less our baby looked like me the better, as the slideshow moved on to a series of photos from our wedding at city hall—the fourth anniversary of which had come and gone a few weeks before—at the sight of which we fell silent. In one, Ella, at the officiant's invitation, was placing the ring on my finger, wearing a smile that even to think of makes my heart ache, whereas in the instant the photo was taken, the instant I became her husband, I was glancing at something the camera didn't catch, as if it were possible, at that moment, for anything at all to be happening out of frame.

■

As the heatwave continued in the next few days, the passage of time became even more obscure. In daylight hours long periods passed in silence, which we broke only occasionally to name cool places we could think of: the abandoned train tunnel, the ocean floor, the dark surface of the moon. I spent these hours transcribing from notes, or re-creating from memory, things I'd heard people say to each other, or things they'd said to me, regarding events of the world that touched their lives. I like to stay outside, the woman in the hijab had said: I have many friends in the neighborhood and we sit around on benches, chatting about this and that. For months these transcriptions had occupied the time I'd previously spent trying to write fiction: I would approach strangers with my notepad out, my voice recorder running, and introduce myself as an American journalist, a modest, aspirational lie, the results of which I'd typed into a file labeled streetview.docx, though I had no idea how this document might be organized into a cohesive work. From the time I woke up until after dark, during the heatwave, I let this problem occupy my mind, as meanwhile my metabolism seemed to slow and longer and longer intervals passed before I was stirred by hunger, another of the heat's warping effects on time.

I remember I was writing up some observations about the boy with the ears—about the charm of his ungainliness and the impression of gentleness he gave—when I got a text from a friend, saying that the party he'd planned for that evening would have to be postponed until after the heat broke. That was a shame, Ella said, meaning roughly that it was not a shame, that nothing appealed to her less than drinking lemonade or grape juice while my expat friends got trashed. I tended to agree: I'd been developing a reluctance to show my face to the people who knew me best—who knew it was my ambition to become a novelist, for example; who knew that if they made gracious excuses to pay for my drinks I'd never refuse, that the months of July and August represented a further period of retrenchment in my life, which was already, to their way of thinking, monkishly austere. Having taught my final lesson of the year, the next paycheck I received would be my last until my stipend began in the fall, and though neither of us said so aloud, Ella and I both realized we'd soon be living on my credit cards again, because her income had recently dried up as well: not since winter had she gotten a call to assist any of the casting directors who had her phone number, in part because her most reliable source of work, a casting director named Flore, had given birth in February and taken maternity leave that was now stretching into its seventh month. Though she still called from time to time, it was never for a job, but rather out of desperation to leave the house, to get coffee or to see movies she'd cast the year before without Ella's help. In motherhood Flore was truly, absorbingly radiant, and for Ella, recovering from these outings was a days-long ordeal, though she had no choice, in the interest of her stunted career. But meanwhile, because my salary from the various freelance teaching contracts I'd cobbled together didn't quite cover the whole of our monthly expenses, she'd taken the only job she'd been able to find, as a part-time nanny for a young woman who lived nearly an hour away by train, and who for some reason wasn't in a position to take advantage of the generous family leave and material support the state offered most new mothers. Sometimes she'd Skype me during bath time, and though it made my heart swell to see her so happy, I'd joke that I didn't think it was a good idea to broadcast video of someone else's naked child. She had use of a bassinet, but to keep him from crying she took him everywhere on her shoulder, on errands or just to stroll, all of which she'd report to me on the phone, often in real time: He's asleep! she'd say. I loved to picture her out in the world like this, I pictured her beaming, absorbing the warmth of this tiny body, swaying gently side to side. But of course there always came the time she had to hand the boy over to his mother, a nurse's aide in a nearby hospice, or else to his grandmother, a heavyset woman from Guadeloupe who sometimes took over in the afternoons and who, in her brusque Caribbean competence, reminded Ella of her own mom. All to say she felt too vulnerable to see even her closest friends. On the way to the metro one afternoon late that spring, we ran into her driving instructor, and she introduced me as her husband from New York, as if to demonstrate how grand her life had become. And where are you living, he asked, because he'd seen us come out of the building where she grew up. Are you living at home? Later that same day, at a picnic with friends of mine in Buttes-Chaumont, we were sitting on a loose ring of blankets when someone asked Ella what she did for a living. I'm a nanny, Ella said, and from the tightness in her voice and the stiffness of her grin, her discomfort was so transparent that, before I could think better of it, I added that she was a gifted actress and that she'd recently signed with a powerful film agent, a thoughtless lie that the rest of the group took as their cue to assure her it was a rite of passage for any aspiring artist to take on work beneath their dignity. My friend Azra, an aspiring writer for whom the dignity or indignity of work was utterly theoretical, remarked that it should be easy for Ella to make it in the entertainment industry because of her family's proximity to some of the great filmmakers of the twentieth century, whose children were now making films that represented the promise of the twenty-first. We were barefoot, the lot of us, Ella was the only person who hadn't removed her shoes. The conversation moved on, someone observed that Buttes-Chaumont gathered in peaceful coexistence the very best of humanity, people from all walks of life, from every corner of the globe, harboring ambitions of every imaginable sort in their unknowable hearts. A guy from UNESCO in an OBEY t-shirt told us about his job on a construction site the summer after tenth grade and the little notebook in which he cataloged the idiom of his coworkers. For a long time, Ella remained silent, and when I glanced her way it struck me that the slight dampness that had risen in her eyes lent a heartrending elegance to her beauty. Before long, she left, taking care to kiss everyone's cheeks, and insisting that I stay and have a nice time. When I got home it was dusk, and I found her in the half-dark apartment, flipping through a stack of headshots she'd gotten made in New York. The dampness was gone from her eyes, replaced by a hard fury that I now understand was directed at herself. Since I was a little girl, she said without looking up, I never told anyone I dreamed of being an actress, because it's such a pathetic thing to want. It was so rare for her, in that period, to open herself up to me in this way, and I think now she must have been reciting these lines in her head as the light died and she waited for me to come home. And I was riveted. Better for people to think you want nothing, she went on, but of course they find out you're taking classes, they find out you're going on auditions, they find out you invited a casting assistant to lunch and couldn't pay the bill. For the privilege of changing diapers she'd been making ten euros an hour, and running a monthly deficit that the bank wouldn't countenance much longer, and she hadn't wanted to tell me but now the baby's mother had taken her vacation days to visit her family in Basse-Terre and had decided not to return.

By the time my friend canceled his party, we'd begun to retreat not only from the world but from each other as well. There were still five days until Ella could test her urine for the presence of hormones produced in a developing placenta, and she took the occasion of her nakedness to watch her body for signs of what it would it do, signs such as change in appetite and irritability, such as spotting, bloating, cramping, and fatigue. In French, we reflected, so many words could mean their opposite: *dessous* and *dessus*, *plus* and *plus*. *Hello* and *goodbye*. Standing at the mirror she tested her breasts for tenderness, as I sat at my computer, adding English subtitles to TV shows and movies that were already in English. That night, and all the next day, we watched *Homeland*, which I'd downloaded from one website and encoded with subtitles from another, with the result that, because of some compatibility issue, the crude pairs of eighth notes that typically announced background music in standard closed captions were for the entire first season rendered in QuickTime as ÅçâçâçÅ, which was in turn rendered phonetically in my brain as *AH-kah-kah-KAH*. The subtitles I'd downloaded for the second and third seasons didn't announce the music at all, but by that time whenever the score picked up, my brain, in what I thought of as a breathy whisper, said to me, *Acacaca*. I'd begun to think of myself as sweating openly, a distinction that seemed to have to do with the animal indifference that now attended my sweating, although *indifference* was perhaps the wrong word; I'd have done anything at all to have stopped sweating, anything that didn't involve spending money. Beneath my neck, beneath my arms, behind my knees, my skin touched itself, an intolerable state of affairs, though the sweating wasn't the worst of it; that honor belonged to the uniform burning sensation on the surface of my skin, as if my entire body were immersed in a pot slowly approaching a boil. Ella soaked a pair of our largest towels in cold water, and we tucked ourselves beneath them at opposite ends of the mattress, having discovered how powerfully the heat of our individual bodies was increased by any proximity between them, the way in a fire pit two logs that are merely hot, as they approach each other, burst into flame. Our bodies, we agreed, had become our oppressors, and hers in particular, she added, had become a totalitarian force in our lives, not only that week but that year, during each of the first six months of which, at the same time every night in the ten days leading up to the procedure, in order to precisely control the passage of her ovum from her ovaries into her tubes, I had given her a shot in her belly, using a marker-sized apparatus that in New York would have cost the same as a used Peugeot, or as passage to Greece for a single Syrian emigrant. While she selected a fresh site for the shot and swabbed her skin with alcohol, I affixed a fresh needle, dialed in the dosage, and flicked the syringe for air bubbles just as I'd seen done on shows like *ER* and *M*A*S*H*. Ella detested needles; while I counted to ten one-thousand, per the instructions, she squeezed her eyes shut and went away in her thoughts, so that in a sense she was absent from what I'd come to think of as an act of consecration. But the moment I withdrew the needle from the tiny wound it made, she'd collapse and throw her arms around my neck, a small but powerful moment of intimacy that nearly compensated for a long hiatus in our actual intimate life that Ella attributed to these shots, whose possible side effects included diminished sex drive, as well as precipitous weight gain, a prospect that had made her so body-conscious that, until the heat made it absolutely necessary, she refused to let me see her in any stage of undress, though I tried to persuade her that if she'd gained any weight at all, it was imperceptible even to me. Meanwhile, she fixated on small rashes she developed, though the doctor insisted they weren't side effects in fact but an effect of stress, and at night as she slept her feverish scratching, together with her violent twitching, often kept me awake until dawn, so that in the dead of night while she thrashed beside me, without quite knowing why I'd sometimes inspect the chart she kept of her daily temperature, which indicated, for those who knew how to read it, when we were to have sex, a program we adhered to without the slightest deviation.

∎

Though now, with Ella in a state of continual nudity, I was tempted to deviate in a serious way. To defuse this temptation and spare myself the embarrassment of rejection, I suggested we order bo bun, which I offered to pay for and to fetch, I figured it would be good to get out of the house, to mosey around collecting observations and impressions to share when I got home. We lived at the edge of a zone that, according to pundits like K. T. McFarland and Bobby Jindal, lay beyond the reach of the French government, where Muslim immigrants were intent on colonizing Western culture and radical Islamic clerics enforced sharia law, and into which it was unsafe for non-Muslims even to set foot. The third week of Ramadan had begun, and it was out of my way, but I went through Place de la Réunion, where the streetlights were coming on and in dusk's deepest phase of blue the gold fountain seemed to glow; beneath these lamps, teenagers crowded onto benches and stood around on cocked hips, holding close to their faces foil packages they'd been anticipating all day, wearing serious expressions and speaking softly among themselves, savoring, I suppose, like all teenagers, the resentment they felt toward a world they didn't ask for but whose rules they nonetheless felt compelled to obey. Younger children, drenched in sweat, were flirting with the idea of getting into the fountain, for which no one would have blamed them and which in fact no one was discouraging them from doing, least of all their parents and grandparents, who were gathered at the edge of the square, throwing bedsheets over the picnic tables, smoothing the creases with their palms, at the direction of the woman who wore ice packs beneath her hijab, who, when she saw me, broke into a warm and natural smile and gave me a little wave. To have encountered this scene—the sense of community it conveyed and my momentary sense of inclusion in that community—as a source of well-being would have been, as I understood it, a signally patronizing exercise of both white liberal guilt and white liberal smugness, if those two things were even distinct. But there was no better term than *well-being* for the feeling that swelled in my heart as I crossed the square to rue des Haies, a narrow and meandering street where I liked to imagine one day owning a home, although that aspiration became less plausible every year for the precise reason that I shared it with so many people who already had the kind of money I hoped to make by writing novels about my life. In Ella's youth, many of these buildings had been abandoned, had fallen into disrepair, and had come to be inhabited by squatters from North and sub-Saharan Africa, who sent their children to schools named after Victor Hugo and Henri Matisse, where they joined children of other recent immigrants who lived in public housing nearby. My mother- and father-in-law, when they moved into their partially roof-less, partially floorless top-story walk-up around the time Ella was born, had become what could be called the neighborhood's first gentrifiers, in that by owning the place they lived they contributed to the transformation of the neighborhood's economic landscape. When she was young this street had been a gauntlet, one where Ella had been catcalled and spat upon and physically assaulted, though out of stubbornness and pride she always re-fused to go the long way around. In front of the bakery, in her telling, was where at seventeen she'd slapped the face of a man in his twenties who'd told her as she walked by that he wanted to fuck her in the ass, and who'd responded to being slapped in the face by punching her in the head. Now, as I walked by this bakery on my way to pick up bo bun, I perceived for the first time how often and how eagerly I'd repeated this story in the company of Americans, not only, as I could now see, to convey a vague impression of the authenticity of Ella's childhood, but also to convey a vague sense of proximity I felt, in the gritty margins of Paris, to the broadly European his-tory of the world, which in my leafy, suburban Connecticut childhood had seemed impossibly remote. Along the length of rue des Haies—outside bars, tea salons, tobacco shops, a hookah lounge—the sidewalks were crowded with people who in Connecticut would be subject to loitering ordinance. On the Jordan Legacy Court, for the inauguration of which Michael Jordan himself had appeared in a bucket hat only a few weeks before, the kid with the enormous ears, still shirtless, but without his band of acolytes, was inexpertly practicing hook shots in the paint, all but completely neglecting the ice cream sandwich that was melting in his free hand, until the ball bounced away and he stood for a minute as he ate, looking at a spot on the wall where, beneath the Jordan mural, someone had wheat-pasted a photo of a little girl in bare feet, wearing a wounded expression and holding aloft a stenciled placard that read NOT AFRAID—a phrase that, since it had come into popular use that winter in connection with #jesuischarlie and #coexist, became less convincing each time it appeared. At that moment, a thought occurred to me that I continued to refine as I carried on past the decrepit residential hotels that had absorbed most of the squatter population in the decades since their buildings had been bought up, and past the stately public bath that was doing brisk business on the corner of rues des Haies and Buzenval. I was still refining it as I watched a striped cat make its way along a narrow ledge on the face of the public bath from one open window to the next, and I was refining it further still when I finally reached the end of rue des Haies and crossed the street to Bistrot Zen, where Estelle, who was chewing ice like popcorn, greeted me in her usual manner: by observing in a kind of singsong that madame always called the order in and monsieur always picked it up. But the entire train of thought evaporated, the way thoughts do as you drift toward sleep, when, as I stood waiting, my eyes fell upon a pair of beckoning porcelain cats, which always made me think of Chris Marker, who for decades had lived on the ground floor of the same building that Ella lived at the top of, where he sometimes hosted her for tea to discuss the films he'd lend her and where now, even three years after his death, he still sometimes received junk mail that I secretly collected in a file I kept in my desk. It was the idea that Chris Marker would have admired the thought I'd now brought to an advanced stage of refinement that caused the thought to disappear, though it was soon replaced by the thought that Chris Marker would also admire the tall and elegant black woman who at just that moment came in and, excusing herself from the call she was on, passed the time chatting amicably with Estelle in what Estelle, in her heavily accented French, told me after the woman left was perfectly unaccented Vietnamese. Estelle had gotten a perm, I noticed, and this is what I told Ella when I got home: that Estelle had gotten a perm and the heat was doing a number on it.

You stupid, Ella replied.

■

All week we took pains to track the flow of air and sun. At sunset we threw open all the windows and oriented the fan to the west, toward the highest of the skylights, in order to vacate the hot air that had gathered all day, and then at dawn we rose to cover the east-facing windows, at which point the room would finally cool off enough to sleep until ten or eleven, when the heat would stir us from bed. Leaving the sheets in gnarled tangles on the mattress, cushions strewn about the floor, our sweated-through undies kicked into the corners of the room, we'd spend the early part of the day with our computers in our laps, until at some point mid- or late afternoon, overcome by a restlessness the heat wouldn't accommodate, we'd put on another episode of *Homeland*, or else another episode of *L'héritage de la chouette*, a series of discussions on ancient Greece that Chris Marker had directed for French TV, which included a segment on the chaotic origins of democracy and another on the democratizing power of vowels—for hours we'd sit around completely absorbed by one or the other of these programs, or we'd idly thumb through the books that had fallen to the floor when a shelf collapsed without warning, getting up occasionally to rotate bottles of Perrier from the freezer to the fridge and otherwise remaining as still as possible, like zoo creatures, waiting for the return of night.

Three days remained until Ella could take the test when her phone rang. She took the call without moving from the place where she lay, twisted in the sweat-damp sheets of our nest on the floor. She covered her eyes with her free hand, exchanging pleasantries in a heavy voice for long enough that I gleaned it was radiant Flore, and that radiant Flore had cut her maternity leave short to work on a film that was already a few weeks into preproduction. Ella asked a few polite questions about the director, about the actors who were attached, the production team, and, listening for a moment to Flore's voice over the line, she bolted into a posture of alertness.

Oui, she said. Oui. Tout à fait.

Then for a long time she said nothing, but only made listening sounds, the kind of glottal, apprehensive monosyllables to which—though maybe it's only in retrospect that I can say so—the French resort in response to either bad or good-but-destabilizing news, such as the offer of a job. In the vaguest possible way, I may have guessed this call would abruptly upend plans and contingencies that had taken us months to hash out. I could make out Flore's zipped-up voice pressed against Ella's ear, but not clearly enough to decipher her French, and so I focused instead on the transformation Ella seemed to undergo, the steady heaving of her chest in the heat and the way her face went blank, so that it seemed she was looking through me, or that I was dissolving under her gaze; it was an almost shamanic ability of hers, to be absent from herself when she was on the phone, as if, in order to project herself into a world she couldn't see, it was necessary to blind herself to the world before her eyes, which is why I didn't like it when she took calls while she was driving.

Through a tiny hole in the roller blinds, a sunbeam cut through the dark room, and I was watching Ella try abstractedly to brush away the shiver of light it made on her bare chest when, all at once, the shiver leapt as she threw her head back and laughed, getting to her feet to pace the room. I admit, she said, I don't even know where Macedonia is, if you'd asked I'd have guessed *Game of Thrones*. It was her sudden cheerfulness that caught me off guard—her cheerfulness, the warmth of her laughter, the way it seemed to bring the world into her command simply to feel and express delight. It had been so long since I'd seen her exercise this gift, which had once defined her in my mind, an instantaneous pulling taut of the wires in a room that wasn't merely a charm she could turn on and off, but a spontaneous function of her feelings.

Stage mothers, she said to Flore now: I see exactly what you mean, this is the kind of woman who weighs her baby's turds.

She felt it, too—I could see her feeling it, like a bird who, waking from a ponderous dream of broken wings, launches itself into the air and rediscovers the joy of flight. As she paced, she picked up whatever her eyes fell upon, the teakettle, for example, a notebook of mine, a deformed candle she'd dug up that winter when the power went out, all kinds of flotsam that, as her conversation continued, she examined and weighed in her hands and even sniffed, as though she might consider buying it for the sheer pleasure of negotiating its price. All these strange ways she had of performing the sensation of freedom. The rest was chitchat and tittle-tattle, from what I could tell, industry gossip. Ah, génial, Ella said, I love Brétagne in the summertime—Us? Écoute, meuf, c'est compliqué, next month my husband is moving to Virginia for school—Creative writing—No, a master's degree!—Exactly, like novels and stuff, j'sais pas, they study creative writing in the US, it's an important step, apparemment, professionally. She went on, brighter and brighter, but I didn't catch the rest, or rather I stopped listening, I'd found the shiver of light where it fell now on the displaced mattress, and I wondered if I could watch it long enough and closely enough to detect the turning of the planet. Bisous, Ella said finally, salut, ma belle Flore, on s'appelle bientôt, and then she hung up and stood smiling to herself for a long time.

Before Flore's call, I'd been flipping through *The Arcades Project*, and I picked it back up now, but I couldn't make my eyes focus on the words, my mind raced, and I felt a certain coldness churning inside me, which only intensified when Ella came to sit beside me on the floor.

My love, she said.

The shoot would begin at the end of August; the position in question wasn't in the casting office, the movie was already cast, but rather on set—

the film, a road comedy that would be shot mostly on the highways of Macedonia, starred two children, and Ella was to accompany them as their handler.

A nanny, in other words, Ella said. It's my precise skill set.

For a long time we lay in the peculiar daytime darkness of our present lives, the fan at our feet oscillating back and forth between us.

It's a stupid project, Ella said. The premise is idiotic and the lead is a literal jackoff. But it's a role with a lot of responsibility, the regulations around having kids on set are really strict. I'll have a lot of contact with the director and the producers, the kind of people who can really help me down the road.

How many hours had I spent, since we'd met, watching Ella's eyes as they roved around the room, dark, fascinating thresholds I was desperate to cross? She was naked except for a black pair of panties, the undercarriage of which was lightly discolored from use. An image returned to me from an early encounter in our acquaintance, during which she commanded me to pin her arms behind her head, grip her throat tightly in those crucial final moments of release. Now, in the flush of her call with Flore, beads of sweat glowed along her sternum and in the creases beneath her jaw. And if she was pregnant, how would that fit into this new hitch in our plans? Momentarily a strong impulse seized me: to press her into the damp mattress, to press myself into her, to force my tongue into her mouth, to look into her eyes, which roved across the cracked and yellowed paint of the ceiling beams. It hadn't always been that our marriage was so chaste.

Plus, she continued, I get to run lines with the kids and coach them in rehearsals. I don't even know if I want to be an actress. I grew up around cinema, I love cinema, when I was a little girl my mom put me in a short film she made, and I just started to believe that if there was a role for me in cinema it would be onscreen. Maybe there's something else—not the babysitting, but the thing that the babysitting leads to.

It's not that I *want* to be away from you, she told me, which seemed like a strange thing to say.

The heat seemed to have joined forces with my pulse: the surface of my skin throbbed and felt like it might burst. I had the spray bottle, and now and then I sprayed cool water into the air and watched the droplets settle over us. At length, my eyes found that shiver of light from the outside world, which had indeed made heroic progress across the room. I mean that I would have sworn up and down that the world had stood still all this while and that the course of time would resume only when the outlines of our future had been defined. With her shoulders, Ella wiped the sweat from her temples and her brow, and I held her clammy hand in my clammy hand, as morning became afternoon and as we talked in circles around the only possible decision, until finally no further delay was possible and we had to say it aloud: I would go ahead to Virginia and she would remain here, at home.

■

The referendum Tsipras had demanded was under way, and I spent the better part of that afternoon reading whatever related material I could find. In both French- and English-language publications it had become conventional to compare Greece to a troublesome adolescent, and the Troika to intransigent parents enforcing a policy of tough love. The type of writer I hoped to become would be able to explain in every particular the course of events that had led to the referendum; I was beginning to see the outline of an essay that would use Greece's geographic centrality to make its financial crisis the intersection of whatever thoughts came into my head: the relation between desperation and greed; the meaning of community; the difficulties of marriage; the anxiety of sharing responsibility not only for my own life and not only for Ella's, but also for a life that currently existed only as an idea that could be carried across the city in a glass tube. In other words, that week I began to see human endeavors large and small, from trade agreements to family planning, each as a point in a long sequence of well-intended bad ideas that could be traced back to the original bad idea of building settled communities over earth we claimed as our own; and while it remained beyond me to make sense of anything related to Greece's debt, I was convinced that if Europe couldn't solve what amounted to a problem of accounting, there was no hope of its solving the myriad problems of acute human misery of which Europe itself was the principal cause. For centuries, Ella pointed out, the nature of borders had been evolving toward its present form, and now had become so staggeringly multivalent that it was impossible to define. As she saw it, she told me later that afternoon, the choice that now lay before the EU and before the entire world was whether to revert to the clearer, more definite borders of the past, or to press forward with the evolution of our present borders until from one generation to the next they ceased to meaningfully exist at all. So many Europeans, she said, felt the continent was being flooded with refugees, and among the vessels that rose on this tide was Marine Le Pen, whose father, Jean-Marie—founder of the party his daughter now led—was in his first term as the municipal councilor of the twentieth arrondissement the year Ella was born there, despite his agenda of sending the bulk of its residents back to countries that within his lifetime were subject to French rule and that even now were subject to French whims. Meanwhile, she said, Angela Merkel, although Germany had accepted refugees at a higher rate than any other EU state, was being depicted in the French press as a pitiless shrew. That afternoon I listened to Ella's end of a phone call with her mother, Clarisse, who was at a theater festival in Frankfurt, where the municipal government was going full guns to prepare for new arrivals; and for her own part, she'd told Ella on the phone, although she relied heavily on Airbnb to supplement her modest pension, she was considering making up the spare bedroom for a family when she returned, and in this small way, as Ella put it, nourishing a larger hope.

I liked the way that sounded, and wrote it down, but Ella didn't have the energy to discuss it. All day at her own computer she'd sat riveted to forum threads on hormone treatments, hypnotic suggestibility, the somewhat cruel and infantilizing bedside manner of certain Paris ob-gyns. As she read, I was aware that a particular intentness of focus came over her that was very like fear; as it turned out, an unmarried woman who'd been trying to conceive for years had finally met with success and bid the group farewell, and this was the cause, I later learned, of Ella's eruption into the convulsive tears she'd been resisting all that week. The only possible thing to do was to hold her in my arms. I have to have a break from this, she managed to choke out, my whole life has become this pinhole—by which she seemed to mean something about admitting light. The heat of our bodies, and the heat of the room and the heat of this particular place on the planet, at this particular time, contributed to my feeling that I was at the center of something transcendentally real. At that time, I didn't have my own strong feelings, though later I would, about having a baby; it was something I'd always wanted for myself but that had always belonged to an abstract future, which had yet to take on tangible contours in my mind. But my wife was in pain. There was nothing, I'd begun to understand, that I could do to relieve it. This I felt strongly about. It tormented me, in fact. From somewhere deep in her core, her entire body shuddered and thrashed, and I tried to hold her tightly enough to absorb these spasms with my chest, my arms, my face. So primal and ululating was her howling that I didn't at first realize that it contained words and phrases it would be impossible to reproduce, but whose essential meaning was that when she saw new mothers, she wanted to murder their babies before their eyes.

What kind of monster, she wailed.

My love, my love, I cooed. I've wanted to murder babies for far less.

For almost an hour, this went on. In the calm that ensued when she'd finished, we retreated to our separate ends of the mattress, having brought perspiration to new heights, and I refreshed our wet towels with cool water, and after some discussion we decided that *Homeland*, because it was both suspenseful and fanciful enough to get us out of our heads, was just the thing.

It was dusk, actual dusk, and the kids on the tracks, silent except for their footsteps, were on their way to the tunnel, when we picked up somewhere in the middle of the third season; by the time they emerged, speaking in soft voices that nonetheless carried clearly off the walls, it was nearly dawn, and we'd begun the fourth. I'd forgotten to find subtitles for this season, but by now it was beside the point. Near the middle of the second episode, the central character, a reluctant and career-oriented mother who routinely made decisions that resulted in hundreds of deaths, found herself for the length of a day responsible for the care of her infant daughter, whom at the day's end she bathed sternly and efficiently, in silence, splashing bathwater over the child's pudgy arms and silken hair. It was, of course, an accident when the baby slid beneath the surface, and the mother quickly retrieved her. But something took hold of her then, and she let the baby sink once more into the water, and held her there, her face going blank. It was two days now until Ella would be able to test her urine for hCG. Somehow, without our noticing, the sound and the image had gotten out of sync, and only once the scene resolved itself in the inevitable decision not to drown the child did the ominous music the scene obviously required begin.

Acacaca, Ella said.

■

When, a little more than a month later—after I'd moved to Virginia and Ella had started her new job—I adapted the events of that week into a short story, I set the climactic scene at the party that had eventually taken place at my friend's apartment. For dramatic effect, I presented my friends in Paris, a loose collection of expats from all over the world, as more obnoxious, more vapid and superficial, pettier and more self-centered, than any of them is in the real world; and at the same time, more attractive, better dressed, quicker witted and more vital. So it was that Knox, the fictional party's host, compared with my gentle and inquisitive friend Michael, was a monstrous prick; that Pauls and Azra, about whom the worst that could be said was that they were slightly, harmlessly out of touch, in the story became the frivolous and self-obsessed Niks and Ruya, objects of some unkind jokes. The médecin sans frontières who made a series of racist remarks about the fertility of Nigerian teens was in reality a médecin avec frontières whose racism was more discreet. The fatuous reporter from Reuters, who in the story kept citing Greece's finance minister by name, was based on an actual Reuters reporter who was guilty only of tucking his shirt in and wearing a braided belt. I think now that the violence I did to these people on the page was an act of atonement—for having betrayed my actual wife at a crucial moment during the actual party, to dramatize which I invented a more obvious betrayal, having to do with a freelance war correspondent with long blond hair and great skin, who corresponded to no one in the actual world.

The fictional party took place precisely the night before Odile was to take her pregnancy test; and so it was in life. That Ella, at this party, was horrified to think someone might notice she wasn't drinking and take for granted what she dared not even hope—that was in the fiction as well. Ella, and Odile, at this party, were not so much alienated as exquisitely vulnerable and exposed. All night, hugging her stomach, she hovered at the margins of conversations, picking things up and turning them over in her hands, often failing to notice when people addressed her with questions or remarks intended to bring her back to earth; she drifted from one end of the room to another, and settled finally in an armchair with a plate of cheese and dried meat that for fear of listeria she didn't touch. She came to life briefly to ask Pauls, a professor of applied mathematics, to summarize a physics concept he'd mentioned in passing: Bell's theorem, which described the possibility that the same particle could exist in two places at once. The idea of such a world, I could see as Pauls spoke, touched something in her imagination, and for a moment her face softened. But, maybe because the idea alone wasn't enough, she hardened again and, in front of the whole room, accused Pauls of mansplaining, adopting a tone that perfectly split the difference between affectionate teasing and callous torment. After a moment of stammering, Pauls protested that she herself had asked him for an explanation, and on a subject he'd studied extensively, and that in those two key ways his conduct didn't match traditional definitions of the crime.

Tell me *all* about mansplaining, Ella said, tilting into anger; I'm not sure I understand. For a moment the room went quiet, and helpless tears stood in Pauls's eyes, as he waited for someone to come to his defense. My own blood went cold. Oh, Pauls, she then said, I'm only winding you up. She leaned forward to squeeze his hand, before settling back in her chair, where she remained for the rest of the night, though she was simultaneously somewhere far away.

■

Not for the same reasons, I felt the same way: I wanted nothing more than to be back home, but without missing the chance to get drunk among people I was desperate to impress. As I tried to lighten the mood after Ella's outburst, a compulsion for making people laugh seized me, to the extent that the guy with the braided belt asked if I had any cocaine. In the kitchen, where people were taking turns standing in front of the freezer, and in the stairwell, where people were sharing a joint, I found myself holding court, ranting about French bureaucracy, about the small-mindedness of French metro riders, about the un-picked-up shit of French dogs. Waiting for the toilet, I asked bewildered Pauls and Azra if they wanted to watch me eat a banana I'd found on Michael's desk. Soon we'd reached the early hours of the morning, but the heat had yet to abate; when I returned to the living room, the entire party had moved from the furniture to the floor, and everyone had stripped off most of their clothes, so that now they were all lying about in their underwear, shining with sweat. And immediately I began to remove my shoes, noticing only then that Ella, who had calculated to the hour the latest that implantation might take place, was still in her armchair, her arms wrapped more tightly around herself than ever, and alone among those in the room in remaining fully dressed. *Any decent human being,* was the phrase that appeared in my mind. Our eyes met, and at that moment it wasn't too late for me to keep my clothes on and lead her out of the room; but then a moment later it was too late, my shoes were off, my socks, my shirt, my shorts, until I stood there in the doorway in just my briefs and my cap; and what I wanted to convey with this scene in my story was that between Arthur and Odile, from that moment, nothing was ever the same.

■

Now, the entire world is confined to their houses, with no end in sight. With time at a standstill, there's little to do with my days but reflect. So the other night, I dug that story out and read it again; the story, the feedback I received, and all the notes I made in the year that followed, and in the four years since, years that have made that week—the Greek financial crisis, our attempt at conception—look like a mere stalking horse for the local and global disasters that would follow. I think the betrayal I was trying to write about was not that I'd taken off my clothes and left her feeling self-conscious and alone; nor was it having stayed so much later at the party than I'd promised; nor having dragged her there in the first place. Rather, these betrayals all followed from the more fundamental betrayal of always being elsewhere, always having my eye on something out of frame. I remember how, almost exactly a year later, at her bedside in a silent hospital in the dead of night, in a room lit only by the TV, I looked back over the intervening months and saw all the pretenses upon which I'd based my life falling away. And I remember how, not quite two months after the party at Michael's, on the very day that the story I'd written was discussed in class, there was a total lunar eclipse, and I went up to the roof of the town house where I lived alone, in which my boxes were yet to be unpacked and my furniture yet to be arranged, and sat for a long time watching the moon move into the Earth's shadow, or, to put it another way, as the Earth got in front of the sun.

It had been on the roof of our building in Paris that I'd found her that night, when shortly after I undressed she'd disappeared. I'd searched for her throughout Michael's apartment. I searched the hall and the stairs. Outside, buttoning my shirt, I asked the prostitutes hanging around there if they'd seen her go. For reference I showed them a photo of the very moment I confirmed my vows. She's about yea high, I said helplessly; she's got deep brown eyes. It was on our roof that I'd found her: the moon had set, and the sun was rising, the hour of her pregnancy test had passed, and there she was hugging her knees, trails of tears shining on her face; and although I suppose it had been in my mind all along, at that moment the idea took definitive hold of me that I would have to write all this down.

2
Full Speed

At the beginning of August, Ella arrived in Skopje and started sending me these long, ruminative emails, as many as three or four per a week, written in elegant French prose that, with nothing better to do, I made a project of translating into English. Ella enjoyed reading, but she'd always been suspicious of writerly self-seriousness, so it was both thrilling and alarming to imagine her there in her hotel room—wrapped in a fresh bathrobe, her hair twisted in a towel—set to the serious task of organizing her thoughts. I hadn't been sleeping well myself, I wasn't adjusting well to life in Virginia, where the insect noise was deafening, where there were vanity plates in galling concentration, where the house I lived in, and my body, too, swelled with the moisture in the air.

Her arrival, Ella wrote in the first of these emails, was the occasion of a rupture she didn't know how to explain. Flight gave her an uncanny sensation. After the intensity of the heatwave and the numbness of the weeks that followed, to fly to a foreign city was, in her words, like turning from stone to sand. The rest of the crew wasn't due in Skopje for another week. Traveling alone, she'd gotten to the hotel after dark, and it sent a chill through her when the porter told her she was the only guest. She took a muscle relaxant to get to sleep—a whole rather than a half—and woke up in the early afternoon. In the shower, she wrote, the water came down over me in a continuous, breathtakingly hot torrent. Lit from above by a single recessed bulb, my naked body was reflected in three panes of glass, so that I had the feeling of being cornered by myself. You know when you repeat a word in your head until its form dissociates from its meaning? That was how I felt, but the word was me, my being entire, everything seemed strange, I had no thoughts, little corded rivulets raced over me and eddied in the drain. I stood who knows how long in the steam; eventually the water went cold, and still I didn't move, though the shock of it took my breath away. And then, I don't know how to describe the relief that settled over me. A pressure, an affliction, internal and external at the same time, had suddenly disappeared. It was as if the heat broke—it was like the first cool morning after those long days of annihilating heat: you wake up, you feel the air on the surface of your skin, you remember what it is to be human and free.

■

Tu te réveilles, tu sens l'air, tu te souviens. I thought of that morning, the morning after the party at Michael's, with the windows thrown open and a fresh breeze moving across the floor. At the time I'd compared that feeling to the moment, after being kicked in the nuts, that the nauseating pain in your stomach suddenly vanishes, and you're overwhelmed by a feeling of gratitude, and you say to yourself that never again will you take for granted the feeling of not being kicked in the nuts. This comment was not appropriate. Ella gave me a murderous look, but remained silent until evening. Did you get kicked in the nuts a lot? she asked me only later, maybe the next day. She meant, was this related to our trouble reproducing? Now, she was telling me that trouble was gone, or rather, that it no longer troubled her, and all it took was a cold shower in a landlocked Balkan state.

Ostensibly, she'd been sent a week ahead of the crew to prepare for the children's arrival, to make sure there wouldn't be any problems. Under French law, working with actors under the age of sixteen was a high-wire act. Ella was responsible for the logistics of complying not only with the labor code but also with the children's and their parents' every wish and whim, for which she was being paid a wage and even receiving a per diem in euros that when converted to denars became truly extravagant. But there wasn't enough actual work to fill her days in the empty hotel. She felt lost and alien to herself, but also free, as if, she wrote, she'd been dropped into a video game whose object was to discover its object. Dans l'hôtel désert et lumineux, she wrote, je flâne à droite et à gauche, à la recherche du fin du jeu. At some point during that first week, having committed the exchange rate to memory, she found the hotel bar empty even of staff, though there was music playing and the tables were set.

She stood awhile, waiting for someone to appear. Then, retreating to her room, she found her hallway changed in some way she couldn't put her finger on. Not her hallway, she'd gotten off at the wrong floor. Finding her way back to the elevator she discovered a room-service tray in the hall, beside a door numbered 6032. She stopped there. It made her blood go cold to know there was in fact another guest in the hotel, she wrote; it made her feel even more like a ghost than she already had.

For a moment she stood silently before the door, listening for signs of life from within. She heard nothing. On the tray, reflecting the strange light of the hall, a silver bangle caught her eye. She bent to inspect it, attracted by its brilliance. Without thinking, she slipped it on, held her arm away from her to see. It was simple and elegant, like the lighting of a cigarette, she said. Folding her knees beneath her, she took the untouched fruit cup from the tray and, for a moment, sat eating in vacant silence. Then a feeling came over her, or a slight, possibly imagined movement in the corner of her eye. She looked up at the peephole in the center of the door. Was it only her imagination that the peephole was staring back? As quietly as she could she rose, and fled on cat's feet down the hall and into the stairwell and back to her room.

■

She called the front desk and they sent up a pack of Gitanes. Dumping what was left of the fruit cup, she stood barefoot on her balcony and put the soiled little dish to service as an ashtray. It had been years since she'd smoked, and now, striking a match, she held her arm in front of her, to admire the cigarette between her delicate fingers and the flash of the bangle on her wrist. The city was dark and cool, it was late, and she felt closer to the sky than the earth.

She left the bangle on the nightstand the next morning, when she started on a sheaf of production materials the UPM, Mounir, had asked her to render from French to English for the Macedonian crew. It was exquisitely dull work, and there wasn't enough of it to get her through the day. Just for the headache, she arranged calls with the heads of craft and catering to review the children's various allergies and emphatic personal preferences. It was no small thing to convince such men that these conditions were non-negotiable. They wanted to speak to Mounir, which Ella was hoping to avoid. The production office resented the power the children wielded, and from what she could tell, they resented her as an emissary of that power. The entire production depended on the parents' cooperation. The older child's parents were lawyers, which wasn't ideal, but it was the younger kid she worried about: Stephane, whose mother, Fatima, still tied his shoes. Stephane was ten. Ella had spent an entire day with him before she left for Skopje, for instruction in managing his daily life. He wasn't allowed to run, for fear of an injury to his face. Because of myriad life-threatening allergies, none of which, it emerged, confirmed by medical diagnosis, his diet was limited to white rice and pasta with butter. Fatima bathed him herself, by hand, and for this purpose she required special pH-neutral soap, which was marketed for washing vaginas.

Espèce de conasse, in sum. When, if ever, she'd stopped breastfeeding him, Ella dared not ask. At the time, it destroyed her to think that the universe permitted such a woman to have a child. Now Fatima was merely a nagging, distant source of unease, a horizon of acid rain. She'd withdrawn Stephane from two productions with half or more of his scenes left to film, and in neither case could she be sued for breach of contract because of minor code violations she cited as cause. A mother's love, she'd said to Ella, allowing a hint of poetry to enter her voice. So it wasn't entirely unwelcome news that there were problems with the highway where they were scheduled to shoot, and the production was again indefinitely delayed.

■

Afternoons she stood on the balcony as the sky changed, listening to the noise of a city the existence of which she'd never given a moment's thought. Entire days passed during which she didn't speak more than a few words. The same porter, a sunken-chested man in middle age, brought each of her meals and, eventually, a new pack of Gitanes. She poured her thoughts into these emails to me, but inside her head, it wasn't to me her thoughts were addressed. The bangle remained where she'd left it, on the nightstand, she dared not put it on again. But the unknown other guest entered her mind at random, and more than once, though it made her heart pound, she returned to the sixth floor to look for a tray in the hall. In the pleasant vacancy her wish to be a mother had left behind, a craving formed: to connect fleetingly with a stranger, the luxury and intensity of that. The production delays continued, no one could say when the rest of the crew would arrive, but it could be any time now, Mounir insisted, there was no sense in her flying back to Paris only to turn right back around. Her room was already paid for, and they would try to find her something else to translate, but in the meantime, he said, she should try to enjoy herself, if she could.

■

This phrase—*essaie de t'amuser*—troubled me in a way I didn't really understand. I was having my own trouble enjoying myself. Things in Virginia weren't going well. Classes wouldn't start for weeks. The apartment I'd rented was huge and mostly empty, I had nowhere near enough furniture to fill it, I'd torn open all my boxes but couldn't find most of my clothes. From one of the empty rooms upstairs, where I wanted to make an office, there emanated the very distinctive smell of cat piss, which the general unearthly dankness of the place made much worse and which management suggested I counteract by leaving an open can of coffee in the corner of the floor. Despite the headache this and other odors gave me, I left the house infrequently, it was just too fucking hot, and I didn't have a car yet, didn't know how to get one, though I did walk periodically to the Food Lion down the street, arriving drenched in sweat and lingering in the cool aisles, filling my basket with frozen pizzas and peanut butter and frequently asking the cashier to split my balance across two or even three different cards. But Ella's relief, and the effusion of thought and language it gave rise to, was a relief to me as well—it relieved my guilt about having left. I loved to imagine her roaming that hotel, claiming its vacancy as her own. I dug out my Larousse, in whose pages I looked up words like *ruisseler* and *revenant*, and I kept her emails open on my phone, read them and reread them, in hope that her relief would hold.

■

From this distance, though, after everything that's happened since, it seems like our relief was relief from each other. Morning after morning when Ella woke, the TV screen had gone to blue, the curtains glowed in the early light. Her per diem was enough to cover lunch, dinner, and access to the spa, pool, and fitness center. The treadmill, she said, gave her the unsettling feeling that she was at the mercy of the ground beneath her feet. In the sauna, with her pores wide open, the events of her life seemed strange to her, like they belonged to a narrative she'd memorized from a book. It sounds unkind, my love, she wrote, but our life feels like a dream evaporating from my mind: Who is this girl who cut her hair short and left for New York with $900 in cash? Last night it occurred to me that at the outset it was you who insisted on the provisional, administrative nature of our marriage. Do you never think about how many of our friends who married for papers have since split up? It's been eleven days since I got here, and apart from the balcony I haven't set foot outside. The patter of my footsteps echoes in my mind, and sometimes I think I hear it from my bed and go and stand at the peephole staring into the empty hall. There's this electricity in my life here, occasional traces of this mysterious other guest: in the locker room, the faint but unmistakable odor of menstruation hangs in the air; in the sauna, as steam fogs the glass-paneled door, a handprint appears, longer and leaner than my own, alongside the delicate imprint of a face in partial profile. Pressing my own face to the glass, I can't tell who's haunting whom. The water in the air and the water in my body gather together on my skin, and again I find myself wondering where it all goes. Like an epileptic who hasn't seized in months or years, I keep waiting for this affliction to return, take control of my body and brain. But no, I pound the treadmill, race my heart, and then at the ice fountain I freeze my blood, filling and refilling my lungs.

■

The film concerned a plastic surgeon who, on holiday with his family, finds his minivan's voice-operated cruise control stuck at maximum speed, and has to steer a safe course through the obstacles ahead, as his family looks back helplessly through the rear windshield at the destruction they leave in their path. Il voudrait bien s'attarder, she wrote, réveiller les morts et rassembler ce qui fut brisé.

Mais du paradis soufle une tempête. The cause of the delay, she soon learned, was a scramble to secure permits for a new stretch of highway for the shoot. In normal circumstances, Macedonia was a perfect stand-in for southern France, because the highways there could be closed for hours every day and nobody would make a fuss. But because of rampant xenophobic violence along Greece's border with Bulgaria, the highway they'd arranged for had become a corridor for thousands of Syrians on their way to western Europe. This corridor had opened less than two months before, when the Macedonian government, responding to pressure from the European Council, and doubtless with its candidacy for EU membership in mind, changed its asylum laws to address the arbitrary detention of migrants passing through the country, who suffered barbaric, systematic abuse at the hands of the Macedonian police. All this was right here, within miles, Ella wrote, and yet it was as remote to her senses as it might have been on the other side of the planet.

A general sorrow took hold of her, under the cover of which she feared her private sorrow would smuggle itself back into her heart. Feared but also maybe hoped. In a fresh bathrobe she became absorbed by the hundreds of images available online that documented what one article referred to as the *migrant experience*, photos that showed men, women, and children of all ages hauling their belongings in heavy black bags they hugged to their chests or hoisted over their shoulders, marching in columns that stretched way out of frame into the distance, reclining here and there in the grassy median with their hats pulled over their eyes. Photographs felt like knowledge, and therefore power. According to Susan Sontag. Photographs did and language, too. The word *migrant* itself suggested a pivotal event in the history of a species. Carefully examining dozens of photos, she realized she was subconsciously trying to provoke a certain anxiety in herself: that the world was getting more crowded, more hostile, that its habitable spaces were getting fewer and farther between. Among the fashionable remarks people were always making at dinner parties when we lived in Brooklyn was the giddy prediction that the wars of the future would be fought not over oil but over water. It made their eyes shine to say so, because it sounded dangerous and exciting, something for pundits to warble about in the autotuned version of the news. After the hurricane, even, Ella remembered hearing this kind of talk, by candlelight in the bar: there was something so sinister about the certainty of our feeling safe.

She'd put it in roughly those words, she said, in a Skype conversation with her therapist, Katia, who told her it was normal to feel overwhelmed. It stung me to discover that Skype calls were possible; Ella had told me that on Hotel Ezero's wi-fi video or even audio calls were inconceivable. Her emails had an estranging quality, I needed to see her face and to hear her voice. Instead, she left me to settle for the newswire photos she'd been looking at, which she began to attach to her emails, and because my experience of these photos became entangled in my experience of her thinking, in her consuming intensity and in the intensity with which I missed her, the photos assumed an important role in my emotional life as well.

What good was served by seeing them? That shady commerce between art and truth. Maybe they gave us a chance to feel despair on equal footing,

STATES OF EMERGENCY

as helpless outsiders looking in. Sweating like a madman among my tattered boxes of books, I examined the photos she sent as I imagined she examined them, and I did feel genuine despair. In one, a toddler had loosed a lock of his mother's hair from her headscarf and held it closed in his pudgy fist, his face half buried in her neck, staring fixedly into the camera's lens. The totality of his trust that she would keep him safe made me wish for the end of the world. Que l'univers permette. The weight of him in his mother's arms over thousands of miles, the evenness of his breath, the sweetness of his perspiration, the warmth of his sleeping and waking—all this knowledge Ella felt gather inside her own body, she said, as she herself slept and woke. I let it gather in my body as well.

■

By now it had been August for what felt like years. Empty peanut butter jars piled up in the sink. I plugged the TV in and kept it on at all times. The number of migrants crossing through the Balkans continued to rise, and the Macedonian government declared a state of emergency, calling upon the military to reinforce the police presence along its southern border. On a train headed to Paris, several people were wounded during a terrorist attack, which was thwarted by a pair of American servicemen on leave. At a town hall in New Hampshire, Donald Trump promised to end birthright citizenship for the children of undocumented immigrants: the Fourteenth Amendment is very questionable, he said. Six days had passed since I'd heard from Ella when, just for something to do, I waited in the blistering heat for the bus, which I rode in the direction of campus, getting off a few stops early at a local bank, where a teller reluctantly took a crumpled five-euro bill in exchange for $5.60 USD. With the five dollars, I bought a coffee and bacon-egg-and-cheese at a bagel shop across the street from campus, which I'd not laid eyes on until now.

Wiping the grease on my pants, I followed a brick path to the library, where I used the sixty cents to print my translations of Ella's emails. I wanted to put them on the wall above my desk, to motivate me if I ever did any

53

writing of my own. But the library was a large, drafty building, with lots of different halls. It took me a long time to find the machine I'd printed to, and when I did, a woman about my age with green eyes and long, vividly auburn hair was there collecting her own materials, inspecting each page as it emerged and assigning it to one of ten or twelve piles. Her headphones were turned up loud enough that even over the roar of the printer I could hear she was listening to Kendrick Lamar. She kept looking over her shoulder at me, like I was lurking, which I was. When she finished, she packed her things and went away, and I waited for my own print job to start.

It didn't start. I caught the redhead as she was boarding the trolley. I might have caught her sooner, but there were some undergrads around, and I was too shy to run or shout. Now she was on the phone. For fuck's sake, she was saying. Why is noncollated even a thing? She turned when I tapped her shoulder. I think some of my pages may have gotten mixed in with yours, I said, breathing hard. I saw that she had a nose ring, which accentuated her huffing. She removed an earbud, and I repeated myself. Because she was slightly taller than me, I stood up as straight as I could: I think you have some pages that belong to me.

She had an Irish accent. No, I don't think so, she said. That doesn't sound right at all.

■

Ella's fixation on the migrant crisis—she wrote in the long, long email that ended that excruciating week of silence—marked a shift in the emotional currents of her isolation. In a state of heightened moral sensitivity, she felt a sudden urge to watch the films she'd brought on her computer. The first was *Persona*, in which—so Sontag wrote in a review, Ella said—language is presented as an instrument of fraud and cruelty, and intimacy as a kind of looking glass that distorts the boundaries of self. When the movie opens, an actress named Elisabet Vogler has for obscure reasons taken a private vow of silence. Happily, her nurse, Alma, does enough talking for both of them—notably on the subject of a porny encounter on a beach and a subsequent abortion. Relative to Ella's fixation on the migrants, a pair of images that she'd dismissed when she'd originally seen the movie as cheap shorthand for psychic turmoil, struck her now in a new way: news broadcast footage of the self-immolation of the Buddhist monk Thích Quảng Đức in Vietnam, and the famous photograph from the Warsaw Ghetto Uprising. We're meant to guess that these images inform Elisabet's anguish somehow; photography made the world discontinuous with itself, according to Sontag. It also made the self discontinuous with itself. Words were supposed to do the opposite; words were supposed to make us whole, put the world in order—so says Sontag: only that which narrates can make us understand. But alas, Ella wrote, Alma talks and talks, and the more she does, the less clear it is what's what, who's who. Not long after she watches the footage of the burning monk, Elisabet is presented with another image: enclosed in an earnest, oblivious letter from her husband, a picture of her son, which she glances over and tears in two. Later, after she's spent long minutes examining the Warsaw photo, she reassembles the torn halves of her son and looks at them anew. Turns out, she hates this gorky, thick-lipped runt, she thought she craved motherhood, but actually it's a major drag.

Anyway, Ella wrote, there's really no better psychic preparation for watching Persona than a long stay in an empty hotel. I mean, if you really want to get deep in your head. What she needed was a human body, a face to gaze into, the incidental contact of hands, shoulders, legs. When the film ended, sometime after dark, she found herself once again descending to the hotel bar, where the same peculiar music played at a just barely audible volume, and colored towers of light cast shadows around the room. This is where she found the occupant of 6032 stationed before a sweating glass. And yet, Ella's email continued, Emina insists our first conversation was not in the bar but in the sauna, where we and not our drinks were sweating. It's strange she'd remember these encounters out of order, because our conversation in the sauna picked up where our conversation in the bar left off, and led to a series of excursions, first out into the Skopje streets and then into the surrounding countryside. It was in the bar that we first met, I watched her set her drink aside and eat her cocktail olives one by one. She caught me staring, and invited me to share a drink.

She was magnetic, Emina. Her easy laughter, her relaxed posture, and her good looks made it natural to feel close to her. She had a way of conveying with her whole body a willingness to take you seriously: with her eyebrows, with her shoulders, with her very breath. Later I learned that, for a report on human rights abuses, she spent her days interviewing people about the most intimate and traumatic aspects of their lives, and I wondered if she earned their trust as easily as she earned mine. By the end of the evening I'd shared the entirety of the long saga of our troubles conceiving, I'd shared a number of embarrassing sexual anecdotes, among which an account of the spatula debacle that made her laugh so hard she cried. And I told her about the heatwave and, now, the sudden evaporation of my wish to be a mother; I said that perhaps to bring a child into the world was unfair to the world and the child alike. Emina touched my arm. Don't do that, she said; I needn't rationalize how I felt, my mind may one day change back. Her own boyfriend only *thought* they were trying to conceive; the idea of being pregnant repulsed her, and she'd been taking birth control on the sly. She just didn't want *people* coming out of her vagina, she said. Our martinis were just very cold glasses of gin. We'd toasted to the notion that to be human was to degrade the very ground you walked on, but also kind of fun.

What else can I tell you? Emina smelled strongly of chlorine. She closed her eyes when she laughed. Later, I learned to recognize a certain violence in this mania that came over her at night, a phantom of her daylight self. She made the barman turn the music up. Olives for dinner and maraschino cherries for dessert. We laughed until our stomachs ached, matched each other drink for drink, sank lower in our seats, closer each round to the floor. Whenever we needed his attention, the barman, who was otherwise absorbed in a ladies' magazine, assumed an air of theatrical exasperation. We made him take one of the quizzes from his magazine, to determine what sort of lady he should be if he hoped to attract a mate. To be a woman is one great picnic! Emina cried. It is one great big piece of cake! Did she notice the glances he stole at her bare shoulders and thighs? He had, Stojan, a wonderful way of moving, he was tall and knuckly and all night he danced in the minutest way you can imagine, the way one hums to oneself, and the music he played was enchanting, a mixture of American and Balkan pop, but also occasionally something more traditional, these keening ballads of the cruel past. One in particular I remember clearly, a kind of bluesy lament, Emina explained, of the Ottoman Empire, named for and presumably set in the remote lowlands of the Vardar basin—which is to say, the present-day former Yugoslav Republic of Macedonia—in which a young woman, her mother's only daughter and the apple of her father's eye, reflects upon isolation, her ennui, her hopeless prospects, the impossibility of leaving, the impossibility of remaining, the burden she's become, and the sight of white geese whose flight over the distant mountains, which is not dissimilar to the elegance of girls in heels. So you see, Emina said, already laughing, we at least are the girls in heels, though in fact we were both by that point barefoot, our soles rimmed with dust. Maybe best not to describe the dreams I had that night, my love. Emina helped me to my room, and I awoke with the suspicion that, in the absence of anyone to help her to her own room, she'd stayed there in my bed, and left while I was still asleep. I seemed to remember, in snatches, rolling over in the night and being comforted by her presence there. But later when I woke again there was no sign of her, and if it hadn't been for the throbbing pain behind my eyes I could easily have convinced myself I'd imagined the whole thing. There was nothing within reach to drink, and I was in too much pain to move; for a long time, I watched a shaft of light make slow circles above the bed. That's what I was doing when the front desk called, to say that they'd found two pairs of shoes in the bar and that whenever it was convenient they'd send someone up with both so I could identify which was mine. I sat up to take the call. In plain view where I'd left it on the nightstand was the bangle. I stared at it for a long time. If Emina had left in darkness, was it possible she hadn't seen it? I swept it into the drawer, but all morning, as I flopped around in bed, with a pounding headache and mild nausea, the curtains drawn shut against the sun, its presence drummed in my mind. In the afternoon, to distract myself, I texted Samia, who's screening submissions for Sundance, and she gave me a link and password for a horror movie set in Tehran during the Iraq-Iran War. The main character is Shideh, a former student activist and mother to an only child; when her apartment building is struck by a missile that fails to detonate, her daughter becomes convinced that djinn have taken up residence in their home, and Shideh begins to lose her grip. Something about the threat of destruction becoming more destructive than destruction itself. How is it that so much of what I felt connected me to Shideh—her vulnerability, her self-doubt—was contained in the determination with which she keeps pace with her Jane Fonda workout tape, even as bombs are falling from the sky? In her sweat and her heavy breathing and her dark, knitted eyebrows, I recognized my own efforts to summon an inner strength I wasn't sure I had, pounding the treadmill in the basement of the Hotel Ezero. Nothing else in the film—the horror of war, the wretchedness of political persecution—corresponded to the experiences of my life, but down to my bones, I felt this ownership of her desperation to keep her daughter safe. The shadows in my room grew longer, then fainter, the sky grew dim, and a steady wind rose and whistled against the glass. I wanted to explain this feeling to Emina. Forgetting the bracelet, I went downstairs and found her in the pool swimming laps, and stood for a while to admire her deliberate stroke and her long body and the various hollows her muscles formed, and the blades she made of her long, fine arms. When she joined me in the sauna a little while later, as she continued panting I told her about the movie, *Under the Shadow* is what it's called—sometimes, I told her, my dreams were so vivid that during the day when I met the people who'd appeared in them I'd feel an intimacy between us that didn't exist, which is how the movie made me feel as well. As if it were a memory of my actual life.

This was my first glimpse of another side to Emina, her daylight self. When I finished speaking, she didn't say anything, she just looked at me sidewise. This was when I remembered the bangle she may or may not have seen. The door panel fogged over, her handprint appeared, and I matched it with my own, spreading my fingertips against the glass. Don't you know, Emina said then, it's bad luck to compare hands?

I watched her chest heave as gradually her breathing steadied. Had she gotten her shoes back, I asked her, just for something to say, and at length, maybe in connection with shoes and shoelessness, she started telling me about her work, the research that filled her days. Did I realize, she wanted to know—apropos of what, I wasn't sure, but it felt like an accusation—that Mother Teresa was born here in Skopje, a Kosovar Albanian of the Ottoman Empire, born a stone's throw from the very spot where we now sat? For six months Emina had been traveling to Skopje and around Macedonia to document its treatment of migrants, she said, patting the sweat on her brow with a dry washcloth, leaning her forehead against the panel in the sauna door to look out at the glow of the pool.

The sauna made me woozy, and in order to stay upright I focused on the taste of my sweat. There was a faint, radioactive trace of anger in Emina's voice. You get a pretty fair idea of the conditions inside a detainment facility, she continued, from a straightforward description of its plumbing. The detention facility right here in Skopje was designated to house around a hundred inmates and was equipped with two working toilets, a single shower, and three sinks, from none of which flowed potable water. For a hundred people these provisions were already criminally inadequate; by the admission of the minister of the interior, in a letter Emina had extracted from him, there were never fewer than 250 *persons* receiving *accommodation* in the Gazi Baba Reception Centre for Foreigners. Drinking water was in short supply as well; bottles were available for ten euros in the so-called informal market operated by the guards, where soap was available at the same markups and likewise toilet paper, and pads and tampons, though some of the women had confided that, from a combination of stress, paranoia, and depression, they'd stopped menstruating altogether. There was no heat, no hot water, they slept on the tiled floor, some without mattresses or even blankets, huddling in the winter for warmth. *Furthermore*, Emina continued, most detainees in the Gazi Baba Reception Centre for Foreigners were not permitted outdoors even once for a moment's fresh air during stays lasting as long as seven months, and it was typical not to have any contact whatsoever with the outside world: a one-minute phone call cost no less than thirty euros, and there was no access to legal counsel, or anyone at all who might tell them when they could hope to be released; and those who asked guards questions of this sort were severely beaten with fists, batons, the studded heels of boots, though of course you could be severely beaten, one young woman told Emina, for almost anything—for laughing, for speaking, for smelling sour—and afterward they'd douse you with cold water but it would be weeks before anyone cleaned your blood from the floor.

People blame it on a lack of resources, Emina said after a moment. Impossible to imagine cruelty like that in the more civilized nations of the world. But it's baked into the very idea of borders, that some people are more human than the rest. The problem isn't resources, she said; the problem is the human heart.

She laid her hand against her own human heart as she said this, and it was as if I could feel it pounding in my chest.

■

I'm not sure why I've written this part, my love, Ella's last email continued. The new freeness I felt was also an emptiness. I was using Emina to fill it, to find my way back to the world. I'm in a bus now heading to the hotel, and that's what I started out telling you. I don't know how much longer my battery will last, I'm not sure how long the ride might be, and in the bus I swear to you it's as hot as it was in the sauna, or during the heatwave in our apartment. Across the aisle there's an old woman traveling with a baby, who hasn't made a peep. The old woman keeps getting up to talk to the driver about something, and when she does, she leaves the child with her seatmate, a large man with a strong neck. With the baby in his lap, a smile appears on his face, something private and withdrawn. He has a tired, hard-ridden face, but he makes cute noises and plays peekaboo. Then when the old woman returns to her seat, he hands the baby over, and very gradually the smile fades.

I feel a weird ownership of the small relationship that's developed between these three. Maybe just by having set it down here for you. I don't really have any concept of where I am. Only that I'm headed back toward Skopje. This week has been so strange. Emina drinks most nights the way she drank the night I met her. This mania that overtakes her, at first I thought it was the alcohol that brought it on, but now I think the reverse is true. She'd kick a chair over, or spit olive pits across the table at her empty glass. She'd help herself to my Gitanes and let her ashes fall where they might. At night when we talked, we mostly talked about me. Thank *God* you're here, she kept saying. I would spin off the *planet*. Then in the daytime, that brittleness. She'd call my room and tell me to meet her in the spa before she went to work, then treat me like a puppy she was training not to beg. Sometimes I felt sure she'd seen the bangle on the nightstand, or that she'd been at the peephole and watched me try it on—that she was tormenting me as punishment for this minor sin.

When she did speak, she returned always to the subject of human vileness, with a heat of reproach in her voice that brought her close to tears. *Vileness* being her word. Did the name General Bernard Janvier mean anything to me, she asked at one point. Janvier, she said, began his military career as a special forces chief in the Algerian War. He served in Madagascar, Beirut, and Iraq. As the commandant of the UN peacekeeping mission in Bosnia, he advocated for neutrality in the slaughter of Bosnian Muslims by Bosnian Serbs. He urged the UN to scale back its mission and leave the belligerents to resolve their differences alone, and meantime the French foreign ministry complained internally that the Bosniaks were manipulating the media to exaggerate their plight. Islamophobia was chromosomal in French foreign policy, Emina said, so it was natural enough for its leaders to feel some unspoken affinity for the Serbs. In the spring of 1995, when several hundred UN peacekeeping troops were taken hostage, Janvier secured their release in a series of meetings with the Serbian commander Ratko Mladić by pledging not to interfere with the Serbian offensive against Srebrenica, a supposed UN safe zone where a ruthless campaign of ethnic cleansing had nevertheless continued in plain sight for years. Over the course of a few days that July, thousands of Mladić's men overran the town, as a company of lightly armed Dutch soldiers on the ground begged Janvier to authorize air strikes to prevent what everyone knew would follow. As promised, Janvier refused, and Mladić stuck to the plan: the systematic execution of eight thousand Bosniak men and boys, and the rape and torture of thousands of Bosniak women and girls. Mladić's term for this was *neutralizing terrorists*, Emina said. What phrase was better calibrated to warm a French general's heart? With her middle finger and her thumb, she made a circle in which she lightly twisted her left wrist, a delicate, grounding gesture. Janvier was promoted in the Legion of Honor, and for years the French government dragged its feet in capturing war criminals, gumming up the works in The Hague, lest its record of peacekeeping be too carefully examined in open court. If you don't know the name Janvier, Emina went on, it's because la gloire de la république ne permet pas—but here I interrupted: My ancestors were Jews in Algeria and slaves in Martinique; I didn't need lessons in the infamy of the French state. Emina narrowed her eyes before she responded. I'm not talking about ancestors, she said, more quietly. I'm talking about now, as we live and breathe, the things we let happen in our name.

But I have to admit it was exhilarating, all this rage pooling behind a dam. I wanted to drink from it, to follow it to its source. I tried not to pepper her with personal questions, but our conversations left these dark spots around her life. I found myself searching along the edges of her towel for scars. When she admitted she was dreading her upcoming thirtieth birthday as much as I was, I managed to extract that she was born in Sarajevo the same month I was born in Paris. I took this coincidence as proof of a bond between us. Ten million people are born every twenty-eight days, was Emina's only remark. But she was so beautiful, and funny, and even her testiness was a thrill. That night she made me dance with her until we both collapsed in a sweaty heap. Then the following day, in the hot tub, she announced that her research was complete, she'd gathered enough material, and with a few days to spare before she flew back to her boyfriend in New

York, where she'd prepare her report, renew her birth control, then set out again to report some new horrible thing. The news that she was leaving was a blow. But something softened in her, she evened out. For now, her days were as empty as mine, and she said that in her empty days she liked to walk the streets to clear her head.

■

The Vardar River runs through Skopje from west to east. We went over one bridge and another, the famous Stone Bridge, the famous Art Bridge, the famous Bridge of Civilizations, *famous* being a near synonym for *vile*, in Emina's vocabulary, but one she used now with a certain sardonic fondness. In the streets, though a few weeks had passed, there were still some traces of festivities—tattered posters, grease-stained skewers, horse shit stamped flat and fossilized in the sun—connected to Ilinden, Saint Elijah's Day, the national celebration of a 1903 uprising against the Ottoman Empire. Despite her fine bones, Emina walked with heavy, insouciant steps, flat-footed, like Serena Williams or Angelique Kerber between sets, and in the searing light of those afternoons I was surprised to find that her face, which I'd only seen in the peculiar light of the bar and of the spa, became new to me: her hair was dyed a very dark brown, almost black, and recently cut, and her skin was much fairer than I'd realized, with long lashes that added to the overall impression of seriousness she gave even when she smiled. She smiled a lot, but there was a gravity to her new steadiness that transformed the ground beneath her feet. At every step we passed memorials, statues of heroes, statues of beggars, ruins of premodern forts, which in Emina's presence became reminders of civilization's millennia-long record of vile behavior: of invasions, occupations, and assaults; of enslavement, despoilment, political murder, murder for spite and vengeance, for honor, for religion, for general bloodlust, beginning even before the famous campaigns of Alexander the Great, an inordinately huge statue of whom occupied the intricately tiled central plaza beside the river, a powerful and contentious symbol, Emina told me, of Macedonian ethnic pride.

Here and there we passed traditional restaurants where clusters of men in bad clothes were to be found in a perpetual state of ruminatively stirring sugar into their tiny cups. What sort of work was available to these men? Were they porters, night clerks, prison guards? Were they gaffers and grips? Emina and I stopped from time to time for a glass of rakija, observing the custom of speaking very little and acting as if we were numb with boredom, or as if we were trying to plan a robbery but didn't know quite where to start. At first I wasn't sure Emina noticed the attention she drew from the men in bad clothes. But it would have been hard not to, it gathered like smoke. It was suffocating, I mean. When it got too thick to bear, some of them would start to actually purr, and this purring escalated until one of them inevitably spoke, the ones with glassy eyes. Brief, hard words, voices like the sudden flash of an ember into flame. They always start by asking if I'm married, Emina told me. It would have been easier to just say yes, she said, but that felt like giving her consent to their arrangement of the world. Instead, she'd respond by turning slowly in her chair, looking the man up and down with frank contempt. Or sometimes she raised her face to mine, as if to let that contempt pass between us like a secret. Her eyes were the same slate blue as yours, and they gave me gooseflesh. And a little chuckle that felt genuinely dangerous—nothing gets at the brutality of manhood like a woman's laughter. But the men were largely unmoved, they returned to their coffee and their boredom, the smoke cleared, we were left in peace. Until finally one day—hier, putain—one of these men with glassy eyes addressed his remarks to me.

Emina slammed her hands on the table with a suddenness that made our glasses jump. Before I understood what was happening, she'd leapt from her chair and flew at the little man with her palms and her knees and her teeth. *Throwing hands* is the exact right term. And a barking, rhythmic invective. The man was stunned, he raised his arms in a vague way to defend himself, but it was the barkeep—a broad-chested man with a flat head and a flat nose—who pinned Emina's arms and gave her a quick, sharp slap in the face that made everything stand still.

Only now did I realize I was on my feet. There was a mirror behind the bar, and I tried to read the expression on my face. Had I frozen? Our glasses were overturned, and one of them now rolled over the edge of the table and shattered on the tiles. There was raki in a puddle on the tabletop, and sticky on my forearms. Never before in my life had violence erupted more quickly than I could react. The shame of that would hit me later. For now my mind was blank.

The man Emina had attacked turned to the mirror as well. (I never did find out what he'd said to me. Later, looking down at the river, both of us would burst into tears, and we would argue about whose tears had pro-voked whose, but Emina wouldn't repeat the words that set her off.) He was a small man in his fifties or even sixties. My guess is he took me for an Arab. In the mirror, I watched him lift his hand to his cheek. His face was scratched and he was bleeding. Emina gave the barman a half-hearted shove in the chest, and he raised his hand as if to hit her again. All around, the men in bad clothes stirred their coffee. I grabbed our bags and grabbed Emina's wrist, tugging her back out to the street.

■

I washed the raki off my arms, but I could still feel the salt of tears caked on my face late in the afternoon, when I found myself in Emina's rental car with the windows down, on our way through the bright, shrubby hills to the Vardar's source, Lake Mavrovo. We were going to spend the night there, and then drive on to Lake Ohrid in the morning to visit an old professor of hers, an ethnographer who was studying Orthodox water rituals. It must have been the lake that finally rinsed the salt away. On the little beach there I applied a thick layer of high-test sunscreen to Emina's back—she's very sensible about her skin—and then for a long time we lay in the sun. Emina flipped the pages of a book, as if on behalf of us both. The sky was unspeak-ably clear, both as it appeared overhead and as it was reflected on the lake's motionless surface, and apart from the distant calling of birds it was silent all around. Occasionally she read passages aloud, reaching out to touch my arm. The book was a biography of Olympias, née Polyxena, a barbarian princess married off upon her father's death to Philip II of Macedon, to whom she bore the child who'd become Alexander the Great. She fucked snakes, apparently, Emina told me at dinner. We'd gotten a room in a sort of bed-and-breakfast within sight of the lake. The innkeeper was a soft man with crooked knuckles, and his daughter moved around us, eager and shy, as we ate and as we smoked in the dark on the porch. She was seven, Emina learned, motherless, not enrolled in school. When her father carried her off to bed, we returned to the lake to swim, there was nothing, Emina said, like a night swim in a lake. Above us the sky was almost perfectly black, and for a long time we floated in the shallows, talking about this and that, until, after a period of silence, Emina told me her own story of loss and grief and rage. She was six, she said, when she was awoken one night by the sound of artillery fire: the distant reports of the cannons and the whistling of the shells through the air, which preceded a sickening, earsplitting impact by a matter of milliseconds. Shells like these had landed by the dozen within a hundred meters of her apartment on a daily basis: each one shook her building to its foundation, knocked glass out of windows, dishes off shelves, brought ceiling plaster raining down in her hair, while outside the shrapnel rained down from the sky. There's almost no way to describe what happens inside you, she said, the hollow, helpless, gut-sick feeling—which often returned to her when she tried to sleep—as you listen to an artillery raid draw closer and closer with each strike. For four years, more than three hundred artillery rounds fell on the city each day. On some days, it was close to four thousand. She remembers always having a headache, always tasting bile in the back of her throat. And the insanity that overcame some of the children in her building as the result of the shortage of food, the shortage of drinking water, and the shelling and ceaseless sound of gunfire that reached them through their blown-out windows at all times of day and night.

A sniper killed her father. A mortar round killed her mother while she waited in line for water at a makeshift tap. She left the city at the end of 1994 with a family from her building, a husband and wife whose two toddlers it became Emina's job to look after over the course of the next few months. What horrors those months entailed she couldn't bring herself to describe. Bringing with them what they could carry in their arms, they proceeded on foot in the dead of night to the border, where they spent weeks in a refugee camp. A pair of smugglers brought them into Croatia, and after several weeks living in a basement they somehow secured funds for the forged Croatian passports they needed to cross borders into Slovenia, Austria, Germany, and Denmark, until finally they arrived in Sweden, where in an asylum center their ordeal continued for years. When she read about Olympias, Emina said, making slow circles beneath the water with her hands, she heard the story of an orphan girl, taken from her home and deposited in a world of strange, hostile men, where she nurses her rage in her womb and sets it loose upon the world.

She left her story at that, maybe there was more to say. For a long time neither of us spoke, but remained mostly submerged in the lake, listening to the insect noise, the passing of cars behind the trees, and to the water's faint lapping over the shore, and over us as well.

■

It was last night by Lake Mavrovo, my love, that I began writing this email. As Emina spoke, the bangle became involved in my mind with the story of her escape from Sarajevo, I was convinced it was some sort of token of her past. I was glad, when we finally went in, that our room had only one bed; it was soothing to be near her, to feel the warmth of her where I slept. This morning, we got up early and made the drive to Ohrid, taking in the scenery and withdrawing into our private thoughts, and I devised a plan to return the thing: I'd simply wait until evening when our conversation resumed, and I'd work my way toward explaining honestly how it came into my possession. As we drove, I ran this scenario through my mind so many times that it felt real. But when we arrived in town and I connected to wi-fi, I discovered I had an email from Mounir, announcing, among other things, that the children are to arrive this evening; Emina put me on a bus and wished me luck, and I doubt I'll ever see her again, so I guess the bangle is mine to keep.

It's been a long ride, with frequent stops in dusty burgs. The grandmother and the baby are gone, and their seatmate is asleep, head lolling, mouth agape. I remember when Emina told me about her report on the detention center, she mentioned a study showing that trauma altered its victims on an epigenetic level, and that when they had children they passed these alterations along. Everyone inherits history, she said; some people have it in their DNA. That thought keeps returning to me. Because what I wanted to tell you about was the movie we watched last night, Emina and I, after the lake, the laptop nestled between us on the bed. One of Marker's earliest: *Le mystère Koumiko*. Now that I've seen it I remember Chris telling me about his first trip to Tokyo, he said that something about Japan quickened his heart. It was probably the girls, I remember telling him; that made him laugh. He'd arrived intending to cover the Summer Olympics, but instead he became bewitched by a young woman, who is amazed to find herself starring in a film that bears her name.

At one point, Koumiko mentions she was born in Manchuria, meaning she was born at the heart of the conflict that drew Japan into World War II, and although she would have been too young to remember, the global history of her early childhood haunts the film. When the Olympics end, Chris returns to Paris, and receives by post a series of Magnetophon tapes on which she's recorded her answers to a questionnaire he's left her—though it soon becomes obvious he's written the answers for her himself, a sort of novelistic conflation of selves that reaches a crescendo at the end of the film, in Koumiko's car during a downpour, when Chris begins to ask a question he can't bring himself to finish: But what do you think of . . . He trails off, but a quick series of images from Dachau, Pearl Harbor, and the *Enola Gay* makes it clear what he means. Did that, he asks, inform your sense of what could happen to you—to you, Koumiko—or did it happen in another world?

No, she replies there in the car, it could happen to me also; it's like a wave, rolling over the sea. And her voice in the car trails off as well, and we hear from one of her recorded letters in which she elaborates upon this thought: we see her in a train now, alone, gazing out the window at the passing scene. When I was a small child, we hear her taped voice say, I lived by what I tasted with my tongue, or by the sweet smells I followed through the streets, while at the very same time, mankind was suffering: men went off to war, and were made prisoners, they resisted and wept, their flesh was mutilated. And yet, when I learn about all this today, I'm astonished that I didn't know of it for so long a time, I'm appalled each morning at how little I understand, because soon, the results of all these events will arrive, like a wave rolling over the sea when there's been an earthquake in the distance, a wave that advances on its way, so to speak, until finally it will reach my feet.

■

With that, emails from Ella became fewer, and briefer, became not emails at all but iMessages, containing only the most basic sustaining platitudes of marriage, as the production began and her days got full. I don't know what I made of her relationship with Emina. I didn't know if it brought us closer or drove us further apart. It seemed to me that in some ledger of personal seriousness, it set her way ahead. But on the other hand I'd spent so much time with her emails, I'd translated them with such assiduous care, that I felt like I'd written them myself, or that I shared in their moral strenuousness and their intensity, their way of embedding beneath the kinetic surface of things a coiled, haunted stillness—qualities I'd come close to but never achieved in my actual writing and which, now that I'd found a way to simulate them, or rather to misappropriate them, became a kind of drug. It was the end of August, and with less than a week now until the semester began, I should have been getting started on work to turn in for class, but instead I began writing a monster email of my own. In it, I described in exhaustive detail the various aggravations of my daily life: the heat and humidity, the circumscription of carlessness, the featurelessness of Virginian culture, a long list of vanity plates in particularly poor taste. Each week, my copy of the *New Yorker* failed to arrive in the mail. The Food Lion, I wrote, didn't have the kind of peanut butter I liked, and its Fuji apples, when it had Fuji apples, were invariably mealy and bland. Somehow, since the heatwave, I told her, so many of the things I'd once valued—art, beauty, sentiment— had come to seem petty and absurd. In the welter of orientation activities I'd met my cohort, who were as soft and shapeless as me. Sitting with them in bars on the downtown pedestrian mall, with Ella's emails still echoing in my mind, our collective fatuousness was overwhelming. One of them kept saying that the year had gotten off to an inconspicuous start. Another, a Bay Stater named Adam for whom I felt an instinctive dislike, knew the proper demonym for residents of every single US state, which I was convinced he'd memorized only so he could trot out the word *demonym* itself whenever he pleased. His fiancée, Helen, was a year ahead of us in the program and seemed to have appointed herself as our shepherd and ringleader; she was Irish, and when she addressed us as *youse*, I always thought I detected a note of disdain intended specially for me alone. Maybe because, though I left this out of my email to Ella, Helen was the redhead who'd taken my pages off the printer. When I mentioned to the group that my wife was in Macedonia, Helen looked at me in alarm, then recognition, and I knew for certain that my translations were the basis of her contempt. So you're all alone here, she cooed, you poor little man.

There's a mean lady here named Helen, was all I wrote to Ella, but I like her and I think you two would get along. I wrote that I had a trial subscription to Hulu and had already watched several seasons of *Grey's Anatomy*, several seasons of *Elementary*, and now I was starting in on *The Good Wife*; already I was daydreaming about dropping out of my program before it even began and trying instead to become something useful like a doctor or lawyer, or a private eye. I wrote, and this was true, that without her smile and the sound of her laughter my existence was joyless, that more and more I was letting hygienic lapses go unaddressed, and that in our apartment, if she chose to join me there, she could have the office upstairs all to herself.

You stupid, Ella addressed her reply, though it was hard to detect the affection this phrase typically implied. This was after another silence of about a week. She was still waiting, she wrote, in English now, for me to say something about her no longer wanting to start a family, and to try to persuade her to change her mind. If I'd spent so much time reading and rereading and translating her emails, how had it escaped me that this was the invisible current that ran through them all? Her work, she said, was exhausting, her days were full of the minutest anxieties one could imagine, on which the fate of the entire production nonetheless relied. Fatima's perfume made her eyes water, but her relationships with the children were satisfying in ways she hadn't anticipated. That day, on the way to set, the massive convoy of trailers, set cars, camera cars, and tech vans had found its way blocked by a clot of news vans parked on a single-lane overpass, beneath which a long line of migrants was passing on their way north and west. With Stephane and Capucine following her, she'd gotten out of the car, and while the three of them stood for a long time among the cameras, looking out over the procession below, her thoughts of course turned to Emina, who carried within her the same horrors that were written on these hundreds of faces, coded into her DNA. All afternoon, the idea had made her feel utterly hopeless and very small, and now she'd been thinking, she said, about the tendency, when people are talking about interconnectivity in high-flown terms, to emphasize that our existence is based on carbon that originates in the cosmos—the stardust from whence we came and to which we shall return. Because tonight by the pool, she wrote, Stephane, who despite everything about his mother is charming, said something that resonated with me—relative to what, I'm not sure—in the offhanded way of children: that if it's true that 60 percent or more of our bodies is composed of water, it must also be true that they're not always composed of the same water; that the water inside our own bodies must at one time have been inside other bodies, plants and animals, other living and nonliving things, and in the ocean and in the very air around us, in various places around the planet at various moments since the beginning of time. Et alors, his mother said, flicking the pages of a magazine. Et alors, ma vie, so what?

3
Love Stories

In June 1958, two residents of Virginia—a black woman named Mildred
Jeter and a white man named Richard Loving—were married in the District
of Columbia; shortly thereafter, according to court documents, they returned to Virginia and established their marital abode, whereupon in the
dark of night they were arrested by Sheriff Garnett Brooks, a cussed and
violent man with a high-pitched voice. Richard was released on bail; Mildred, who was six months pregnant, was detained in the rat-infested holding
cell for four days before the couple appeared for arraignment before Judge
Edward Stehl, a self-described racial moderate who decades later would
disinherit his eldest daughter for marrying a black man. A grand jury issued
a felony indictment, charging the couple with violating the statewide ban
on interracial marriages. The Lovings pleaded guilty and were sentenced to
one year each in prison; however, the trial judge suspended the sentence for
a period of twenty-five years on the condition that they leave the state and
not return.

After their convictions, the Lovings took up residence in DC, but
soon—because Mildred missed the feeling of grass beneath her feet, and
Richard missed drag racing his car—they filed a motion to vacate the judgment, citing the Fourteenth Amendment. A three-judge panel continued the
case, allowing the Lovings to present their claims to the Virginia Supreme
Court, where it was found that the conditions of the Lovings' suspended
sentence were unreasonable, but that, as the US Supreme Court put it 1888,
marriage, as creating the most important relation in life, as having more to

do with the morals and civilization of a people than any other institution, has always been subject to the control of the Legislature, thereby remanding their case to the original court so the Lovings could be sentenced once again.

Neither of us knew anything about the Lovings on the long-ago Tuesday morning that we were married in Manhattan. It was the summer of the heatwave, and the following fall when I arrived in Virginia and hid myself away in the Alderman Library stacks, that my endless reading of Supreme Court materials led me inevitably to the famous case that bears their name. When my first year of grad school ended in the summer of 2016 and I was back in Paris, they came up again: until Ella's hospitalization I hadn't had much to do but walk the streets, and one day Ella surprised me by agreeing to tag along, she said she liked to see her city through the eyes of a stranger, by which she meant foreigner, by which she meant me. So during an hours-long conversation by the banks of the Seine, she described the Hollywood version of the Lovings' story, which she'd recently seen at its premiere in Cannes.

We'd been talking about our own wedding, which took place in June 2011, on the morning of the summer solstice, when we'd known each other a little under a year. Even as we rode the subway into the city, the concept of lifelong commitment remained a pleasant abstraction. At the moment we said our vows, the thought of having children was no closer to my thoughts than it had been the moment Ella first appeared in the bar where I worked, wearing cutoffs and holding her résumé in both hands. She might have worn cutoffs to the wedding, too, if we hadn't been instructed to make it look legit. Instead she wore a vintage dress; I wore the same bad suit I wore to all weddings. It's amazing it's only been five years, she said now by the river, it feels like another life. I felt the same. Sometimes, I said, I woke up at night with a powerful longing to return to that day, to reabsorb the optimism that carried us home from city hall.

I'm not sure how long we'd been walking by then. The days were getting longer, afternoons stretching well past dinner, a reminder, Ella pointed out, that in fact the return of that day was coming up fast. We were watching the carrousel at Hôtel de Ville, where soldiers in fatigues were standing guard. The Seine had swelled its banks and risen higher than it had since before World War I, bringing a hush over Paris. The passage of time collapsed, and, everywhere, tourists teetered over their feet, under the destabilizing influence, it seemed, of a certain nervy ardor, hitching their pants up over their hip bones, as if they'd all left their belts in the airport; and in the circumstances it was strange to walk among them, to be confronted with their distrait, mammalian scratching, stunned and disoriented as they were by the rising water and its slight distortion of the familiar world. Our conversation turned on the idea, as my wife put it, that to the same extent that the present is attainable only because its future is *un*known to us, the past is *un*attainable for the precise reason that its future is *known*. Which is to say that though we'd begun by discussing how we might celebrate our anniversary on such a severely attenuated budget, we soon found ourselves talking about that original year, the year we met and got married, the first lifelong commitment either of us had ever made and, accordingly, the first time either of us had in any meaningful way understood our lives as delimited by eventual death. Imagine, she said, you could interrupt us on the night we met, you could pull us aside to say we'd be married by the first day of the following summer—what would either of us have made of *that*? We agreed it was almost unthinkable—having spoken to her only briefly during a second visit she made to the restaurant where I worked, and considering that I routinely found myself cowed by the prospect of contacting even women who had given me their phone numbers with the clearly stated expectation that I would call—it was unthinkable that on a night off I would take the train across Brooklyn to get her number from the résumé she'd left, and that I would dial it that very minute from the bar, to my own astonishment and to the astonishment of my coworkers looking on, who knew me as hapless and shy and catatonically irresolute. And what's more, she said, getting to her favorite part of the story, that she would agree to see me, would suggest we meet that very night, either at a party that I planned to attend, or a party she planned to attend, or at any of the places she or I might visit along the way. It was on this occasion, as the night wore on and our signals continued to cross, that I became familiar with what I came to think of as her house style: her insistence on sending her erratically punctuated text messages in all caps, as if to convey an ongoing baseline of enthusiasm and disquiet she'd felt since arriving in New York—at the thrill of being young, of being abroad, and alone, of being broke and unemployed and a little bit afraid—a baseline to which no further typographical emphasis could be added, even when it developed that we were about to pass within a few feet of each other, riding trains in opposite directions on the Williamsburg Bridge, and even hours later, when we finally found ourselves within striking distance and she sent me the name of a bar, the worst of the many dives within a six-block radius of my house, where when I arrived, having missed last call, she invited me to share her drink, the drink that like all her drinks that evening had been paid for by her date, a nice man named Rob, to whom she introduced me cheerfully before thanking him for a lovely time and taking me by the hand back into the street.

By the Pont des Arts, we descended the steps to the water's edge, where the lowest branches of a white birch dragged in the current, and sat for a moment listening to the river and the cries of gulls. How thrilling it must have been, I said, a little sadly, to be in the streets with you in that cool hour before dawn—to be speaking loudly, staggering theatrically, giddy in anticipation of each other's bodies. I remembered catching our reflection in the dark storefronts we passed, and now I wondered, to what extent were we pretending, to what extent was it possible ever to feel so good? Because we were on my very block when in the shadows ahead of us a girl went down on her bicycle with breathtaking suddenness, as if she'd been blindsided by an invisible linebacker. When we rushed up to help her to her feet, she was bleeding heavily from her chin; more blood than they'd have let her donate had already stained her face and arms and the white front of her shirt, her bare legs, and the pavement at her feet. Once her eyes stopped rolling in her head, she took in the sight of her blood, and began to shriek and thrash about, not in pain or shock, but as if she thought we were responsible for her fall.

Only a few weeks later, Ella remembered now, this same girl, her chin bandaged tightly, came into the restaurant and, without giving the faintest sign of recognition, sat in Ella's section; Ella wondered how much of her blood had needed to be replaced. We'd learned her name was Virginia Hale. That night, the night of her fall, it had taken most of an hour to get Virginia on her feet. Ella sat her down, helped her breathe, assured her she was safe but that she was in urgent need of medical attention. Not least because she didn't have health insurance, Virginia refused to move from her perch on the curb until her roommate, a nursing student we'd managed to reach, arrived to collect her. We watched her go, and the several thick pools of blood she left behind soaked into the pavement; and even after the street sweeper had come and gone the following week, the faint traces of these stains remained, I studied them from my living room window, from which they looked like continents on the map of an unfamiliar world. And now I think it was standing there at my window, I told Ella by the river, where in those days some of my finest contemplating took place, that my present admiration for her began to form. In view of the grace and firmness with which she'd brought this small emergency under control, and made this flailing, braless white girl calm, it was clear to me, I said, that the fecklessness and whimsy that had carried us toward daybreak was in my veins, whereas she was coursing with stronger stuff.

■

It was at the river's edge that Ella mentioned the film she'd seen at Cannes; I was annoyed to hear that Hollywood had gotten its hands on a subject I'd invested so much idle time in myself, not because I hoped to write a Hollywood version or any version at all, but because if people started talking about it I'd have to find subtle ways to indicate that I knew all about this stuff before it became a film.

In a strange way, my interest in the Lovings had to do with a disequilibrium in our relationship, Ella's and mine, a distinct internal pressure that during the month of Ella's emails from Macedonia built into a swallowed panic, as it became obvious that a decision I'd made without hesitation—to move to Virginia and spend two years of my thirties studying, as Ella put it, how to make up stories in my little brain, leaving her behind in France without access to my iffy genetic material as her ovarian reserve dwindled month by month—as it became obvious that this decision, and really the entire enterprise of writing and reading fiction, was extravagantly pointless and vain. It had to do with that invisible ledger of seriousness; for a long time I'd been unconsciously resisting the life I was meanwhile committing myself to live. Beginning months before the heatwave, as I've mentioned, this resistance took the form of a sudden enthusiasm for reading case law: decisions and dissents and transcripts dating as far back as the nineteenth century, many of which, in their intertextuality, in their authoritative clarity of thought, and by their impact in the nation's culture, exhilarated me in a way fiction never had. So many of these texts, too, expounded upon ideas about what was and wasn't natural to marriage and procreation (an area in which I welcomed any instruction I could find) and did so with nimbler imagination than fiction could almost ever hope to do. Well before the case of *Obergefell v. Hodges* was decided by the Roberts court that summer, I'd realized that the Lovings' story put anything I'd ever read in a novel to shame.

It didn't endear me to my classmates that I went around saying I wished I'd applied to law school. In the library, I found the legal basis for the Lovings' conviction, which turned out to have originated a short drive from where I now lived, with an initiative of the Charlottesville chapter of the American Anglo-Saxon Club to classify all residents of the state as either *Caucasian, Negro, Mongolian, American Indian, Asiatic Indian, Malay, or any mixture thereof.* According to a bulletin published by the Virginia Board of Health, the Virginia Racial Integrity Act of 1924 would correct *a condition which only the more thoughtful people of Virginia know the existence of: that there are in the State from 10,000 to 20,000, and possibly more, near white people, who are known to possess an intermixture of colored blood, in some cases to a slight extent it is true, but still enough to prevent them from being white.* I mentioned this bulletin, one night after a poetry reading, to a Caucasian guy named Nolan Trucks, a recent graduate of my program who now worked as a gardener on a large estate. Nolan's ready response was that he had colleagues he saw every day who'd say it outright that the very thought of *miscegenation* made them a little sick. A lot of my conversations around that time went this way. I always felt out of step and tried to keep to myself. With the gray sky hanging low as we walked along the muddy river, I told Ella how, in the solitude of my apartment, I developed a kind of barometric alertness, how I sat at my window when the sky grew dark to watch the sudden downpours, or the hailstones bouncing on the deck, or a heart-stopping bolt of lightning above the tree line, whose beauty, for only a split second before it disappeared, made me feel artistic and grand. Always wheeling in the sky when it was clear, meanwhile, atop towering, invisible thermal columns, were great black vultures in search of carrion: I'd watch them in the afternoon, then at dusk I'd watch the bats come out, who followed altogether different forces through the air, and mornings after being up all night my chaotic dreams would be interrupted by a tinny, hectoring voice on the outdoor PA at the elementary school down the street, a voice that, against the myriad voices of unseen birds, never failed to create the illusion in my sleep-fogged mind that I'd awoken to a state of emergency the nature of which I couldn't discern.

In class I kept my cap pulled low, and avoided making even momentary eye contact with anyone by taking copious notes. My classmates turned in stories about hunting, about train travel, about succulents, about photography and lithography and taxidermy, always with a faint element of the supernatural—ghosts, telekinesis—that was in vogue at the time. When called upon to comment on these pieces in class, which took place around a teak midcentury dining table set with a pitcher of iced tea and exactly enough glasses for all of us, I claimed to admire them, I defended their tasteful magic against our exasperated workshop leader, Lynn, who accused us of using magic as a crutch, but my critique letters, which at the time I thought were thoughtful and generous, I can see now were a bit heavy-handed, not so much with respect to the work itself as with respect to a broad insinuation that fiction in general, and short fiction in particular, while not as bad as poetry, was a childish and self-indulgent way to spend one's time. As a result, I didn't have a lot of fans, and when my story about the heatwave came up for discussion, it was a very polite but total bloodbath. I'm not certain, they'd say, the finely wrought framework of this work of short fiction doesn't risk buckling under the weight of 1,200 words about the Greek financial crisis. I just worry, they'd say, that maybe, in a work of short fiction, there's a *limit* to how many films you can summarize. Conception is magical, right? they said. So maybe just lean into that a little bit? I wrote all this down, I wrote down even that, as the discussion proceeded, Lynn's piercing blue eyes locked in every time someone took a sip of iced tea, until she was satisfied the glass had been replaced squarely in the center of its coaster, and I remember vividly, for example, the way the late-afternoon sun glowed in the very fine white down—exactly like the down on my earlobes of which I'd been ashamed all my life—on the cheeks of a twenty-three-year-old woman named Constance, when she said, not unkindly, that I seemed to be implying that women were defined by a compulsion for bearing children. At department functions, I never knew whom to talk to, and affected an air of mild bewilderment, chewing the dead skin on my thumb. During a reception for a visiting writer whose lecture consisted mostly of football metaphors, I joined a conversation between Helen, the Irishwoman; Lynn, the steely-eyed department chair; and the laced-up visiting writer himself, just as Helen was explaining that the stress of planning her wedding was giving her hemorrhoids so bad she couldn't sneeze. Lynn, who had forbidden us from using the word *orifice* in our work, was struck dumb by this remark, which I took as an opportunity to natter endlessly about my own wedding—the seven-minute ceremony, the party where we served mac and cheese—in the transparently self-righteous style of someone who doesn't own a TV. I don't know how long I'd been talking when Lynn blinked once and led the visiting writer away, leaving Helen to glare at me while I tore at shish kebab with my teeth.

You have this intuition that your marriage is the most interesting thing about you, Helen said to me, and your writing on the topic is hypnotic. But you should find something else to talk about.

I had the idea that most evenings, and on the weekends, we all took the opportunity to retire to the isolation of our separate lives, to watch trashy television and look up at the wheeling vultures and make up stories in our little brains. But in fact my classmates, under the ringleadership of Helen, met for drinks several nights a week. For this and other reasons, when I finally got a car, I made it a habit, every Thursday after dinner, to drive seven hours to Brooklyn, where I'd stay for the weekend on my brother Owen and his fiancé's couch, spending my days reading case law on their terrace and my evenings visiting old favorite bars, where for some reason Steely Dan was always playing and where I complained to whoever would listen about all of this, the vultures, my classmates, the biblical storms, bitterly and tirelessly, excusing my powerlessness to shut up by rather puppy-doggishly invoking the inordinate amount of time I'd been spending alone.

Sundays I'd hit the road at sunset, driving back the way I came, which is to say west into Pennsylvania, south into the Blue Ridge Mountains on I-81, east in the small hours of the morning through the Shenandoah Valley and across the Rockfish Gap, where without fail I'd hit a wall of fog so dense that I'd often pull off the road and get out of the car to feel it rolling past me; and from that moment, resuming my place at the wheel, I'd begin counting down the days until I could leave again, all the time forming a fantasy in which I didn't return at all, but stayed in New York, went back to bartending, until I'd saved enough cash to get back to Paris, where I'd get a nice French job with a lifelong contract, thirty-five hour weeks, a generous pension—a fantasy that would grow more vivid all week, until I found myself driving north again and it seemed almost real, so that when I left for my brother and Noah's wedding one Thursday in October, I packed for weeks rather than days, and then upon further consideration loaded fifteen boxes of books into my car as well, the only things in my apartment I wasn't prepared to leave behind for good.

■

Only because she'd mentioned the Loving movie did I tell Ella any of this—the way this distant history had become embroiled in my own psychic conflict, which I perceived for the first time when a guest at my brother's wedding mentioned having read the script while it was still in preproduction, a fairly banal coincidence that I took as evidence of the connectedness of all things.

At the ceremony, which was conducted mostly in silence at the austere Quaker meetinghouse on East Fifteenth Street, the officiant kept confusing the grooms, who had the same haircut and the same sharp jaw. My dad's sister had a bad cold and, throughout long periods of silent reflection and brief speeches we were encouraged to regard as the voice of God, kept hawking and clearing her throat. At a certain moment my mom, the spirit having moved her, spoke stirringly about the sacrament of marriage, which she said created a bond that was larger than the sum of its parts; while she was talking, my aunt was consumed by a fit of coughing that didn't subside until the very moment my mom sat back down.

Owen and Noah lived with roommates in a three-bedroom near the Graham stop, in a brand-new building that the landlords rent-stabilized not long after they moved in. The apartment was small, but the building was tiered, and they had a private eight-hundred-square-foot rooftop terrace. I told Ella how I'd found myself describing my situation—the countless hours I spent in the car and the feeling that I never quite slept and never quite woke—over and over that day, in conversation with, for example, a white-haired man in a Perfecto outside the meetinghouse, my twelve-year-old sister, Evie, and Noah's broad-shouldered mom in a taxi across the bridge, and anyone who'd listen at the reception, refining my delivery with each telling in order to tease out a comic futility that would make people think I was actually fine. But seldom did I elicit more than a blank stare or, worse, an earnest, vaguely condescending expression of sympathy, so that by the time I'd performed the latest version of the whole shtick for Owen's boss, Marisa, she caught me off guard by not blinking wordlessly or assuring me everything would work out, but instead fixing me with a thoughtful expression, and asking matter-of-factly whether Ella and I planned to have kids.

A few minutes earlier, my aunt, breathing through her mouth on account of her inflamed sinuses, had asked the same question (When would we start a *family*, she'd said). Marisa meant it in a different, more human spirit, but I told her the same thing I'd told Karen: that the world didn't need any more of my DNA. But I felt exposed and lowered my eyes. As if I were teetering on the deck of a ship, Marisa reached out and held my arm; and without letting go, she dropped her voice into a more intimate register, in order to tell me about the earlier years of her own marriage to the man we could both see at the railing, picking at a fistful of pistachios and filling his pockets with shells.

My brother often talked about Marisa when we lived together, and from the hours he'd spent decoding her smallest gestures, I expected her to be withholding and opaque. But actually she was remarkably direct, with a narratorial streak that reminded me of regulars from the bar. For her own part, she began, she'd never had any interest in children; on the contrary, as she reached her thirties and friends from college and from law school started to pair off and reproduce, she developed a reflexive contempt for the entire institution of the nuclear family, the fatal germ cell of society. At the time, her own career as a film scout was just beginning, and Peter—then her boyfriend—worked for Children's Services in the Bronx, which, vis-à-vis his idealism (he was fond of saying now), was like getting an enema with a fire hose.

It was true that idealism was the heart of the problem. No one gets into social work because they hate poor people, she said. Peter grew up in a working-class neighborhood in Minneapolis, the eldest son of a single mother whose resilience was no less impressive for the support she got from the state. For reasons related to his mom's past, his family was served by a social worker named Pam, who hovered benevolently at the edges of their lives and made their existence feel less precarious than it was. It was Pam's compassion and efficiency that formed the basis of Peter's conception of government in general and later, when he realized how rare these virtues were among her peers, of his conviction that the system's only shortcoming was its failure to recruit high-quality people into its ranks.

Marisa released my arm and, having quaffed the last of her drink, folded her own arms against the cold. She had dark, intense eyes in which there flashed a look I recognized as horror—a shy person's horror at being seized by an irresistible compulsion to talk. In New York, she went on, Peter's illusions about government quickly dissolved. As a child welfare caseworker, the paradox of social work was inescapable. On the one hand he was supposed to provide material support, to prop parents up for the benefit of their kids. But the better part of his work was surveillance and intervention, protecting children from their parents' failures. As the Clinton years wore on and social programs disappeared, for many parents Children's Services became the only adequate source of relief, which only reinforced a general resentment of the department's agents; the access Peter provided to government benefits was contingent upon his continued approval of your life, and any time he pleased he could cut your benefits and take your kids away. In the course of his investigations, he had to gather information from neighbors, relatives, teachers, anyone who might have knowledge of his subjects' private lives. His notepad made people edgy, and neighbors suspected each other as his spies. It sometimes happened that they settled unrelated scores by filing false reports of abuse, but typically his presence turned people against each other in more subtle, pernicious ways. Black children were dramatically overrepresented in foster care, and even without access to the official figures, it was obvious to residents in Peter's caseload that they were at the mercy of a system that was devoted to criminalizing their lives. Many of Peter's colleagues had grown up in solid, middle-class suburban homes that their parents bought in the postwar boom and, having no personal basis for sympathy with the communities they oversaw, often viewed those communities as fundamentally adverse to the well-being of children. Peter's insight, by which he felt personally oppressed, was to recognize his role in reinforcing that adversity. Although he understood the daily mechanics of poverty and the psychosocial toll of economic marginalization, as he sat at kitchen tables in Tremont or Grand Concourse, unsnapping his attaché case and opening his legal pad to a clean page, his clients eyed him silently, as if through a pane of bulletproof glass.

Finding her plastic cup still empty, Marisa made a thoughtful, sullen face. Her cheeks were flushed, and when she continued speaking, I noticed a faint slurring of her speech. Before long, she said, Peter's frustration curdled into despair. Each night when he came home, he tugged his shoes off and unwrapped a frozen pizza, then loaded a bong he'd bought in college, forgot the pizza in the toaster oven, and watched Comedy Central until he fell asleep sitting up. In the glow of the TV, he openly picked his nose. He rented movies like *Friday* and *Clockers* and racked up outrageous late fees Marisa eventually paid herself. It was around the time Jon Stewart took over *The Daily Show* that Marisa discovered she was pregnant. She and Peter had always agreed they didn't want kids, and anyway she wasn't sure she wanted to raise a child with someone who brought frosted Pop-Tarts to work. But the weeks slipped past and she did nothing, she covered Peter with a blanket and switched off the lamp each night and ate his forgotten pizzas for breakfast each morning, and although she took care to hide her pregnancy, she thought fatherhood might give him the boost he needed, a small sphere of influence where his good intentions didn't turn everything to shit.

That's what I told myself, she said; in reality it was something deeper that she couldn't put into words. Well into her second trimester, Peter hadn't noticed anything amiss, and meanwhile she'd started browsing rental listings, knowing she'd have to make a decision soon—but at this moment Marisa paused to observe the commotion surrounding the arrival of the pizzas: twenty-five pizzas no one had made space for on any of the folding tables situated haphazardly around the terrace. My other brother, Thomas, a former Marine, from behind a stack of pizzas balanced on his arms, was trying to take charge. Ignoring him, Owen and Noah led the retinue of pizza bearers from one corner of the terrace to another, until the proceeding devolved into a scene of minor chaos, whereupon Noah's uncle, an Baptist minister from Ohio with a deep, commanding voice, stood on his chair and, whistling sharply through his fingers, secured order, though no sooner were the pizza boxes arranged and a line formed than a very fine, cold mist of rain began to fall, and a volley of groans went up, and chaos was restored.

■

In the scramble to get pizza before it got soggy I lost Marisa. I tried all evening to find my way back to her, in order to hear what became of her pregnancy before she was too drunk to speak. In the kitchen where I was fixing a drink, my aunt found me again, famous aunt Karen, who always managed to convey her disapproval that Ella never appeared at important events, that she already harbored doubts that we were a *real* married couple, which Ella's absenteeism did little to dispel. Now, after some remarks freighted with that implication, she asked once again whether Ella and I planned to *start a family*. We are a family, I told her. But you *know* what I mean! she said. Her face contorted in the advent of a sneeze. A mixed-race baby would be just so *cute*! Assuming she knew how babies were made, I said that at a distance of three thousand miles, starting a family in the way she meant would be an impressive feat. With a slight nod of my head and a modest swivel of my hips, I pantomimed ejaculating in the general direction of France. Karen gave her head a little shake; her mouth still hung open, but the sneeze had been a false alarm. Even for me! I said, hitching up my pants like a cowboy. She furrowed her brow, pretending not to understand. She was a close talker, her face was right in front of mine. I suppose, I said into the hot miasma of her breath, I could rinse out a jam jar and send it by post.

Now the sneeze arrived without warning, catching me squarely in the face, thousands upon thousands of tiny droplets of snot and spit in my beard, eyes, and mouth. Half blind, I staggered away, to the so-called master bathroom, where I gargled vigorously and washed my face three times. For a minute I stood panting before the mirror. I didn't like being sneezed on.

A little fantasy kept replaying in my head, where Karen came right out and said the things she typically left herself room to plausibly deny—hateful, unambiguously racist or homophobic things to which I'd respond with a diatribe so trenchant and devastating it would ruin her life.

■

It wasn't only that I didn't like being sneezed on, I told Ella. Just then I missed you a lot. Sitting on the bed, I massaged my face and scalp and drew air deeply into my lungs until my anger dissipated. As if on cue my phone rang, and it was her. At which exact moment entered Javi, Owen and Noah's roommate, to change out of their thigh-high boots. You look like you're in hiding, they observed. I sent the call to voicemail, and explained I was hiding from my aunt's mucus. Javi understood immediately: *Your* aunt is the mucus lady? Not even by marriage, I said: I'm related to that person by blood. Javi had her pegged as Noah's family, the Florida branch: You know they're *all* supporting Trump? Well, I said, Karen's from Connecticut, she has a Bernie Sanders sticker on her car. I asked if my face still smelled like snot, and they brought their face close. Smells like face, they said. My phone buzzed, Ella had left a message, which when I listened to it later broke my heart. So, Javi was saying, examining a framed photo of the grooms: Who made an honest woman out of who? They were undressing and I was trying not to stare. I said for neither of them did I think respectability was in the cards; Javi gave an approving cluck of the tongue. No peeking, they said. While they unlaced their boots, they told me about the life the three of them shared in the apartment, the drag shows they hosted, the strobe light they'd bought, the chart they'd made to divide household chores. Pulling up a chair, Javi pointed a heel at me; with some effort, I tugged off each boot. Your Doc Martens also smell like face, I said. They stripped to the waist and selected a long *Æon Flux* t-shirt from Noah's dresser. A glimpse of rib cage quickened my pulse; addressing myself to a row of Noah's puppets on a high shelf, so as not to gape at Javi's naked chest, I began to reminisce about the years we'd all lived together—Ella and I, Owen and Noah, and a childhood friend—but Javi cut me off. You're just *adorable*, they said, and, pulling the t-shirt on, planted a loud kiss on my cheek and returned to the party with bare legs.

The childhood friend was Marco, whom I found with Owen by the fire on the terrace, eating cake from a plate in his lap. Javi seems to think, I said, that your present roommate situation is better than ours on Havemeyer, just because you have drag shows and own a George Foreman Grill. My brother laughed. Owen, Marco, and I lived together for six years; in the fourth, Noah and Ella had joined us, and at the beginning of the final year Ella and I were married, and then we'd all had enough and were relieved to go our separate ways. But in memory that period had a special sheen. On Sundays, we took long walks in the neighborhood in search of Brita filters and potted plants. Owen and I took Marco shopping, and helped him choose clothes for dates. He worked on *30 Rock*, Marco, and he stole us craft-service bagels and lox. From the walk-in at work, I stole hanger steaks that we cooked on the fire escape and served to a rotating cast of our disparate friends. Once, Owen had taken his vacation days to visit a man in Frankfurt, who dumped him the moment he arrived; when he returned, I hugged him tightly while he cried, and then Marco made a pot of chili and we watched four hours of *Game of Thrones*. On the way to buy groceries or to swim laps at the pool, we cut down Fillmore Place; in our thirties when we were rich, we said, we'd go Dutch on a town house and each take a floor. I never wanted to be married, I blurted out now by the fire; I just wanted those years to go on and on.

The rain had stopped, and scattered all around the terrace were the damp carcasses of towels, which Javi had brought out so people could dry their seats. Marco put his paper plate in the fire, and we watched what was left of his icing caramelize and turn to smoke. He remembered that time fondly, too, he told us; until then, without quite realizing, he'd always resented the vaguely adversarial nature of his relationship with his friends.

He'd said this to me before; I knew it meant he was about to launch into a story I'd heard many times. But even before he began, I could see his attitude toward the story had completely transformed. He began with the habitual disclaimer that the events he was about to describe predated the movie *Catfish* by five years. He was living in Boston at the time, in a large house on Linden Street that he shared with five other guys. And though 88 Linden, as they called themselves, wasn't exactly *Animal House*, he said, nor was it really the most reflective or sensitive bunch. They shared a Brazzers subscription, and on their refrigerator was a season-long scorecard for sock hockey, which they played in the unused dining room Sunday nights.

It was in the fall of their second year there that Marco created a MySpace account under the name Sara Hope, to which he attached a handful of photos of our high school's homecoming queen. He invented a constellation of interests for her: she liked Weezer and Damien Rice, for example, and *Groundhog Day* and *Space Jam*. As the days got shorter and colder in the weeks between Thanksgiving and Christmas, he began connecting with other college students in the Boston area, and particularly at Northeastern, where Sara was a member of the class of 2008. By the time the house on Linden had emptied out for the holidays, Sara had a network several hundred strong; that was when, one by one over the course of about two weeks, she connected with Marco's housemates as well. People had begun to gather around, and Marco stopped for a moment, as if the thought of what came next was more than he cared to confront. After Christmas the energy in the house shifted immediately, as it emerged that they'd all become MySpace friends with the same chick, an *actual cheerleader*. They were thrilled to discover so many of her interests overlapped with their own: she shared Morgan's love of *Space Jam*, and Hammer's love of Soundgarden, and like Anand she was a marketing major who'd worked at the Best Buy in her hometown. It was Gil who, emboldened by their common tree-nut allergy, sent her a message to introduce himself; with that line of communication open, Sara was free to initiate contact with the rest of the house. Each night, one of them would receive a message, and though the rest would seethe with jealousy, they also welcomed any development that would more deeply involve her in their social world.

It didn't take long for Sara to become the animating force behind the entire communal life in the Linden house. He hadn't expected how reverent the discourse around her would become, Marco said; sometimes, as if they'd remembered themselves, they'd make vulgar comments about her body, but when they did it always felt half-hearted and pro forma, until one morning Gil, with her profile open on his laptop, remarked, Yup, she got them good dick-sucking lips. The rest of the group glared at him: Dude, Morgan said, grow *up*, and from that moment, the emotional stakes escalated dramatically. I can remember—Marco told us, looking into the fire—the excitement that came over them when they learned the name of her dorm, and the hush that fell when, crowded around Morgan's laptop, they typed the address into MapQuest and learned it was only two stops away on the T. It amazed me how isolated I began to feel, he said, not only because I was alone with the truth, but because they believed themselves to have access, through Sara, to a higher plane of feeling that wasn't available to me because I didn't have a MySpace account.

But neither had he expected to assume, for the same reason, the role of private confidant to them each. He could remember a conversation with Hammer: they were in the supermarket, and Hammer, who'd gotten in the habit of touching up his chinstrap daily, kept taking random items off the shelves and examining them in his hands—a honeydew, a pasta turner; there were just so many *things*, Hammer said ardently, that he'd never paid any mind, the whole world felt brand-new. Marco had to understand, never in his life had a woman of this caliber *stepped to him*—To me, Hammer! he'd said—and he felt sincerely that, come what may, he was learning a lot in the process, about himself and about what it meant to be a man.

In February things escalated precipitously. The housemates were planning a huge party for the sole purpose of inviting Sara Hope; having anticipated something like this, Marco brought another MySpace account he'd created into play: Leon Tavarra, Sara Hope's volatile on-again, off-again boyfriend, a community college student with dark, intense eyes and a chinstrap that made Hammer's chinstrap look like a pantystrap. In many of his photos Leon was shirtless, revealing a bulky, sculpted physique and a startling number of animal tattoos. All to say, he made the housemates nervous even before he began sending them messages featuring menacing emoticons, and when he warned them that, because they so often referred to themselves collectively online by their exact address, he knew exactly where to find them, they began to discuss canceling the party altogether.

Naturally Sara contacted them right away, to apologize for Leon's behavior; beneath his admittedly troubled surface he was basically a decent guy who she didn't really think was dangerous. She hoped they'd go ahead and throw their party, but for now it was best if they left her alone. A furious argument ensued, in which the opinion prevailed that any argument for inaction—respecting her wishes, giving her space, admitting that in fact they didn't know her all that well and should maybe just mind their business— was a smokescreen for the shirking of their manly duty. Still, the possibility had to be considered that Leon belonged to a more violent, less forgiving world than they themselves. Let's be realistic, Morgan said. We've all seen *Training Day*, maybe we're in over our heads. Hammer had some boys he could call, boys who had his back no matter what, but Hammer's boys notwithstanding, the debate proceeded in circles throughout the course of the next week, by the end of which it was too late.

During all of this, their patience with Marco ran short: the triviality of his everyday concerns annoyed them, they'd come to regard him as a fundamentally unserious person. To provoke their condescension, he'd leave notes in the kitchen claiming someone had, say, finished his grapefruit juice, and then he'd march into their individual rooms—where they lay in the dark daydreaming about Sara Hope—and ask them whether they'd read the note he'd left in the kitchen about his grapefruit juice. They'd resolved, finally, to send Sara a carefully worded message, saying they didn't think anyone had the right to tell her what to do, and that if she chose to come to their party, at which there would be a keg of Sam Adams and a terrific amount of nachos, she'd be safe there, and further, that if there was any other way they could be of service, they were available for that as well.

On the night of the party, Anand overplucked his eyebrows, and somehow this became a tiny crack through which escaped the cumulative insecurities of the entire group. They bickered ceaselessly all afternoon, and their habitual banter took on a caustic edge. By comparison to his squirrelly roommates, Marco seemed preternaturally charming and relaxed, and because they were fixated on Sara Hope, he benefited from the undivided attention of numerous women who existed in flesh and blood, one of whom followed him up to his room. He told her about his sense that the life he was living was not his own, that the feelings he felt were not his feelings, that his voice was merely an echo in the void. She herself often felt there was a secret side of her she could never share with anyone, as if she were in fact two people or more. Yes, Marco said to her, he told us on the terrace, that was exactly right. Because her name turned out to be Sarah, he felt newly committed to seeing his prank through to the end, and after she'd fallen asleep, as the party continued downstairs, he crept into each of his housemates' rooms and emptied their dressers onto their beds; back in his own room, he wrote to them as Leon, to the effect that Leon had come to their party incognito, that he'd walked among them, that he'd watched them from afar and could see the fear in their eyes, a hollowness and desperation almost strong enough to smell.

Among the people who'd gathered to listen was Marisa, whose face, lit by the fire, showed an expression of woozy dismay, and Javi, who clearly thought Marco was a sociopath. Karen, meanwhile, kept having to be reminded which characters were real. Marco explained that because Hammer was selling pot out of his room, and because Anand maintained an ample stash of coke, he'd managed to convince them not to involve the police. Over the next few weeks, the housemates became almost as obsessed with Leon as they were with Sara. It was decided, on the basis of what Marco dared not guess, that he was South American, and it galled them to find he shared a lot of Sara's interests, too: the thought of Leon and Sara watching *Space Jam* together made Morgan feel unwell, and it seemed unlikely, they all agreed, that his appreciation for Jeff Buckley was sincere. He's manipulating her! cried Gil. For a week or so, Sara dropped off the radar, causing them all a great amount of distress. Marco was spending two or three nights a week at Sarah's house, which turned out to be only two doors down, and sometimes in the morning he'd come home to find the housemates gathered silently in the kitchen, drinking his grapefruit juice, numb with concern. What's so special about this girl? he once asked, and speaking for all of them, Gil, who slept with his socks on, said they didn't expect him to understand, which seemed to imply some slight against Neighbor Sarah, as they called her, whom they regarded as an imposter of some sort.

By this point, Marco said, I was beginning to think I'd be forced to maintain the secret identities of Sara Hope and Leon Tavarra forever, to live in the space where the fiction of their world intersected with the reality of mine; and in moments of weakness I got nearly to the point of confessing the entire plot. But he resolved that the only way out of the mess he'd created was to carry it through exactly as planned. Unprovoked, in the spell of a jealous and (the housemates speculated) possibly drug-fueled rage, Leon began firing off antagonizing messages, and in the dead of night, Marco often found himself committing minor acts of vandalism and theft against his own house, smashing the mailbox, stealing the PlayStation, egging the porch. It was mid-March, but there was still snow on the ground, in which he created footprints leading to the kitchen window, where he created handprints and evidence of a nose pressed against the glass. Standing alone in the dark street during the hours before dawn, he told us, I knew I'd crossed some threshold, and I wondered if there was a difference between insane behavior and insanity itself.

When, near the end of March, Sara reached out to Morgan to say she could really use a friend, the housemates leapt into action. Immediately they made plans for another party, a blowout even bigger than their last. At the supermarket with Hammer, gathering materials for nachos, Marco's knees were weak from the effort of containing the turbulence in his heart. I just want to hold her, Hammer said, weighing an enormous block of orange cheese in his hands, I just want to hold her and to tell her everything is going to be okay.

Because there was strength in numbers, they decided that even if it would distort the ratio of males to females, they'd all feel better if they invited Hammer's boys. Leon knew about the party, he'd been taunting them all week, but it was too late to back down now, in Sara's hour of need. When the night arrived and the house began to fill with sweaty bodies, the housemates remained tethered to Gil's computer. Sara had written earlier to say she was having dinner with her cousin nearby. She'd made a definitive break from Leon, she said, and tonight she just wanted to get wild, to let her hair down, to feel young and carefree in a way she hadn't for years. Meanwhile, there'd been no word from Leon, and—though there was a minor crisis when it transpired that Hammer's boys had finished the nachos, despite Gil's specific instructions to leave some for Sara—spirits were generally so high that no one noticed how often Marco was slipping away to his room, where he had two computers running on his bed. When word arrived from Sara that she and her cousin were waiting for the check, the housemates started losing their cool. For the occasion Morgan had shaved his chest, and now in his giddiness he couldn't stop scratching. Hammer kept dropping to the floor to do push-ups, and asking Marco if his triceps looked great, which they did.

As the wait dragged on, however, their spirits sagged, they grew surly and made unkind remarks about each other's haircuts and personal odors. After nearly two hours, another message arrived, not from Sara but from Leon. Leon knew what they'd done, he said, he'd hacked Sara's MySpace and knew about the messages she'd been sending behind his back, knew what they'd said about him, knew she'd soon be at their house. They'd been warned, and he was sick of playing games. He was around the corner, he told them, with a group of friends, and in no more than five minutes they'd be out front.

In five minutes the housemates, together with Hammer's boys, were ready in the street with bats, lacrosse sticks, empty wine bottles, with the plastic hockey sticks they used for their games on Sunday nights. Their eyes were wide. The color had gone out of their lips. Beneath the streetlamps they turned in circles, not knowing from which direction the attack would come. When they spoke, it was in whispers, as if their adversaries were hidden in the bushes, waiting for the chance to strike. It felt to Marco like a very long time before someone noticed that the mailbox, which they'd yet to replace, was open, and there was something inside. It was a scrawled note from Leon, instructing them to check Sara's profile now, see if they still felt tough.

Sara! someone breathed. What have we done? With no further thought for their own safety, all of them rushed inside, and waited for the page to load. Sara Hope's profile picture was now a picture of Marco, unsmiling, in his red plaid shirt. A long moment passed before anyone even moved. So wait, Gil said quietly, are you Leon? He's everyone, Anand replied, more quietly still. They were all still holding their weapons. Marco stood at the edge of the room, completely motionless, wishing he could disappear. He could feel, he said, the tumult roiling in each of his housemates' hearts. A sob went up, maybe from Morgan, and then was immediately gulped back. Neighbor Sarah, he noticed from the corner of his eye, quietly withdrew from the room. By now it was after midnight, a new month had begun. In the photo, Marco held a sign that said APRIL FOOLS.

∎

A thick, sodden haze hung in the air, glowing in the firelight. The crowd on the terrace had grown thin. But someone had passed out blankets, and the small audience around the chiminea had listened in rapt silence until this climactic moment, which they met with an appreciative gasp. Now they chattered in excitement, as if they'd seen a play. It was agreed that Marco was unwell, but to my surprise and I think to his, no one expressed full-throated outrage; rather, they admitted to a grudging admiration, the kind of grudging admiration that isn't even really grudging. You had them in the streets with baseball bats, someone said, you had them shaving their pubes; imagine what else you could have made them do. The fire had died down, Javi squatted beside it to add a pair of logs, holding their hair back to blow on the embers. Everyone wanted to discuss why his housemates were so easy to fool, and Javi ascribed it to the strength of a universal human need to connect.

Javi, my god, put some pants on, my brother said. You'll catch your death. People started getting up for new drinks, and to pick over what remained of the pizzas. Marisa stayed put, her knees pulled up to her chin, and, not having spoken or even moved for as long as she sat there, now produced a cigarette and asked if anyone had a light. I'm not so sure, Marco said in reply to Javi, cupping a small flame before Marisa's face. Since that night ten years have passed, and in that time, every one of those fuckers has gotten married—a few of them to women they met online. It's only me, he said, who seems to have been marked by the story of Sara Hope. He explained that whenever he got close to someone he was dating, he began to doubt whether she existed for him except as Sara Hope had existed for his housemates—as an external source of approval, like a flattering fitting room mirror. That was the lesson: that what so often passed for love was mostly a desperate construct of your own vanity, a steamroller with which the self pressed the other flat until a smooth, reflective surface was all that remained. Little wonder that tears brimmed in Anand's eyes when, having drunk himself into a sullen stupor at Morgan's wedding, he pulled Marco aside to ask whether Morgan's new wife, Julie, was hotter than Anand's own new wife, Julie. A few of us laughed, and Marco laughed, too. He poked the fire and drank his beer. To think this way, he continued, is to resign your personhood, to renounce thought, feeling, connection, to live in the sphere of goal-directed verbs—to become a thing in a world of things. And I guess that's what people crave. You see them gathered together with their families, you see all these Julies and Morgans and Anands, you hear the speeches and the syrupy vows, and sitting there with your chicken-or-fish getting cold it's impossible to imagine these people have any inner life at all, impossible to imagine they have any living attachment to the human realm, and then they come out and do this stiff little dance and everyone cheers and hoists them up on chairs, and you think, what—fucking *this* is society's most sacred bond?

Ella had not tried calling back. Her voicemail said she'd been offered a job as a casting assistant; she'd be responsible for organizing auditions for each of fifteen child roles. Only just the night before she'd booked a flight for November 12, which now she had to postpone by a month. My love, she said, if I knew it would be this long, I'd never have let you go, I'd have thrown a fit to make you stay. Her voice so serious and sad, and exhausted, somehow. That was what broke my heart. By now the terrace had cleared, and Marisa, much sobered, sat drinking a Gatorade, smoking one cigarette after the next. That Marco, she said. Imagine what kind of mind. I told her I'd heard him tell the Sara Hope story many times, but never so urgently as he had tonight. As if in the telling the act could be redeemed. That happens at weddings, Marisa said in a sleepy voice: people tend to lay it on the line.

At her own wedding, she said—as extravagant and precious an affair as could be thrown together before the baby was due—her father, who spoke a very charming English he'd learned in Cambodia as a boy, gave a toast to the effect that it was marriage, and the resulting families, that transmitted a culture through time, but that it also provided an opportunity to lay claim to the future on your own terms—a political act in the same way the golden rule was a political tenet; inherent in either was an assertion about how the world should be. Her father was a small, bespectacled man, Marisa said, a devoted gardener whose nailbeds were always rimmed with dirt, and since his death a few months before, she found herself returning to the videotape of his toast, which struck her now with new force.

It began to rain again, and we went inside to stand by the window, as on the terrace my brother Thomas and Marisa's husband, Peter, holding empty pizza boxes over their heads, oversaw a group of drunk people un-rolling cheap fake turf upon which to set up a handful of borrowed tents where some guests from out of town would spend the night. Marisa turned her head slowly side to side, examining her dim reflection in the glass. She'd never wanted to get married, she reminded me. As her pregnancy progressed, she saw how much energy she sank daily into Peter's despair, how little energy she had left for herself and for the critter taking shape in her womb. From a pile on her desk at Miramax, she read one screenplay after another about the million ways life could go wrong—schlocky Oscar bait in which children were separated from their parents, in which husbands lost their wives, cancer movies, Holocaust movies, movies about the deaths of pets. A shapeless pessimism formed in her; she'd get on the subway and, finding the pole warm and damp from strangers' hands, feel a marrow-deep disgust with humankind. Peter was barely functioning, it was only a matter of time until he lost his job, and she no longer had the strength to keep him on his feet. As an undergrad, she'd photocopied a passage from Invisible Cities, which said the inferno isn't the world to come, but rather it's the world we live in every day, that we create simply by being together. And now that she'd reached her third term without making a decision, these words echoed in her brain. She dug the photocopy out of a closet, and kept it folded in her purse. Calvino, she explained, says you can escape suffering in the infernal city of the living in one of two ways: by becoming such a part of it that it becomes invisible to you, or else by learning to seek and recognize what, in the midst of the inferno, is not inferno, and to make it endure and give it space. Ridiculous as it sounds, she said, in that notion I discovered a perspective from which my pregnancy made sense.

A warmth had been spreading through me as Marisa spoke, a recognition of how seriously she lived her life, how assiduously she applied her mind to the duties of existence, how readily she turned to literature to make sense and meaning of that existence, and how easily she managed to do so without seeming pathetic or overwrought, which is how I seemed to myself when I did the same things. Through the window we could hear the wind howl, and the frustration and hilarity in the voices of the people setting up their tents. Marisa, who as my brother's boss had special dispensation to smoke indoors, lit still another cigarette, running her finger around the rim of her cup. Since *Obergefell* was decided, she said, she'd been thinking about marriage a lot. She'd gotten her hands on a screenplay, not long before the *Obergefell* decision came down, that told the story of the Lovings, Richard and Mildred. In her Fourteenth Amendment class she'd studied this case in detail and knew that, even irrespective of their name, it was a story ready-made for film: the Lovings were not recruited by an activist organization, as the plaintiffs in *Lawrence v. Texas* would later be; nor did they deliberately break a law in order to establish standing to challenge it in court, as Estelle Griswold had done a few years before. Neither Richard nor Mildred was especially civic-minded, they had little interest in revolution or reform. Rather, they loved each other, and their children, and their home. But sometimes cultivating one's own garden means turning the entire world upside down. By 1963, they'd already been arrested once, when they'd returned to Central Point for Easter Sunday, and in her fine cursive Mildred wrote to Attorney General Robert Kennedy, asking for advice. It wasn't within the power of his office, Mr. Kennedy explained, to intercede directly on her behalf, but she ought to contact the ACLU. She promptly did just that, explaining that while she understood she and her husband could never live in Virginia again, she'd like at least to be permitted to return from time to time so her children could visit their grandparents without having to see their mother and father hauled off to jail.

Marisa admired the filmmaker who had been hired to write and direct the film, she said. But of course the trouble with narrative was that even when it made you feel bad it made you feel good.

Yes! I said. This is what I keep trying to say to my classmates at school!

Marisa gave me a stern look. Your classmates don't need to hear that kind of thing, she said.

But at a subtextual level, she resumed, in the context of an *Obergefell* decision that relied so heavily on *Loving* for precedent, it was inevitable that a feature film about *Loving v. Virginia* would portray the civil rights movement, the tenure of the Warren court, the entire countercultural revolution of the sixties, as a final messianic disruption in the course of history, the aims of which were now achieved. As much as the two cases resembled each other, Marisa pointed out, *Loving* was decided by a unanimous bench, whereas four justices voted against *Obergefell*, and implicit in their dissent was a repudiation of *Loving* as well.

It wasn't long after she told him she was expecting that Peter quit his job, and they started their life from scratch. Now it troubled her to think that if she'd felt compelled to marry him for the sake of her unborn child, she must have agreed with Justice Kennedy that *without the recognition, stability, and predictability marriage offers, their children suffer the stigma of knowing their families are somehow lesser.* Currently her son was in the wretched throes of puberty, Marisa said. She wanted to tell him it'd get better, that in the adult world his tormentors and their opinions would count for nothing and that the cruelty, conformity, and pettiness they enforced would disappear—that the meek would inherit the earth. It's felt that way, hasn't it, these past eight years? Among the arguments against both miscegenation and same-sex marriage presented to the Supreme Court was the contention that the children such unnatural partnerships produced had an exceptionally hard time navigating the prevailing biases of the larger world—an argument that failed to demand that bigots make the inverse consideration on behalf of their spawn. But on the other hand, Marisa said, breathing smoke, she'd wondered if this argument didn't succeed in diagnosing an intractable state of human affairs in which the infernal always got the upper hand.

■

On the other side of the window from where we were sitting, Karen was asleep on a soggy deck lounger, snoring raggedly. From where I sit now, as lockdowns persist around the world, Karen sneezing on my face looks like an act of terrorism, one that's shockingly consistent with the politics she's developed since. Having learned nothing from Marco's story, she's come to worship at the altar of the anonymous entity known as Q. She believes in preserving monuments to the Confederacy, and she believes the virus is a hoax, and I'm being sincere when I say that I hope she catches it and dies a long and painful death. But at my brother's wedding, watching her sleep off a mixture of white wine and Robitussin, I gratified myself with the more modest wish that she would startle awake from sleep apnea or unpleasant dreams and fall violently off her chair. But she didn't startle awake. For a while Marisa absently watched her chest rise and fall. It seemed like she was trying to work something out. Leaning forward, I found myself filling the silence with thoughts about my own marriage that I'd never spoken aloud. I told her about that first date, about Rob and the bike accident and the pavement soaking up blood. When I moved to New York in 2007, I said, I found a culture that authorized self-absorption and preciousness as badges of artistic sensitivity, and in that spirit, I'd actively avoided any sort of entanglement that might interfere with my program of wearing tight pants and listening to Grizzly Bear and futzing with a ponderous novel set in a bar. But Ella, when I met her in July 2010, was already scheduled to fly back to Paris in September, where she had a boyfriend whom—although he'd been on the lam since killing an Ultra in a brawl—she was hoping to see again. There was zero risk we'd become seriously involved. She didn't know her way around, and I thought it conferred a measure of status upon me that I could show her the ropes. But she didn't care about the ropes. To dinner at Five Leaves, Bozu, Dressler, and Rye, she wore the same faded floral-print dress from Urban Outfitters, which she pronounced with a long *i*, so that it sounded like she was describing hand-to-hand combat in the city streets. Severe, tat-sleeved barmaids at Commodore and Union Pool flared their nostrils when she ordered salted margaritas, but within minutes she had them giggling like little kids. When she was ticketed for peeing between parked cars in Greenpoint or for jumping the turnstile at Marcy Ave, she gave the police a fake name. When she got a paycheck, instead of buying a new dress, she bought a mound of coke to share with her French friends. I didn't do coke, I couldn't speak a word of French, I tried to impress her a thousand ways and failed, but she kept returning my texts. What do you *like* about me? I asked her one night on my roof. Do you want *me* to kill someone in a fight? She answered without hesitation: she said she liked that I made her laugh, she liked that I knew right from wrong, and, while she didn't know whether my writing was any good, she liked that I approached it with seriousness and discipline, even though it was probably a waste of time. The night before her flight to Paris, we went with Marco to Walter

Foods and spent the night at the bar. Who knows what we talked about; all I remember is that we laughed a lot, that I was proud of her wit and dauntlessness, and the way her raucous laughter carried around the room. I remember that the bartender kept giving us shots of fernet, that a plan eventually developed to stage a threesome in my bed, and that, having worked out in great detail what this threesome would entail, we'd made it back to my bed and out of our clothes, whereupon I'd promptly fallen asleep. I remember, I told Marisa, half opening my eyes sometime before dawn and finding myself wedged between the two of them, and then again, in the blue half-light of morning, watching her collect her things and tiptoe out of the room. For a moment our eyes met, and her face was stern and blank; later, when I awoke properly, I told myself it was for the best. I understood, I'm not sure how, that she and Marco had carried on without me, if only briefly before losing heart, and I walked to her apartment beneath the bridge convinced I was on firm ground to make a clean break.

While she made us tea, I tried to compose my thoughts. Over the top of her mug, however, she looked at me with an openness that stopped my heart. She said it made her so sad that things would end this way. In these words, she told me I'd badly hurt her feelings, that I'd made it clear she meant nothing to me, that I thought of her as a whore to be lent out to friends. The thoughts I'd composed had vanished. Her dignity, the steadiness of her gaze, and the absence of anger from her voice opened a space inside me: I couldn't have said so until that moment, but my feelings were badly hurt as well. I didn't know whose idea the threesome had been, maybe it began as a joke, but it gutted me to think she'd agreed so readily, and I'd gone along with it only because I didn't want to be controlling or possessive, and didn't want her to think I was a prude. We talked for a long time, and the realization settled in my gut that I cared about her a lot more than I knew.

Since then, we've frequently drawn on this capacity—to levelheadedly confront a crisis together from opposite ends. But at that moment it was without precedent in my life. We'd humiliated each other, and it would have been natural to freeze over or to lash out. Instead, it was as if we'd stepped out of our bodies to communicate calmly and honestly over the tops of our own heads. I felt this new space inside me expand. Our tea got cold, and we lay down on the stripped bed. Then her cab came and took her back to France.

Marisa remembered my brother talking about my wedding at the office; she remembered him explaining that, for the time being, it would be a marriage on paper only; we had no plans to move in together, and no expectation of being committed to each other for life. She remembered he was fairly skeptical, and he said our wedding guests, many of whom we barely knew, were flummoxed as well.

Things were no clearer in our own minds, I said. Following the summer we met, Ella spent the fall at her mom's, working in a fondue restaurant where she spilled melted chocolate in a woman's hair. She arrived back in New York on Christmas Day, just hours before a blizzard that left the city under three feet of snow. We linked arms, took pictures of the ice-lacquered trees, but by the time the snow had melted, it was clear I'd made a huge mistake. She moved into a prewar building just two blocks from mine, a filthy two-bedroom she shared with some Italians, Arturo and Pierro, who had loud sex, not always with each other, for hours on end. Inevitably, she relied on me for everything: help opening a bank account, finding a job, speaking to customer service reps on the phone. I went to Ikea with her and assembled her bed. When she saw a mouse in her bedroom, she showed up at my door unannounced in the middle of the night, drew a bath, and stayed for two weeks. My friends, coworkers, and bar regulars reacted viscerally when I reported these developments: what set us apart as New Yorkers from the rest of the world was our right to catastrophize even the slightest impositions on our time. *You* need to set *boundaries*! they all kept saying. When she enrolled in an acting program, I lent her $3,600 for tuition and then, as gently as I could, sent her back to her apartment, claiming I had important work to do. But the trouble was that I loved spending time with her. She had a radiant smile and when she laughed, her cheeks crowded her eyes shut. Because of her idiosyncratic accent and vocabulary, each sentence she spoke held a delightful reinvention of the world. Around March, the ESL program that provided her student visa was shut down, giving her three months to make other arrangements. At Bozu one night, when she offhandedly suggested we get married, my blood went cold, I could scarcely eat. She didn't see why I was making such a fuss: compared with our friend Nissa, who was paying a parolee $30,000 in installments to pose as her husband for five years, this was minor league, we were an actual couple in actual love.

It was her casualness that sent me over the edge. Over the course of the next few weeks, I refined a theory of my attachment to her as flimsy and solipsistic, not unlike Marco's unified theory of Sara Hope—I didn't love *her*, I told myself; I loved the way she made me *feel*. I affected a kind of pro-phylactic coolness in my attitude toward her, and her continued insistence hardened my resolve. Soon she realized she'd overplayed her hand, and she became diffident, made shy attempts to restore the lightness of summer, always fidgeting, always watching me from a corner of her eye. It wasn't easy to be so callous; in sharp conflict with my determination to live according to the principles of self-devotion I'd adopted as a New Yorker, I had a powerful impulse to protect her, which conflict destabilized me in strange, unrelated ways, processes of my own brain that should have been natural or automatic became difficult to trust. I had difficulty sleeping, and I kept leaving the house without my keys. Her voice and the wonderful innovations of her English echoed in my mind as she slept beside me. I remember, eating a bagel one day in spring, suddenly finding myself incapable of deciding when I'd chewed enough to swallow. Meanwhile, her dark eyes and soft voice. It was clear I was causing her pain, and after a series of conversations with Owen and Marco, I convinced myself the time had come. Once again, I went to her apartment feeling utterly justified to break things off for good. That was the end of May. We were married by the end of June.

■

Ella listened quietly to all of this, as we strolled beside the swollen river, weaving through herds of tourists by Notre-Dame and pausing to examine the strange reliefs that appeared on the bridges and above the doorways, the death-fraught idylls of Paris through the ages, the two of us standing sometimes even close enough that I could smell her hair. When I was finished, I realized it disturbed her somehow to hear me tell the story of all these stories. Had I forgotten, she wanted to know, the boilerplate prenup I'd printed out—not because I had any assets to protect, but because I wanted things between us to be clear. You said when we were ready to be married for real, she reminded me, we'd tear up the prenup, in a ceremony of our own design. But we never had the ceremony, she said, turning to face me. We never signed the prenup, we were so dizzy we just forgot, and then the small misfortunes of ordinary life began to accrue, and we gradually took for granted that our fates were bound.

That's just what I told Marisa! I said. That's what I told Marisa, and then for days afterward, I felt like I was at the threshold of an insight I wasn't quite prepared to face. I spent the week after the wedding on Owen and Noah's terrace, in one of the better tents: each night I built a fire, where Owen and Noah sometimes joined me, treating me with the kindness you show a rescue dog. I told them the thought of returning to Virginia was a cold terror, and I described my classmates' weird and self-important habits of speech and mind, like how they were always saying the words *liminal* and *diachronic*. Do you think you feel such contempt for them because you feel such contempt for yourself, they asked, or do you feel such contempt for yourself because you feel such contempt for them? If you don't go back, they asked, what would you do instead? Go to Paris, join the circus, take a silk-screening class in Tulum? I didn't know exactly, these were difficult questions, and the temperature sank lower each night, so mostly they left me alone, staring into the flames or breathing hard in my zippered tent, with a sense of foreboding drumming in my ears, a sense of foreboding that was actually Karen's cold coming over me, to outpace which in the daytime I compulsively walked the streets, unrecognizable though they were since I'd moved away. With demented tenacity, to escape the flocks of paralegals in their V-necks and the baristas smoking self-importantly at the curb, I walked over the Williamsburg Bridge into Manhattan, over the Manhattan Bridge back into Brooklyn, over the Brooklyn Bridge back into Manhattan, back over the Williamsburg Bridge again at nightfall, hoping to recover a sensation of fullness—that anamnestic intoxication, as Walter Benjamin put it—that I felt more or less continuously when I first moved to New York, and that the novel I'd spent most of those years writing had been an elaborate attempt to record. I still knew the code for our building on Havemeyer, so one night I climbed the stairs to the roof, where the view no longer looked out over the skyline but at a barrier of steel and glass. All week I'd been getting worried emails from classmates and professors, I told Ella, and I realized I'd never had any intention of disappearing from school, of abandoning our things and starting a new, more serious life, and so I would have to slink back to the life I already had.

■

The following Saturday, therefore, I drove through a storm and hours of traffic—west into PA, south down I-81, back east out of the mountains—to be at Helen and Adam's wedding, whose decision to marry likewise related as much to matters of immigration as to matters of the heart. I missed the ceremony at town hall and arrived late, with a smudged tie, a low-grade fever, and a runny nose, to the bar where the reception was being held, and where I found the bride's parents, the bride's brothers, her many cousins and uncles and aunts, who'd all arrived that day, giddy with the thrill of being gathered together so far from home. They'd already been so proud— I'd been told by a ruddy aunt, Aunt Sue, a charming woman in her sixties who didn't once sneeze in my mouth—they'd all been so proud already, Sue said, to have one writer in the family, and now here they were with two. I must have grimaced. It's a fine thing, to be a writer, she exclaimed, gesturing around the room. Someone has to make sense out of—all this mess.

You know, I said, Helen is the only person here who likes my work, she always stands up for me in class when the rest of them are tearing the flesh from my bones.

This was true. In class the day before I left for my brother's wedding, Helen had made a little speech on my behalf: we could all agree this character was flailing, she said, and his fascination with geopolitics, with injustice, with his wife Odile's suffering, and with the ferocity of her body's needs was a way of repudiating the blitheness of his existence and borrowing from the world around him the makings of a heavier, more meaningful life. I didn't know if this was true, exactly, or I hoped it wasn't, and I didn't bring it up with Aunt Sue, I'd been avoiding thinking about it since it happened, but now I remembered how in class that day, hearing Helen's lone voice come to my defense in this way as the rest of the room straightened their backs in their wishbone chairs, I'd been overwhelmed by gratitude, and tears sprang to my eyes, which I concealed in my usual manner, by keeping my face close to my notes and my cap pulled low over by eyes. Sue smiled and raised her glass: It's a fine thing to be a writer, she repeated. Not that you'd catch me dead.

Sue dragged me onto the dance floor, where in the course of an hour she and I worked ourselves into an ecstatic sweat. And it was maybe an effect of the good feeling she imparted that, though I was still uneasy among my classmates, I found as the night went on that I was very happy to look around and see them in their best clothes, picking lint off each other's jackets, straightening each other's collars, steadying themselves on each other's arms—I felt an admiration for the hope they shared, words to describe which I couldn't find, though I thought I might have better luck the more I drank.

To that end the bride and groom had advanced a massive sum of cash against the bar tab, a sum—enough for another Peugeot, I told Ella—it soon became clear we wouldn't make it even halfway through if we didn't get serious, as Helen put it, standing on a barstool, in a stirring address to the gathered crowd. Indeed, the bride in her lovely white dress made it difficult not to take this duty seriously, and she took it quite seriously herself, periodically ordering more tequila shots than there were mouths available to drink them and taking it upon herself to drink the balance, a pattern that had been developing for a few hours when I found myself part of a small, cross-eyed group of wedding guests to whom she was explaining, with poise and authority, why she was no longer wearing her dress in the usual way.

Having gotten on the outside of so many tequila shots, she said, I went into the women's bathroom and vomited all over the outside of my dress; but because I didn't want to appear in photographs of my wedding day with vomit visible anywhere on my person, I thought it would be better to turn the dress inside out. The inside of my dress, which is now the outside of my dress, is vomit-free, especially relative to the outside of my dress, which is now the inside of my dress, and which is absolutely *covered* with vomit.

It was here that she flipped up the front of the dress to illustrate her point. This was when I knew for certain you'd love Helen, I told Ella on our walk, because later in the year she and Helen did in fact become dear friends. The vomit, she'd said, I told Ella, which until recently was inside me, is now being smushed, by the outside of my dress, which is now the inside, against the surface of my skin, which is for all intents and purposes the outermost extreme of my existence, a state of affairs she'd have to tolerate for the rest of her life.

Part 2
Winter and Spring 2016

4
Ministère de l'Intérieur

Probably because of the thunderstorms that so often passed overhead at night that fall of my first semester in Virginia, as the summer heat faded and Halloween came and went, or maybe because of the angry voices I sometimes heard from the next apartment, or because of the plague of moths whose shadows fluttered through my room, I started having these tormented dreams, in which Ella and I were pursued across ruined landscapes by an obscure danger that never quite came into view. As it happened, Ella was fascinated by other people's dreams and, after she'd returned to Paris from Macedonia, demanded I relate mine to her in as much detail as possible when we spoke on Skype. Let's hear it, she'd say. Don't be shy.

So when she visited over Christmas when the semester ended, I tried to tell her about the recurring childhood dream from which I thought these apocalypse dreams originated. My dad was always watching war movies on TV when I was a toddler, and I had this dream where my family was chased out of our safe suburban house by soldiers or men with guns. But Ella cut me off: I'd rather tell you now, she said (this was a favorite phrase of hers): Whenever you talk about your dreams, je te mute, directe.

But *you're* the one who always asks to hear them, I said.

I mute your ass, she repeated. I just like to watch your face.

Since the terror attacks in Paris the month before, things between us had relaxed; we'd spent hours at a time together on Skype, mostly just going about our business in each other's virtual presence, but also flirting and teasing each other with more enthusiasm than we had for years. Now that we were together in the flesh we kept it up. You can't get enough of that shit, Ella was saying. Watching your face when you describe your dreams is like looking in a funny mirror—I recognize your self-seriousness as my own. We were sitting outside together as she issued this judgment, a few stray clouds in the sky above us edged in moonlight. I'd forgotten the way Ella's voice sometimes caught in her throat, as it did now—a kind of swallowed chortle—when her thoughts sounded particularly brazen or ludicrous. You're just lost in La Mancha, she said, giving my head a little pat—another favorite phrase of hers. You're lost in La Mancha just like me.

■

At that moment, Ella and I were on the outs with my entire family, and it felt to me like we were allied against the injustices of the entire world. This was in the eastern Catskills, where we'd all gone splitsville to rent a farmhouse for a week: Ella and me, Owen and Noah, Thomas and his wife, Jess, and my parents and their little terrier Norman and my twelve-year-old sister, Evie, and her school friend Addie P. The Gibson Memory Palace—as Addie dubbed it, because of the museum labels affixed beneath just about everything—was a farm complex that, not including a hilltop outhouse where a David Lynch poster was mounted beside the commode, comprised five buildings: the main house, where we were staying; a converted chicken coop; a one-room cottage; a former stable in service as a woodshed; and a massive converted barn and silo, which housed what Dr. Gibson, a neuro-biology professor now in his mid-eighties, called the "Dreamatorium," a surreal, homespun laboratory where he'd conducted oneirological research for decades, which we'd broken into that afternoon while the rest of the family was out for a walk. It wasn't La Mancha, the Dreamatorium, but I'm not exaggerating when I say it's one of the world's great unknown monuments of quixotic self-seriousness. The walls were packed with decade upon decade of press clippings and awards. Museum labels were affixed beside each door—THE OFFICE OF DR. ALLAN J. GIBSON; THE LIBRARY OF DR. ALLAN J. GIBSON—and the doors themselves were cordoned off with velvet rope. Ella and I had spent more than an hour in the silo alone: a spiral stair-case ran up the center, and the walls were lined with books. The fourth floor was dedicated to Gibson's own work, remaindered copies of a great many academic volumes, but also a memoir and an entire shelf of private diaries and dream journals dating back to 1941, when he was eight years old. He was born in the Depression, I told Ella now: It's seventy years of dreams about food.

By this point it was sometime after dinner, a few days before Christmas, and we'd gotten a fire going in the fire pit behind the house, just the two of us bundled in our parkas, and somewhere out there the dog as well, while the rest of the family gathered around the hearth inside, where Addie was teaching them to make paper flowers. Earlier there'd been some confusion about whose night it was to cook: while we'd been exploring the Dreamatori-um, everyone assumed we were at the store, and when we came in sometime after eight, there was nothing in the house to eat. Although everyone pretty much knew the fault lay with Tom and Jess, the pair of them had managed, by dint of the hectoring bravado they were perfecting in law school, to persuade my parents of a narrative in which it was Ella and I who'd screwed the pooch, and it fell to us to make a last-minute dash to the gas station for a stack of tortillas, an assortment of commercial salsas, and a pillow-sized bag of Monterey Jack; we cooked quesadillas two at a time and served them in icy silence, making sure everyone had seconds before taking our own plates outside. I loved Tom and it had always troubled me that he and Ella didn't see eye to eye. I will never forget this, she'd said while we built the fire. To my dying day—I'd rather tell you now.

But she did forget it, momentarily at least: we finished eating and shared one of her Gitanes; soon the exhilarating strangeness of the afternoon in the barn settled over us again, and we stayed out until well past midnight talking about Dr. Gibson's dreams. In her dark, damp eyes, both the fire and the moon were reflected in miniature, and it hardly needs saying that as she spoke they danced. You can't get enough of that shit, she said. Actually, I'm the same. I guess it's everyone who's haunted by their dreams.

I like smoking with you, I told her, I feel like I could burn the whole world down—a remark Ella acknowledged only by holding out two fingers so that I could return her cigarette.

In Gibson's library, she went on, she'd read about the neurochemical process that enables us to distinguish the things we *see* from the things we *think of*, so that the thought of a bear, for example, wouldn't trigger the same response as the sight of a bear—a mechanism, in other words, for distinguishing fear that originates around us from fear that originates within us. During sleep this process was suppressed, and that was why we experienced our dreams as so uncannily real. But the difference, she said, patting me on the head again, is that for you this fear is a form of beauty, because in your waking life you experience nothing of the sort.

■

In the moonlit dark, beneath the day-old snowfall, the Gibson property seemed to glow, rising behind us to the south toward a distant tree line and falling away before us to the north into a modest valley plain, at the far side of which, against the sky, could be seen the crested silhouette of Overlook Mountain, where we'd promised my dad we'd all do some hiking. It actually heartened me how candidly Ella spoke about my psychic faults—it was a sign of the equilibrium we'd achieved, as if my personality, like her body, had become an external difficulty for us to surmount. Looking up at the actual moon now, which was nearly full, I started rambling about the perfect waxing crescent moon that had caught my eye in Virginia on the night of the attacks in Paris the month before—in connection, maybe, with the question of real versus imagined fear. When I received her message that afternoon, I said, I was in the locker room at the graduate rec center, in a pleasant endorphin fog after a long hour swimming laps. All around me, business school kids with sausage fingers were waving their squash racquets around like machetes, massaging their triceps, and, inexplicably, blow-drying their pubic hair with the hair dryers mounted by the sinks. In my underwear, I read Ella's message as it arrived, a quick series of messages, in fact: a shooting of some kind was under way in Paris; she was with her friend Samia, whose boyfriend, the manager of a restaurant near the canal, had heard gunfire not far off, and locked himself and his staff and their customers inside behind the gates.

In the pocket of the coat she was wearing Ella had found a bag of sunflower seeds. She'd been eating them one by one at her usual abstracted pace, cracking the shells with her teeth and launching them off the tip of her tongue into the flames, like a first baseman, I thought.

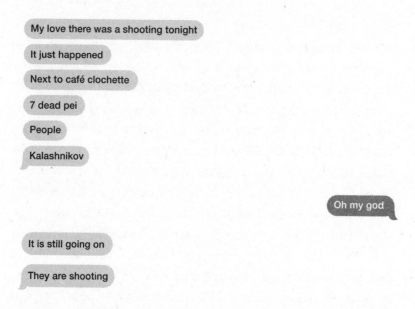

My love there was a shooting tonight

It just happened

Next to café clochette

7 dead pei

People

Kalashnikov

Oh my god

It is still going on

They are shooting

Sitting there in the silent Catskills with the smell of woodsmoke burning my sinuses, it was easy to blame the close, damp quarters of that locker room, its echoey din, the billowing steam, along with the endorphin glow I've already mentioned, for the equanimity with which I received word there was a shooting in progress. To be fair, my most pressing concern—that you were safe, I said to Ella now—she'd preempted by texting me before the news broke. I imagined an attack on a much smaller scale: a police officer, or a squad of soldiers who stood guard at the doors of synagogues since the *Charlie Hebdo* shooting and Kosher market siege. I rolled my wet swimsuit into my towel, and walking down the hall, I peered into a large, mirrored dance studio, where rows and rows of women in spandex were practicing arabesque turns en pointe.

I'd been planning to leave the next morning for New York, and had a number of errands to run before I did. In the car I checked my phone again, and found in neither French nor American media any report of an attack. By the time I reached the dry cleaners, I'd found reports of an explosion at the stadium in Saint-Denis. I texted my friend Michael, who as it turned out was locked down in another bar in another neighborhood, having also heard gunfire nearby. He was in touch with our friends Pauls and Azra, who'd seen people fleeing near Nation. Likewise did the reports and rumors flying around on Twitter add to a sense of ubiquitous carnage. What number of men were stalking through the city, discharging automatic weapons indiscriminately, was anyone's guess; making my way homeward through traffic with my phone in my lap, I started picturing the most horrific and improbable scenarios; and by the time I noticed the crescent moon that had risen in the evening sky—incontrovertible evidence of the planet's continued turning—Ella began reporting gunshot victims in our immediate social orbit, and in my imagination an army of hundreds had the entire city under siege.

The fire had begun to die, Ella raised her hood and pulled her parka more tightly around her. Behind the cottage was a stack of snow-dusted logs, an armful of which I arranged over the glowing embers. I crouched beside them as they caught fire, and the two of us watched the flames grow. It was true that whenever I remembered the terror of that night, I felt a vague regret that it had faded. A passage returned to me from Dr. Gibson's memoir, *Dream Life. Consider three cardinal dream emotions: anxiety, elation, and anger*, he'd written. *Recent evidence suggests that these emotions are existential elements of the self, integral components of our autocreative armamentarium.* Was this related, I asked Ella, getting settled again, to what she'd said about my nightmares being beautiful to me? Speaking readily, half chortling, she said I could be forgiven if I found the experience of imaginary fear morally clarifying, or if it made me feel more human.

I don't think I told you, she went on, but a few days before the attacks, I had an appointment with a hypnotist in Montmartre, who'd relieved a number of my friends of various compulsions, fixations, and phobias: overeating, a hatred of dogs, the need to be liked—so they'd sworn. And I thought maybe he could do me, too. The longer I'd been back from Macedonia, the more intractably I returned to this empty place, a feeling like wrenching loss I'd really begun to hope was behind me. Remember *Nights of Cabiria*, the scene where Giulietta Masina gets hypnotized? And she takes the stage, quaking with apprehension, the magician with devil horns under his hat. It was my mom who made the appointment, a birthday gift. Monsieur Carvalho had dark eyes and an endless network of creases in his face. As soon as I saw him, I believed he might cure me once and for all of wanting a child. His office was cramped, and the smell of his aftershave made my eyes water. Everywhere you looked were art objects of indistinct African origin, wood carvings mostly, a few discreet pieces of ivory, the sorts of things that are commonly found in medical offices in France. On his desk was a photo of a woman carrying a basket on her head—white people love the woman with the basket on her head. Is that your friend, I asked him, and he gave me a bewildered look. Still, I found myself unable to look away, unable to resist projecting onto her face a self-possession and defiance I craved to find in myself. And I imagined a basket in which I would place the burden of my own hope, or fear, whichever it was, and soon I found myself saying all of this aloud, gradually coming under his spell, laid out on the sofa with him crouching beside me like a gargoyle, performing a series of rituals to help me relax.

Now that he was right on top of me, his aftershave was overpowering, it made me feel faint. This man stinks, I said aloud, which he was very professional about. But so remember Cabiria, her hypnosis consists mostly of a reality the magician creates in words, a beautiful flower garden she can inhabit by closing her eyes, so that her dingy, claustrophobic real life disappears. Whereas my eyes stayed open, I was aware of the office, and the world outside, from which the voices of people in the street reached me with intense clarity. But at the same time, lying there, I watched myself enter another reality, guided by my own voice. At Carvalho's mild prompting I described the scene precisely: a bright, sunlit apartment I searched room by room, barefoot over the cool floorboards. I knew I was looking for a basket and that, when I found it, Carvalho would ask me to discard its contents in some decisive or violent gesture. But I felt no urgency about it, I felt calm and detached, like I was wandering through a museum on a long winter afternoon, the Dreamatorium, say, or pacing the floors of a perfume ad in the magazine that was open on Carvalho's desk, the pages of which I could hear shifting in a draft through a missing pane of glass. But I never thought I'd want a child, either, I said aloud. There's a moment in the *Cabiria* scene where a hush falls over the crowd, as Cabiria, in her crown of white flowers, submits to the illusion of a better world. It's like she's brought the impossibility of such a world to life for them, like she becomes not just a spectacle but a work of art. By this time the smell of aftershave was so preposterously thick I could feel it on my skin. I never found any basket. I paid the man, and then, feeling like the shadow of myself, I went outside, where a light rain began to fall.

The coat Ella was wearing—a large, hooded parka—was not her own coat, she'd found it in the house, it belonged to Dr. Gibson, as did, presumably, the packet of sunflower seeds she'd found in the pocket, which she continued cracking in her teeth as she spoke. Around us we occasionally heard the jingle of Norman's collar, as he darted around in the snow. It was only now that she was putting all this into words, she continued, that it began to seem so unreal, like a train of thought you follow through a sleepless night, which in the light of day makes no sense at all. But on her Uber ride home, the memory of that clean, untroubled interior was still fresh in her mind.

Because of construction on the périphérique, the entire northeast quadrant of the city was gridlocked, and her driver, Djamel, arrived promptly, but it was an hour before she was home. Djamel drove with both hands on the wheel, and kept the radio turned down low. In her ongoing state of receptivity, the gentle sound of rain on the roof, and the gentleness of his demeanor, made it easy to listen to him talk; soon she'd learned that until recently he'd lived in Setif, the city of his birth, where he'd been a florist, and that less than a year ago he'd moved to France with his wife, Mira, a Franco-Algerian woman who worked at the mairie in Aubervilliers, where they were living with her parents. He liked Paris, he said when Ella asked, he liked the food and the rich diversity of its culture. Nationwide, a strong middle class enjoyed an exceptionally high quality of life—he liked that, too. He liked the feeling it gave him to be accepted into Mira's family, and to take part in the rooted existence they'd led in the same neighborhood since just after World War II. Now and then after dinner, he sat with his father-in-law until very late, listening to stories from nearly three-quarters of a century in France—a car fire he'd seen as a teenager coming home in the dead of night, a half-drowned dog he'd pulled out of the canal—intimate conversations that, moving freely between French and Darija, and backward and forward through the course of decades, gave Djamel a strong feeling of peace.

Still, he said, the long months of gray skies made him lethargic. The hard water made his hair chalky and dull. He felt lonely in a way that he never had back home. People looked away when he met their eyes in the rearview mirror. He missed working with flowers, he said, which had given him a daily opportunity to reflect upon the nature of beauty and the goodness of God. The etched, shadowed features of his face and his heavy accent made it difficult to find steady work. At Mira's insistence, he'd taken part in the massive solidarity march after the *Charlie Hebdo* attacks, the so-called Marche Républicaine, where the sound of chanting and "La Marseillaise," the fevered crush of bodies, the carnival atmosphere on the train and at République, the painted faces and funny hats, and, more than anything, the dubious refrain *not afraid*, made bile rise in his throat.

Yet, this was Mira's home; he knew she wouldn't like Setif, and France was a good place to start a family. Though as to that, he said with a sigh (coming now, Ella sensed, to the heart of the matter), it was starting to feel like a moot point. Essentially since the night of their wedding, he and Mira had been hoping for a baby; in fact he'd even gone so far as to ask her to join him in prayer, despite their unspoken agreement never to discuss religion. He just wanted her to be happy. Some women are made this way, he said. You know how it is. And at this point Djamel stopped himself, Ella said, searching her face in the mirror, a delicate, silent way of asking her permission to continue. Yes, she told him, meeting his eyes, she thought she understood. For a long moment as traffic crawled forward, Djamel was silent, pausing at the threshold of a still further realm of confidence. Only a few months ago, he continued in a lower voice, it seemed our prayers were answered. We could scarcely believe it, we'd done nothing differently, same position, same time of day—it seemed impossible, the only explanation was maybe the phase of the moon, with the bodies of women it's always the moon. When the technician showed them the tiny dark spot on the screen, nothing more than a shadow really, Djamel knew he could be happy in Paris or anywhere else. He'd never seen Mira so luminous. She made the whole world glow.

The rain continued to fall, and on the sidewalks beside the Buttes Chaumont intrepid joggers in calf-high socks wore expressions of misery. Only a few blocks remained until they'd reach Ella's father's place, where she was looking after the cat. Ella, scarcely breathing, watched Djamel's face. Two months had passed since the miscarriage, he continued, Ella told me. Suffice it to say, Mira was shattered; it was hard to imagine she'd ever again be whole. Her doctor had put her on medication, and she'd taken a leave of absence from work. She sat by the window sometimes for hours, staring into the empty courtyard, listening to the cheerful practice of the flautist who lived on the garden floor. The light in her eyes, that quality of responsiveness Djamel loved, went all but completely dark, and sometimes when he watched her—standing at the sink, for example, or lying awake in the early morning as sunlight gradually filled the room—it seemed she was no longer among the living, she was so far gone.

And meanwhile, his own life barely deserved the name. He was working longer hours but taking fewer fares; he'd drive in silence, or park and simply walk the streets. More than ever, he said, he was committed to the promise they'd made each other of equal partnership, but it wasn't possible for him to share equally in her pain. That morning, out drifting when he should have been behind the wheel, he found himself standing before a flower shop, watching the water that leaked from beneath a display of May lilies and filled the cracks in the pavement at his feet, whereupon he dissolved in a flood of tears. I feel so lost, he said to Ella as he pulled up to the curb to let her out; I feel so lost and helpless, and there's no one to tell me what to do.

■

One of the peculiar, unintended results of being hypnotized, Ella would later tell me—not that night in the Catskills but the following summer, as we strolled beside the flooded Seine—was that her lifelong fear of sleeping alone in a dark room was gone: that very night, without giving it any thought, she'd put out the light and slept more soundly than she had for years, and likewise the few nights that followed, though it wasn't until the night of the attacks that she even noticed, because that night she didn't sleep at all, staying up until dawn instead with Anaïs, smoking one cigarette after another, soaking up the images—the disembodied moaning, the blue wash of sirens and bright pools blood—that looped on BFM throughout the night. It felt wrong to watch, she told me by the river, terrorizing people is BFM's entire business model, but it felt more wrong to look away. By the time she mentioned this we'd been walking all afternoon, we'd already been from the east end of the city to the west and back again, but sunset was still hours away. For long periods we lapsed into silence, and each time we resumed talking a new discussion began, on such topics as—in addition to the Lovings and Virginia Hale's bicycle accident—the inevitable collapse of the GOP, the upcoming referendum on the UK's membership in the EU, the previous summer's referendum in Greece, and the hours we'd spent watching videos of John Berger, whose remarks on the vacuousness of European oil painting could so easily be applied to the carefully composed Instagram photos people were taking all around, and whose large features and massive head, together with his gentle voice and generous spirit, made her think of Djamel. I followed her eyes across the water and up toward the gray sky and over the faces that went past, the soldiers we kept crossing, who patrolled the entire city now in teams of three, outfitted in full fatigues, with flak jackets and patrol packs and sidearms strapped to their chests, and to the sugar she watched a homeless man at the water's edge stir into a tiny coffee cup printed with clouds. Occasionally we'd drift apart, according to our separate whims, and I'd watch Ella at a distance, in her specific relation to the world; and when we came together again, I always had the impression that the idle thoughts we shared belonged to the diffuse, ongoing conversation we'd been carrying on all afternoon, which itself belonged to the diffuse, ongoing conversation we'd been having since we'd met. Conversation, that's the ticket, I said. Our whole marriage is this one conversation, repeated with variations at appalling length. Other couples have sex, whereas you and me, we like to converse.

■

You like to converse, Ella said. I don't much care for it. But she pointed out the link between our long walk that afternoon, our weaving course along the banks of the Seine and over its many bridges, and the days she spent walking by the Vardar River in Skopje. That was already nearly a year in the past, but on the night of the attacks in November her return from Macedonia was still fairly recent. Having finally fallen asleep near dawn, she woke in full daylight, in a state of tremendous confusion, and momentarily took the sleeping figure beside her not for Anaïs but for Emina. Only once her eyes found the muted TV set in the corner of the room did she regain her bearings; and her initial disorientation conferred upon the present circumstances, as the memory of the previous night returned, some of the disembodiment and unreality she remembered from her time in Skopje. All night, in fact, as the attacks and their aftermath unfolded both in the city around her and in her imagination, she reflected as her head cleared, she'd heard an echo from the shadows of her consciousness that now she understood to be Emina's voice. The previous night was all a blur, but she remembered how, between ten and eleven, she, Anaïs, and Samia had watched in near-total silence as one attack after another was reported in the city's eastern districts, and how her blood went cold whenever she recognized another storefront or street corner from her daily life. And she remembered that Romain, Samia's boyfriend, was still locked down in Café Clochette—exceedingly drunk and presiding over the collective disaster euphoria of his staff and customers—when people she knew in France began to mark themselves safe on Facebook, and people she knew in the US began superimposing their profile pictures with a translucent image of the French flag: #prayforparis and #jesuisparis. By then hours had passed since Romain first texted to say he'd heard the sound of gunshots. In the meantime, when they'd learned that the shots Romain reported hearing had killed fifteen people on the terrace of Le Carillon and inside Le Petit Cambodge, less than a hundred meters away from where he was now in hiding, the color had drained from Samia's face, and she'd spent at least an hour trying to get him on the phone, an hour during which she also learned that her cousin Ana had been sitting on the terrace with her friend at Café Bonne Bière when the shooting began: Ana had been wounded and couldn't remember anything except a few frames of memory in which, across the table, her friend was shot and killed. From the streets, all night, came the sound of sirens, at various distances, moving through the city in various directions, and difficult to distinguish from the sirens on TV, which may have been the same sirens anyway, broadcast live on a slight delay. The exact numbers of dead and wounded were still unclear; even before the police stormed the Bataclan, estimates on BFM put the toll as high as 160. At La Belle Équipe, a café on the corner of Anaïs's block, where Ella and I had occasionally shared an Orangina, it was reported that dozens of people had been killed; the younger brother of another friend of hers, also named Samia, was among the wounded there. Ella had watched these numbers obsessively as they rose, until at a certain point Hollande appeared on TV. The substance of his message to the public was that the scope of the attacks remained unknown, that the threat to French lives was ongoing, and that it was correct to be afraid; for the foreseeable future, he explained, this attitude, under the legend état d'urgence, would be the law of the land. *France must be strong,* he said; *it must be great and the state authority must be firm. You must put your faith in the state's power to defend you.* Ella excused herself to use the bathroom, where time seemed almost to stand still, and she became lost in a surreal sensation like drifting in empty space. Samia left sometime after two to be with Romain; Ella stood by the window to watch her cross the courtyard and step into the empty street. How close would a bomb blast have to be, she asked herself, leaning against the same windowsill again toward dawn, to blow the glass out of the pane? She remembered the breeze in Carvalho's office and the rustling pages of the magazine. And now with that thought in the morning she rose, and another sensation returned to her: floating beneath the night sky with Emina, on the surface of a lake. Careful not to wake Anaïs, she crept out to the kitchen to make a cup of tea, over which she held her face as she waited for it to cool. The anger she felt swelling inside her—she wondered whether it had been there all along. When Anaïs came into the room in a Betty Boop t-shirt Ella had dug out of the closet for her to sleep in, they were faced with the problem of how to interact in a dramatically reordered world. It was two full days before either of them went outside.

■

Some of this Ella repeated for me, at my prompting, during our walk; but I heard her account of the attacks in its entirety for the first time at dinner with my family on Christmas Day, for which occasion my mom had laid the table with an ancient silk tablecloth she'd found in a linen chest—which we recognized from photos of the dining room that hung on the dining room walls, from occasions dating back to the early fifties, per the labels Dr. Gibson had affixed beneath them—as well as with delicate china she'd found on a high shelf, which was clearly marked NOT FOR USE BY GUESTS. And now my parents had opened another bottle of wine. My family learned a valuable lesson that week about crossing Ella: a few days had passed since the quesadilla debacle, and she wasn't yet satisfied that she'd extracted her .45 kilograms of flesh. Tom and Jess she was outright ignoring. On rare occasions that they spoke to her she'd blink twice and turn away; and when their night to cook arrived (which is to say, our night), they prepared a beautiful lamb ragout—à la Antillaise, they claimed, the same dish Ella's mother, Clarisse, made at Christmas every year—and Ella left it untouched on her plate. Aren't you hungry? my poor mom ventured, and Ella showed her teeth. I'm sure it's very good, was all she said. But Tom and Jess weren't the only targets of her wrath. My parents, for so readily accepting a bogus version of events, she treated with exaggerated, impersonal courtesy; and Owen and Noah, our former housemates who'd failed to rise to our defense, got flared nostrils whenever they tried to revive some memory or inside joke. Only Evie and Addie were spared, though the warmth and charm she showed the two of them was really just another instrument of her contempt for the rest.

All this was deeply satisfying to me. I felt a vague responsibility to smooth things over. But in fact, I didn't like it any more than she did. Still, angry as I was, especially at Thomas for how he'd spoken to her, and great as it felt to be aligned with her against the world, it was Ella whose forgiveness the whole family was falling over themselves to earn; it was Ella who had the power to ruin or salvage what was left of the week. My dad, like a helpless puppy who'd been whipped, kept bringing her things to look at, animal skeletons and scraps of birch bark to sniff. You want to see something neat? he'd say. My mom kept asking her opinion about any topic that came up: What do French people think about Obama? she'd asked as we all sat around the fireplace in our slippers the day before. As it happened, "Strange Fruit" had started playing on someone's Spotify channel, and Ella decided to remark upon that instead: Oh my, she said. What a cozy song.

And now it was Christmas. In the center of the table Noah had arranged a basket of the paper flowers they'd all folded, and their uniform whiteness had a sepulchral effect. It was his and Owen's night to cook; they'd made macaroni and cheese from the same recipe Ella and I had served at our wedding—

another peace offering—and it was sitting heavily in all our stomachs, we were sinking low in our chairs, some of us softly groaning. While they cleared our plates, my sister passed around a GIF in which Donald Trump's nose had been removed, folding his eyes and mouth into the middle of his face, with the result that he looked like the representative of a devolved, post-humanoid race in a dystopian future. In fifty years, my mother said to me, someone will write a dissertation on all the alternate histories where Trump wins; you should start writing yours now. This was the month Trump called for the closing of the nation's borders to all Muslims. That man, Addie said, turns oxygen into evil with his lungs. Tom nodded: It's barometric, there's no such thing as an external threat, we manifest violence out of thin air. And it was true that a few nights before, while Ella and I sat by the fire outside eating soggy tortillas, a cluster of supercell thunderstorms had descended upon the Midwest and the South, producing nearly sixty tornadoes that tore the roofs off schools, flattened churches, and scattered grain silos into the air like chaff from Michigan to Mississippi, where brick houses were razed to their foundations, mobile homes were tossed high into the air, and school buses were turned into surreal, grotesque husks, and where the devastation continued even now on Christmas night as Owen and Noah set out dessert, a platter of chocolate chip cookies they'd made with store-bought dough and a six-ounce container of raspberries they hadn't washed.

It was raining here at the Gibson Center as well. Tracing with a fingertip the intricate patterns embroidered in the tablecloth, which formed approximate shapes of flowers, I described this destruction at length—I'd been watching the footage all afternoon—and I said that disasters of this sort felt consonant, somehow, with the image of noseless Trump. Someone had lit a pair of kerosene lamps mounted to the wall—ORIGINAL 19TH-CENTURY FIXTURES, their labels claimed. It was one of those antique houses where at night there hangs a faint haze. Now and then my father leaned over the table to top our glasses, filling each to within an inch of the rim. Noah got up to let the dog in out of the rain, and spent a few minutes doing dishes before returning to the table. When he came back, somehow I'd gotten from the tornadoes to the fact that Dr. Gibson was a direct descendant of Roger Williams: What were we to make of that, I demanded. As it turned out, Noah was raised in the Baptist church, which Roger Williams founded, Noah said, wiping his hands on his shirt, when he was banished on pain of death from the Massachusetts Bay Colony for speaking out against the confiscation of Native American lands. He was driven from his home in the dead of night, into the frozen wilderness, and with the help of the Narraganset he survived the winter and established a settlement called Providence Plantations, where he passed the continent's first antislavery legislation, in the 1650s, though he never managed to get the surrounding settlements to sign on and after his death Rhode Island became the center of the slave trade in the New World. As Noah spoke I looked up to find that Ella, with a slight, complicit smile, was carefully and patiently forming little sculptures in her tea saucer with drippings from the several candles my mother had lit, little misshapen pillars of wax she added to a drop or so at a time, while on either side of her Addie and Evie watched in rapt, unfaltering attention, enchanted, I think, by what must have seemed to their twelve-year-old sensibilities a wanton breach of the table etiquette they'd been learning all their lives. Why I found this so touching, I'm not really sure—how modest it was, as demonstration of resistance, of their own power to deform the familiar world. Even when the discussion moved from tornadoes to tsunamis, from the slave trade to the Bermuda Triangle to hurricanes and floods, to Eric Garner to Dylann Roof to the rising seas, even as I agreed with Noah that civilization stood at the precipice of an expansive void, I felt I could see signs in these three lovely, candlelit faces a version of the future in which that void might become an abundance—though an abundance of what, I couldn't have said. At any rate, the conversation soon turned to the attacks of November, and this was when Ella described that night, speaking in a detached, level tone that was unfamiliar to me.

Before I picked her up at the airport, she'd asked me to bring some books from the library; by the fireplace all week she'd been reading work by and about Frantz Fanon, and now I could hear her translating his French for herself, as she reached the end of her personal account and began a kind of commentary. She'd set the candles she'd been playing with down in front of her, and, ever so faintly, their flames registered in the tablecloth's silken sheen. Likewise in the silver bangle that, I noticed only now, she was twisting around her wrist. Leaning against the wall in her father's apartment, Ella said, there was a large, slightly rippled mirror whose imperfect reflection of the room, throughout the night of the attacks, was always somehow in her mind—and now, reading Fanon's work and biography, this detail kept returning to her. Before he became a revolutionary, Fanon was a psychiatrist, and after World War II, when he was studying in Lyon, he observed that the mysterious pains suffered among the North African men who lived in the city's crowded tenement district on rue Moncey, which his white colleagues attributed to the indolence and dishonesty of the Arab mind, might better be explained as the psychosomatic effects of racial persecution, which, from the very beginning of France's involvement in Algeria, was not merely incidental in a loosely governed colonial world, but rather a deliberate and systematic aspect of a carefully outlined colonial project. It might surprise us to hear, Ella said, that Alexis de Tocqueville, having just finished an encomium on democracy in America that's celebrated as a testament to Western liberalism to this day, became the chief ideologist of French colonial policy not long after the conquest of Algeria began, and advocated for a policy of total war that included the burning of harvests, the extermination of livestock, the expropriation of lands, the destruction of cities, the subjection of native peoples to separate laws, their forced relocation and internment, and the ruthless subdual of resistance by a scorched-earth doctrine that sometimes involved the slaughter of entire villages, measures that had reached genocidal proportions by the time he delivered a report in praise of the colonial administration's *able and glorious* conduct in war. Complete submission, he insisted, was only a matter of time, but in fact, year after year, as thick clouds of smoke and ash hung in the air where villages and cities once stood, the people of Algeria grew more determined and resilient, even as the nineteenth century ended and the twentieth century began.

By this point I knew what Ella was up to. Her voice was even and precise. Before their eyes, she was measuring out their existence on a whole new scale. No one dared interrupt. My brother Owen, however, had invested his attention in the tall stack of Pillsbury cookies on his plate, each of which he was now topping liberally with whipped cream—a process Ella interrupted herself to observe, until he put the can down and sat up straight. In the first half of the twentieth century, she then continued, intelligence analyses reported an increase in settlers' complaints of arrogance among the native population, who spoke disrespectfully to their European employers, who insulted white women in the streets, and who even went so far as to *denigrate French culture*. Ominous nationalist graffiti appeared wherever you looked, LE CHÂTIMENT APPROCHE, for example, and FRANCE À LA MER, until on May 8, 1945, just as victory in Europe was declared, a loose collection of Algerian nationalists—many of whom had been conscripted into the war— took to the streets not to celebrate the liberation of France but rather to protest their own subjugation to it.

As thousands of demonstrators peaceably assembled, police throughout Algeria promptly deployed their batons, their boots, their barking voices and bare hands. In the city of Setif, a crowd of young men raised the out-lawed Algerian flag, and a group of affronted settlers sitting on the terrace at the Café de France rushed to tear it down. It was then that a young farm-hand named Bouzid Saâl moved to secure the flag, and the police opened fire, striking him dead. Witnesses, Ella said, even to this day recall the shock of seeing Saâl's lifeless body in the dusty street, in the wrinkled, faded blue uniform of the Muslim Scouts. After a long moment of silence, according to Theldja Nouar, who was twelve at the time, a wild, rhythmic, piercing ululation went up among the women present, a ritual lament that was already ancient when Herodotus described it in his *Histories*, which later became a battle cry of the Front de Libération Nationale. Then the shoot-ing resumed, Madame Nouar's account continues, Ella said: further shots rang out and more bodies fell, as in a panic everyone ran this way and that, and the four policemen in their starched gray uniforms coldly bolted and rebolted their rifles. In the ensuing backlash, throughout the departments of Setif and Constantine over the course of the next few days and nights, Algerian demonstrators killed 103 settlers, the so-called pieds-noirs, and set fire to a smattering of their businesses and homes. According to reports in the colonial archives, eight Frenchwomen and girls were raped. With the blessing of the Ministry of the Interior, whose leadership had made its bones as functionaries of the Vichy regime, the colonial authorities declared a state of siege, and undertook to punish the whole of northeastern Algeria, mobilizing the army and organizing vigilante civilian militias, so that within a few weeks twenty thousand Algerian civilians were killed by aircraft, naval bombardment, artillery shells, tank treads, lynch rope, buckshot, and rifle fire in the streets and in their homes. As Ella enumerated these horrors, my father and Jess were eyeballing the last cookie; at the very same moment that their eyes met and they began to make mutual gestures of deference, Owen leaned forward and not only took the cookie for himself and put it in his mouth entire, but also swept the crumbs from the platter onto his plate, which he then lifted to his mouth one by one with the tip of his forefinger, as Ella explained that it wasn't long after the massacre in Setif that Maurice Papon, former supervisor of the Service for Jewish Questions, became the Ministry of the Interior's vice director for Algerian affairs and, later, the prefect of Constantine, in which capacity he began adapting the techniques of conquest Tocqueville had outlined in the nineteenth century for use in modern times: mass arrests, open-ended detention, torture, asymmetric retaliation, and extrajudicial execution, but also a Foucauldian campaign of psychological warfare that included ethnic stereotyping and the public encouragement of violence against supporters of the Algerian cause—among whose ranks, point being, Ella said, could be counted the Martiniquan headshrinker who was at just that time researching the effects of racial marginalization on mental health. For my part, I listened to all this with my heart pounding in my chest, as if it were a piano recital or a floor routine. All along Ella had kept her eyes on her hands, twisting her bangle and examining the creases in her palms. But now momentarily she cast a glance around at us, and a beseeching expression flashed in her eyes. The rain had stopped. For a while I'd been watching Tom as he sat listening, my brother Thomas who as a lieutenant in the Marines had deployed to the Helmand Province of Afghanistan in 2010, in the troop surge that was supposed to get that war under control. Which of course Ella knew. As she spoke he was not only silent but utterly, grimly still. He, too, loved cookies, but he hadn't so much as touched the ones on his plate and didn't appear to notice when Jess quietly expropriated them to her own. In college he'd majored in history and political science, this material was doubtless familiar to him. And yet in a way it seemed like he was hearing it for the first time. In popular imagination, Ella went on, Fanon was seen as an impassioned advocate of violent insurrection, often mentioned in connection with Eldridge Cleaver and Malcolm X—and it was true he was a soldier, that he was wounded fighting side by side with the FLN. True he'd written that the violence that governed the colonial world, which the colonizer with a clear conscience brought into his victims' homes and minds, would be repaid when the colonized swarmed into the forbidden cities and blew the colonial world to smithereens. Admittedly stirring passages like this were often cited in reducing Fanon's work to rabid incitements, but in actual fact, he merely recognized violence as a politically and psychologically intelligible response to centuries of humiliation. To Ella's way of thinking, she said—taking care, I could tell, not to let any emotion rise in her voice—Fanon's theory of revolution was best articulated in a piece he wrote for the newsletter of a hospital in Algeria where he once worked, in which he described it as an act of heroism to approach the world with conscience and love.

Here Ella abruptly paused, and sat up straight and tall, so it seemed like she might have more to say, only to sink the next moment back in her chair and fold her arms across her chest, as if suddenly overcome by exhaustion. With that she began to eat her own share of the cookies, and for a moment the only sound was the rain on the roof, on the windows, on the patio slate, as Addie and Evie put the finishing touches on an elaborate structure of hot wax they'd made on the lovely tablecloth, which my mother noticed only now, whereupon the evening devolved into a heinous scene.

■

My father's habit of bursting into my room in a state of high enthusiasm about the day while I was still asleep, which as a teenager sometimes annoyed me nearly to the point of tears, was now, in my thirties with Ella in bed beside me, so supremely annoying that it achieved a certain charm. It was the morning after Christmas that he roused us for the hike we'd promised, waking me from a dream in which I could dunk from the foul line, which I related from the back seat of one of the two cars we took on the way to Indian Head Wilderness, back seat middle, no less, where Tom and Owen had trapped me using an old trick they should have outgrown. Not that I was in any position to complain: they'd taken pains not to lord it over me, but they'd gone splitsville on my share of the rent on which we'd all gone splitsville. So I accepted my place pressed between them, unshowered, mute, drinking burnt coffee from a go-cup someone had put in my hand, and also eating a stale doughnut I'd found on the dashboard, chewing it to paste as the sensation of dunking from the foul line faded from memory. Is there *anywhere* on the court you can dunk from? Noah asked.

It was Ella's playful idea that the boys and girls ride separately. She rallied Addie and Evie to the cause. The rain had stopped, it was a cloudy, bright white day. This is how it was then: Ella was the weather. She helped my dad marshal us all out of the house, arranging us in a file and handing us our shoes and hats. When she was in a decent mood it was enough to simply hear her voice to make anyone around her smile. But it hadn't escaped my notice that this sudden burst of warmth didn't apply to me. What have I done now, I kept asking myself. In the woods, I watched her walk beside my dad, and it made me envious to see the way her attention energized him: the way he identified trees along the trail, pressing his palms to the bark like a mystic, making sudden, wild gestures, and thrusting his hands so deeply into his back pockets that his pants sagged toward his knees. Off the trail, meantime, Evie, Addie, and Norman romped around in the brush. From the car we'd seen the nighttime rainfall evaporating over the hills in ribbons, but now up close, the tree bark, the thick layer of fallen leaves, the ragged fungi that grew on everything, the rotted trunks of trees, toppled and teeming with larva—all this was rain-slick still, and the smell of dampness, the overall atmosphere of decay, overpowered me, I felt a sort of rupture, a slightly dreamlike sense of omnipresence that I think now may simply have been doughnut sugar in my blood.

By this point we'd come upon the ruins of the Overlook Mountain House—a hotel built in the early nineteenth century as a destination for Manhattan society types drawn to the region by the paintings of Thomas Cole—which on April 1, 1875, was destroyed in a blaze that began as a chimney fire, the first reports of which the management took for a prank and ignored. Although it was less accessible from rail stations or steamboat landings than its competitors, the Overlook Mountain House enjoyed a certain distinction in the 1870s and '80s. Its visitors included Ulysses S. Grant, who on the first morning of his stay led a hike to the mountain's summit, where after a stirring chorus of *America, America!* he allowed a group of small girls to tie wildflowers in his hair. By 1917, however, when a hotelier named Morris Newgold bought the property, the Catskills had become a destination for working-class gentiles and middle-class Jews, and meanwhile residents of artist colonies like Byrdcliffe and Maverick, who wore strange clothes and gave each other provocative haircuts, were in constant conflict with the ornery locals, from among whose number the Ku Klux Klan was recruiting with ever greater success. For which reasons not only the Overlook's but the entire area's prestige in aristocratic circles had faded, and still more so when Newgold leased the grounds to the Unity Club, a recreational division of the Ladies' Garment Workers' Union, whose membership included a great many Russian and eastern European needleworkers with Bolshevik sympathies, which is how, in May of 1921, the Overlook became the site of a secret meeting of America's fractured communist leadership, who checked in under the cover of night and were the only guests for the length of their stay. For two weeks they paced the halls, paced the floors in the musky ballroom, smoking intensely, stoking the hearth, discussing the difficulty of organizing the American proletariat, and the inevitability of armed insurrection against the bourgeoisie, and no doubt also standing outside now and again to breathe the mountain air, to look out over the valley, contemplate a historical cataclysm they were certain was near at hand. By the time they left they'd formed the unified Communist Party of America, or so the doggedly anti-Red United Mine Workers claimed in a broadside published two years later, mere weeks before the All Hallows' Eve that the Overlook once again mysteriously burned to the ground. Its ambitious reconstruction, after nearly two decades of false starts, was finally abandoned in 1941, when Newgold died a sudden death, and his grandson Gabriel, having enlisted in the army, boarded the project up and left it to await the end of the war, by which time the site had been picked clean, though it would take two more fires and seventy more years of abuse and neglect to reach the advanced state of disintegration in which we found it on Boxing Day of 2015.

■

None of which did I learn until later that week. On the long drive back to Virginia, Ella mostly slept, and when I dropped her at Dulles, she gave me a limp hug by the curb and insisted it wasn't necessary for me to park and come inside. Back in Charlottesville, to escape my cat-piss apartment, where Ella was all I could think of, I spent long hours poking around the library, pursued through the stacks by unintelligible whispers that always turned out to be the heat coming on, or the stutter of wonky fluorescent bulbs. At such an altitude, three thousand feet, the Overlook Mountain House was situated above the clouds, like heaven, according to an 1873 dispatch in the *New York Times*, and though the hours-long stagecoach ride from the nearest station of the Ulster and Delaware Railroad was frequently sodden and gray, guests would nevertheless sometimes discover clear blue skies upon arriving and would stand on the portico in amazement, looking out over the tops of rainstorms or banks of fog through which they'd just ascended. This was not our experience on stumbling upon the ruined hotel that day, though, because while we were wandering through its skeletal remains, it emerged that Evie and Addie were nowhere to be found.

We didn't exactly panic. The wilderness around us was vast, but only on the scale of the Northeast. But Addie's parents were a fucking nightmare, in my mom's phrase. The temperature was dropping, and it looked like it might rain. And there were copperheads to worry about, according to my dad. For a while we took turns shouting into the mist. Jesus H, my mom said, I could wring their scrawny necks. Thomas had a trail map, and he spread it out on a patch of moss. Dropping to one knee, he divided us into teams of two and assigned us each a sector. My dad and I were to stay put at the hotel, in case they turned back up. I couldn't help feeling there was some slight to my competence intended by this assignment. But in the silence that ensued after the search party left, my dad and I both experienced a certain heightening of sensitivity, a feeling that time had suddenly opened in both directions, toward the future and the past at once, or anyway this is what I said at the top of a grand, curving staircase that simply ended in open space above what must have been the lobby: that the destruction of what's gone before, he agreed immediately, anticipates the destruction that awaits, a notion he illustrated with the image of two waves collapsing on the same spot.

The girls are probably fine, I said.

For a minute we were quiet, as he stroked his mustache, until at length, removing his glasses and cleaning them with the tail of his shirt, he started naming the trees whose tangled roots formed the lobby floor: birch, beech, oak, and ash. The sky remained gray overhead, and a wispy fog drifted among what was left of the walls. In all the morning's hubbub I'd forgotten the long, tense conversation Ella and I had in bed the night before, about when the time would be right to begin the process of IVF. I wanted to wait, she wanted to start right away. For all the world I couldn't remember whether we'd reached an agreement before we fell asleep. It made no sense to do it now, to have a baby would ruin all our plans; on the other hand, it would be so liberating, to be reduced spontaneously to this one thing you have to do. A rabbit hopped across the lobby. For a while I moved from one room to the next, standing at the threshold of each and trying to rebuild it in my mind. My dad wandered off down the front steps; through the trees I saw him standing at the precipice, looking out over the valley. Imagine, I said to myself, he was twenty-five when I was born. And I said to myself that this man was an excellent father, that despite being related to his sister Karen he had a tender way of living in the world. He had four children who'd never once doubted his love. This was the small, vital imprint he'd leave upon the earth, and it could be my imprint as well.

Somehow I'd never perceived the prospect of fatherhood this way. Ella sometimes said I'd make a good father. With that thought in mind, I decided to apply myself to the problem of finding the girls. It would be nice to have her look upon someone who had saved the day. Norman was missing as well, and I worked out that he'd probably started chasing some small animal—a rabbit, say—and Evie and Addie had bounded after him. If I were a rabbit and Norman was chasing me, I asked myself, which way would I go? Naturally I'd go downhill, and through the thickest brush possible at that. Thomas's plan was based on the premise that they wouldn't be far from the trail. I now knew that to be incorrect. I explored the area on his map. To the south the falloff was too steep for a rabbit, but on the more reasonable northern slope there was a vast, densely wooded area through which no trail was cut. I told my dad to hold the fort, and strode off before he could object.

The fog thickened as I set out. I soon found myself looking over the submerged detritus of a flooded outbuilding. No sign of the rabbit, Norman, or the girls, but on the plus side, I felt like I'd stepped into a scene from *Stalker*, a film in which the future—a postrevolutionary Marxist utopia—has failed to arrive: as I continued downhill, I found myself waxing poetic about the Zone and the Room and the claim of placeness some places make only once they begin to disappear, submit to the claims of nature, become hostile to the exact demands of civilized life they were designed to fulfill. How long would it be, I wondered, until all the world was such a place, a vision that in my present overcaffeinated mood I found quite soothing, and one that, as I shambled through the brush, soon became indistinct from my actual surroundings: to think of the grass growing up through the cracks in the sidewalk, telephone poles rotting, listing, and toppling over, rain that would fall on no one and would pool inside of tire swings along the banks of rivers, saplings that would push up through the floors of not only hotels but of banks and schools and auto dealerships, first one tree and then the next, until the floor was the ground and everywhere was the woods, and meanwhile all mankind united in being dead and silent— though I may have added this last bit later, when I reached the bottom of the mountain and followed a creek upstream to a beautiful lake in the woods, by which time my blood sugar had dropped precipitously and I decided to take a little rest, letting the pleasure of lying down spread through my body, letting the thought form in my mind that I hadn't saved the day but ruined it, and letting myself understand that this was a waking-life problem and could make it go away simply by closing my eyes.

■

Later, once again riding back seat middle, I would think about that lake—the feeling of desperation that seized me when I awoke beside it, the thousands upon thousands of concentric ripples that appeared on its surface when a light rain began to fall, and the residue of a dream of fatherhood so vivid and so warm that it caused me physical pain to feel it evaporating from my mind—as we drove in grim, helpless circles because no one's phone had a signal, and my father's eyes in the rearview mirror conveyed a sense of disbelief of the exact sort David Byrne described in the song that had just come on.

And it was when this excellent song came on that I started noticing signs along the roadside marking the former sites of townships, where beyond a narrow strip of woods there was nothing but water, in the glassy stillness of which you could watch the shifting skies. This, too, entered into my idle reading in the library the following week: I learned that these villages, with names like Olive, Eureka, Bittersweet, and Neversink, had all at some point in the past century been submerged in the reservoirs of the Delaware and Catskill watersheds, which, together with Westchester's Croton watershed, supply New York City with its famous water. During the days I spent in the empty library, collecting digital copies of documents published in the early twentieth century by the New York Board of Water Supply, and reading the work of a historian named David Soll, I had no idea what purpose all this reading and compiling and note-taking would serve, except as a way to avoid going home, where the smell of Ella's shampoo still lingered after the single night she'd spent there a few weeks before, which made me miss her so much I couldn't sleep, could only watch the shadows shifting on the walls as the moon made its way across the sky, in which state of exhaustion the obvious resonances suggested by the title of Soll's book, *Empire of Water*, finally became vivid in my mind.

The municipal government's long career in what Soll calls *democratic resource imperialism* began with the Old Croton Aqueduct in the 1830s, when the sorry state of the city's original water system caused a cholera epidemic that claimed 3,500 lives, many of which in Five Points, the slum to which the city's free black and immigrant Irish residents were then consigned, where they didn't have access to private distribution reservoirs like the one built on Chambers Street by the Manhattan Company, which would later become Chase Manhattan Bank. The Croton system of reservoirs submerged hundreds of acres of farmland in the counties of Westchester and Putnam, and this water was conveyed to the city by a forty-two-mile aqueduct running underground. When the City of Brooklyn annexed itself to Greater New York, it was largely for access to Croton water. Ditto Richmond, as Staten Island was then known. The city's population doubled virtually overnight and continued to grow at a yearly rate of 157,000 persons, each of whom requiring, the newly created New York Board of Water Supply estimated, a hundred gallons of water per day. The Catskills' Esopus valley had barely recovered from the ravages of the logging industry, which left entire mountainsides denuded of trees, and of the tanning industry, which stripped thousands upon thousands of acres of hemlocks of their bark, and of the mining industry, which emptied the hills of bluestone with which to pave over the Manahatta Island of the Lenapes once and for all. After the ravages of these industries poisoned the groundwater, choked rivers and streams to a trickle, and left what remained to burn to charcoal in wildfires that spread unchecked, the city's public relations apparatus emphasized the undespoiled character of the region, which would be made more lovely by the addition of vast, pristine bodies of water where your thinking man might have occasion to contemplate the glory of nature and the bottomless ingenuity of humankind. With the construction of the Catskill water system, it wouldn't be going too far to say, city officials went so far as to say, New York City would earn comparison to Babylon or even ancient Rome, whose own famous network of aqueducts was likewise a testament to Western civilization's commitment to progress.

Critics of the project suggested that it was a perversion of nature, but the city contended that it would prove mankind's ability to exist *in harmony* with nature, and to restore the natural world to its natural state; after all, hadn't geological surveys revealed that the footprint of the Ashokan Reservoir would coincide almost perfectly with a glacial lake of the Devonian period, some twenty-five thousand years in the past, and if so, wasn't it true that this land belonged not to the bumpkins who lived there but to the water that would soon return? To me, this sounded a bit like Tocqueville, vis-à-vis relieving the Arabs of the Maghreb, which in his view rightfully belonged Kabyle and other Berber peoples who'd occupied the deserts and mountains there at least since Herodotus wrote of them that they saw no dreams in their sleep—and who, he insists, might in the absence of their half-savage Arab compatriots be conquered in the peaceable Christian fashion, exactly like the Indians he'd seen on his tour of the United States. Point being, all this came to a head when the secretary of the Mayor's Catskill Aqueduct Celebration Committee composed an elaborate pageant in celebration of the Ashokan Reservoir. *The Good Gift of Water* was conceived in seven parts: a prologue, in which an Indian village on Manahatta Island performs a winsome Rain Dance; five allegorical performances articulating *the Great Uses of Water*; and an epilogue, in which the great Chief Ashokan makes the abundant water of his native mountains available to the people of Greater New York and joins the city aldermen in affirming the goodness of God, from whom all blessings flow. The pageant was to be presented in Sheep Meadow, with some twenty-five thousand schoolchildren taking part. Invitations were sent to President Wilson, and Colonel Roosevelt. No expense was spared. Absent from the proceedings, however, was any representative or representation of the present-day inhabitants of the Catskills, though finally the slight was mooted on a Friday afternoon in the autumn of 1917, when Mayor Mitchel connected the aqueduct, sending a jet of water eighty feet into the air, and thousands of New Yorkers turned their faces toward the sky just as a heavy, unrelenting rain began to fall, and the pageant had to be called off.

It's doubtful, however, that this would have been any comfort to the residents of the Catskills, who by then were more than a decade into an ordeal that had nevertheless only just begun. The city discovered it was more cost effective to burn down the houses that came with the land they requisitioned than to sell them at auction back to their original owners, to be dismantled and reassembled elsewhere. Even as the embers of these homes smoldered in the dirt, the city, in an attempt to reduce its tax burden, applied to have the thousands of acres of developed commercial and residential property and fertile farmland it had razed reassessed as *unimproved*. Meanwhile, towns that had reconstituted themselves on higher ground soon found that the local economic landscape had indeed been unimproved in ways that were hard to gauge. Butchers' regular customers moved away, or went broke, or bought their meats from large cut-rate outfits who'd set up shop to supply the construction camps. Families who ran boardinghouses found their new locations held no appeal for formerly loyal guests. The new fields farmers bought were all but impossible to till. In the legal apparatus established to assess these sorts of damages, locals who brought legitimate loss-of-income claims were pressed to account comprehensively for their past earnings, a process that often ended in humiliation, as certainly was the case when a washerwoman named Laura Every was asked to perform a problem of simple arithmetic under oath and, failing to give the correct answer, was essentially laughed out of court. The recreational paradise officials had promised as a boon to tourism and to their own quality of life, meanwhile, never materialized; rather, to ensure residents never got near enough to pollute the water impounded in its new reservoirs, the city deployed a force of guards to patrol the entire watershed, whose salaries it was far cheaper to pay than it would have been to build and maintain a treatment plant downstate. By the time the aqueduct was connected in 1917, the surface of the Ashokan Reservoir was untroubled by even so much as the hull of a canoe. Silent beneath it, too, along with thousands of acres of farmland that owed its fertility to decades of cultivation, were eight towns and villages, the total populations of which exceeded 6,000 people, not including, of course, the 2,700 departed souls buried in the ground there, whose remains the city had required the living to disinter.

For the dead the indignities associated with the water system ended there, but for the living it just went on and on, I told Ella as our walk continued along the Seine, and as the gray afternoon stretched on for hours without giving the faintest hint of evening: it went on and on, I said, until the towns of Cannonsville and Rock Royal were razed to make way for a final reservoir in March 1962, the same month Algeria won its independence from France. It was true, I said, that in the seventies the city's clout in the affairs of the Empire State was diminished, and its hold on the watershed began to slip. But since 9/11, its properties upstate have been more carefully guarded than ever before. Ella stopped as I spoke, watched me advance a few paces before trailing off and turning to face her. A heat flashed in her eyes when I did, followed by something softer, and sadder. We kept walking and had gone some ways before she spoke.

I remember standing on your rooftop that night, she said, having released Virginia Hale into the care of her roommate: I remember looking out at the glittering Manhattan skyline and feeling a sense of triumph grow inside me that's become more elusive every year since. I remember how lovely it was to stand beside you, to steady myself on your arm, experience the fullness of the world as nothing more than light. I felt good then, in short, she said, like myself.

Why she circled back to that memory, I didn't know at the time, and still don't now. But I date from that moment, near the end of our walk, a new phase of the coldness between us. I could tell she wasn't listening, a moment later, when I asked her to imagine the women of the Ladies' Garment Workers' Union strolling the Overlook terrace on a Friday afternoon in October 1917, stroking their chins and tapping their ash, whispering in maybe Russian, or Armenian, or Bohemian, or Yiddish, about the world to come, gazing out at the vast, newly built reservoir that was at that very moment being connected to their homes.

■

On the Île Saint-Louis we found a bench and sat to rest our legs. I don't know why you had to go charging into the woods like that, Ella said. It was Ella who'd found the girls that day: just uphill from the ruined hotel, at the very peak of Overlook Mountain, there was a fire tower, which rose to a height of sixty feet; and when Ella saw it looming overhead, she said to my mom she was sure she'd find them at the top, as indeed she did: they'd stolen one of Ella's cigarettes and were trying to figure out how to get it lit.

It turned out they'd told me that's where they'd be before peeling off from the group—I have no recollection of it, but I don't doubt it in the least, I was probably just lost in thought. Ella lit their cigarette and smoked it herself, then led them back down the metal stairs. Little cretins, she said. Not ten minutes after I'd charged off into the woods, the entire family reconvened on the former portico of the hotel, and little Norman came trotting up as well. Two hours later, not long after I arrived there myself and fell asleep, Thomas found me by the lake, Echo Lake it turned out to be called, and we followed the Saw Kill back out to the road. I don't know why, Ella said again now, laughing a little and with maybe a hint of affection in her voice, you couldn't just do as you were told.

I didn't know how to answer that question. I wanted to be a man of action, I could have said, but that wouldn't have been quite true. Ella watched me as I stood up and paced around. The same soldiers went past, smug in their vigilance, the one with short legs, the one with the big mole beneath her eye. I'd read somewhere that, since the attacks in November, applications to the French armed forces had tripled. The same had happened in the US after 9/11, I said, wanting to change the subject and performing a series of half-hearted stretches. I didn't remember much from that day, but I remembered how the boys kept talking about *joining up*. That would have been at the beach. I remembered standing around in a loose crowd of my classmates, many of whom hadn't yet heard from parents who worked in the towers, the smoke and dust from the collapse of which we could see clearly on the horizon forty miles down the coast. My own father worked only a few minutes from my school, and I'd spent the morning in his office holding back tears, as he tried to reach a close friend who worked on the eighty-second floor of the South Tower, which we'd seen come down live—I remembered that as well, I remembered feeling powerless to inwardly match the gravity of external events as they unfolded; this is what it's like, I kept telling myself, to be alive during history. I remembered the hours we spent riveted to our TV, my family, the way none of us dared sit, but paced the margins of the room, maybe leaned on the arm of the sofa, or perched on the very edge of the coffee table, careful to avoid any posture of relaxation that one might associate with the passive entertainment that defined middle-class American life throughout the 1990s. Beyond that I didn't remember much at all, I told Ella now. But during the few nights I'd spent at my parents' on my way back to Paris from Virginia, I'd found a box of old notebooks, filled mostly with poetry that slackens my bowels even to mention—and it was in one of these notebooks, point being, that I discovered numerous pages of strikingly candid observations dated September 12, 2001.

I had no memory of making these notes, but in them I found a quality of attention I'd achieved in precisely nothing I'd written since. At the beach, I'd wondered whether the boys around me, affecting a certain gravitas, were, like me, in some small corner of their minds exhilarated by the authenticity of this catastrophe, a catastrophe we could not only see blooming against the sky in the distance but could feel in the air around us, and if the resolution they kept so solemnly repeating, to join the military after graduation, didn't express a secret wish to claim that authenticity as their own. Was this covered, I'd written, by the phrase *feeling confused*, one of several emotions our principal had said over the loudspeaker we could expect to experience, and if so, wasn't imprecise language of this sort the hinge on which our culture of self-absorption, complacency, and rationalization turned? The fineness of the scene made a strong impression: the water lapping at the rocks, the clear blue sky, and the calls of gulls that wheeled around us, which with my eyes closed I could imagine as cries of human distress. One kid, forgetting himself, predicted that defense industry stocks would soar, and in a way I admired him for it, I wrote: such a grown-up thing to say. In a bulleted paragraph stretching to nearly a page, I described the behavior of a classmate named Alexi, about whom I now remember nothing, but whose mother, according to my notes, worked in the WTC and had yet to be in touch. With hours of tears dry on her face, Alexi sat perched atop the lifeguard stand, dusting sand from her ankles, from the soles of her feet, the webbing between her toes. Not long before, I'd gotten word my dad's friend had made it safely out of the South Tower, and now at the beach I wondered, though it was true Karl was like an uncle to me and I cared for him a great deal, whether I'd really been so afraid to lose him, whether the intensity of feeling I'd experienced didn't pertain to something else.

On the night of the twelfth, my dad and I visited him at home, where we found him in an alcoholic stupor. Over the course of several hours, in fits and starts, and with long intervals of silence and occasional interruptions to take calls from the spouses of coworkers wanting to know if he'd seen their loved ones in the stairs, Karl told us the story of that day. This story left a profound mark on me. In my notes, which I realize now I must have made immediately upon leaving his house, I warn myself against the temptation to repeat it every chance I got in the years to come; until now I've mostly managed to resist that temptation whenever the subject has come up, and so I'll mostly resist it now, except to say that 90 percent of the company where Karl had worked for more than twenty years was killed that morning, having aborted the initial evacuation on instructions from security, or having never in the first place left their desks. It's true that for my own benefit I recorded what he told us that night in every sensational particular, as nearly as possible I tried to use his exact words, and to preserve on paper not only his voice but his gestures, his sudden silences, the dampness that rose in his eyes, and the way he'd rubbed his fingers together, like a bellhop, to describe the texture of the air, but all of this always with a view toward the overwhelming shame I felt to think of how I'd spent the previous afternoon.

Nowhere do I mention the fate of Alexi's mother, but the following day, the morning of the twelfth, we learned in the local paper that no one from our town was killed, which we all agreed was miraculous. At any rate, Alexi was still searching her palms for sand when a friend of mine, Matthew, discreetly suggested that our standing there on the jetty accomplished nothing, an early version of *don't let the terrorists win*, any objections I might have made to which were soon defeated by the prospect of piling into his pickup with his girlfriend's friends, all of us pressed close in the bed of his little '85 Toyota, speeding out of town to a secluded spot whose beauty we promised the girls would still their hearts, where between two high cliffs gathered a deep, clear pool in the east branch of the Saugatuck River, just downstream from the reservoir that supplied our homes—a reservoir, I couldn't resist mentioning to Ella, that during the Depression had displaced the hamlet of Valley Forge. It looked like a painting, one of Taylor's friends observed when we arrived, whether Nina or Amanda my notes don't say. For a period we sat around in silence, on an outcropping above the river that couldn't be seen from the road. We held our heads in our hands, lit cigarettes and heaved great sighs. With a twig, Taylor drew intricate patterns in a patch of dirt, and swept these patterns away. I found a book of matches in my pocket and practiced striking them one-handed, until I'd burned through them all, by which time the gloomy atmosphere among us had lifted, so I'd written, as the duty to assert our freedom as Americans developed clearly in our minds. Soon we were speaking in our full voices—about what, my notes don't say, though with a certain sense of inevitability they record that Taylor was the first to swim, that she stripped to her underwear and without a moment's hesitation leapt from the cliff, that she dropped forty feet into the water below, that we'd watched the surface of the water for a long moment, waiting for her to reemerge, and that when she did her face had opened into an exhilaration that instantaneously spread through the rest of us, so that in short order we, too, had stripped out of our clothes and lined up along the edge to await our turns, first Matt, then Joey B., followed by Amanda, until it came to Nina, whom I'd had a crush on for years, and who turned to me to say she was afraid to jump alone.

Fifteen years have passed since that day—at that age, I said to Ella, it's hard to see how much closer you are to childhood than to adulthood; you look so much more like an adult than a child, you're intent on putting away childish things, turning away from the world of make-believe in favor of what's real. At a certain point as Karl told his story, according to my notebook, I relived the moment when Nina and I, lacing our fingers, stepped out into empty space and experienced the sensation of falling exactly as it's experienced in dreams—with none of the heaviness of actual life, none of the inevitability, only the eventual silence of submersion and shock of cold. Whereas later that afternoon when I arrived home in bare feet, with my hair still damp and my wrung-out boxers balled in my fist, and as early estimates reached twelve thousand dead, gravity was restored. It was the sight of bodies, Karl told my father and me, as if the thought only just occurred to him: it was the sight of the bodies, which he watched—standing at the window with his colleagues before any of them knew what was going on— dropping out of windows in the tower opposite, only moments after the first plane struck, that had triggered in him an irresistible instinct to flee.

And specifically, Karl said, it was the sight of a man and woman who leapt together, holding hands, after a pause in which what passed between them he couldn't guess.

■

The day of our hike up Overlook Mountain, in our hopeless circling in the car, we came upon a diner, the type of place whose authenticity made us tingle, where we agreed to ask directions and meanwhile stop for lunch, ravenous as we were from all the walking, from all the searching, those of us who hadn't found a doughnut or had a nap.

The diner sat at the center of one of those impossibly quaint Northeast downtowns. The car parked next to ours was an old 4Runner, and the guy getting into it had his t-shirt tucked into his jeans. He looked us over—representatives of a whole class of ingrates and parasites—with open contempt. At just that moment, a soldier came out of the post office across the street, an army kid in service greens; the guy with the 4Runner barked at him, Thank you for your *service*! It was obvious we were the intended audience for this remark, and Thomas winced. Ella picked up on it as well. *Connard,* she said under her breath.

What did she call me? the guy snapped, addressing no one in particular.

She called you connard, Tom said without a moment's hesitation. I think it means asshole but you'd have to check with her.

Ella chortled, and touched Tom's arm. *Sir,* she said, this man was in a war, do you want to salute him, too?

The guy slammed his door and sped off. On his rear windshield was a sticker that said NEVER FORGET.

It gave me a peculiar feeling, neither pleasant nor unpleasant, to hear Ella refer to my brother as a man. Because of my ridiculous stunt on the mountain, no one besides my dad would look at me. A jovial camaraderie had developed among the rest. Ella held the door for my mom and Jess and followed them in, pursued by the soft rattle from a chain of faded bells that reminded me of the stolen bangle on her wrist. I was starting to remember more of our disagreement from the night before. Getting settled into bed after dinner, I'd told her how proud she'd made me, the way her history lesson had put my family in their place. That's just so typical of you, she said. I'd rather tell you now. But she didn't tell me now. Instead, she said she wanted to start the IVF process as soon as she got back to Paris. I said that if we started now, the baby would be born in the fall and I'd have to drop out of school; better to wait another year. You don't understand what a year represents for me, she said, and for a long time, we went back and forth on that topic. It's so typical, she'd said. You're oh so proud of the historical suffering I've inherited, but you have zero interest in my specific, personal pain. I'm very interested in your personal pain, I'd said. That was the phrase that returned to me outside the diner when I heard those bells.

The ten of us crowded into two booths, and once more I found myself tricked into the middle seat. I'd had enough of my family, it always made me tense to be in restaurants with them, my mom talked too loud and my dad was always clearing bits of food from his mustache with his tongue. At the counter, next to a white guy reading *Between the World and Me*, a white guy with floor-length dreadlocks was muttering about the hazards of cell phone signals, and his voice became difficult to distinguish from my thoughts. After the silence on the mountain and the racket in the car, the soundscape here was disorienting, all noises seemed to reach me at equal volume: knives on plates, the radio in the kitchen, trucks braking at the crosswalk, a wait-ress's Crocs on the tiles. But then all at once the background noise faded as Thomas, in what connection I'm not sure, described a candlelight vigil at a park in East Haven the week the towers came down, where the mayor crowed that it was *a good night not to be in Afghanistan*—a remark that earned raucous applause but sat poorly with my young brother. He remem-bered those words, he said, on the night of September 11, 2010, as he descended the open cargo bay of the C-17 that carried him to Camp Dwyer, where for a stunned moment he paused to contemplate the beauty of a crescent moon. His military service now complete, and with three semesters left in law school, he'd turned down lucrative offers at white-shoe law firms in favor of jobs in the Department of Defense and the Department of Justice, and as a clerk to the chief judge of the DC Circuit Court of Appeals. His entire identity was predicated on the belief that American institutions were a force for good in the world. But he could remember, he said, standing in the crowd that night in East Haven, and standing at the back of that plane in Afghanistan nine years later, feeling the prickle of doubt grow in his mind, as he perceived how easily those institutions could be corroded by human vulgarity. And that prickle had returned, he said to Ella, tracing the lines in his palm, as he sat pinned to his chair during her disquisition on Fanon and Tocqueville the night before. Here Thomas paused and, as if he were about to ask her something, looked up into Ella's face, the first instance of eye contact between them I'd ever witnessed.

There was something almost breathtaking about it. I suddenly felt protective of them both. Since then he's served his year apiece in the DoD, the DoJ, the DC Circuit, and even the Supreme Court—mastabas now, all of them, sinking in the sands. And I wonder if he remembers that moment that his eyes and Ella's met. If he could have spoken his mind plainly, I think he'd have asked her to forgive his behavior around the dinner mix-up, for his shameless, blustering bad faith. But before he could say anything, my mother asked Ella if she thought the attacks in November would form the basis of a culture war in France of the sort that had dominated American life since 9/11—one in which, my mother went on without waiting for Ella's reply, the attack in question would give form to a sense of victimhood that was always invoked as the final word by those least represented among the victims of that attack—meaning, I suddenly hissed, the vanishing class of backward white people like the locals all around us, who would face the final verdict on the relevance of their lives when the election results were announced in the fall, whereupon they could crawl back into the sunless holes they came from, where with any luck they'd suffocate from the reek of their own foul breath. Ella patted my hand, like the forbearing owner of an excitable dog. The rest of the table ignored me. Certainly, she said, turning to my mother, it disturbed her profoundly to see, as the attacks were still unfolding, that a cousin of hers had posted *DEATH TO MUSLIMS* on his Facebook page. It was a common enough sentiment in France. Still, in a way liberals bothered her most of all. She could remember the dull fury that came over her like a cluster headache when she realized that the trauma she was experiencing near at hand was being addressed in the culture as a series of new and recycled hashtags, flag overlays, and variations on the bromide *It's our freedom that they hate*. After the worst of our fights, she said—her fights with me, that is—she was often struck by the deep satisfaction it would give her when I'd finally crossed some line, broke a plate, say, releasing her of any responsibility to examine her own behavior. And this was the emotional mechanism she saw at work that night: never was Western culture so exultant as when it could credibly don the mantle of victimhood. Witness, for example, the viral clip from *Last Week Tonight*, in which John Oliver described the attackers as petty nihilists motivated by nothing more than envy—for France's literary tradition, its viticulture, its revolution, and its macarons— his voice reaching a height of emotion in which outrage and triumph were indistinct.

■

Most of us ordered the Reuben, and Ella ordered a tall stack of blueberry pancakes with bacon, sausage, hash browns, and a pair of over-easy eggs. This isn't going to be pretty! she kept saying. I'd rather tell you now. Now I reminded her of that meal on our bench by the Seine. We'd recently watched *Ways of Seeing* together, and now, surrounded by tourists, it was clear how comprehensively Berger's program on oil painting had pegged the hypocrisy around the attacks in Paris on social media, relative to the silence around attacks that same week in Baghdad and Beirut. On Twitter and Facebook, people attributed this to a callous indifference, on the part of the media and the general public, to the suffering of black and brown people. No doubt this indifference governed in many of the largest and the smallest affairs of our world, but in this case I didn't think indifference quite covered it, it was better described as a glibness that had become so deeply entrenched that it amounted to a kind of psychosis. Only a few days before the attacks, I told Ella, I'd heard Claudia Rankine read from her book *Citizen*, and during the question-and-answer period a man who introduced himself as the president of the local chapter of the NAACP asked her when white people would recover from the mental illness of white supremacy; later, at a bar, a classmate of mine mentioned a study that found medical students at the university hospital consistently rated the pain of black patients lower than the pain of white patients, as just one concrete example of what the NAACP guy meant. Fanon said it in the fifties, and Baldwin said it in the sixties, and Berger said it on the BBC in 1972: one can only conclude that such a culture is mad. Imagine a world where even the futility of Roger Williams's best intentions gets so diluted by the course of history that it ends up as a silo full of Dr. Gibson's scribbled dreams. What happens in Beirut or in Baghdad, I said to Ella, or what happens in Ferguson or Flint or Baltimore, happens beyond the frontier of the dream world within which Western society locates itself, a dream whose borders are fortified by the hypnotic philosophy of consumerism, which commands the better part of our autocreative armamentarium and leaves little for the essentially autocreative work of compassion; so that when those borders breach, point being—when the violence and chaos of the outside world upset the peace and order of the dream—it's only natural that we respond in the dream's own language, a visual language in which value is conveyed in a richness of physical textures and in a system of symbols of prestige. Macarons and wine. All to say, it upset me, too, when, even as sirens blared in the city streets, people one after another in my Facebook feed overlaid their profile pictures with French flags or, worse, changed their profile pictures to photos of their vacations in Paris, photos in which, for example, a platter of croissants and strawberries foregrounded their hotel room's view of the Eiffel Tower, or in which they themselves, shopping bags hooked over each arm, appeared in sunglasses, baring their wine-stained teeth beneath the Arc de Triomphe or Notre-Dame.

And in no case was this more infuriating, I said, than in the case of Matt and Taylor, who'd remained together since high school and who at some point had quit their jobs to travel the world, an adventure they soon turned into a profession, taking extraordinarily lush, symmetrical photographs of each other with high-end leather goods or in designer sunglasses, or straddling surfboards and gazing out to sea. If it was true, as Ella said, that Instagram succeeded in conflating the aim of oil painting and the aim of advertising—respectively, to consolidate the owner's sense of his own value and to manufacture envy in the hearts of a target audience—then Taylor and Matt succeeded in flattening their very lives the exact same way. They were impossibly photogenic: wholesome, sun-kissed, always in clothes of earthy, undatable good taste, sturdy clothes that nevertheless hung loosely on their shoulders, and in colors that matched the sky or grass or rippled dunes. Just the other night, I'd spent a long time looking at these fucking photos, I went on, mainly for the purpose of invigorating myself with contempt; I'd pored over thousands of photos featuring antique Jeeps and stacks of surfboards, hermit crabs, windswept reeds, but also monks receiving alms in Laos, shoeless merchants of spices and flowers and knives, baby elephants, every type of cloud; or variously grass tennis courts, clay tennis courts, balloonists in Cappadocia, fishmongers in Marrakech, sugar cubes in Zurich, handsome doors wherever you looked, a cricket pitch, porters on Kilimanjaro, a Kenyan woman with a basket on her head; midcentury furniture in sunlit rooms, a glass of crushed ice on a pressed-tin bar, tightly rolled towels in sunlit rooms, stands of sunlit bamboo framed in the window of a sunlit room, every image a study in slight overexposure, in desaturation, rectilinearity in all things, the ends of docks on foggy days, waterfalls, mirror lakes, infinity pools, the ocean swelling at dawn, a houseboat in the Mekong Delta, dhows in the Indian ocean, hot springs, reservoirs, squat toilets, bathtubs, hot tubs, lap pools, and of course no shortage of swimming holes, in Thailand, in Canada, in Colombia, and outside our hometown. It wasn't enough, according to Barthes, for a photo to make you want to visit the place it depicted: it had to make you want to *live* there, and this was what Matt and Taylor achieved, for who would refuse the world these images promised, in which every difficulty—in which shame and unloveliness and critical thought—was abolished in favor of elegance, comfort, and light? In comments, many of their followers had independently arrived at the same conclusion: that Matt and Taylor were *living the dream.* I wouldn't have argued otherwise. At the end of October, just a few weeks before the attacks, they'd traveled to Paris on behalf of a service that made fashionable, well-appointed apartments available to tourists for rent—an Airbnb for the luxury market. On the night of November 13, Taylor posted a photo of a vintage bicycle parked in a sunlit Parisian courtyard, to which, along with the salient hashtags, she'd appended the remark that Paris was on her mind.

For me this was a breaking point, that night. I, too, had watched hours of BFM that afternoon, and in the horrifying footage I recognized familiar landmarks of my life—squares and street corners, greengrocers, metro stations—made strange by the bodies scattered among them, by people fleeing in alleys from the sound of rifle fire, by the blue pulse of sirens on the walls, triage stations, shattered glass. In the most literal, immediate sense, I said to Ella, the world that was being depicted onscreen was our world, and this was difficult to process. But it was the same recognition—on the part of people who'd visited Paris, or spent semesters abroad here, or had simply seen the Woody Allen movie—that motivated the response that so offended us both. That very day, I'd seen a news item about the bombing in Beirut and hadn't even clicked the link, I said, not because the lives of Lebanese people meant less to me than the lives of French people, but because the deaths of Lebanese people didn't transform my world into one in which I wasn't perfectly comfortable and safe. Which is to say, the public outpouring of sympathy and grief that night was less an expression of empathy than a basically selfish expression of fear. As I pressed through traffic toward my apartment that day in Virginia, Michael continued sending me updates from the bar where he was locked down, within earshot of the Bataclan. I'd just come out of the dry cleaners when you called me. Among other things, you said you were scared. Now in Virginia the sky had only just started growing dark, the moon was low, everyone was on their way home from work. The faces of drivers in the stalled cars around me were blank and indistinct, registered no awareness of the tragedy taking place, and my disdain for their innocence became the vessel of a dark sort of pride. Soon the geography of the attacks began to emerge, and I realized they formed a roughly straight line along boulevard Voltaire between République and Nation, the precise route that as many as two million people, Djamel among them with his wife, Mira, and me and Ella, too, had followed in January, in solidarity with *Charlie Hebdo*, and as a high-handed demonstration of France's republican ideals. When finally I made it home, I told Ella, I sat fixed in my chair with my computer in my lap, as new information accrued and new trends developed and new graphics appeared, all in a swirl around the central fact of the death toll, which wasn't a fact at all but only another rumor, one that became more abstract as the number continued to rise but that, on the other hand, increasingly seemed like the only way to measure with any clarity how much the world would change. All this seemed to be happening in my chest, I said, I felt a shift of some kind taking place inside me, and, my love, I know it was stressing you out, but I couldn't help barraging you with text messages, messages that communicated nothing, except maybe a sense of helplessness and a degree of shock. When people I knew in the US began to change their profile pictures, to compress their sympathy behind hashtags and solemn memes, the resentment I felt toward them was colored by my lack of contact with you, I knew you were safe but I felt a strong need to be near you, to be with you in that room—and on Facebook it felt as if the whole world were intruding upon something that rightly belonged to us. I understood that there was too much going on for you to answer my messages or my repeated calls on Skype, there were too many people you'd yet to hear from, too many people who'd yet to hear from you, there were still hostages inside the Bataclan, sirens still wailing all around. New footage began to appear on Twitter, recorded on cell phones and security cameras, and I found myself studying each new video like the Zapruder film. In one I found a tiny moment when a shattered victim seems to show the faintest sign of life. In another, what seemed to be a golden pool of lovely satin, which had somehow come into the hands of a dark, crouched figure, who carefully spread it over the body at his feet. It was with particular attention that I inspected the pavement in these videos, where in many cases vast quantities of blood leaked toward the gutter, or ran between the cobblestones like a network of canals. How likely it began to seem, point being, that in the ordinary course of your day you'd crossed that very pavement only hours before; it was so easy to see, the slight bounce that inflected your stride, and the look of mischief, or impatience, or delight, that would cross your features when you were in your thoughts. I was tormented by an image of your own blood, and I was soon convinced that only by happenstance had you escaped being covered in golden silk, so that by the time Taylor posted that Paris was on her mind, it occurred to me, even as I continued sending you texts, that I was intruding on something that rightly belonged to you alone.

I must have been ridiculous to you, I said. I was ridiculous to myself. From a certain point in the years since we met, I'd been afflicted by a peculiar feeling of vulnerability; it seemed my eyes were always damp, unaccountably, as if I were never far from tears; and it seemed almost anything might undo me—a Mercedes commercial, for example, or a puppy, or a well-arranged bouquet—though of course even when I was alone I never failed to keep myself under control. Having seen Taylor's post that night, the undefinable pressure in my chest reached the point of bursting; I rose from my seat and packed a bag. On the East Coast it was ten o'clock. By this time in Paris you must finally have been asleep. I don't know why it suddenly felt so urgent to leave; but all night I drove in silence, watching the blacktop faintly glow as it disappeared behind me in the rearview mirror. From time to time, to stay awake, I spoke aloud to you, exactly as if you were beside me. I drove slowly, and my thoughts grew clear, and though the pressure inside me remained unrelieved, it now became an aspect of a new moral climate I felt I'd found. You talk about being hounded by this new anxiety, a fear of losing the people dearest to you, my love, and I sincerely understand. Among the many changes, I said aloud in the car that night, that marrying you had effected in my life was that now my life could so easily become pointless, from one moment to the next. Virginia was dark and silent. Pennsylvania was dark and silent. The New York skyline appeared before dawn, and then I crossed Lower Manhattan to the Williamsburg Bridge. In Brooklyn the bars were shuttered and nothing moved. It was light out when I found a parking spot right beneath my brother's building, and when I let myself in, no sooner had I connected my laptop to the wi-fi than your call appeared on my screen.

And there was your face, my love, inscribed with fear and exhaustion and resolve, at the sight of which, finally, I was helpless not to weep.

5
Bon Courage

It would never have occurred to me, what it turned out Ella had in store—
she must have been planning it for some time. I certainly didn't know anything about it on the first day of 2016, three days after I dropped her at the
airport and returned to my apartment in Virginia, when I awoke with a bad
headache and a powerful impulse to watch *Métisse*, the 1993 motion picture
whose title was scrawled in spray paint all over the door to our apartment in
Paris. After the chaotic week with my family at the Gibson Center, waking
up each morning in an empty house left a residue of perplexity upon the day.
I remember thinking the sunlight cutting through the hanging dust seemed
like something larger than it was, and that I'd had the same thought the night
before about the shower of sparks issuing from a Roman candle I'd been
given to hold as midnight struck, embers that turned to ash in the space of a
heartbeat, the heat of which I was tempted to test with my free hand, with
the predictable result that I suffered a burn whose severity I appreciated only
now in the stark light of day.

This was in the street in front of my house, a prefab town house in the
other half of which my neighbors hosted a party, the neighbors I sometimes
heard fighting through the wall, who turned out, I discovered when they
knocked on my door, to be a landscape architecture student named Laurie
and that weird guy Nolan Trucks, the graduate of my program I was always
running into at department events. You?! he said when I opened the door.
With the usual preciousness of the amateur bartender, he made me a Negroni,
then went away on some hospitality errand for Laurie, leaving me to wander

the room alone. Now that I was here, it occurred to me there was no reason, upon accepting their invitation, I couldn't have changed out of my sweatpants. I'd recently switched to a nonaluminum deodorant, a transition that had been more difficult than I expected, so after circulating a bit and introducing myself to a group of architecture students who smelled really nice, I decided to stick as much as possible to the kitchen, where the air was thick with the odor of foodstuffs, mostly spanakopita from Trader Joe's, and where I once again found Nolan, who it seemed also used nonaluminum deodorant, in his case at zero detriment to his confidence. When I walked in the room, he was already talking, to whom it wasn't clear, about his job as a gardener, gardener-slash-groundskeeper, he said, which afforded him plenty of time, in the winter months, to hole up in shuttered outbuildings and work on a science fiction epic that, at nearly 2,500 manuscript pages, was getting a bit out of hand. How's your beverage? he asked, reaching out to squeeze my shoulder. It's revolting and you know it, he added. I think people just get a kick out of saying the *word* Negroni. The terrible taste makes people feel sophisticated, and meanwhile they get to go around saying Negroni this and Negroni that, it gives them this little frisson. This was the consumerist small-talk phase of the party, and I was meant to say something nice about, for example, his Restoration Hardware cocktail shaker. In fact I had the same one. But just that moment I myself had a little frisson when I noticed a stack of *New Yorker* back issues on the countertop, each of whose subscription label, I confirmed, bore my name. Did you read the thing about John Boehner, Nolan asked, noticing me noticing the *New Yorker*s he didn't seem to realize he'd stolen from me. The GOP is eating itself alive.

Nolan chewed a toothpick, which he occasionally used to make gestures of emphasis, and he had dirty fingernails and wore a multitool on his belt. He kept his wallet in the breast pocket of his canvas shirt, a departure from orthodoxy I admired. Because the noise around us increased and because he spoke in a low, droning mumble without parting his teeth, I understood almost nothing of what he went on to say, though I gathered it mostly pertained to the things he saw around the forest at work, or around the invented forest where his 2,800-page sci-fi novel-in-progress was set, though I was never sure which details pertained to which world or whether, for that matter, the two were entirely distinct in his mind. At any rate, before long he guided me back into the living room, and had his arm over my shoulder and was breathing on my face, describing some sort of albino or radioactive deer, an important character, from what I could gather, in his book. That was when Helen arrived leading a band of my classmates, who in their bewilderment at finding me there stopped dead in their tracks at the threshold, clutching each other's coats, and spent the rest of the night studiously avoiding eye contact with me, which is why by the time Nolan handed me a lit Roman candle a few hours later, I was in a kind of funky mood. Blinking awake the next day, I felt funkier still. At the Gibson Center, Ella and I hadn't revisited the question of when to begin in vitro, and now I was reimmersed in the preposterous life I was so worried a pregnancy would interrupt. I remember I lay for a long time, contemplating the slippers she'd left behind on the carpet—I lay for a long time contemplating those slippers, and the essence they suggested of Ella herself, little bootie slippers each with a sad little pair of pom-poms she adored—and then without giving the matter much thought I started watching *Métisse*, as if it would fill in what the slippers left blank. The film's main character, who shared my wife's first name and was played by her first cousin, often visited with her grandmother, who was played by Ella's actual grandmother—that is, by the grandmother she shared with her cousin whose character shared her name. The slight family resemblance between the main character and Ella, and the very strong family resemblance between the grandmother and Ella, gave physical heft and immediacy to certain futures of Ella's body (one in which it gestated and birthed a human being; another in which it grew old and died) that had remained abstract in my mind, futures that in connection with the present reality of her body (that it was very far away) and the present reality of my own body (that it had a splitting headache and was badly burnt) made me feel desperately helpless but also made the blood sing in my veins. Through the wall I could hear Laurie and Nolan fighting, possibly in connection with the cleanup from the bottle rockets Nolan had lit in the house sometime near dawn. I had no ibuprofen, and the bacitracin I found in the medicine cabinet had expired years before. Because of my wounded hand, my usual method of serotonin reuptake was unavailable. But I had to admit I liked being hungover, it made my sadness fuzzy and larger than life.

■

Having coffee cakes and frozen pizzas in deep supply, I had little reason to leave the house that day; and no more the next, January 2, the day that Ammon Bundy, acting on orders from God, led a group of armed men from a Safeway parking lot to the headquarters of the Malheur National Wildlife Refuge, a property that Bundy and his disciples, as one of them put it in a tearful YouTube video, were willing to kill for, and would defend from the federal government even at the cost of their lives. Neither did I have any intention of venturing outdoors on Sunday, January 3, the day that Peyton Manning led the Denver Broncos to a fourth-quarter comeback victory against the San Diego Chargers, and the day that Ella, as I learned only later, began a sixteen-day course of gonadotropin-releasing hormone agonist injections, having enlisted the services of a house-call nurse—neither would I have left the house that day, had it not been for a bulletin from the university's emergency alert system, saying there was a police incident in progress and that members of the university community should stay clear of the 2500 block of a street not far from my own, where indeed I found that the police had formed a loose perimeter around a house with torn screens and peeling paint and a sunken wraparound porch.

The house stood in relative isolation from others on the block, cornered against an intersection by a thick grove of poplars. Across the street a crowd had gathered in their slippers and sweatpants to see what would become of their eccentric neighbor, a young man who, I learned from a kid in Umbros, had barricaded himself inside his home with a bottle of high-end vodka, a great bounty of stimulants and barbiturates, and an arsenal of pistols and assault rifles that would have made Ammon Bundy blush. He's got more than a million followers on Vine, the kid told me, pointing to her phone—thanks in part, it seemed, to his signature machine gun noise, with which he punctuated his thoughts, if that's not too strong a word, and which he rendered typographically with the hashtag #gratata.

It didn't take long to detect a palpable mistrust in the air, mistrust and mutual contempt, it was a group of people who were obviously not accustomed to being gathered together in a public space, and in the same relation to the law. A pair of uniformed cops were having a hard time with the yellow tape and kept having to chase us back out of the line of fire. You think he'll start shooting? someone said to no one in particular, without quite managing to sound like she was hoping he wouldn't. There was *nothing* this kid wouldn't do for attention, a woman in a Redskins jersey explained; after all, his career in show business had begun as a *gay-for-pay* porn star. She kept repeating that phrase, *gay-for-pay*, with disturbing relish, as if it were an emblem of her worldliness: every crisis develops its own lexicon (*credit default swap, bump stock, herd immunity*), and to have entered this term into the glossary of the Declan Foster standoff gave her a feeling of authority. Look at this crowd! she said. She'd known him since he was a boy, and she was certain he was in there *eating this shit alive*.

Law enforcement's original interest in Declan Foster wasn't immediately clear, but I learned from the chatter around me, as much of which as I could I recorded in my notes, and from his Facebook page, where I glimpsed for the first time a corner of the American psyche I couldn't quite fathom, it had to do with an early-morning domestic dispute with his seventeen-year-old girlfriend, which had ended when he'd threatened her with a firearm and she'd fled to call the police. Now, under the influence of the drugs and alcohol he kept posting photos of, he broadcast a series of freestyles, rapid-fire couplets that each rhymed *gratata* with itself, during which he used both real and imaginary guns to pantomime how he intended to handle the SWAT teams that were outside suiting up behind their trucks. In the comments on each of these posts, his detractors, on the basis of his complete chinlessness, the prominence of his front teeth, the extreme highness and unevenness of his cheekbones, and the unnatural distance between his eyes, kept referring to his striking resemblance to Sid, the Paleolithic ground sloth from the *Ice Age* film franchise; his numerous supporters, meanwhile, expressed their admiration for the strength of character he was demonstrating in adverse circumstances, and defended his right as a white person to self-identify as a *real-ass nigga*, in view of the education he'd received from a young age in the ways of the streets, the streets where this very minute his neighbors were eating chips.

For a long time nothing happened. But this was a mild day, and no one seemed to have anywhere to be. At the tops of phone poles, turkey vultures came and went. Maybe an hour had passed when Ella called: My love, she said, there's something I really need to talk to you about, but I cut her off, walking away from the crowd in my eagerness to describe the scene. You wouldn't believe this shit, I said. I told her about Declan Foster's arsenal and texted her a link to his Facebook page. I told her about the bored SWAT team and wandered close enough for her to hear their radios.

Wait, she said, you're there now?

Switching her to video, I left my phone peeking out of my breast pocket and took her on a tour of the crowd. By now, the people of the neighborhood—the quality of their interactions, and the complex interplay of sincerity and insincerity that underlay the various moral claims they made, and the frankness of their wish to be entertained—had eclipsed both the immediate drama of the standoff itself and the melodrama of the standoff as it existed on social media. Just blow the door down and shoot the guy! we heard one kid say. I just hope they don't hurt his dog, his friend said.

When it emerged that the teenage girlfriend who'd fled the house that morning when Declan Foster threatened her with a loaded gun was here among us, opinion was divided between those who regarded her as a fucking snitch, and those who regarded her as the underage victim of a sick fuck who'd deserve whatever he got. Jesus, Ella said in my ear. White poverty had always fascinated her in a way that made me uneasy. But I pointed out that the girlfriend controversy was only one among many readily apparent faults along which the crowd could be divided into haves and have-nots: those who referred to the police as *twelve*, for example, and those who referred to the police as *police*. More saliently, Ella observed that the white trash (she pretended to be, but wasn't completely, innocent of the malice the term implied) could be distinguished according to their attitudes toward Foster himself: those for whom his stupidity, precisely because its defining feature was an inability to recognize itself as stupidity, was a form of heroism, as compared with those for whom his stupidity was proof they deserved their superior station in life. (To this second group she added a subset, in which she included the two of us, comprising those for whom his stupidity was a proof of our superiority but for whom the impossibility that he would ever recognize our superiority, that he would ever look in the mirror and see Sid the Paleolithic ground sloth, that he would ever face the objective truth that he barely deserved to live—those for whom the injustice of these impossibilities—was a source of torment for which our appetites were a bottomless pit.)

But for the moment they had in common their impatience, a dissolute Sunday bloodlust for which American football was no longer enough. The police had finally got the tape up and parked their trucks and cruisers in such a way that we had no direct view of the house—for our own protection, they said; hope remained that shots would be fired. I don't need to be the fastest guy, I heard a man in a fleece pullover say to his kids. I just need to be faster than the slowest guy, he said, casting a look around him at all the obvious ways—obesity, respiratory disease, gout—his neighbors passed the contingencies of poverty along to their bodies, which in an active-shooter scenario would have made them sitting ducks. There were now not only chips but Oreos in circulation, a kind of block party atmosphere had developed, and the desire for entertainment, the frustration of this desire, and the scattershot irony in which the frustration was expressed all had a unifying effect, reminded everyone of their common humanity, if that's not too strong a word, beside which the differences and resentments among them were trivial. Gay-for-pay! the woman in the Redskins jersey cried when

Foster posted another #gratata video. Gay-for-pay, that's how he got the money for all them guns!

Nah, the guy in the pullover replied. It's residuals from *Ice Age 3*!

Looking back now, that was the moment we should have known. There followed a long volley of such remarks—It's like the moyen-âge, Ella whispered in my ear; it's like a hanging in the public square—which gave the triviality of their differences new meaning. The woman in the Redskins jersey was streaming the Redskins game on her phone, and the man in the pullover, whose lanky teenage son was wearing a long-sleeved Blackwater t-shirt, was standing beside her to watch. When a new detachment of police arrived, he bellowed that, the entire police force being tied up here, it must have been Thunderdome over in Fifeville. No one needed this remark explained (the woman in the Redskins jersey merrily clucked her tongue); Fifeville was a black neighborhood across town, where the blue wash of sirens was constant night and day.

I narrated some of this for Ella. The only black family present—a middle-class family whose son I'd earlier heard ask when the term *twelve* had replaced the term *five-oh*—was standing close by, I told her. The man in the pullover, I'd gathered, was their next-door neighbor, and I'd seen them exchange pleasantries, I'd seen their kids running in and out of each other's houses for Gatorade and snacks. But still, it was hard not to imagine an invisible shroud that hung around them, within which they were isolated from the rest of the crowd. The son was off chasing a soccer ball around with the kid in the Blackwater shirt, but the mother, father, and daughter were standing near enough that I could make out the private household matter they were discussing, which I have no intention of relating here except to say it provided a stark contrast to the gleeful cruelty of the crowd. Ella said I was reducing them to emblems. But I'm reducing everyone to emblems! I objected. And you're the one throwing around the term *white trash*!

It *was* interesting, though, Ella had to admit—to her ear, though it was difficult for her to pick out accents in English, the voices of the black family sounded white, whereas the white trash voices all sounded black. Fresh in my mind was an anecdote Claudia Rankine told at her reading that fall, about taking a well-meaning white lady to task for making a similar observation about black voices: And I said that's racist, Rankine told us. Out for drinks after, with a lot of hemming and hawing, my all-white cohort had tried to puzzle this assertion out, but now, suddenly, it seemed self-evidently true. On the other hand, I confessed to Ella, I thought Van Morrison was black until I was twenty years old. My love, Ella said (her voice broken by that brassy chortle), don't you think it's a little creepy how much time you spend thinking about black people? But how else to be white in America, I said; that was the invisible shroud. Many of the so-called white trash here, who spoke with so-called black voices, stole occasional, openly contemptuous glances in the black family's direction. Did this contempt surpass their more general contempt for the middle class? A line from *Métisse* returned to me, which I now jotted at the top of the page as a kind of legend to my notes: when the main character's white suitor receives rough treatment at the hands of the police, as meanwhile his black counterpart is treated with dignity and respect, he observes that *it used to be white and poor was better than rich and black*. Whether this had ever been true in France I couldn't have said. But I don't think it's going too far to suppose that many poor white people might have agreed the same was true right here in central Virginia, despite obvious evidence to the contrary: that beyond the yellow tape dozens of cops equipped with tactical assault gear stood by in full awareness of explicit threats made against them, and that nevertheless Declan Foster was still alive.

∎

I said all of this and more to Ella on the phone, I'd spent my whole life thinking about being white, and I just went on and on, only to discover that at some point the line had gone dead, my phone was out of juice. I stuck around for a few more hours, hovering at the margins of the crowd, writing things down verbatim, and then I wandered home and sat for a while on my back patio, reviewing my notes. Nolan was out there, tending his compost heap, chewing his toothpick, possibly the same one, and eventually I started telling him about poor Declan Foster, until we fell into the sort of searching, painstaking conversation that's only possible between very earnest straight white men. After the two days I'd spent more or less in bed, I told him, the strangeness of the standoff had struck me with especial clarity. In the mild weather the spongy lawn had squelched all afternoon beneath our variously shod and unshod feet, and somehow this sound lent the scene a kind of swampiness that struck me as particularly American. As I spoke, Nolan did background research on his phone, unearthing relevant tidbits, such as the tidbit that the original domestic disturbance had erupted when the teenage girlfriend had told Foster that she might be pregnant. It was interesting, I said, ignoring this detail, which like all reports of unplanned pregnancies gave me a sudden hollow feeling in my gut, how quickly upon the arrival of the press the fragile détente among the onlookers broke down. Local news outfits soon turned their cameras away from the house and began looking for bystanders to interview, and attitudes once again split tidily along class lines. When one correspondent, who'd described the atmosphere outside the cordon as *fraught with apprehension*, asked if anyone cared to speak with her who knew Declan Foster personally, the poor-white contingent went silent, shifted squishily back and forth on the sod: I'm not saying shit, they grumbled. Nor were they surprised that the boy in the Blackwater t-shirt—to whom they affixed the epithet *schoolkid*—jumped at the chance to be on TV; as did a woman roughly my own age, who spoke in a pinched, nasal voice that would have made Ella twitch; and as finally did a guy in a barn jacket, who said he was shocked to discover that ignorance of this kind existed in his neighborhood, under his very nose, without his ever suspecting, and who gloated to his friends without self-consciousness when his interview was finished that he'd knocked it out of the park. That the reporter, who *had millions of dollars* and who could relate to Foster's circumstances *in no exact way at all*, would even bother with these three was a source of bitter resentment: this *college boy*, the woman in the Redskins jersey complained, was going to be a *lawyer*—they were all lawyers or future lawyers—and might she not be a lawyer herself, she said, were it not for her kids and her two motherfucking jobs. Might Declan Foster not have been a lawyer, were it not for the appalling circumstances that had led him to do gay-for-pay instead? They extended their disdain for journalists to me as well, I told Nolan, they asked me outright what I kept writing down and to whom I'd been whispering and for whom I worked, but soon enough they forgot about me and began to freely share among themselves their intimate knowledge of Declan Foster's life and times: many of these details, dating back to Foster's childhood, were not in the public record, and though they were shared in a public space without any reasonable expectation of privacy, and with full knowledge that I was present taking notes, and though I repeated them with a certain twisted relish to Nolan that day and to many other people besides in the days and weeks that followed, here I'll let it suffice to say that their sum was a personal history of such sensational sordidness and violence and sorrow that I was halfway convinced Declan Foster had actually come out rather well.

Though maybe not quite so well as he claimed, Nolan said. He'd found a clip from Foster's appearance on *Tosh.0*, in which Foster compared himself favorably, in terms of realness, with Jay-Z, whom he went so far as to dismiss as a fufu lame. And didn't this track neatly with Ammon Bundy's recent comparison of himself to Martin Luther King Jr., on the basis of the dauntlessness they shared in the face of their respective people's oppression? Or, further to that, Nolan put in, with a meme he'd seen recently, posted in response to nascent local agitation for the removal of certain monuments to the Confederacy, which suggested that by the same logic, monuments to Dr. King's legacy should likewise come down in recognition of his opposition to same-sex marriage? Chief Justice Roberts's convoluted parallel, for that matter, I added, between the injustice of the *Dred Scott* decision and the injustice of the *Obergefell* decision could be added as a more sophisticated but no less disingenuous entry to the same list; as could Norman Mailer's identification, in his 1957 essay "The White Negro," of the postwar existential tumult in white America with what he perceived as the pathological and nihilistic hedonism of the black American outlook that resulted from the precariousness of black American lives. Still, Nolan went on, flipping his toothpick from one corner of his mouth to the other and back again, his own passion for Delta blues, a passion he owed mostly to Moby and the Coen brothers, felt like a manifestation of the same impulse: the impulse to claim affinity with an aesthetics, with a morality, or with an authenticity of blackness without giving the experiences of actual black people a moment's thought. Indeed, I said, quite so. We stayed out there quite a while, Nolan and I, there in the early darkness, speaking across the no-man's-land of brush and ductwork between my back patio and his. Soon the night grew colder, Ella called, I let it ring. My wife says I spend too much time thinking about black people, I said. As if he were raising the stakes on a bet, Nolan confided that, although he was what some people would call a white guy's white guy, what with his pickup truck and his fly-fishing gear and the collection of hunting knives he'd forged himself, it was a profound, secret regret of his not to have been born black. Or at least Jewish, Nolan added with a sigh. It was a symptom of a peculiar American pathology, he said, an impulse to frame our personal narratives according to the template of our historical narratives, in which every momentous turn of events is framed as a struggle of the righteous, to quote Quentin Tarantino, beset by tyranny and inequity on all sides—Tarantino being a notable example of one form this pathology could take: the state of arrested adolescence that Declan Foster, Ammon Bundy, and Norman Mailer all likewise typified. Like me, Nolan was educated at the height of the multiculturalism movement, and in fairly progressive northeastern public schools, where the curriculum included picture books, chapter books, and children's histories on such topics as the Indian Removal Act, the Underground Railroad, the Holocaust, the internment of Japanese Americans during World War II, the immigrant experience on Ellis Island in the early twentieth century, and, perhaps most emphatically, the courageous, nonviolent acts of resistance promoted by the likes of Rosa Parks and Dr. King; the struggles of minorities in America had always loomed large in his civic consciousness, and though it was true that many of these stories highlighted a kind of messianic broadmindedness on the part of a small cohort of white people, from an early age he'd formed the idea that oppression was a precondition of heroism. It had never been his privilege to be oppressed, he said, his mouth twisting into a self-conscious grin, and so his strength of character would remain his whole life long pleasantly, hypothetically abstract.

■

Indeed, I said, quite so. A better definition of heroism was on the tip of my tongue, but I couldn't quite place it. Ella called again; again I let it ring. The sky was going dark. I shared Nolan's wish to keep our conversation going, it was nice to talk, and more than that, I felt a strong aversion to going back inside; once I did there was no telling how long it might be until I emerged. But on the other hand I'd reached my daily threshold of being a white person talking to another white person about black people. Worrying at my blistered palm, I tried instead to describe to Nolan how strange it had been to watch *Métisse* in Ella's absence, how real and tangible the idea of Ella's pregnant body became for me as her cousin's simulated pregnancy progressed onscreen, and how the presence of the slippers she'd left in the middle of the floor became a kind of focal point for this effect, or rather formed a sort of bridge between the real and imagined spaces of my life, so that later, half asleep, I felt distinctly that she'd materialized in the room and stood unmoving in the wide, flat-footed stance of these slippers, her fingers laced over her belly, waiting for me to wake. This was the most I'd ever said to anyone on the subject of pregnancy as it concerned Ella, and that night, as the oven preheated and I stood studying the network of deep scratches in the patterned linoleum, I wondered whether even to have said this much wasn't an egregious violation of her privacy. I tried returning her call, but it was much too late, she was asleep. The longer I inspected the scratches in the floor, where there'd amassed decades of grease and dirt, the more clearly I perceived how crucial it was to find some diversion to fill my days. It was the next morning that I filled my thermos and walked to the library to begin my pointless research on the New York water system; and it was the day after that, January 5, that Michigan governor Rick Snyder declared a state of emergency in Genesee County, in response to a crisis that was already halfway through its second year. A week passed this way, days and nights that I never opened my venetian blinds, and each morning when I stepped outside, under the spell of perplexity I've already mentioned, it was like the entire visible world reconstituted itself only as a trick of light, everything quivered, as if in anticipation of a thunderstorm that never arrived. This sensation was continually renewed by the tedium of the research I was conducting and the peculiar stillness of the empty campus, broken only occasionally by the sudden kinetic appearance of, for example, a squirrel that dropped out of a tree as if struck dead, or a bead of water that gathered in the mouth of the tap and fell silently into the open drain, in the depths of which it landed with a sound so brief and clear that it rang in my mind for hours. And all this suited me just fine, for the remainder of the break I made my life into a kind of sensory-deprivation chamber, deviating from my daily routines in not even the slightest ways, and limiting my human contact to the clerk in the bagel shop, chance encounters with Nolan on the front steps, and sporadic Skype check-ins with Ella, during which she was alternately distrait to the point of comatoseness or else just impatient to get off the line.

■

Paris at this time was beset by January's usual spell of cold and damp, which only added to the atmosphere of grief and paranoia in which the city had been suspended since November. At the sites of each attack memorials had appeared: the tea lights and the flowers, heaped and wilting in their cellophane, and the washed-out photographs of the dead. It was overwhelming, Ella said, to have to pick her way through the crowds that often gathered, among whom it was difficult to distinguish the true mourners and pilgrims from those who had come just to gawk. The largest of these was in Place de la République, which had become a focal point of generalized shock and sorrow on the night of the *Charlie Hebdo* attacks the previous January, when a candlelight vigil organized on Facebook had drawn as many as forty thousand people. That vigil had been the starting point for a ten-thousand-word reported essay that, in a last-ditch attempt to make something consequential of my ambition to be a writer, I'd written that month on spec, and naturally this essay never saw the light of day, but now Ella, as the anniversary of those events came and went, unearthed a copy of it on her computer. And having reread it, she called me one night to deliver herself of a long, anxious rant. That same week, the week of the *Charlie Hebdo* attacks, while I was working on that piece, we began a course of injections in preparation for our very first attempt at IUI, a fraught nightly trauma the traces of which she felt she could discern on the page. It gave her a nice, tender feeling to recall the determination with which, playing at man in the street, I pursued the story through the city that week, the quixotic pride with which I'd described various minor acts of daring, the uncertainty in my voice as I read out to strangers the questions she'd written in French on my pad, the recorded answers to which she'd later translate for me at our kitchen table, where we'd dip the day's stale bread in honey as we worked and where she'd then leave me typing furiously until the early hours of the morning. Such a hustler, you were, she exclaimed now on our Skype call, I was proud of you, I'd never seen you work so hard. And now that the country was recovering from another attack, the attacks of November 13, each time she passed through République she thought of me, there was always some journalist searching the faces in the crowd for someone to interview. And wouldn't you know it, my love, last night it was my face picked out of the crowd, by some British guy with gold-flecked pale blue eyes just like yours. He fumbled for the words to ask my origins, I think he hoped I was Muslim. Anyway, I ignored him, instead I asked if he'd seen *La haine*, Mathieu's second film, after *Métisse*, which is set during a riot after a young man's brutal beating by the police. The film begins with a voice-over, the parable of a man in free fall from a height of fifty stories, who keeps reassuring himself: *Jusqu'ici tout va bien*—so far, so good. It was dark at République, a light drizzle began to fall. Around us everyone was fussing with the damp wicks of candles, striking their lighters to no effect. The journalist pulled his hood up, his face was folded in shadow, but his eyes caught the light in a way that gave me the illusion he might understand. C'est ça, la France, she said. It's not falling if you never land. If you never land, it's a dream. So actually I told him about your essay on the *Charlie Hebdo* attacks—the part about the little boy in Nice whose entire family, when he refused to chant *Je suis* Charlie along with his class, was hauled into the police station for hours of interrogation and investigated for *apology for terrorism*; how his own teacher taunted him in the classroom, how the teachers' union flagged his father, on the evidence of his thick beard and his wife's hijab, as a legitimate threat to security; and how his principal refused to authorize the blood sugar tests he took daily to monitor his diabetes, explaining to the boy that for wishing death upon others he deserved to die himself. That's how far the revolution's liberal humanism had fallen, she said I'd written, after two hundred years of flapping its arms as if they were wings.

I don't think I wrote that? I said to the pixelated image of her on my computer screen. I don't remember that at all. But I had written it; she read it to me, it was the first time I'd ever heard my words in her voice. Sometimes, my love, she said, I think you think I value your writing far less than I do. It was Monday, January 11, the day the protocol Ella had undertaken in secret introduced a second daily injection, this one containing 150 ccs of the follicle-stimulating hormone preparation Gonal-F, in addition to the GnRH regimen that was in its second week; but I didn't know that, I was at the kitchen table when she called, spreading peanut butter on apple slices and scanning the news; I knew that El Chapo was in custody, and that Officer Caesar Goodson's trial for the second-degree depraved-heart murder of Freddie Gray had been abruptly postponed. I had *La haine* on my hard drive, and I watched that opening sequence now as Ella spoke—all that riot footage from the nineties, the tear gas cans and firebombs, the Cité des Muguets. City of May Lilies, I thought. Praise from Ella usually pertained to small acts of what she saw as selflessness: maxing out another credit card to send some nonprofit a hundred bucks, or having dinner ready when she got home from work. Rarely did she have kind words about my writing, and, not knowing anything about her secret IVF plans, I had no way to account for the sudden, nervous generosity of her mood. But I was overcome by an intense longing to be near her, to listen to her speak and follow her eyes around the room. She'd been thinking about the phrase *bon courage*. She'd gotten into an Uber Pool that day and found a young man in the back seat crying hysterically. For the length of the ride, the only other sound inside the car was the wipers on the glass, and only when it was time for the crying man to get out did the driver, finding his eyes in the mirror, quietly wish him *bon courage*. In the circumstances, it struck Ella as exceedingly human, a gentle, gracious way to acknowledge pain in another person's life—pain, or adversity, or trauma: to acknowledge, in short, the need to be brave. It would have been close to dawn in Paris, and I wondered if she'd been up all night. If and why. I didn't understand what she was trying to tell me; for a minute, stupidly, I thought it was her way of saying it took courage to try to live a writerly life. Now I know it was her way of wishing courage for herself. This was the week the Oscar nominations were announced. That Saturday Ella had a blood test and an ultrasound, as scheduled, and then on Monday, as Americans were celebrating the memory of Martin Luther King, she injected herself with ten thousand IUs of human chorionic gonadotropin, in order to trigger a final maturation of oocytes, which after roughly thirty-six hours would be ready for retrieval by a process she'd undergo at the Hôpital Maternité des Vertus, where she'd furnish the doctor with a document of consent bearing her best approximation of my signature and a six-liter cryogenic dewar in which was packed a vial of my frozen sperm. Now on the phone, she said only that for months, with increasing frequency, she'd been plagued by vivid dreams of becoming pregnant, of sharing the news with our family and friends, preparing the way for a new life, and, in quiet moments, holding herself in her arms, at a height of joy she'd not thought possible. Joy but also a nameless fear. Like a dream of flying, she said: jusqu'ici tout va bien, you wake up before you land, and the exquisite, agonizing memory of the sensation keeps you up all night. . . It was raining again in Paris, when her voice trailed off I could hear it pounding on the roof, and I told her in as many ways as I could think of how deeply, how viscerally, I missed her and how painful it was not to be able to hold her in my arms, but then I heard how deeply and evenly she was breathing and realized she'd fallen asleep.

■

There was a storm brewing, Nolan told me, in those exact words, inspecting his toothpick, when we crossed paths in our shared front yard the following day. And indeed by the end of the week the entire town was making preparations for a blizzard some predicted would paralyze the region for weeks. The semester would start soon, and I didn't have enough money for books; I took the reading list to the library to check out what I could: *Call It Sleep*; *Pale Horse, Pale Rider*; *Let Us Now Praise Famous Men*. On the way home I stopped at the Food Lion for supplies, backed my car up the driveway, and flipped my wipers out, following the example of my neighbors up and down the block. That evening, Friday, as the first fat snowflakes began to fall and something childlike took hold inside me, Nolan knocked at the door and asked me over for a glass of whiskey. It was awfully pleasant to sit in their living room by candlelight, on their handsome, modern furniture, most of which they'd salvaged from yard sales and junk shops and restored themselves, and to watch in the frame of their rear picture window great whorls of snow come down in the floodlit backyard. I admired that they had a coffee table, I told them; and in such a handsome room, it was easy to imagine spending uninterrupted hours, getting up periodically to move from one piece of furniture to the next, with any of the novels or story collections that were stacked along the baseboards. Lately, I said, that was what I liked most about reading fiction: it was a nice way to appreciate the space around you—a park, a train car, a well-appointed café, the pleasure of straddling worlds. Oh, me, I'm all about straddling worlds, Laurie said.

Nolan rolled his eyes. Landscape architect, he explained, that's her whole thing.

It was true, she went around all day, she said, thinking about the delimitation of interior and exterior spaces, and metaphorical and experiential effects you could achieve by complicating the transitions between them. An obvious example was a house she'd just been writing about, which a young architect named Sou Fujimoto had designed in 2008 and built in the city of Oita for a retired couple and their dog. House N, as it's known, employed a concept of nested boxes, each of which clearly defining a domain—the garden, the house proper, and a domestic inner sanctum—which nevertheless leaked light and air into each of the others by way of the large rectangular apertures arranged at seeming random on their surfaces, so that, as Fujimoto put it, each space is interior and exterior both, anywhere on the property you were both indoors and outdoors at once. I couldn't quite picture what she was describing; instead, Helen came to mind, her ruined wedding dress, her vivid little speech about the smushing together of her insides and outsides. Sure, the barf dress, Laurie said, same idea. In Fujimoto's view, all of human life consisted of nested domains of greater or lesser privacy, the same way the human personality consisted of nested selves. Laurie was already quite drunk, I could see, she'd been drinking heavily since midday. But there was a point she wanted to make. Nolan had a handheld whetstone and all this time had been sharpening a knife he'd recently forged, which he tested from time to time on the short hairs of his knuckles. Just looking at the photos makes you feel sophisticated, he said without looking up, as Laurie handed me her iPad to see. City blocks, postal codes, voting districts, nation- states, she went on, all expressed, according to Fujimoto, extrapolations of a scalable original concept of fortification upon which the earliest human settlements were founded—in the Indus Valley, in Mesoamerica, and in the city-states of Sumer as far back as Jericho, for example. Certainly the construction of supposedly impenetrable defensive walls formed no small part of the mythos of such tyrants as Gilgamesh, who erected the ramparts of Uruk upon foundations laid by the Seven Sages, or Nebuchadnezzar, who rebuilt the walls of Babylon and the sacred Gate of Ishtar. Laurie refilled her glass and folded her legs. The nature of borders was changing everywhere you looked: social

media, transnational commerce, global finance, salmon fishery, terrorism—
Or further to that, Nolan put in, sitting up suddenly in excitement, so-called
cryptocurrencies, a concept he claimed to have invented independently of the
developers of Bitcoin in his 3,100-page sci-fi epic in progress, in which the
multiform nature of borders was both the prison in which galactic society
was captive and the key to its final release. He cleared his throat as if to launch
into an impassioned speech he'd been preparing all his life. By then I understood there was ample precedent for Nolan's steering of a conversation,
whether by way of Bitcoin, aerosol technology, Nicki Minaj, or anything
else, to his sci-fi epic in progress, and only a brief moment passed, during
which there flashed on Laurie's face a look of seething contempt, before an
argument, a bona fide domestic dispute, erupted so precipitously that I
jumped in my seat, unsettling my glass and spilling whiskey all over my lap,
a misfortune neither of them registered, rising from their seats and com-
mencing to stomp around the half-lit room, attacking each other's essential
character in wild flights of invective, and also breaking things, small things
at first, like a clementine, and then medium things, like the Richie Havens
record that we'd been listening to a third consecutive time, which shattered
into three unequal portions that flew through the air and came to rest in
discrete corners of the floor. With a recent issue of my own *New Yorker*, I
discreetly covered the knife Nolan had by now made razor sharp, but otherwise I remained motionless until they'd chased each other upstairs, where
their fight continued for only a short while, then with a slamming of doors
went silent. The snow swirling in the picture window, and beyond it the
dark, heightened my sense of the room's new stillness. Maybe because of my
conviction, formed in childhood, that in a blizzard the usual standards of
behavior didn't apply, the obvious next move—to go home and go to sleep—
didn't occur to me. Righting my glass finally, I poured myself another whiskey,
and then, for how long I can't say, I looked through the photos of House N,
studying each intently, in an effort to see through my own feeling of refinement to whatever Laurie had been getting ready to say. Even the least idea of
what it was like to be inside House N was elusive: that to understand what a

space achieved you would have to experience it in three dimensions, from within; to sit, for example, in various corners and watch various patches of sky for passing clouds, or to listen for the sound of rain on the roof, for rainwater racing in the gutters, wind racing in the alleys, or to watch the patterns of light and shadow move across the walls through the course of the day. But nevertheless, it seemed to me that to resist visiting these spaces in your imagination, and to resist accommodating your worldview to the psychic impact of these imagined visits, was to be less meaningfully human. By now it was morning in Paris, Ella had set her alarm and, before it was fully light out, she was in a cab. Because the various hormones caused her to retain an unnatural amount of water, her fingers had swollen to the point that to wear her wedding ring had become a torture. Three days had passed since a scant six eggs had been retrieved from her ovaries, each of which had been intracytoplasmically injected with as well formed a sperm cell as could be found among those we'd frozen, and now the single, morphologically middling embryo that had resulted was to be transferred back into her body with the hope that it would implant in the lining of her uterus and eventually become a child. By the time I awoke in Nolan and Laurie's chair and found that the snow had risen past the wheel wells of my car, Ella was home, lying on her back, staring at the soot and grime and bird shit on the skylight, and trying to detect the slightest tremors inside herself as signs of what might be taking place there.

■

The snow continued falling all day Saturday, and it was still falling late that night when I went out walking, to experience the peculiar atmospheric coldness of falling snow, which was unlike regular coldness, was in fact more like warmness, as the result, I'd read someplace, of snowflake formation being an exothermic reaction—that is, a process that released heat into the surrounding air. How was it, I wondered, snowflakes didn't melt each other the very moment they began to exist? Ella loved the snow, she loved to be confined to the house and to sit at the window to watch it fall. I spent the day in bed, and sometime before dawn that night I awoke with a start; with my heart pounding and unable to get back to sleep, I put on the first movie that caught my eye, a chambara film set during the Meiji Restoration called *Lady Snowblood*, in pursuit, I told myself, of the refinement the House N gave me—a feeling I associated with all things originating in Japan. Just like me not to have made any conscious association between the title and the snow that was still falling in the actual world, I remarked to Nolan the following afternoon, while we shoveled that same snow from our respective driveways and as I described the plot of *Lady Snowblood* in exhaustive detail.

Nolan worked tirelessly, with impeccable form, and wore an expression of intense focus, pausing occasionally only to defrost his mustache. We shoveled for hours; it was dusk by the time we finished. The ache in my arms and in the small of my back gave me the pleasant sensation of having earned my place on the planet. Nolan suggested we eat dinner at a bar downtown, where, when we arrived, a cold wind blew in the deserted, snowed-under streets. How seductive it was, Nolan mused, to imagine you'd be around to enjoy the end of the world. Later, the bartender having cleared our plates, I sat absently peeling the dead skin from my burn, pushing it into little piles on the bar top, a revolting thing to do, I now realize, but on the other hand there were very few people to revolt. In the far corner of the dark room, the only other customer, a white guy with a ponytail, played rack after rack of pool in his little wedge of light without ever once acknowledging our presence. Meanwhile, as the irregular clack of pool balls continued behind us, Nolan and I were glued to the screen over the bar: there was football to watch, the conference finals, six hours of harrowing collisions that excited in me a series of feelings I usually identified with an urge to dance. Nolan likewise, I think; we scarcely spoke, but we seemed to be operating on the same wavelength when, on the way home, he turned into the empty and unplowed Food Lion parking lot, asked for help unloading the sandbags from the bed of the truck, and disengaged the four-wheel drive.

The night had become bright and clear, the wind had died, the air was still. Not since I was a teenager had I driven doughnuts in the snow, but for maybe an hour, that's what Nolan and I did, with the stereo off and the windows cracked, doughnuts and fishtails and bootlegs, taking turns behind the wheel. I wasn't sure what to call the hunger this satisfied in me, which watching football had awakened. During each stunt, there was a period of weightlessness—between the exhilarating moment the tires lost their grip on the earth and the vaguely dispiriting moment they regained it—during which I had time to reflect that before long all this snow would melt, and the world would be the same as it was. Classes began the following day and life resumed its usual pace. I still couldn't bring myself to read anything that had been assigned. Instead I pored over the daily news. In Hanoi, a beloved 360-pound turtle named Cu Rua, one of the last of her kind, expired at an advanced age. The stock market plunged as the price of oil continued its steady decline. Danish lawmakers passed legislation permitting authorities to confiscate valuables from migrants, as a tax that would fund their access to health care and education. Ammon Bundy was arrested on his way to a speaking engagement, along with eight of his followers; a ninth refused to surrender and was shot dead in his cowboy hat by the side of the road. According to the WHO, Zika was spreading at an astonishing rate in more than two dozen countries, which pregnant women were discouraged from visiting; in El Salvador, the government advised women not to become pregnant at all. Ella started a new job in the casting department of a TV series about casting agents and never really had time to talk. In an upcoming British TV show about 9/11, Joseph Fiennes would be playing Michael Jackson. Donald Trump declined to participate in the Republican debate in Des Moines, where in hope of lending a whiff of authenticity to various wholesale fabrications, Ted Cruz cited the popular John Adams quotation that *facts are stubborn things*. In a nighttime raid in Dalori, Nigeria, Boko Haram abducted dozens of children and left as many as a hundred people dead before turning the entire village to ash. The European Commission issued a report finding Greece seriously negligent in its duty to stem the tide of migrants arriving on its shores, a conclusion that enabled EU member states to continue fortifying their internal national borders in direct contravention of the EU's purported ideals. At Gobbler's Knob, Punxsutawney Phil saw no shadow, foretelling an early spring. The following day Ella left early for work and stopped at a medical laboratory, where they drew her blood, in each milliliter of which, it transpired, there were to be found .0064 IUIs of hCG. Forty-eight hours later, that figure had increased to .0138, and forty-eight hours after that to .0297, at which point it could no longer be put off to call me with the news that we'd successfully conceived.

■

So much has happened since the moment Ella told me she was pregnant— years have passed that felt like days, and weeks have passed that felt like years. Many times over, the end of the world has come and gone. We talked for hours, from midmorning until late in the afternoon. It didn't even occur to me to be mad she'd arranged the whole process behind my back; it didn't even occur to me I'd been deceived. Together, we consulted a graphic that charted the baby's growth in comparison with various food items. On this day she was about four weeks pregnant, and the baby—we seemed already to have settled on that term—was the size of a poppy seed. I remember thinking it was a kind of displaced expression of our feelings, which we couldn't articulate in any satisfying way, that we fixated on this sort of detail, on matters of technical and practical concern, and on the difficult logistics of the months ahead, the intricate series of blood tests, doctor's visits, and sonograms Ella would have to fit into a demanding work schedule. It was hard to imagine how we'd afford plane fare, but it was also inconceivable that we'd be apart until the end of May. At this point Ella was in bed, the room was mostly dark, and she was using the thumbnail preview on her computer screen as a mirror to remove her makeup—it seemed strange, she said, inspecting the soiled little cotton disk she'd been swabbing her eyelids with, after having wanted something so badly and then having finally gotten it, to nevertheless have to continue going through all the tiny motions of daily life. And yes, I thought I knew what she meant, it made my heart swell to think of her waking up that morning and, after a few seconds, remembering she was pregnant, that she was no longer not pregnant, and then, standing at the mirror after her shower, trying to come back to earth and prepare her face for the day. In her features as she spoke I rediscovered a softness I'd forgotten, having to do with what was essentially happy in her; and the pain of being able to see that softness plainly but being unable to reach out and take her in my arms was both unbearable and somehow exquisite. In my giddiness, the only plan I could think of was to drop out of school the very next day and return to Paris on the soonest flight. Ella ignored this suggestion and suggested instead that, since we could afford only one ticket, and not even really that, it would be best if we divided the time we'd be apart neatly in half: I'd come at the beginning of April, when her present contract would expire, and her pregnancy would reach twelve weeks, by which point the sonograms would be more vivid and it would be safe to share the news; and in the meantime, she promised me in an indulgent tone, with her mother right next door she'd be in excellent hands until I arrived.

At a certain point Ella carried her computer into the kitchen, our flimsy little Ikea kitchen, where she made herself what she called a tartine, which is to say she made herself toast with jam. And promptly upon taking the first bite, her tartine flew out of her hand and landed facedown on her keyboard. This small commotion precipitated a kind of diffuseness between us: as the sky deepened, we moved on to other, lighter things, not because we'd exhausted the heat of emotion we'd been stoking for hours, but rather because, exactly like a real fire, we needed to back away from it the more brightly it burned. For a while we looked at flights together, and then with what was left of my monthly stipend check I bought a ticket for April 3. What would happen, I mused, if I simply stopped making payments on my credit cards, beyond the destruction of our credit and the disintegration of our future? Your credit, Ella said; your future. She was actually doing okay; she had a side project coming up, a perfume ad based on a concept by a famous street artist, which would be shot in the Louvre: the concept was *diversity*, a term that was used with deliberate imprecision in the casting call she'd typed up and sent out. How humiliating it all was, how degraded

181

she felt, as a human being, to walk down a hall lined with professionally tall women whose thighs didn't touch, and to call them one after another into a small white room to perform a series of basic maneuvers, such as standing, sitting, walking, and tossing their hair. There was still jam on her keyboard, I think, in the spaces between keys maybe, and she kept absently touching the tips of her fingers to the tip of her tongue. I told her about the snow, clutching my breast, I told her that its beauty reawakened something in my sensitive, poetic soul, a compulsion for perfecting descriptions of things that I'd first become conscious of as a child, after a winter storm left a tree in our front yard wholly encased in ice. At this she cackled, and the energy it gave me to hear her laugh took control of me instantaneously; something like adrenaline rose in my blood, and I found myself improvising a bizarre and manic comic routine. Among the supplies I'd bought at Food Lion was a can of cocoa powder, and as I waxed poetic about snow and things related to snow, I brought my computer into my own grimy kitchen to make hot chocolate in my little saucepan, absenting myself from the frame for just a moment only to reappear in an apron of hers, but otherwise quite nude. At some level, I explained as I measured out the chocolate, the sudden impulse to share with her in this sacred ritual of my childhood was probably calculated not only to demonstrate the attentive sort of father I'd be, but to prefigure an idyll of our future life as a family; I was perhaps feeling a bit sentimental, I said, eating cocoa powder from the can with a spoon now, though on the other hand by the time our child was old enough to form memories snow would be a thing of the past. But in that world there would be new beautiful things! I hastened to reassure her. Like mudslides and dust devils and great howling tempests, heat lightning on the horizon at all times. And what's more, I said, counting on my fingers, our daughter (I could feel in my bones it would be a girl) would almost certainly be born into a world where for the first time a woman had been elected president of the United States. In the grip of this preposterous mania, I carried on for who knows how long, while on the screen Ella beamed back at me, looked at me with such naked affection, laughed in unalloyed delight at even my feeblest jokes, the gratitude I felt for which made my eyes damp, until by the time we said good night, I'd reached a state of emotional depletion that was not especially well suited to such a violent spectacle as the Super Bowl, which was shortly to begin.

Nevertheless, with my blood drumming in my ears in the otherwise silent apartment, I got myself situated on the couch in time for the opening kick-off, with a tray of corn muffins I'd been saving for the occasion, into the top of each of which I made a discreet incision, as in a coin bank, large enough to deposit a thick pad of butter. As I sat there I settled into a new kind of vagueness, the brutality of the game didn't reach me, there were too many penalties, too many punts; and strange to say I felt equally detached from the procession of my thoughts, which I tried to account for to myself in real time, the way you might try to account for the course of billiard balls even before they've come to rest after the break. On my palm, I traced the rim of dead skin that had yet to peel away, which outlined a patch of new skin beneath it, pink and rippled and very delicate—less like skin than like the repulsive film that formed on the surface of hot milk—within which, it occurred to me, my so-called innards were contained. And meanwhile, with the better part of my mind I was still contemplating Ella's face, or to put it another way, after the many hours I'd spent staring at it, Ella's face was superimposed on all my thoughts, or became the vessel I poured my thoughts into and whose shape they took. At a certain point I realized that this contemplation had an external aspect as well, in that I'd been trying to re-create Ella's face with my own face, simulating its response to the distant events of the game, her frank expressions of irritation, consternation, con-fusion, and awe, but also trying to replicate on my face certain intangible aspects of hers, the softness I've described, or the depths that opened in her eyes during moments of absentmindedness or introspection. I'd been doing this since we met, with respect to not only her face but her entire physical existence, something about which I couldn't fathom: the imprecise way she rubbed her eyes with her fist when she woke, or threw her limbs around as she tried to sleep, for example, or the way she snapped her head back when she hiccupped, like a Muppet, and above all the exaggerated but somehow businesslike and metronomic lateral movement, not of her hips but of her shoulders, involved in her gait; and of course this was the trouble: that, beyond comparing her with Giulietta Masina, I'd found no good words to describe the way Ella moved, and so I'd resorted, sometimes consciously and sometimes unconsciously, to trying to describe it with my body, trying to move through the world as she did, to blink with her eyes, to speak in her voice, occasionally wearing her robe and wrapping my head in her towel; trying to impersonate her, in short, to incorporate an essence of her into my own. Such were my thoughts—that I would never fix Ella's existence in permanence and contain it within me to express at will—as I sat there on my couch eating corn muffins, nude except for her apron, as the first half of Super Bowl 50 came to a close and as, after a Doritos commercial about a fetus, Chris Martin took the field in multicolored shoes. Naturally I knew who Chris Martin was, and I understood that he enjoyed a global reputation for good-heartedness, serious-mindedness, and maybe the sort of abstract melancholy to which everyone could relate. But I had no idea what he looked like, had never seen so much as a photo, and so when the halftime show began, I was astonished to see how terrible he was: it was as if, I said to myself, someone had taken all the emotional and aesthetic content of a pair of aquamarine capri pants and used it to make a man. So imagine my relief, point being, when Bruno Mars appeared and then, only a minute later, Beyoncé—though relief was only how I put it to myself at the time: in fact what I felt was that familiar pressure rising in my chest and at the back of my throat, and a dampness in my eyes that I kept having to wipe away with the hem of my apron, the source of which wasn't immediately clear. Likewise did the costumes, though I learned only later that they made explicit reference to the Black Panthers, contribute to my feeling that history was collapsing on the present moment: fashion, as Walter Benjamin put it, is a tiger's leap into the past. Until that moment, I hadn't yet referred to myself in my thoughts as an expectant father (a term that nowadays brings tears to my eyes), and it's true that even without having registered the political semiotics of the costumes, and not only because the way Chris Martin moved bore the same relation to real dancing that capri pants bore to real pants, it was difficult not to perceive in the entire affair a parable of race relations that could be summarized by the grandiose refrain *I used to rule the world*.

But actually, given everything that's happened since, I'd say that the Super Bowl 50 Pepsi Halftime Show illustrated a broader political distinction: a distinction, let's say, between optimism, which is for idiots, and courage, which teaches that the state of emergency in which we live is not the exception but the rule, and whose business it is to bring about a real state of emergency, in which the past will be redeemed and what's smashed will be made whole. When Chris Martin reclaimed the stage, he looked more than ever—if I can borrow a phrase from Declan Foster—like a fufu lame; sitting at a piano, he incorporated snippets of previous Super Bowl acts into a song of his own, while meantime a video montage of these acts was superimposed over his own image on the screen, so that at times it was difficult to distinguish the present from the past, an effect that seemed to vindicate a conception of history as, rather than a chain of events, a single, ongoing catastrophe that keeps piling wreckage upon wreckage and hurling it at our feet.

■

Later, when it was finally time for bed, I stood in the middle of the floor of my bedroom staring at the slippers Ella had left. Where a slat had broken the moonlight streamed through the blinds and seemed to leak from the edges of everything, and I wondered what I'd feel next. I know that first of all I expected the nagging suspicion that in the world of adults I was an imposter to fall away. I also knew that many men, when they learned they'd be fathers, experienced a surge of animal pride. I was three thousand miles away when my defrosted sperm was injected into my wife's ovum without my knowledge, so animal pride wasn't really in the cards. I'd eaten a tray of corn muffins for dinner, so neither did I feel especially grown up. Rather,

I thought of all Ella's talk about dreams of falling and flying, which at the time had struck the chord of a memory I couldn't quite place. Now, in connection with the surge of pride I anticipated but did not experience, it came to me. Mounted on the wall in the waiting room of the lab on rue Drouot was a large television, where there repeated a twenty- or thirty-minute montage of extreme sports footage—BASE jumping, cliff diving, paragliding, heli-skiing, kitesurfing, and motocross—which, the very first time I'd visited, I'd watched at least twice through in a trance, confirming that it showed the final outcome of not even one of the many flights it recorded, before my number was called, and I was led to a small room where a video of an entirely different nature also played on a loop and was given instructions for collecting a sample of my sperm that would be analyzed, frozen, and stored for the eventual purpose it had now fulfilled.

It was strange to think that if I were to order all the events of my life, the conception of my child, which most men could trace to a few glorious seconds, would in my case correspond to the events of an entire year. And as I stood there in my dark bedroom, what I eventually felt was this: how astonishing it sometimes was to look back and find disparate threads of your history running through the same moment, though even at the time they seemed not to intersect. So this was near the end of November 2014, that I first saw the adrenaline video and that I filled the sterile cup (if that's not using the word *fill* too generously), capped it, and left it by the sink, per the printed instructions taped to the wall—the same day, it now came to me, that my career as an ersatz journalist began, when a controversial art installation in Saint-Denis was the subject of a protest that had briefly turned violent.

This was at the Théâtre Gérard Philipe, where a performance installation had gone up the night before, an artistic re-creation of the human zoos of the nineteenth century. In a large, open space a winding corridor had been constructed, along the walls of which a cast of fifteen black actors and singers were displayed in various Western and indigenous costumes and contexts—on pedestals, in cages, in servants' quarters, shackled at the neck and ankles, muzzled, bare- breasted, bearing baskets of fruit, seed, and severed hands, in cotton dresses, in head wraps, shut in broom closets, powdered and painted. These tableaux had titles, such as *Found Object*, and the placards that described them listed the actors among the materials of their construction. Audience members were to wander through the exhibit one at a time in order to absorb its impact in isolation. The director was a white South African who'd grown up under apartheid and who'd spent his entire life, by his own account, wrestling with the legacy of colonialism; and the result of this wrestling was a collection of shattering images of black pain the very existence of which was unconscionable to a great many black people: previously, in London at the Barbican, a crowd of protesters, with the support of a petition that had collected twenty thousand signatures, had succeeded in shutting the show down permanently; and on opening night in Saint-Denis, too, the crowd had swelled the barricade and two men had broken a glass door—according to an eyewitness who recounted the scene to me later, they demanded that the exhibit be vacated, and though both men were arrested, they succeeded in shutting the performance down until the following night, the night I was there with my tape recorder, when five companies of riot police were deployed to ensure the show could proceed.

In the days after the Super Bowl, I rediscovered this material in a notebook, and started thinking about how it could be turned into fiction. Ella and I had already fallen into the habit of logging on to Skype for hours each day, not necessarily to talk so much as to share space, so that as I sat nipping at my keyboard, in a little window in the corner of my screen I could look up to find Ella in her headphones, absently eating an avocado with a spoon as she watched the day's audition tapes and compiled them into a single reel. I loved watching her face (superimposed, so to speak, on my thoughts) in these blank moments of focus, she was so calm, the things that previously had caused her so much irritation or anxiety seemed far away. Her presence gave me a great surge of confidence in my abilities as a writer, and also incited me to think more rigorously on the page than I ever had before. At the time of the exhibit, I told her, it wasn't my opinion that it should be shut down. But the French press had reported the controversy as if the protesters, by accusing the show of racism, had disastrously misapprehended its intentions as identical to those of the original human zoos it was modeled after, whereas in fact the piece was a powerful indictment of the racism and dehumanization it portrayed, and that it was therefore a logical impossibility that it also be racist—as if, that is, the black people who lived in Saint-Denis, through no fault of their own, simply didn't understand art, didn't appreciate subtlety, and wouldn't listen to reason. I didn't see how any of this could be true. The evidence provided was limited to the slogans written on signs the protesters carried, and chants they led, and a few carefully selected words from the mouths of the protesters themselves, usually presented in something like scare quotes. It was typical of race discourse in France, as I'd later learn, that the ruling class discussed racism at a fifth grade level, but treated everyone else like children. This was only a few days after a grand jury in St. Louis County declined to indict the officer who'd killed Michael Brown, and it struck me that journalists across the ideological spectrum covered the human zoo controversy the way Fox News covered Black Lives Matter. They all agreed that the angry tone of the protest, together with its flirtation with violence and, above all, its unthinkable attack on free speech, released them from any responsibility to give serious consideration to, or even to accurately report, the protesters' actual concerns. They all carried an official statement from the minister of culture—who *condemned the protests as an attempt at censorship and intimidation, based on forms of intolerance that had no place in the Republic*—and a number of them argued that the piece was a good faith effort to provoke an important conversation. But no one seemed interested in the conversation the piece had provoked, though it was true that to open the second night of the show, the theater's program director planned a panel discussion, to which my mother-in-law had been invited to express her view that the show couldn't be dismissed as an elaborate history lesson, that it provoked in its audience emotions more complicated than pity or guilt, and that in a forceful and visceral way it traced the subtler violence of contemporary racism and dominance to its monstrous roots. Whether anyone on the panel had been invited to express an opposing view, I never found out, because at the last minute, out of an abundance of caution, the event was nixed. By that time, more than 250 riot police had assembled outside the building, which, when I got there, glowed like a palace over the heads in the crowd. Within minutes of arriving, armed with questions Ella had written on my pad as I'd rushed out the door, I'd recorded statements from numerous people, each expressing a nuanced personal opinion. Of course it was only later that week, during the hours I spent listening to the interviews I'd recorded with Ella, pausing every few seconds for her translations, that I appreciated the volume of insights I'd gathered that somehow no actual journalist had put into print. A man in a corduroy jacket named Loic objected not so much to the fact of the exhibit as to the theater's having presented it in a predominantly African community without any historical contextualization and without any input from community members, whose perspective he thought should be consulted in some minimal way. According to Sonia, a woman in her twenties, it was galling that the theater, which was underwritten by the Ministry of Culture, occupied such a prominent place in this neighborhood, but made so little effort to serve the people who lived there, though that was in fact part of the mandate attached to its funding, and while the other public services—parks, housing, and, above all, schools—were meantime in advanced decay; it was insulting, she said, that the government would spend tax dollars on a work of supposed art about black pain in a neighborhood where there was so much black pain it was neglecting to even notice. Though she understood perfectly well, another young woman, Aïssatou, told me, that the piece was meant to denounce the consumption of black pain as entertainment, the fact remained that, irrespective of the question of artistic merit, white people—and here she nodded up at the brightly lit windows of the theater at which theatergoers, quite possibly, I thought, including Clarisse, stood looking down at us—were paying money for what they considered a benefit, the benefit, as she put it, of *feeling something*, to be gained by seeing black actors degraded and abused.

It was obvious to me even at the time how far out of my depth I was, trying to report this story, and now, trying to write it up as fiction, I told Ella, I was further out still. By this point, weeks had passed since the Super Bowl. Our baby would soon graduate from green pea to blueberry. The payment dates on my credit cards had come and gone. Declan Foster had appeared before a grand jury and was indicted on charges of abduction and possession of a firearm by a convicted felon. Antonin Scalia was dead and buried, and Merrick Garland, who had just hired my brother as a clerk, had been nominated to fill his seat, and still I hadn't written a word, I was in a phase of my creative process that mostly involved looking at photographs of Mitch McConnell and perfecting a fantasy in which I suffocated him with his own neck wattle on the Capitol lawn. Ella, nestled in the corner of my screen, though she had her own work to do, took it upon herself to keep me on task: Would it be a good start, she suggested, simply to continue telling her the story in as much detail as possible, and then from memory to transcribe what I'd said? I could remember that as I listened or pretended to listen to Aïssatou, a great phalanx of protesters advanced toward the barricade, until they were chest to chest with a row of policemen, who took shelter behind their Perspex shields; in bright windows above us, still more theatergoers crowded together to watch. And the image they formed there, their silhouettes, their imperviousness, haunted me the following week, I told Ella on Skype, when the show moved to an arts center in Paris called the Cent-Quatre, and we went to see it ourselves. In the week since the show's run in Saint-Denis had ended, a grand jury in New York had declined to indict the officer who murdered Eric Garner, and I was surprised by the strength of the anger I felt, a tightness in my chest that had yet to relent when Ella and I picked up our tickets at the box office and found seats in the subterranean waiting room, where red and white wine were available in plastic cups. All week I hung around the lobby and, introducing myself as a journalist from a publication that didn't exist, interviewed people in the stunned minutes after they'd emerged from the exhibit. This is how I met a South African woman who'd been living in France for forty-five years, who told me the show had brought back a memory from her university days: a museum she'd visited in Cape Town, in the mid-sixties, she said, at the top of Adderley Street, where she saw an anthropological exhibit on the lives of the San, which featured, as she put it, a bushman—a living bushman!— who'd clearly gone mad. Because it had recalled that earlier trauma so distinctly, it had been hard, she told me, so very hard, to confront the present exhibit; it was hard to be a white South African, she said: you sustained an enormous amount of guilt about the way you lived back then, about the many servants you kept, about how easy it all had been; one put blinkers on, she explained, one didn't think about politics, one didn't speak about politics, and how guilty one felt now, she said, when one looked back.

∎

At the Food Lion the only evidence that remained of the snow, which had been piled into an enormous mound at the center of the parking lot, was the faint outline of salt and grit this mound had left on the pavement when it melted, which I remember contemplating at unnatural length one afternoon on the way to my car, thinking of how I'd describe it to Ella later when we spoke. Before sunrise that same morning, she'd called me from the medical imaging clinic, where she was looking at an ultrasound that showed, in the darkness of her womb, a mottled island of gray roughly the size of a raspberry. Listen, my love, she'd said, and the soft patter I then heard, which I immediately recognized as a heartbeat, had been echoing in my head all day. (It's echoing in my head still.)

By then I'd begun a draft of a story centered on Arthur, the central character of the heatwave story, and it all started pouring out. But when I'd arrived at this moment, the South African woman and the grotesquely tone-deaf things she said, I'd once again found myself stumped: how to convey, in the mixture of revulsion and triumph that rose in Arthur's chest as she spoke, the recognition of something secret about himself that he would never say aloud. Listening to these recordings, I could hear myself circling a question I didn't quite know how to ask, having to do with who and what art is for. And then on the tapes, when an answer begins to present itself, I can hear myself backing away, like I didn't really want to know. During the week I spent lurking around the lobby, I spoke with a few of the actors, the ones who spoke English, and they all had thoughts on what the work accomplished, and on how the same racism it portrayed was present in their daily lives. But in fact their answers were fairly pat, and while I didn't doubt the sincerity of what they had to say, they were also actors, and the polish of their self-presentation had the corrosive residue of self-regard. Meanwhile, I occasionally caught glimpses of the creator of the show in his Uggs, skulking at the edges of the room, but I kept telling myself he looked busy and that I'd speak with him another time. The truth was I didn't need to interview him, I knew what he had to say. On Facebook, he'd posted a photo of himself, enclosed within one of the cages from the show, looking defiantly into the distance. *Rage, rage against the dying of the light,* he'd written. On French TV, he'd insisted that the protesters who had actually seen the show had changed their minds, had blessed it as non-racist, expressed their heartfelt gratitude, begged his forgiveness. He had a pointy beard, and wore a porkpie hat, beneath which he also wore a patterned kufi. Around each wrist he wore a tangle of cotton bracelets. If blacks in the United States, he'd said somewhere, liked to refer to themselves as African American, it was reasonable to think of himself as Euro-African. Whenever I looked at him, that week at the Cent-Quatre, I felt certain that art existed primarily to serve the egos of the people who created it and the people who consumed it, and that whatever else it might do it had no truer purpose than this.

■

Over the course of a month or so, our idle conversations covered topics such as *Lady Snowblood*, Bernie Sanders's surprise win in Michigan, the Turkish government's negotiations with Brussels to take back hundreds of thousands of migrants in order to brighten its prospects of joining the EU. I told her, in earnest admiration, what I'd gathered so far of Nolan's 4,300-page sci-fi manuscript and its unusual distortions of the standard struggle between good and evil. Ella ate olives in terrific quantities, always with an expression of dismay, as if there were something about them she couldn't understand. We made lists of names, we asked ourselves what sort of parents we hoped to be, what sorts of values we hoped to transmit, though the ecstatic feeling it gave us both to do so was too much to sustain for very long; the future had become magical to us, and its power over us was exhausting. By this time I'd watched the "Formation" music video dozens of times, the choreography from which I often found myself performing in my head, though any attempt I made to perform it with my body went catastrophically awry. Why it had become so important to me to do so I couldn't say, but I think it was related in a way I still can't quite articulate to the kind of somatic wisdom I hoped to gain by my tiny, private impersonations of my wife. On YouTube I found a tutorial, and one afternoon I made Ella howl with laughter as, standing back from my desk, I thrashed about in my shorts. That day I'd finally finished a draft of the story about the human zoo exhibit, and the thrill of finishing something had quickened my blood. While she read it I kept busy with an article about the human rights abuses that had intensified at the Macedonian border, though all the while I watched the corner of my screen for the minutest flutters of emotion in the wry expression fixed on Ella's face as she read. When she finished reading, she spoke at length, as if her words originated from a space inside her to which she no longer attached any importance, and without reference to either the story or even the original incident that had inspired it. It made her think of *La haine*, she said, of how carefully the film tracks the attitude of its three main characters toward the television coverage of the riots in their housing project, to which they turned as a metric of their relationship to the outside world. They were variously incensed by the media's gleeful sensationalism, dismayed by the indiscriminate destruction, and envious of their friends who'd made it into the frame. It was from a bank of TVs, after a report on the Bosnian War, that the boys learned a friend of theirs had died at the hands of the police. In another scene, a newswoman pulls up to a disused playground with her cameraman, looking for a hoodlum to interview but refusing to get out of her van, exactly as if, one of them says, she were on a drive-through safari at the Thoiry Zoo. Representation is sticky wicket, Ella said. But of course the question was, to what extent could the film itself be accused of more sophisticated versions of the same sins? Her father had been the film's chief camera operator—it was impossible to spend much time behind a camera without being troubled by the power dynamic cameras express, she said. So much of the moral logic we applied to the pain of others was so cravenly self-serving; and she'd been thinking about this—she continued another day, midway through March now, when the baby was the size of a kumquat—not in connection with the exhibit in Saint-Denis but in connection with the Magnum photographer Antoine d'Agata, a recent collection of whose she'd found lying around at her mom's, a collection that (if we were to make anything of its title, Atlas) suggested a new way to map the long shadow of colonialism. They were indeed shadowy photographs, distorted by motion and by their unusual, artless perspective. To be found in them were nightmarish images of exploitation and neglect—prostitutes, mostly, and drug addicts, on dirty beds in Bamako, in Havana, in Phnom Penh, for example, writhing, faces contorted in apparent pain. Far from invisible, the agent of this pain as often as not appeared in the act of causing it, off-center in small pools of light: this was d'Agata himself, a sordid, ghoulish figure, bald, with long fingers and a curved spine, a thick, warped cock and hollow cheeks, bent grotesquely to various depraved acts of penetration. In the past few years, she said, as our demands for a higher social consciousness in our art and discourse increased, our art and discourse had been overrun by performances of morality that often amounted to little more than the passing of blame. D'Agata had rejected this pretense long ago. Rather, he created a kind of situationist template for art that enacted the sins it portrayed, deliberately and transparently—he became a character in his photos, he said, because the photographer's traditional, impersonal position behind the camera was an act of obscene dehumanization. It was impossible to look at his pictures and derive any of the usual feelings art targeted. You felt revulsion, and contempt. But still, you felt somehow that to denounce his photos would be beside the point. They implicated you not only for consuming them but for turning away from them, in search of less troubling, more righteous art to consume. It was equally unforgivable to refuse to look at d'Agata's photos as to look at them: you lived in this world; you gave your consent to the suffering it inflicted simply by failing to take up arms against it. Whereas in the moral framework of the human zoo exhibit, you could earn absolution simply by feeling horrified, or guilty, or ill at ease.

It was nearly April by the time Ella made these conclusive remarks, only days before my flight to Paris—and in the meantime, since she'd read the piece, it had received from my classmates grudging but unanimous praise. I remember she was wearing an clay mask, and that as she spoke, in order to insulate myself from the impact of her words, I was exploring Paris on Google Maps. And it occurred to me how very like the whole of my life it was, to have not only the softness of her features but the clarity of her thoughts superimposed on my navigation of the world. She was making a case against self-justification, I remember her saying. Photography, according to d'Agata, had to be accountable to the role it played in the situations it recorded—and why shouldn't the same be true, she said, for performative or narrative art forms as well? In interviews and in public statements, the director of the human zoo exhibit emphasized the non-racist power of his work to shed light on the hidden history of colonialism: it had been suggested to him, he'd claimed on TV, that all the children of Europe and all the ministers of the European Parliament should be required to see it, such was its potential to shape hearts and minds. In my story, one character proposed that a more honest version of the work would feature a transparent account of its own creation—the rehearsals, for example, at which the director submitted his performers to all sorts of emotional abuse, mocking and prodding their naked bodies, barking racial slurs, pushing up his sleeves as they broke down in tears. But the story itself—Ella said—was toothless satire at best.

In it, I'd made my fictional counterpart, Arthur, for the sake of simplicity, a fluent speaker of French. This was pernicious bullshit, she said. I'd pretended to powers of comprehension I didn't possess, and left out the only interesting thing I had to report: the scripted caveat I'd read to the protesters

I interviewed that first night in Saint-Denis, explaining that I didn't under-stand the questions I'd be asking, and wouldn't understand their responses, but would translate them later with the help of my wife. What kind of story would it become if it were framed by the moment of that translation, she wanted to know: Arthur with Odile at the kitchen table, and whatever passed between them, listening to him simulate an attitude of sympathy for a cause he knew nothing about, when they both knew that in truth he was on a drive-through safari of his own, hoping secretly to see some car fires and broken glass.

Of course she was right. But I was crushed. That night, lying in bed, I replayed Ella's assessment in my mind. In fact I was angry. But more than that, I worried that my writing had resurrected an ambivalence in her feel-ings toward me that her pregnancy had put to rest. In the darkness of my bedroom a sensation returned to me from the heatwave, that week we'd spent together waiting for news that had not arrived, and this sensation became a part of the confused final stage of consciousness before I fell asleep: the flutter of her blinking eyelashes on my neck, just below my ear, as I held her in my arms, and the feeling of fullness if gave me to realize that all this time her eyes had been open, even as her body was racked by sobs. As if not a moment were to be missed, as if even in misery every second of time might be the strait gate through which a new world would arrive to redeem the old. I fell asleep with this thought, lying on my side where I could see her slippers. And then hours before dawn I was awoken by a rustling in the woods beneath my window: I pushed aside the blinds to see what was there. Only after a long moment did I understand that the large, brightly glowing figure moving ponderously through the brush, an enchanting and also terrifying sight, was in fact an albino deer, a buck with a broad rack of antlers, which I watched pick its way through the trees to the top of the hill, where it disappeared. My phone rang then, it was Ella. Even before she spoke I knew what she would say. She was with the doctor, Docteur LeFebvre. In a soft and broken voice, she apologized: I'm sorry, my love, I'm so sorry, I'm so sorry it didn't work out.

6
Erosion

Lady Snowblood opens at night in a women's prison, during a blizzard that will produce more than a meter of snow. Above the swirling wind, the voice of a wailing infant can be heard, and this voice belongs to Lady Snowblood herself, newly born in the seventh year of the Meiji era, a period of social reform in Japan that was inscribed in the very DNA of the previous regime, the Tokugawa shogunate, which in 1603 had unified the fractured nation by a shrewd combination of economic and military domination, legitimating its authority through the invocation of a higher power and cultivating in the national psyche a tenacious commitment to the status quo, which fifteen successive shoguns of the Tokugawa clan maintained for a total of 265 years, transforming the previously vibrant and heterogeneous culture of Japan into a comprehensively regimented feudal, agrarian society, whose intricate Confucian hierarchy was determined by birth. To preserve the uniformity of this culture, the shogunate cut off all but the most glancing points of contact with the outside world, outlawing the construction of oceangoing ships, sealing borders from both sides, and both informally stigmatizing and formally prohibiting foreign ideas and practices of all sorts.

But the very mechanisms by which the strongmen of Tokugawa sought to freeze Japanese society in time were also the mechanisms that would propel it inexorably into the future. Witness, for example, the program of alternate residence, according to which each feudal lord, or daimyo, was to reside in the capital city of Edo while his family remained at home, and then, after a period of six or twelve months, when he returned to his domain in the country, to install his family in the capital, as hostages, essentially, in case he got any funny ideas. Even irrespective of the safety of a daimyo's family, this system made any serious challenge to the shogun impossible, merely by virtue of the crippling financial burden of maintaining a massive retinue of servants and samurai at an estate in town, with the unforeseen result, however, that the servants and samurai began to develop a taste for city living, so that a trend toward urbanization and capitalization disfigured the Tokugawas' agrarian utopia by imperceptible degrees, until by the mid-nineteenth century population centers swelled all over the country, in support of which former subsistence farmers sold ever larger surpluses of their crops, and soon were growing rice, sesame, tobacco, and sugarcane at commercial scale, in parallel with escalating production of sake, woven cotton, and silk, as well as entire industries devoted to the transport, storage, and distribution of such goods. Meanwhile the samurai, who in former times had supported ascetic but dignified lives in the countryside, found that in town the value of their rice stipends was far outpaced by currencies now in circulation, so that they were soon buried in debt; while officially their loyalties remained with their masters, the daimyos, in fact they were beholden to a new urban class of merchants and bankers, who by birth ranked at the very bottom of the social ladder but nevertheless controlled the new Japanese economy, forming together with their industrial and agricultural peers in the countryside a nascent bourgeoisie.

Added to all this internal turmoil were pressures from abroad—from Britain, which had taken control of Hong Kong during the Opium War; from France, which had been eyeballing the Ryukyu Islands; and from the newly formed United States, which, in need of coaling stations along the route to Shanghai, was making increasingly importunate overtures for Japan to open its ports. The shogun's standing army of samurai was nowhere near equal to putting off an invasion by Western powers, whose military capabilities were centuries ahead and, in part because Japanese manufacturing, too, lagged far behind its Western counterparts, the trade agreements that the shogun eventually signed heavily favored Western industries, wreaking havoc on the Japanese economy, so that the suspicion and fear with which the general populace had always regarded foreigners grew into a feverish xenophobia at the exact moment the forces of globalism became impossible to resist.

Needless to say, the shogun realized it was all going up in smoke. When his heart failed in the summer of 1866, the newly ascended fifteen-year-old emperor Mutsuhito, whose predecessors had been mere figureheads, ordained himself Emperor Meiji, the Enlightened One, and quickly set about reinventing Japan according to a model of statehood that Napoleon had spread through Europe, and according to a model of economy the British fleet had spread throughout the world, pursuing the ideals of modernization and liberalization under the legend *Fukoku kyohei*—enrich the nation, strengthen the army—to achieve the latter part of which the samurai were replaced with a modern military, into which all able-bodied men older than seventeen and taller than five-foot-one were conscripted to serve. Invoking Western peoples, the government described this conscription order as a blood tax, or ketsuzei, and in the provinces, the peasantry read this vivid phrase into a legend dating from Japan's first encounter with the Christian ritual of Communion, that demons stalked the countryside dressed in white from head to toe, abducting young men and feeding on their blood, a misapprehension that gave rise to the Blood Tax Riots of 1873, during which a beautiful woman named Sayo is widowed and brutally raped when she arrives in a remote village to which her husband, a schoolteacher, has been assigned as part of the emperor's program of civic enlightenment, where his fine white clothes make him an easy target for bandits exploiting the chaos of the times. Sentenced to life in prison for the murder of one of her four assailants, Sayo seduces a guard in hope of conceiving a child, the sole purpose of whose life will be to exact revenge on the remaining three. Indeed, she dies giving birth to a little girl, named Yuki after the blizzard howling outside, and this child becomes Shurayuki-hime, or Lady Snowblood, whose inherited mission of vengeance is the subject of the film that bears her name.

■

In late May, with less than a week until my flight back to Paris, I found that the boxes I'd spent the entire year neglecting to properly unpack had nevertheless spilled their contents into the apartment to such an extent that to repack them was going to take far more time than I had. I'd broken the lease on my piss-smelling town house and, my credit cards all being canceled or frozen for nonpayment, had paid cash for the first month's rent on a storage unit in the outlying county, without any thought as to how I would get my stuff there. In the strictest sense, I had no friends in the area with whom I was close enough to ask for help. Most nearly fitting that description were Nolan and Laurie, but they'd flown off to some kind of yoga retreat, leaving Nolan's pickup parked in the driveway where it did me exactly no good. My classmates, meanwhile, were for the most part unreformed in their antipathy toward me, and none more so than Helen, who'd made history by vomiting on her wedding dress and turning it inside out. I asked her anyway, and to my surprise she agreed not only to help me move the heavy furniture but to come over and help me pack everything away.

For three long days, Helen and I packed the house, speaking mostly of Ella the whole time. That was the price of Helen's help: that I listen to her endless reflections on the character of my wife, on whom she'd developed an immoderate fixation. That was what we shared, Helen and I—with respect to Ella, a lack of moderation. Well, Helen explained, I'd read so much about her in your work, hadn't I? The heatwave story, the Macedonia story, and the human zoo story; the story of the bicycle accident on your first date. The Macedonia story wasn't a story, I pointed out. It was an email that got mixed up in the printer with Helen's own work. Helen was unfazed. Right, she said. Well, anyway, it was ages that she'd been on my mind.

She didn't drive, Helen, and arriving on foot, she'd stood at the door for a moment to finish a cigarette, peering in at the scattered debris, the loose cutlery and stacks of magazines and stray dish towels, then tamped out her butt on the doorjamb, expelled the last of the smoke from her lungs, and said she'd expected far worse. I was impressed she didn't spend even a moment asking herself where to start, which, although I'd read on the internet that it was a habit of highly ineffective people, is exactly what I'd spent most of the previous week doing, to say nothing of my entire life before that. I'd gotten only as far as acquiring a stack of flattened grocery boxes from the Food Lion; without hesitation Helen began to revive them to three dimensions and then, choosing a corner of the room, to fill them to capacity and seal them shut, tearing the tape with her teeth and pressing it flat with the edge of her fist. Choosing another corner, I did the same, copying her technique of just throwing shit together willy-nilly, shaking the box now to let it settle into the negative space. Because I'd spent so much time speaking to her in my head as I read and reread her work, I told her, I felt a bit awkward in her presence. That's how I felt when I met your wife! Helen said. I felt like I knew her from your stories, but I was never sure where Odile ended and Ella began.

Partly for that reason, what had been a mild obsession took new dimensions when at the beginning of April she spotted Ella across the room at a drinks reception on campus. It was maybe just the uncanniness, Helen said, having read your fiction all year in class, of encountering one of its principal characters out in the actual world, like she'd roamed out of a dream. She didn't look the way I'd imagined; her face was more open, and she was smaller, the way celebrities always are. There was a charge around her, the electricity of grief, it was like she caused these ripples in the air. But I didn't know it was grief at the time, I thought it was just Frenchness, so before I could think much about it I went up to her, reminding myself only just in time not to call her Odile to her face.

Odile is all wrong for her, by the way, Helen said. It's too dour, too priggish; an Odile wears Mary Janes and can't move her eyebrows because she braids her hair so tight. In the closet beneath the stairs, she'd found a duffel bag full of duffel bags, into one of which she was now packing the various shoes Ella had left in storage when we fled New York—flip-flops and snow boots and various flats and heels, each of which in turn she submitted to a frank appraisal as she spoke. But there *is* something about her, isn't there? she said. She held up Ella's slippers, the slippers that between Christmas and Easter hadn't moved from their place in the middle of the bedroom floor: she was holding them up not to appraise them but rather for me to see, as if—I immediately understood—to show me that whatever invisible essence of Ella it was that inflamed protective instincts in both of us, which was so hard to explain, these abandoned slippers expressed perfectly. She gave the grimy pom-poms a little shake. I gave a slight, helpless nod of my head, and in that instant I think a new sympathy developed between the two of us; the faintest hint of a smile appeared on Helen's face. It was the reception for Caryl Phillips, she went on. She was radiant in her awkwardness, Ella was, Helen said. Haven't you got a drink? I asked her, following her eyes across the room. Don't tell me that wee fuck went schmoozing and left you standing here alone. With her head bent and her eyes cast down at her empty hands, her eyelashes formed a kind of veil. I proposed we share my cider, I passed her my plastic cup. She lifted it to her lips and wrinkled her nose.

It was too sweet, she said. But she'd meant it as an opening. She said she liked the fabric of my dress, reaching out to touch it. Her way of laughing made me feel like we owned the room, this brilliant, generous, complicit laughter that made me homesick for my school days. Without a word about it, she started eating the coconut shrimp I'd piled on my little plate. We started talking about food, and from there we got to general likes and dislikes, to celebrity Instagram accounts, to favorite memes, to the exultant, valedictory atmosphere of Obama's final year in office and to the captivating strangeness of American life. On the wall there was that portrait of Jefferson, and how we got from there to horses I'm not sure, but it emerged that we'd both ridden as children, and soon we'd made plans—Ella was emphatic she'd arrange the whole thing—and when the appointed day arrived, she picked me up in your car and out we went into the hills, where a woman named Marjorie kept horses to rent by the hour, and where the potent smell of manure caused Ella's nose to wrinkle the same way the cider had done.

■

Horseback riding belonged to a list that included sushi and oysters and trampolines; that's what I thought when Ella told me she was going riding with Helen and needed the car. But until Helen told me, I hadn't heard the first thing about what happened that day.

Through the windshield, Helen said, Marjorie's farm seemed to have been fashioned from the stuff of Terrence Malick's soggy dreams: the tall swaying grass, budding leaves, sagging fences and a weathered barn, sunlight at the edges of a single galloping cloud. The smell of manure, Helen said, wasn't entirely unpleasant, and Marjorie herself, with a bandanna tied around her biceps, looked like the type of woman who'd produce with every utterance a sort of careless poetry—like Sissy Spacek, who as it happened lived nearby. But upon closer inspection every charming thing turned out to be in a state of advanced decay—not just tastefully weathered but thoroughly, disgustingly rotten: the sagging fences were sodden with rot, termites had gnawed the barn inside out, the Morgan horses dragged their feet and leaked pus from open sores. Beside the front door there flew an Israeli flag, alongside the Stars and Stripes, Helen said, which puzzled her at the time. As for Marjorie herself, from the look of it she'd been doing some gardening with her teeth. We introduced ourselves, Helen said, and her eyes never quite came to focus; there was a long silence, before, relative to nothing at all, she started sliding off her chair about the loveliness of my accent, the fairness of my skin, and the glowing auburnness of my hair. And then, observing in a low, breathy rapture that I must be Irish, she just sort of wandered off.

Despite her airy manner, Marjorie's voice was taut with the vague menace of southern courtesy. Airiness like a gas that fills a room, sooner or later it would either suffocate you or catch a spark. I knew, Helen said, that Ella was in a bad way, but I thought it was to do with another egg gone off, the monthly sadness, like in your story from the fall—nothing on the measure of what had happened crossed my mind, I must admit. Only later did she learn of Ella's weakness for horror movies, for the gothic and the grotesque. It was so easy to imagine Marjorie as demonically possessed—the heedless shuffle of her feet, the wheezing in her chest—but more than that, like Sissy Spacek's mother in *Carrie*, she seemed capable of doing crazy and even violent things in the name of her god. And even the seeming was violence of a sort. Helen suspected the woman was overdoing it with some powerful prescription sedative, which she'd doubtless been taking at least since a nighttime fire had killed most of the family who rented an apartment on the upper floor of her house, according to the story she'd go on to tell during a tour they hadn't asked for, which included the pasture, the trailhead, an oxidized and sun-faded playground, as well as the barn and stables, the pond, the creek, and the house, which, glory be, had been repaired. This was how it went with Marjorie, the fire was this central horror around which she led them in circles all afternoon. It's never the ones you hope in America, is it, Helen said, who're impressed you're Irish. It's always some bearded eminence quoting Yeats at you, or some ruddy drunk peeling his waistband to show you his shamrock tattoo. And now this Marjorie. Helen's accent filled her with a longing for a bygone world, for the beauty and simplicity she saw all around her when she was young. She described the heady early days of her marriage to the man from whom she got her Irish name, a long, bounteous period during which demand for the horses they raised seemed endless as the hills.

Is he Irish, then, your husband? Ella asked.

America, Marjorie said in the patient tone of authority with which people spoke to Borat, used to be a place you could stretch your legs.

Ella's sunglasses reflected the horizon and the sky. She didn't speak again for the rest of the afternoon. Without transition, Marjorie remarked that of course nowadays one saw blacks in the congregation of her church, that there were blacks among her charges in the day care center she operated; and she'd even given riding lessons to a black man, she said, along with his white girlfriend—black man, white woman, wasn't it just wonderful, after such humble beginnings in this country, the progress the blacks had made here by accepting Jesus into their hearts?

■

As Helen spoke, I wondered whether Marjorie made this remark because she'd registered Ella as black, or because she hadn't. I'd seen it go either way, and they were hard enough to tell apart that Ella often wondered herself. It wasn't only that she was light-skinned. Black Americans recognized Ella without fail; for white Americans, she more often registered as merely *something*, and that something was adequately covered in their minds by her being French. Once, out at drinks with colleagues of mine, when we first moved back to Paris, this white guy in his fifties, with a ponytail to the middle of his back, told a story about a cab ride he'd taken in Georgia, the point of which was that he couldn't discern, from either the cabdriver's appearance or her voice, whether she was black or white. He was defending his nation's honor, someone had mentioned Black Lives Matter and he was trying to prove that even the southern United States wasn't as divided as it was made out. Across the table, Ella wagged her eyebrows at me, like, This is getting kooky. People don't realize, the guy kept saying, as if he'd just learned the word, the extent of the *miscegenation* down there: It's all *miscegenated*, there's no telling what's what.

What's what?! Ella cried in delight, clapping her hands.

But even our friends, people who knew Ella's background, sometimes made comments they'd have kept to themselves in the presence of black Americans—affectionate, admiring comments about, for example, a viral local news item in which a black woman was interviewed after a fire. Or they'd exchange helpful advice: They really don't like it, someone might say at a dinner party, if you touch their hair. Or: I guess it's fine if you're alone in your car. Once, in Brooklyn not long after we were married, I made reference to Ella's blackness in conversation with our roommate Marco, sometime near dawn, after a party at which Marco had removed his pants. Listen, man, he said in a confidential tone, I think I should tell you: I don't know if people really think of Ella as black. Years later, I shared this story with an African American professor of mine. He was reassuring you, the professor said. But that wasn't it, not by a mile. In Marco's mind, he was bringing me down to size. What he meant was, I was making an unfair claim of proximity to blackness, a proximity so many white Americans craved. When we were kids Marco had a VHS copy of *Friday* he watched so many times he could recite the whole thing soup to nuts. Like, he clarified, I don't know if people think of her as *black* black. Her mother's black, I'd said. Do the math: she's as black as Obama. According to Marco, it wasn't the same. The thing is, I could see his point. The next night at work, one of my regulars, a black guy from Flatbush who spoke with a faint British accent when he was drunk, asked to see a photo of my new bride. Ella, I said, handing him my phone. O-*kay*, Kevin said approvingly, she's a *sister*. Well, I told him—so he wouldn't feel hoodwinked when he found out Ella wasn't *black* black—I'm not sure you'd say she's a *sister*. Kevin straightened. He took this to mean I was distancing myself from blackness, and he was pissed. But I just wanted him to have all the facts before he gave me that kind of credit. In our nightclothes, Ella and I had chewed it all over at the kitchen counter the next morning. It was August, but Ella was wearing her beloved slippers with the pom-poms. She put it this way: I'm never sure if I count.

■

How strange that this problematic was a source of closeness in our marriage, I thought now. Whereas the problematic of how badly we both wanted a child only drove us apart. That's what I was thinking as Helen related Marjorie's remarks about the blacks. Which, relative to the sad fate of her tenants the Mohsens, were meant as proof of her broadmindedness. Blessed perhaps with the wisdom to accept the things she could not change. Helen could feel Ella trying to catch her eye. Marjorie pressed ahead. The Lord works in mysterious ways, she said. In relation to what was unclear, but it was soon clear that this, the mysterious will of the Lord, unified her scattered thoughts, whether they pertained to the sinkholes that kept opening up on her road, or to the scummy surface of the little pond, or the furious rash from which her husband suffered every spring. She wanted Helen and

Ella to accept this wisdom as well. Herein the violence Ella feared. It wasn't only her Frenchness that resisted being proselytized to; it was something deep in her bones. All this tyrannical fretting about everyone's eternal soul. Marjorie held that there was no improving upon the world we lived in, notwithstanding the rash and the sinkholes and the sorry state of her Morgans (whose world, Helen pointed out, could easily have been improved with some vigorous brushing and the occasional mucking out of their stalls)— there was no improving on the actual world because there was no improving on the infinite goodness of the Lord's will.

So herein the violence. To hear her tell it, she'd held Hussein and Khalida hostage the same way from the moment they moved in upstairs three years before, having arrived in adverse circumstances, of this much Marjorie was sure. Were they aware that by taking Jesus into their hearts they could make peace with any misfortune as part of a plan that, even before Creation, had been provided for in the most intricate detail in the Lord's mind's eye, and that would culminate in the redemption of those souls who repented of their sins and rejoiced in the truth at the end of time? Marjorie spoke these phrases slowly, Helen told me, always as if they'd just occurred to her and weren't platitudes she'd repeated each a thousand times, peering into our faces, Helen said, like we might throw ourselves at her feet. The Mohsens— it probably went without saying, Marjorie said, Helen told me—were of the Muslim persuasion, and actually Marjorie developed a certain affection for them, the fate of their souls preoccupied her more and more. At bedtime she prayed they might be saved. Some mornings when she walked with Khalida to the end of the long driveway, where the older child boarded the bus, Marjorie, following her pastor's advice, would patiently enumerate the many ways her faith in Jesus's love had enriched her life: her health, the joy of motherhood, the companionship of a good man. Khalida eventually pointed out that she, too, enjoyed such blessings, so Marjorie extolled the patience Jesus's love gave her, the peace it gave her to resign herself to the Lord's care. But Khalida insisted that she already enjoyed these blessings as well, and while she admired Christ's teachings, she and her husband had their own moral instincts by which to navigate their lives. At which point Marjorie was forced to bring to Khalida's attention certain realities that awaited not only her and Hussein but their children as well, if they remained unbaptized until the Final Judgment, when decent Christians would ascend to the Kingdom of Heaven, while even the wisest and most virtuous of nonbelievers would be consigned to eternal residence in a Lake of Fire.

Yeah, Helen quipped, sounds like a no-brainer.

Marjorie ignored this. She was convinced, she said, that the Mohsens had been sent as a test of her capacity to spread the Word of God. For over a year, she tried to bring Khalida around to Jesus. If only she'd had more time. She felt that in a way Khalida had become a friend. She taught her needlepoint and crochet. She was an excellent listener, Khalida, you could speak to her for hours and hours at a time. At this point, Helen remembered, they paused, the three women, to watch a heavy man in a work shirt Helen took for Marjorie's husband, crossing an open meadow along the crest of the hill—a lumbering silhouette making slow progress against the sky, with the kind of patience, Ella would later say to Helen, it would take to dig a grave in the dark of night. It was obvious Ella wanted to go, she kept taking sharp breaths, her brow was creased, she looked around in alarm at every rustle of wings. But Helen pretended not to notice, it was such good material, she couldn't get enough. They were punished, was it? she prompted Marjorie. The Muslims—would they not be saved in the end?

Tim called them the Hussein-Obamas, Marjorie said. That was as close as she ever came to telling a joke. It was as close as Helen got to asking herself if this was all more than Ella could take. The husband disappeared from view, Marjorie turned away, and for a short while they trailed her in silence. When she resumed speaking, it was on the subject of Hussein's grief, about which, because he'd moved into a motel, she seemed not to have much firsthand knowledge, though a strange, jealous energy entered her voice when she spoke of it. It was bewildering, the rigor and thoroughness with which she'd imagined the anguish this man had experienced in the days after his family was killed: the ache at the back of his throat and the throbbing of his temples that the force of his weeping had caused; the endless hours of television he'd watched in the darkened motel room in a state of numbness and shock; his alienation from ordinary phenomena, such as a traffic signal turning from yellow to red to green. A hell she invented for him to live in, no more or less than he deserved. It caused him unendurable pain, Marjorie said in awe, to look at the hundreds of photos of his wife and his children that he kept on his phone, which he nonetheless couldn't resist doing again and again in the dark hours before dawn, when he was consumed by rage and disbelief.

All this was clear in her mind. Her powers of empathy were so acute as to amount to clairvoyance. Now, the three women—Marjorie, Helen, and Ella—were following a swampy creek bed deep into the woods, beneath a sparse canopy of leaves through which shafts of sunlight carved angles in the shade. Marjorie swatted the air as she spoke, as cluster flies buzzed around her head. Later, during a spur-of-the-moment trip out of town, Helen and Ella would chew over the whole encounter and agree that she believed un-ambiguously in the fire as the wrath of God, a punishment the Mohsens could have easily avoided by renouncing Islam and recognizing as their Lord and Savior Jesus Christ. It's misery, Ella would say, hugging her knees in her rocker on the dark porch of a rented cottage. She wants to drown the whole world in her misery like a sack of kittens in a scummy pond. Is that what will happen to me? she asked.

The creek bed they'd followed uphill had led to a small clearing, where without ceremony Marjorie installed herself on a rock and began massaging her calves. This clearing, she claimed, was the site of some minor, unrecorded action or encampment in the Civil War; the property had been in her family for generations, but only recently had her husband discovered, scattered throughout the clearing beneath a thin layer of topsoil and debris, a trove of Civil War relics: a dragoon holster, a bullet mold, a bowie knife, among many others, all representing a windfall that funded the refinishing of the basement, as well as the construction of a playground in the yard and the purchase of a pair of Shetland ponies, investments that made possible the modest income Marjorie's day care center produced, without which they'd have been forced to sell the property ages since. It almost looks like this was a cemetery, Helen observed before she could help it; just how much topsoil did you have to clear away? This caused an expression of lucid hostility to flash in Marjorie's eyes, which in turned caused Ella to reach for Helen's arm and hold it tight. Oh well, Helen offered as conciliation, the past is never really dead, is it?

Of course she'd always taken it for granted, Marjorie said after a moment, resuming her ethereal manner, that traces of the dead were all around us; but to have their paraphernalia scattered at her feet like the fruit of the land made her feel sincerely blessed. It was nearly two o'clock in the morning (it then occurred to her to continue) when Hussein returned to the house from the Birchwood Golf Club, where he worked as a barback, and found his home engulfed in flames: in exhaustive detail, Marjorie described the burning smell Hussein first registered in the car, which he soon connected to an obscure, rushing sound that seemed to approach and recede like a violent surf as he stood on the dark landing of the rear staircase, flipping the light switch on and off to no effect, until a deluge of thick black smoke crashed down the stairs and knocked him backward into the yard.

It was January, and she remembered, Marjorie told them, waking in confusion and rushing outside into the bracing cold; and she remembered the sound of the horses snorting and stomping in their stables, spooked by the dull crack of the windowpanes as they blew out one by one. By the time the fire department arrived, Hussein, using a ladder Tim had rushed off to find, had already made several desperate attempts at the windows, but each time he was thwarted by the intense heat of the flames and the thick, acrid billows of smoke, until finally it became impossible even to approach the house, and Hussein, having sustained numerous burns on his hands and face, could do nothing but stand at a distance of twenty or thirty feet watching the fire consume the roof, while the firefighters launched a thick cord of water into the night sky, and while Tim paced around with his head in his hands, and while Marjorie, seeing the situation for what it was,

trotted barefoot up and down the lawn, drenched in sweat, screaming herself hoarse, as she put it, for Khalida and her young children to *go to Jesus, go
to Glory*, though she knew it was already too late.

∎

We'd finished packing for the night by this point, and Helen was sitting
on the counter, drinking the first of six bottles of cider I'd promised for
her help. In a personal, immediate sense, the visit had disturbed her, she
said—obviously. But in a broader sense as well. Something about Marjorie's
eschatology, and her faith in Providence, were consonant with a dialectical
view of history as an inexorable march of progress, proceeding according to
inviolable natural laws (the way water follows a creek bed downhill toward the
sea), and the final obstacles to which were soon to be surmounted, clearing
the way for civilization to take its final, utopic form. And so forth, Helen
said. What I mean is that in the grotesque folly of Christian historicism,
which is such a powerful force in American politics although it's been obsolete for centuries, the poverty of regular historicism is inscribed plain as day.
When finally Marjorie dismissed them, Ella's relief, which was palpable in
the air, made Helen feel ashamed.

So she was surprised when, during spring break the following week, Ella
texted her in the middle of the night to suggest that the two of them leave
the next morning on an overnight trip to Tangier, an island that had been
gradually sinking into the Chesapeake Bay for hundreds of years, where a
population of fewer than five hundred people lived in such thoroughgoing
isolation that their accent and dialect were said not to have evolved at all
since John Smith first arrived there in the summer of 1608. As Helen spoke
she was flipping through a sheaf of photographs from the day Ella and I were
married, which we'd collected from the iPhones of various friends who'd
been there with us to celebrate and had printed out for inclusion with Ella's
green card application as evidence of our actual love. Leafing through them
she softened, the tension went out of her shoulders, and her face opened to
an extent that was difficult to reconcile with the woman who'd once made

such memorable reference to her own hemorrhoids in the presence of Rick Bass. She held up a photo in which Ella and I, late on the night of our wedding, were shown crouching to collect the shards of a broken wineglass, as the party continued around us. At this moment, the overhead bulb blew out, leaving Helen softly backlit by the floodlight in the yard. Oh my, she said. Without asking whether I minded, she lit a cigarette. At the window behind her, winged insects of every description appeared from the darkness and pitched themselves frantically against the screen. Breathing smoke, she picked up where she'd left off.

■

On the way out of town they passed the aftermath of a wreck. Smoke was still rising and the authorities had yet to arrive. Just missed it! Helen said. Is a bit of excitement in this life too much to ask? Ella connected the sentiment to her own interest in Tangier Island: Everybody wants to own the end of the world, she said. The golden bands of light that fell across the harbor as the ferry made its approach somehow underscored this point, and among the first things they saw of Tangier was a makeshift cross that rose out of the marsh grass, stenciled with the legend CHRIST IS LIFE. The spongy bands of sediment onto which most of the island's construction was clustered—the so-called uplands—rose at its highest point to only a little over a meter above the surface of the bay and could scarcely be described as land: the highest tides not only cinched the island's perimeter tight, but also percolated up through supposedly solid ground and formed ponds that seemed to get bigger each time they returned.

Later, Ella would tell Helen that she herself felt like an island whose edges were being washed away. But even as the ferry approached the dock, Helen could feel Ella shrinking into herself, as she'd done in the woods at Marjorie's farm—that air of psychic vulnerability whose origin Helen could only guess. I mean I thought it was to do with race, Helen told me, and I wanted her to feel me beside her, at Marjorie's I'd left her alone, and now I wanted to make her feel safe. The harbor was lined with shanties that stood on pilings rising out of the harbor, like fishing villages Helen had seen in Cambodia and Taiwan. Even in the spectacular late-afternoon sun, the landscape looked not so much like a scene from Malick as from Tarkovsky: the sodden, silty earth, the rusted detritus, the water tower, the looming church spire, the gnarled stacks of crab cages, the sagging docks and the sludgy dock lines, the distant cries of birds, the occasional tugboat horn, and the harbor chop lapping against the seawall—and more than any of this, Helen said, a Tarkovskian atmosphere of desolation, anxiety, and fatigue that not only hung in the air but was also etched into the faces of the people who watched them coming down from the ferry with something between suspicion and contempt.

We spent that night—Helen told me—in a pair of rockers on the screened porch of the cottage we'd booked, where a stray kitten no more than a few months old crept in the shadows. Both feeling more thoroughly shattered than we could have predicted by the encounters of the day. All that white sadness, Helen thought. Boo-hoo. The trouble was that her protective instincts made her even more than usually combative—preemptively so—in their dealings all day long with people whose bigotry it seemed safe to assume. No sooner had they deboarded the ferry than their eyes fell on a Trump poster: The man is a failed abortion, Helen observed, loud enough for everyone around to hear. You can tell by his wee little hands. I was like a human Twitter account, she now recalled, it was like I was on coke. She told a crab fisherman she liked the Jebus fish on the stern of his boat. For no good reason, she described hip waders, to a woman who was wearing them, as condoms for your legs. Between the white clapboard houses and the white picket fences that lined the street, such as it was, there stood crooked rows of headstones in the grass, the dead standing guard at the gate. From a flagpole in one yard, there flew another Israeli flag. Everyone they met rehearsed the same case, as if it were a civic or sacramental duty: that Tangier not only deserved to be saved but had been chosen specially for salvation by God himself. Helen would say, Well, I don't see what you hope to gain convincing *us*.

At the Methodist church they found the pastor, a large, jolly man who, maybe just to save himself the irritation of hearing them point it out, made a great deal of the irony that with a name like Deluge he'd been assigned to the congregation of Tangier. Ella's contempt for this man felt almost dangerous. It was naked on her face, and in the barbed silence she maintained even when he addressed her directly. Yes, he said, a great many people here felt that the Lord would spare Tangier from destruction, exactly as he'd done so many times in the past; as devoted Christians it was difficult for them to believe that any place so pious as this little island could be punished, while the rest of the nation, under the leadership of a party that supported same-sex marriage, abortion, and the right of deviants to use any restroom they chose, would be spared. Helen took this as her cue to intervene. I was raised Catholic, so I'll warn you, she told the pastor, not to be citing Scripture to me unless you intend to be precise.

With a big, hardy laugh, Deluge showed his palms. In the Bible, he said, water was an illustration of God's Holy Spirit, and although it threatened Tangier's existence, it also gave Tangier life, just as biblical Canaan, the land of milk and honey, was nourished by the waters of the river Jordan on the shores of the Dead Sea.

That's very nice, Ella said. I think I need to get some air.

■

Now, Helen said, now that I know what happened, I keep thinking about that contempt. Not contempt at all, really, more just the moral clarity of grief. And actually isn't it the moral clarity we perceive in black culture, black life, black death, that we-the-whites are always trying to soak up, the way the sea soaks up an island: claiming it as its own an inch at a time? How our hearts swell when we hear the voice of Beyoncé or Obama or Dr. King. Ditto the bereaved, point being. It seemed certain Ella was on the brink of some sort of cathartic outburst or collapse for which she could not be blamed. And I *envied* her. Inside the modestly decorated church, the wind's ceaseless buffeting of the clapboards and the stained glass filled the silences she let hang in the room. Outside, that same wind made wild tangles of her hair. Mine, too. Back at the docks, we met a woman named Sharon, who like Marjorie was charmed by my Irishness and somewhat mystified by Ella's Frenchness, though not in quite the same spirit as Marjorie in either case. Ella softened when she saw her, as if in recognition. She wore a giant, sturdy sweatshirt and chose her words carefully when she spoke, tugging at the frayed ends of the drawstring to her hood. Later, on the porch, Ella and I spent ages trying to describe the quality that distinguished Sharon from other people we'd met on Tangier. She had poetry in her voice but they all had poetry in their voices. She had flinty eyes, but no more so than anyone else. What can you tell me about your fabulous thigh-high wellies? I asked her. She was making her daily pilgrimage to the ruins of the local Canaan, where, she said, each step took her both forward and backward in time. Why not take us with you? Ella asked.

It was a choppy afternoon on the bay. Sharon's little skiff vaulted from one wave to the next through a fine mist of salt that glistened on our skin. Having no hip waders ourselves, with our pants rolled up to our knees and carrying our shoes, we jumped off the bow onto a thick layer of oyster shells, climbed up onto the loamy flats. And the power of the place—something like the force that compels you to whisper in a temple, or in the presence of well-known art. We stood in the wind, turning slow circles to take stock of the wasteland around us. Canaan was the original settlement on Tangier, Sharon told us, until, in the late nineteenth century, as more and more of the shoreline melted into the bay, residents began to abandon their homes or dismantle them to be reconstructed across the channel, on ever-so-slightly higher ground. By the 1930s, what buildings remained in Canaan had been left to rot and be washed away along with the earth over which they stood. As a child, she said, before anyone gave much thought to what might be in store for the rest of Tangier, she often spent entire days here with her father, an escape from life in town to the bucolic paradise the former site of Canaan had then become: she remembered the goats that ran wild, chickens, wildflowers she gathered in her arms, figs she ate directly from the branch, the sweetness of which she could still taste when she closed her eyes. Like life after death, she said. Truth is maybe we were doomed all along. Now there were only the petrified husks of trees long since felled by wind and rot, the sun-bleached shells and windswept grass. At the tops of sagging phone poles even the ospreys had fled their nests. Whatever evidence of the thriving community that once existed here was scattered on the ground. Over the years, she'd collected medicine bottles, tobacco pipes, dolls' heads, cookie jars—and dozens if not hundreds of arrowheads that had once belonged to the Pocomoke who hunted here long ago. Then at the end of 2012, after Hurricane Sandy had nearly washed the entire island from the face of the earth, she told us, pointing to the headstones that littered shore just above the high-water mark, she'd found a pair of human skulls and then, later, femurs, clavicles, vertebrae, and metatarsals, an entire graveyard's worth of bones, each a bracing reminder, she said, that even death wasn't quite so permanent as we tended to believe, or at least not in the way we meant it to be when we laid our dead to rest.

Ella perched on an ancient, half-buried tire, studying the windswept sand. On any ordinary day, Sharon said, you could sit and watch the shore fall away in slabs in the wash of the tides. We did sit and watch. And seeing with our own eyes how each wave claimed its inch of earth for the bay, I remarked that Tangier Island stood about as much chance as a cube of sugar in a pot of English tea. And Sharon looked at me like I'd farted on her breakfast. Maybe I could have been gentler. But on the other hand she's a grown person; and as a first-generation college grad, as an Irish person who's lived in London, and as a woman who's interacted with men, I know something about the chafing rage that grows inside you when a stranger speaks to you like a child. You need to forget it, I wanted to tell her; you need to get on with your life and start something new. But Ella cut me off.

Helen, she said, do you ever shut the fuck up?

■

Helen tipped her ashes into the bone-dry kitchen sink. She lined her empty cider bottles shoulder to shoulder on the windowsill, as if they were to be executed for letting her down. In the smoke that hung in the air around us, I could hardly breathe. I missed Ella so much, and I wanted her back.

There wasn't a drop of booze to be had on Tangier. Wrapped in blankets on the porch that night, Helen told me, they hugged their knees and blew over the tops of their tea. After her outburst, Ella had gone mum. As a demonstration of her contrition, Helen stayed quiet for the rest of the afternoon as well. Back in the boat, they listened to Sharon's continued reflections on time, death, and hope. And that seemed to do the trick. Now Ella ran her fingers through the knots the day had made in Helen's hair. For hours, they talked, as the night grew colder and as the kitten, desperate for something to eat, circled closer, until finally he leapt up onto the little table between them, where they took turns scratching behind his ears. Hopelessness had come over them both, like a spell they'd cast themselves, Helen said—in connection not only with the grim prospects for the island's survival but also with the precipitous erosion of any common ground upon which to base an exchange of ideas with the people who lived there. Midnight came and went, and although it had been a long, exhausting day, neither of them was anywhere near ready to sleep. At a certain point, the kitten climbed into Helen's lap, and as she stroked his fur, he began to nibble at her forearm— he thought her forearm would bear milk, Helen realized, which sent a ticklish sensation up her spine, and made her squirm helplessly in her chair, until the cat leapt into Ella's lap and made the same mistake. Somehow they'd been talking about Marjorie again—it was unsettling, they agreed, how extensively Marjorie had appropriated the narrative of Hussein's pain, and now Ella was saying that on the other hand she found herself endlessly summoning to her mind, in compulsive detail, an unendurable fiction of his family's final moments on earth, as if to test herself against the horror of their deaths. And it was at this moment that the cat jumped into her lap, and began suckling at her arm. Within seconds, her face was stained by silent tears. Actually, she felt genuinely sorry for Marjorie, she went on. Imagine what a life. Was she not infuriated, Helen asked, that Marjorie had claimed the tragedy of the fire for the will of the Lord? The cat continued suckling at Ella's arm, and Ella held him close and tight. It's misery, Ella said. And yet, she couldn't help seeing sadness as the best of us. When her sadness was exhausted, what would be left? The kitten kept suckling at her arm, and suddenly she seemed to lose her breath; soon she was racked by sobs. And I could see, Helen told me: it was the kitten's need of her, that bodily need, his smallness and warmth—and I knew what she would tell me next. For a few minutes, she cried harder and harder, and then softer and softer, until she was calm again. I can feel his heartbeat, she quietly explained.

Only very slightly, Helen continued, did Ella's voice waver as she went on: she explained that back in Charlottesville the night before, while you were at the pool, she'd found your notebook and that, opening it against her better judgment, she'd felt her blood stop cold in her heart when she saw how exhaustively you'd documented not only the news of her pregnancy but the heartbreak of its loss.

It was all there, Ella said, beginning with the moment, after an un-scheduled visit to the doctor, that she'd told you the fetus's heartbeat had stopped—a phone call that had lasted nearly two hours, though neither of you had done much but keen. Afterward you dragged yourself to class, where a story of yours was up for workshop—I remember, Helen said: you had your hat pulled low over your eyes, and looked up not once from your frantic notes, we all thought you were being sniffy about your work. It makes my ears ring, she said, to think of how much you must have hated us that day. Ella said you called her afterward from the car, and burst out crying. The next day, steeling her nerves, she went alone to the surgery ward to have what remained of the pregnancy removed; much of the long day she'd spent in recovery the two of you likewise spent on the phone, she said; in your notes, you'd expanded upon the guilt you felt that she endured this procedure alone, and that you had nothing helpful to say, but actually the fact of your speechlessness was a comfort to her, somehow. It soothed her to hear your ragged breathing and broken sobs, and she was surprised to find in your notes that you'd intuited as much when, after she returned from the hospital, you'd heard the strength and determination that came into her voice when she tried to comfort you; you'd written, she said, Helen told me, that although you knew you couldn't feel precisely what she felt, you hoped that by stoking and nourishing your own pain you might take some of her pain upon yourself. Between phone calls, a profound psychic agony came over her in waves, each of which she could see approaching but was helpless to avoid, and each of which, when it crested, racked her entire being and held her under until she gasped for breath, though there was nothing she could do but surrender control and wait to be released.

So she'd described it, Ella told me that night on the porch, and so it appeared in your notes. When you suggested immediately booking a ticket to France, she insisted on coming here instead. But because of the possibility there'd be complications arising from the procedure, it was ten days before the doctor would clear her to travel, and during those ten days, the initial impact didn't abate in the least. Rather, it was continually renewed in her thoughts, and in the various interior pangs and shudders of her body, and by a cheery voicemail from her doctor's secretary, confirming her twelve-week sonogram in a few days' time. This appointment and several to follow she'd booked in February; she remembered a feeling like pride, setting them down in her calendar. Now she canceled all of them—wishing death for the secretary or at least a cold sore the size of Mars—and booked a flight instead. Arriving in Virginia she found the kitchen stocked with food, and for the first few days after she arrived, you skipped your classes, neither of you left the house. A relative calm took hold of her, almost relief, just to be in your arms. But the tiny caterpillars she kept finding on the walls, when she connected them with the moths whose shadows fluttered like ashes in the dark, caught her off guard and made her feel helpless, broken, and alone. Somehow, whereas while you'd been apart she'd felt closer to you than she maybe ever had, now that she was here with you she felt that a distance had opened. In the dark, she sometimes looked up into your face, illuminated by the glow of the TV, and found there a blankness she ascribed to an innate ability, she said, to be absent from yourself, which she both envied and despised. And at other times, she caught you looking into her face, but far away in your thoughts, and wearing an expression of bemusement. According to no natural schedule or pattern that she could discern, she drifted in and out of sleep, and more than once, half awake on her way to the bathroom in the middle of the night, she found you at your desk, bent to your notes by the light of a weak bulb. Little by little, everyday life began to reassert itself, in conducting which you left the house for hours at a time, maybe even a bit eagerly, and she started to feel like you'd betrayed this sacred thing you shared.

Soon, Ella said, Helen went on, she'd begun to suspect you resented her, whether consciously or not, less for failing to carry the pregnancy to term than for bringing this sadness into your life and making you its hostage. That was when, though your handwriting was all but completely indecipherable, she opened your notebook one night and found that, far from resenting her grief, you were turning it into material. The day after the miscarriage, you recorded a painstakingly unaesthetic description of the ache at the back of your throat, the soreness in your abdomen, the dull pressure behind your eyes. Over the next week, you tried to locate the precise source of your pain, and decided it mostly arose from the thought of her pain. She was touched to see that you'd spent so much time consulting pregnancy blogs and self-help books on the topic of miscarriage's particular brand of grief, and that you'd made an earnest attempt to apply that wisdom toward practical ends. In one entry, you explored your own personal sense of loss, the sorrow that you felt on your own behalf. She recognized her own thoughts in the observation that, in one sense, you wanted to be released from that sadness as soon as possible, that it was intolerable, but that in another, you had a horror of the thought that this sadness would ever fade. But from that point, in a kind of circular way, you began to advance a series of propositions in each of which the very specific fact of a lost pregnancy was more thoroughly transformed into the broader concept of a ruined future, until your sadness, if it appeared on the page at all, had become unrecognizably abstract. Before long, the notes on the miscarriage fell off entirely, or rather were absorbed in an outline you'd been drawing up for a short story, which was to be set on the island of Tangier, upon reading which she was overcome by a powerful feeling of repulsion, and decided she had to get away.

■

When I woke up the next morning, my throat was so dry it felt like choking. I staggered into the kitchen, and let the tap run for a long time, to wash the night's collected ashes down the drain. Four years have passed since that conversation with Helen, and I'm grateful for those pages she described, whatever harm they've caused. I've revisited them many times, and I'll say in their defense that they do give me access to that sadness, they return me to that crushing predawn hour that Ella called from the doctor's office, and to the agony and rage of the weeks and months that followed. Ella has her body to remind her; I only have my notes.

It took two full days to finish packing up the house. Then I reserved a truck with money my brother sent by PayPal. But at the rental office, it turned out the truck I rented didn't exist, though another truck just like it, the lady offered, existed at a location in Richmond, an hour and twenty minutes away. Helen took it upon herself to make a scene on my behalf, though there was no convincing the woman behind the counter that she was under any obligation to have the second truck delivered, or even to comp me the extra 140 miles, or even to stand up from her chair.

We drove to Richmond, and as promised, they had just the truck I wanted. A beautiful truck with a retractable ramp and a furniture dolly thrown in at no extra cost. But my debit card wouldn't cut it, they needed a bona fide credit card on file, and all my credits cards were canceled. I bought Helen a box of Marlboros and a liter of cider to keep her happy on the way back. I got a tallboy for myself, to take the edge off the stress headache behind my eyes. There was Nolan Trucks's truck in the driveway when we got back, caked in the shit of chickadees that nested in the branches overhead. Laurie and Nolan being unreachable, I didn't see how it did us any good. Helen gave me an appraising look. If you're serious about getting those boxes out of your house, she said, you'll have to commit a few small crimes. There was a bathroom on the ground floor at the back of the house, with a small, high window that, if it was like its counterpart in my own apartment, didn't properly lock. I'll give you a boost, Helen said. Wriggling through the window, I kicked her in the head, and she called me a turd. For a long moment, as Helen cursed outside, I stood perfectly still, waiting for my eyes to adjust to the light. Until there I was, in the mirror above the sink.

Absent Nolan and Laurie, the apartment, which was perfectly symmetrical to my own, but furnished so tastefully, and with such care, gave me the feeling of wandering through a version of my life that I'd failed to live. Their midcentury furniture, the slight disorder of their bookshelves, the improvised arrangement of the pictures on their walls, gave the impression of an elusive peace. In the peculiar, shimmering stillness of these rooms, which I tried to disturb as little as possible, I opened drawers and cabinets, searching for a spare key. (You felt like an intruder because you were an intruder, Helen later said.) It was on Laurie's drafting table that I found it, beside a sketchpad on which she'd roughed out an albino deer. In the corner of the page, with a red felt-tip marker, I added a smiley face with x-ed out eyes. Then I passed Helen a bundled stack of my *New Yorker*s, and extruded myself through the tiny window and back into the light.

■

All night, Helen and I drove back and forth from the storage facility in Ruckersville, a forty-minute trip each way, past a succession of abandoned houses, motels, gas stations, barns, and churches, each of which I was tempted to stop and photograph. Hauling boxes, wrestling with furniture, sitting in the musty cab of Nolan's truck, we talked and talked, mostly about Ella but also about ourselves. And then found ourselves blinking into the cool, damp morning air. It was in the early morning that she finished the story about her trip to Tangier Island with Ella, saying that they'd also stayed up talking until nearly dawn, long past the hour that the island's watermen rose from their beds and set out into the bay; and having drawn the curtains tightly shut, they'd overslept and missed the ferry, and were obliged to stay another night. They spent the afternoon mostly in silence, drifting around the island, standing at the ends of docks watching the waves lap at the pilings, and scouring the tideline for arrowheads or shards of pots. But by dinner, their mood had lightened. They laughed and scandalized each other, slouching in their chairs. Helen managed a close approximation of the Tangier brogue. A rich, tidal odor filled their lungs, and Ella asked if Helen was on her period, and Helen pulled her waistband out, as if to check. They exhausted themselves with laughter, it gave them aches. Again, they sat up late in the dark. Helen was reading *Minima Moralia*, and Ella wanted to know what it was about. It was a long catalog, Helen told her, of the ways civilization had degraded human life: as Adorno explained in a letter to Max Horkheimer, the history of Western civilization was a permanent catastrophe, which became only the more irreparable the more doggedly civilization devoted itself to the objectives of dominating nature and capitalizing culture in the name of technological and economic progress. Disintegration was the logical conclusion of enlightenment, she said, like an island that's been sinking all along, or a human who begins dying the moment she's conceived.

Expanding upon this idea, Helen watched Ella carefully brush the sand from her ankles and the soles of her feet, and she brushed the sand from her own. After a deep sleep, they awoke in gritty bedsheets, nevertheless. The whole way home they listened to a podcast about critical theory, which they both took very much to heart. Then approaching town, Ella got an email for a new project, a music video that was to be shot in June, and with the idea that the distraction of work would do her good, three days later she boarded a flight.

■

Ella never said a word to me about where she'd been. For the three days between her return from her mysterious disappearance and her departure for France, I tiptoed around the house, waiting for her to look at me even once. We scarcely spoke, until, at the airport, she broke into tears, which ran down my neck and under my clothes. Now, I dropped Helen off at her house, parked Nolan's truck, and managed to hoist myself back through the window to replace the key, and then slept for twelve hours on their couch. I dreamed of Ella, in the dream I was me and Ella both, and I knew that to give her what she needed from me I'd have to be something other than myself. When I woke up it was twilight, and of course Helen was gone, the house was empty except for me. Behind the bathroom mirror, I found Tylenol with codeine, prescribed in Laurie's name. I took two. In the bedroom I discovered a set of DVDs, still in cellophane, comprising *Lady Snowblood* and its sequel, which Nolan must have bought on my advice. That seemed like just the thing. But whereas the first time through it had been so pleasant to escape into the distant, undespoiled world it portrayed, now a sinking, hollow feeling came over me, as I recognized Shurayuki-hime's world as contiguous with my own. More to the point, it was the same world, one in which the pursuit of ideals rapidly degenerated into the pursuit of power, and growth and expansion were both zero-sum and do-or-die, so that system-wide no one could improve his station except to the detriment of someone else, and redemption became synonymous with revenge.

What had any of this to do with Ella, beyond the basic fact that bearing witness to Ella's pain made everything more vivid and acute? The doctor had told her that failure of pregnancy was not the result of any external or emergent event, but rather was coded from the beginning into our baby's DNA. I could still feel her inside me, I heard her name with each breath I drew. Maybe it was the codeine, or just exhaustion, but sitting there in the dark on Nolan and Laurie's couch, I perceived for the first time not only that having a child is a fundamentally political act, but that hate was a prerequisite of love. Whatever you loved, the world would try to smother; that's what the world was for. Lady Snowblood's mission of vengeance is personal, it's her literal raison d'être, but it's also consonant with the struggles of, as she put it, the powerless multitudes who suffer at the hands of the rich and corrupt. It's to them, she says, as much to the memory of her mother, that she consecrates each grisly kill. *We are marked by karma even before we enter this world,* she explains, meaning roughly, I think, that she feels more keenly than most the weight of centuries bearing down upon her life.

Part 3
Summer 2016

7
Chronique d'un été

Less than twenty-four hours after I'd returned to Paris I was tear-gassed for the first time in my life. On my way to meet Ella at the hospital, I'd idly joined the ranks of a demonstration beneath the great columns that stood at the entrance to Place de la Nation. A detachment of riot police stood by in their gear, shoulder to shoulder, absorbing occasional half-hearted eruptions of abuse from the crowd, who waved their listless banners, chatting and taking selfies, although their faces were hidden behind ski goggles and handkerchiefs and masks—an atmosphere like an afternoon ball game. I was soon distracted by the shallow, rippled water running in the gutter, which was pumped up from the canal on an intricate schedule to clean the streets, and which in its vividness and clarity suggested to my jet-lagged mind a kind of continuity with my former life in Paris, a life that, in my weekly circuit of the city, seemed at times to be carried by these gentle currents—for example when, every Tuesday, after teaching an English class in a public school at Place des Fêtes, I turned the corner onto rue du Télégraphe at the very moment the waters came on and raced ahead of me downhill. And for a moment, now at Nation, I was tempted by the idea that the intervening year in Virginia had been folded into my real life only as a dream is, or a matinee. Nearby, someone was playing a guitar rendition of "El cóndor pasa," the folk song that the previous summer I'd heard three times in the course of a single commute, a coincidence that only reinforced the sensation of time's collapsing—and so on, these were the thoughts in my head when I found myself in a dense, overhead bank of fog that burned my sinuses, provoked a violent fit of coughing and gagging, and of course caused blinding tears to stream from my eyes, an experience that, in part because it coincided precisely with the onset of a severe case of hay fever that would torment me for many weeks, I'd later understand as the first of this summer's many signs of the apocalypse.

Ella and I were scheduled to see the head of the fertility team to discuss our prospects for conception—prospects I was doing all I could not to even think about. The exhilarating pain of being tear-gassed helped in this regard, as did, when finally I caught my breath and opened my eyes to find myself leaning against a cool stone wall, a plaque I took a moment to read in full. It explained that in 1660, when the present Place de la Nation had been only an empty meadow in the border region between Paris and the village of Picpus, there'd been erected an elaborate throne to mark the return of Louis XIV and his new bride from their wedding ceremony on the Pyrenean coast—and it was on this site, at the end of the eighteenth century, the plaque said, that Claude Nicolas Ledoux, a utopist city planner, erected two giant columns to mark the easternmost passage through the newly built Mur des Fermiers Généraux, where to enter the city farmers were required to pay a toll. The government christened the new square Place du Trône, but only a few years later, in the early days of the Thermidor calendar as the river literally ran red with blood, and as the smell of blood rose thickly from the paving stones, it was renamed Place du Trône Renversé, where in the course of about six summer weeks in 1794 Robespierre's guillotine separated heads from the bodies of more than 1,300 loyalists, clergymen, nobles, commoners, and Barefoot Carmelite nuns, who were tried and sentenced en masse, the heads and bodies both then to be carted in piles to the garden of the Picpus convent, where they were dumped into either of two pits, until finally the guillotine was returned to Bastille for the execution of Robespierre himself. Not long afterward, however, during the time of Napoleon, the square's original name was restored, and later, the two great columns, which had stood unfinished for half a century, were finally completed, and mounted one with a statue of Louis IX and the other a statue of

Philippe Auguste. But once again the days of the royal monarchy proved numbered: after another abortive attempt at republicanism and another interlude of imperialism, the square was renamed Place de la Nation, and on the centenary of the revolution, a bronze monument was installed at its center, depicting the figure of Marianne, the revolution's personification of liberty and reason, in the company of various allegorical figures representing republican ideals such as justice, education, and abundance, and encircled by a thrashing group of alligators, representing *threats to democracy*, which were melted down a few decades later by the Vichy regime as a contribution to the Nazi war effort.

The figures of Saint Louis and Philippe Auguste stood at a height of a hundred feet. It was impossible to tell what they made of the modest upheaval below. But likewise—I thought as I went on my way, leaving the roiling protest behind me—in Nebuchadnezzar's dream was the course of civilization represented by a towering statue of a king, smashed to bits in this case by the hand of God and scattered in the wind like chaff on the threshing floor. Or at any rate, that was Daniel's take. To hear him tell it, the commanding principle of civilization was failure. But the succession of failed civilizations the dream describes, Daniel assures Nebuchadnezzar, is itself only a prelude to the coming of the Lord's own eternal kingdom, which would appear on earth in the due course of time. It was in the windowless waiting room, reading Rachel Cusk's divorce memoir, that these thoughts came into focus; relative to the messy breakdown of her marriage, Cusk describes how in the turmoil that follows the collapse of a massive and unified society such as the Holy Roman Empire, inhere inherent the dark, fractured stirrings of creativity that will eventually give rise to something new. And point being that when Ella and I finally took our seats across the desk from Docteur LeFebvre, an ashen-faced woman in late middle age, she applied more or less the same logic to Ella's reproductive apparatus. As traumatic as it had been, she said, now in the aftermath of a miscarriage Ella was likely more fertile than ever, and though she understood that I'd return to Virginia in the fall and that it frightened us to imagine once again being separated in the tenuous early stages of a pregnancy, the time to act was now.

■

Everyone kept asking me how it was to be back in Paris, neighbors I passed in the stairs, friends of my in-laws, the woman from the bakery who called me Monsieur l'Américain. What they wanted to know was whether the atmospheric tension that had been mounting since I'd left—the suspicious packages that were always interrupting train service, the continued rise of social and economic nationalism, the graffiti everywhere and the military patrols—had reached such a pitch as to be apparent even to me. In fact, this tension formed the basis of the general feeling of overstimulation I had, the thrill of living in interesting, dangerous times. The demonstration I'd stumbled into, for example, was in protest of modest changes Hollande's administration had proposed for the labor code; further protests were scheduled on an escalating scale throughout the summer, while in parallel a corps of the faithful, drawing inspiration from Zuccotti Park, had occupied Place de la République, where they'd set up a little tent city and made it the headquarters of a grimy, catch-all movement called Nuit Debout, the sort of public assembly that was officially forbidden under the ongoing state of emergency that had been renewed in May. In public spaces, loud noises and sudden commotions made people flinch, and meantime as hosts of the Euro Final, Parisians were nervous about the arrival in their city of hundreds of thousands of soccer fans from all over the continent, who, I was told, would be intoxicated on a continual basis from the moment they set down their bags, and would charge through the streets waving their arms around and making noises at all hours of day and night. A dense fog settled over Paris at a height of about four stories; at a certain point, I said to Ella one morning, we'd have to call it clouds, and in fact that afternoon a driving rain began to fall and didn't relent for days.

The doughy boy with enormous ears I'd seen the previous summer or-ganizing the distribution of ice cream sandwiches had been transformed by puberty: not much taller, but sharper, more fully in possession of his body. Whenever I saw him outside the grocery store, he was surrounded by kids competing for his attention, which he bestowed upon them with a certain warmth. The condo building next to ours was finished and, apart from the retail space on the ground floor, fully occupied; our new neighbors, whom we saw sometimes in the street deploying their pocket umbrellas or checking the soles of their shoes, seemed somehow more crisply defined than the rest of us, if only because they were younger and their clothes were new. In metro stations all around the city, meanwhile, the destitute identified themselves as Syrian refugees not only with handmade cardboard signs written in both French and Arabic, but also with documents they held up for inspection, passports and asylum papers, in order, I learned, to authenticate the basis of their claim to sympathy, since a consensus appeared to have emerged among the French that these ubiquitous *familles syriennes* were not *syriennes* at all.

It troubled me that the French regarded themselves as vulnerable to such a ploy, whether it was real or imagined—that they would willingly admit that their sympathy was in such short supply. At lunch across the hall at Ella's mom's, I discovered that Clarisse felt the same way. Human rights aren't rights, she said with feeling, if you have to apply for them. The rain fell harder and harder, against the tin roof and the skylights. In Clarisse's apartment there were dozens of plants, succulents and shrubs and orchids of all kinds, lined up on tables and windowsills, clustered on the floor, hanging from the rafters, and as she spoke she stood up from the table to water them. It wasn't uncommon, at meals with Clarisse, to see her pound her fists on the table in frustration, but in the most passionate moments of any argument, without interrupting herself she would often calmly rise from her seat to do something useful—to clear the table or water the plants or check a cake she had in the oven, or fetch the little cookie tin in which she kept her rolling papers and her pot. If you have to apply for them, they're privileges, she said. So okay, fine, but call it what it is. This lunch took place around the time the flooding started. The day before our long walk up and down the river, Ella had finished a project she'd been working on, the casting of an entire classroom of twelve-year-olds in a tough, ethnically diverse public school, to accomplish which, because unlike Hollywood the French film industry lacked an entire subclass of professional child actors, she'd gone looking in the real world of ethnically diverse children who went to tough schools, such as her own middle school, Collège Henri Matisse, just off Place de la Réunion, where she'd sit outside with a book as the kids let out for the day, watching them holler and horse around until it was obvious which were the most natural and charismatic, whom she'd then approach in an attitude that split the difference between openhearted warmth, a kind of charming, ironical flirtation, and levelheaded professionalism, a working process that left her with little emotional stamina to deal with me. For the length of our walk that day, I had her to myself, but the following Monday, she started a new project, a music video, with the result that my own days—once I'd perfected numerous variations of my résumé and replied to every single TOEFL post on Craigslist—were empty; and, because when the sun came out even on mild days our apartment got untenably warm, this meant I was back to wandering the streets and approaching strangers as well.

■

And in truth, despite my debilitating hay fever, despite the awkwardness of my French, and despite the fact that I didn't have enough money in my pockets or in my bank account to buy so much as a glass of beer in any of the exceptionally pleasant-looking places beer was available in Paris, I recognized a certain luxury in the rhythm of these days. The chaos around me (what felt like chaos at the time) was intoxicating. It's hard to imagine now, but that summer felt like being aboard a ship bearing down on a rocky shoal; we all saw it drawing near, but didn't doubt the helmsman's competence to steer a course around it. And my instinct was that the better I understood the danger, the more thrilling would be the eventual near miss. In fifty years we'll tell our grandchildren, I said to Ella, that 2016 was the year we came right up to the brink. (Our grandchildren, Ella echoed.) At night I sat up in bed with Ella's iPad, fanning out in tabs the myriad analyses to be found on the websites of foreign policy think tanks, which all agreed that although it was unthinkable that the Brexit campaign would succeed, the very fact of it, like Donald Trump's imminent nomination as a presidential candidate, served as an alarming index of the purchase populist nationalism was gaining worldwide. Whereas the metaphor of choice for Grexit had been parenthood, for Brexit it became marriage and divorce. In the mornings while I drank my coffee I'd sit at my desk on the mezzanine, sending job applications into the void, watching a tuft of pigeon down that had come in through the skylight drift across the floorboards in the drafts that swept through the room. And then after a long shower I'd wander across the twentieth, across the nineteenth, carrying a deep supply of Kleenex, following vague impulses in the direction of something that seemed to wait around each corner, at the top of each staircase, at the end of each alley, some reward for my attentiveness and my receptiveness that never came into view. In the sandy medians of the boulevards there were always men playing boules. On the terraces of cafés, men crossed their legs at the knee. All sorts of ordinary details were heightened in my experience of them, only by virtue of their relation to the gathering storm. Sooner or later I always ended up at Canal de l'Ourcq, which I'd follow south—past the cafés and bookstores that had been installed in former barges, past a man with a casting rod who looked like Howard Stern—toward Stalingrad, where the metro emerged from underground, in the shadows of whose tracks, and in a park just north, I found that as many as two thousand asylum seekers from places like Sudan, Eritrea, Somalia, Iraq, and Afghanistan had made shelter in tents, beneath tarps, in cardboard boxes, and on mats in the open air.

Matter of fact, this is what I'd come to see, not even really unconsciously— it brought the concept of urban civilization into a new clarity, worlds within worlds within worlds. There was nothing for the occupants of these dwellings, the men and women and children who lived in this place, there was nothing for them to do during the day but wait; under French law, they had the legal right to emergency housing while their asylum applications were processed, but for the moment, according to the Ministry of the Interior, no such housing existed. In certain ways I was reminded of delays I'd endured at LaGuardia, or rather, it seemed possible that the uncertainty, frustration, helplessness, and tormented hope that were evident in this scene of institutional breakdown existed on the far end of a continuum of human experience that also included the unpleasantness of waiting for a flight in a crowded airport—an observation I recorded in my notebook along with a warning never to share it with anyone. But point being people carved out personal space wherever they could, abided the distress of their situation however they could, burying their faces in the crooks of their elbows, shouting into cell phones, turning the pages of paperbacks and magazines. It was difficult to understand how so vast a government, a government that employed 20 percent of the working population of France, could fail so utterly to make something happen here. But like many vulnerable populations, the migrants' main point of contact with the state was the police: one day I arrived at the site to find it abandoned, cleared out by gendarmes with bullhorns and pepper spray and batons: heaps of waste and sodden cardboard and crumpled tents and dirty, disemboweled mattresses, the decomposing ruins of a society that would nevertheless reconstitute itself by the end of the week.

■

Later on some of these afternoons I got calls for job interviews and took the train to distant quarters of the city, where in classrooms strung with clotheslines from which finger paintings hung to dry, my interviewer would listen skeptically as I explained my interest in working with young children, and would then instruct me to pretend she was a toddler and to select a story to read her in its entirety, pausing at teachable moments, such as the appearance of a doggy or a kitty or a tree—and pausing occasionally to stem the flow of snot from my nose with a tissue balled in my fist—an exercise that invariably concluded with an offer of roughly the same salary I'd earned in a hardware store at the age of fifteen, for a position that at any rate wouldn't begin until the second week of September, long after I'd returned to the States.

Afterward, when Ella returned from work, it proved difficult to relate these encounters in a way that both made her laugh and didn't make her feel hopeless about the prospect of my ever making any meaningful contribution to our financial partnership; instead, I'd pepper her with questions about her work, but she was always too exhausted to respond. After I finished the dishes, since she usually still had a few hours of editing and cataloging audition footage to do, I'd once again be overcome by an urge to get out of the house—out of range of Ella's indifference. Night after night I'd take the train to République, where the evening's Nuit Debout program was just getting under way, an erratic schedule consisting mostly of information sessions that were in fact opinion sessions, and a lot of invective spoken through bullhorns or soggy, shoddily wired PAs. All the while, dozens of unaffiliated skateboarders threaded themselves through these crowds at terrific speeds, and performed their astonishing stunts with such aplomb and finesse that by comparison the earnest, un-washed Nuit Debout types sitting cross-legged on carpet remnants all around me, listening to reggae and eating merguez and drinking enormous cans of beer, seemed somewhat less than fully alive.

At home I'd find Ella asleep with the light on, and by the time I'd reviewed my notes from the day and put out the light so that I could sleep as well, it seemed an impossibly long time had passed since I'd visited the migrant camps that morning, and I would awaken the next day resolved to return, without quite understanding why. In the days and weeks that fol-lowed, I became impressed by certain informal conventions that developed there, as compared with République, such as the orderly accommodations that were made for the drying of clothes, or the tidy rows of shoes you'd sometimes see where mattresses were lined up edge to edge. Naturally, privacy was scarce, but on the other hand there were less conspicuous places to assemble camps in and around the city; and though I was ashamed of the need I felt to be here as a witness, the visibility was the very point, the migrants themselves had chosen this place precisely in order not to be ignored—that it was a moral imperative of this historic tragedy to hold it in my mind as the summed grief and suffering of individuals. There were TV crews trawling the perimeters of the camps for human narratives to publicize, purportedly for this very purpose. But the alacrity with which they pursued these narratives—an almost carnal appetite for the personal wretchedness they were documenting, which flashed hotly behind their eyes in the moment before, say, they pulled back a tent flap and pointed a camera inside—made me uneasy about my own intentions, which at bottom of course were the same. For this reason I confined myself to observing from a certain middle distance, from which minor, unrecorded gestures of kindness took on enormous and sentimental proportions for me—a group of people passing around a bottle of orange soda, for example. The smattering of volunteers had a similar effect, individual citizens and grass-roots charitable organizations who brought cauldrons of soup and crates of bread. A woman named Mathilde, a white lady with her hair tied in a rolled-up bandanna, had assembled a neighborhood collective that served dozens of hot meals every night. I asked her reasons for doing so, expecting a diatribe against the ineffectual and disinterested government of France. This is where I live, she told me instead. The French, she said, we expect the government to take care of everything, like spoiled teenagers; that's why there's so much dog shit in the streets. She untied the bandanna and used it to wipe sweat from her neck and beneath her collarbones. There are people in my neighborhood, she went on, who feel themselves to be the victims of this situation; the camps are unsightly, and they smell, and they take up too much space. They're repulsed, is what it is, they're leery of dirty Africans hanging around on their sidewalks and in their parks. And I'm being entirely literal when I say they're talking about organizing a hunger strike, to force the government to move the camps. And so if you do nothing, she said, retying her hair, that's the world you deserve: a world where it makes more sense to starve yourself than to offer to share your food.

■

It was that same day, the day I spoke to Mathilde, that a trash strike began, and already garbage had begun to amass on every corner in stinking heaps. At République that night I was less circumspect in approaching protesters, who, unlike the migrants, I felt owed the world an explanation for their presence in the streets. Relative to how strongly they felt about it, however, very few of the people I spoke with there could describe their objections to the new labor code with any specificity; worker's rights were under siege, was as far as I ever got. Then, finally, hanging from a line strung between two trees, my eyes fell on a handwritten poster that read AVOCAT DEBOUT. The middle-aged man who stood there in a newsboy cap, holding his beer bottle between his knees while he lit his new cigarette with his old cigarette, turned out to be not an avocado but a labor lawyer, whose business here was to offer free advice; he'd grown up in the village of Longwy, he told me, in the north, where his father worked in the iron mines, and so he understood better than most how important it was for working people to have access to the law.

What I liked about talking to Corbin, as he turned out to be called, was that he spoke in slow, simple sentences that I could understand because they were in English, and that he, too, watched the skateboarders raptly, interrupting himself from time to time to admire their most impressive feats. Unlike the people standing all around us, at the Écologie Debout stall, for example, the seats of whose pants were crusted with dirt, Corbin's pants were clean, and this was because, as the banner he was flying implied, standing up was the whole point. In essence, he told me, changes to the labor code allowed for the temporary circumvention of national regulations on overtime, unfair dismissal payments, and vacation time by a local vote, whereas previously such circumventions could only take place industry-wide. For emphasis, he hefted his personal copy of the present code, as if its defects were obvious from a demonstration of its terrific weight. I found it difficult to understand, I said, why workers would so vehemently oppose a law whose effects could only be implemented by their own consent. Sign of the times, Corbin said, of the general atmosphere of distrust in neoliberalism that even the most modest implementation of market logic caused convulsions nationwide. One such example of these convulsions, he added, would follow later that week, when a demonstration in the south of the city was predicted to draw hundreds of thousands or perhaps even a million people out into the streets.

How we arrived there I'm not sure—perhaps in connection with the so-called spirit of '68 people kept invoking, which Corbin felt arose from an instinct to bend historical narratives toward the future—but later in the same conversation, I learned that there was an exhibit of 250 works by Paul Klee at the Pompidou, and that among them was the tiny but extremely famous *Angelus Novus*, which had once belonged to Walter Benjamin and which, on loan from the Israel Museum in Jerusalem, was now returned to Paris for the first time since Benjamin fled the city in 1940, before taking a fatal dose of morphine tablets in the foothills of the Pyrenees when the fascist government of Spain ordered his return to France. I wanted very much to see the so-called Angel of History, but when, the day after my conversation with Corbin, I expanded my daily circuit to include a visit to the Pompidou, I found the square teeming with tourists and street performers, and a line for tickets that curled around the block. So instead, I decided to go another day, and found my way back to the nineteenth, and, maybe out of determination to have an experience of culture, I went past the migrant camps to the Cent-Quatre, the arts center that nearly two years before had hosted the human zoo installation. Having previously visited the Cent-Quatre only at night, I wasn't quite prepared for how impressive the space would be in the daytime, flooded with light and air. Though it more closely resembled a nineteenth-century railway terminal, with its cupola bell, its clockface, its high archways, and the canopied glass roof laid over a cast-iron frame, the building was originally constructed, in the 1870s, on the site of a defunct slaughterhouse, as the operational headquarters of the Service Municipal des Pompes Funèbres, in which capacity, until the end of the twentieth century, it dispatched the mortal remains of roughly 150 departed souls to their final resting places every day. In the wide-open hall of the eastern building, and in its many niches and alcoves, where formerly dozens of hearses had been garaged and hundreds of horses stabled, dancers of all kinds had carved out space to train in their various disciplines: classical and modern ballet, break dance, hip-hop, Afrobeat, soft-shoe, ballroom styles such as salsa and the foxtrot, as well as a number of dance-adjacent acrobatic practices, for example a giant metal ring called a Cyr wheel, in which one became a kind of gyroscopically kinetic Vitruvian Man. For the most part, a security guard told me, these were local residents, members of the immigrant communities of the eighteenth and nineteenth arrondissements, to whom the administration made the grounds available in accordance with its core philosophy of good neighborship. In a vague, approximate way, the space was divided by portable partitions made from aluminum tubing and sheets of Plexiglas of such deeply obsidian black that they doubled as studio mirrors. In one, I watched the dark reflection of a woman doing a one-armed handstand. In another, three teenage girls were rehearsing an irresistible routine of their own invention to a song I recognized as Nicki Minaj—angels of history of an entirely different sort, all of which in the bustling midst of the center's more official structures: art-related shops, cafés, a bookstore, a vaguely organic-looking playroom, lots of signage directing visitors to the bathrooms or to the western end of the complex, where the coffins used to be built. Enchanted as I was, it took me a long time to perceive that in the culture of this space there'd developed a nuanced understanding of what was on display and what wasn't—that is, it took me a long time to notice that none of these other visitors to the cafés and exhibitions and restrooms was openly gawking at any of the dancers, none but me, a transgression that when it came to my attention made my eyes burn with a mortification I promptly sat down to describe in my notes, in a kind of frantic penmanship I'd never be able to read, and looking up from the page not once until I'd finished, only to find myself staring into the inky depths of another of the plastic screens, on the surface of which I encountered a dim, elusive reflection of my face that I would try to reassemble a few days later, in a calm moment after the raging fires of the protest were put out, when I found myself inspecting the scattered shivers of black glass that had melted into the street.

■

This was on the opposite end of the city. Corbin had told me that at the head of the demonstration there was certain to be a group of masked teens and twenty-somethings dressed in black; this was the Black Bloc, whose method was to use the occasion of larger protests to wage war on the state itself. They carried rocks in their bags, and explosives and crowbars and pipes. If I was looking for some action, Corbin said, giving me a little wag of his eyebrows, these were the people I had to find.

In Place d'Italie a kind of fairground had been established: food stalls selling kebab and cups of beer, DJs in every direction playing reggae and classic rock, horns and whistles sounding at random near and far, and, stretching their tethers to the limit in the sky, giant, harmless balloons. The smell of sulfur was thick in the air, and occasionally the reports of flares and fireworks could be heard. Children rode their fathers' shoulders, invariably looking a bit dazed. Adults wiped their greasy hands on their pants and clapped each other on the back. On a flatbed truck, a band wearing Smurf hats was playing a song called "Whipping Post," and there was no clear indication they'd ever stop. A lot of leather, I wrote in my notes: a lot of mustaches, a lot of sideburns, soul patches, mutton chops, crow's-feet, and everyone dressed in shades of red, hoisting signs that said things like WE REFUSE TO BE SLAVES or THEY'RE SUCKING THE MARROW FROM OUR BONES. A large pink man in a denim vest and a Che Guevara t-shirt, who turned out to be a metro conductor from the south, was waving a flag featuring a skull with sharp fangs and a spiky mohawk: this was the logo, he told me jovially, of the Exploited, an anarchist punk band from Scotland that (I learned later) was popular with skinheads, possibly because its lead singer had a swastika tattoo. When I asked the large pink man, the sides of whose head were shaved bald and whose hair was pulled back in a greasy little curlicue, why he was waving this flag, he said only that he was angry, that he was very angry; he didn't look angry, he looked like he was enjoying himself tremendously, but I decided to take him at his word, and asked what specifically made him so very angry. It was the system that made him so very angry, the system that was sucking the marrow from his bones, he said, and he might have said more, but he was busy gnawing on the cudgel of salami he held in his other paw.

The march set out along avenue des Gobelins, where the smoke grew thicker and the hissing and crackling of road flares, which sprayed showers of neon-red sparks into the air all around, grew louder and more menacing. It wasn't long before I found myself caught in a little slipstream behind a column of masked, black-clad guerrillas and self-appointed field medics in bicycle helmets working their way toward the front of the line, from where dense billows of white smoke were rising. A helicopter that flew past overhead, not so high above the mansard rooftops, made my blood race, as did the sight of a potbellied man with his t-shirt tucked in, on his hands and knees at the base of a sycamore, retching into the dirt. Farther along, behind an overturned Citroën, the group I was following paused to get their gear out of their bags. Nearby, a pair of armored policemen was beating a clumsy retreat; I was astonished when a masked figure came running out of nowhere and launched himself through the air to jump-kick one of them in the back: the first policeman hurtled into the back of the second, and they both stumbled to the ground in a tangle of armored limbs. The assailant and the policemen scrambled to their feet; during the long, tense moment that they stood facing each other, I held my breath. Then one of the cops stomped the pavement and gave a little feint with his baton, and the assailant disappeared. And at that moment, even as flames and smoke rose around me, I was overtaken by a memory from adolescence, a game we used to play in the leafy back lanes of my Connecticut hometown after school, which involved calling the police on ourselves from a pay phone and then leading the responding officers on long foot chases through our neighborhood, where we knew all the shortcuts and hiding places by heart; whenever they started to lose the trail, we'd pop out from behind a hedge to show them our bare asses, or out of a garden shed to pelt their cruisers with fresh tomatoes, so that the game could go on and on until finally it was time to go home and eat; prolonging the game was the whole point—prolonging the illusion of danger, because even if it had been possible for us to be caught, being sent to bed without supper was really the worst we could expect.

For the rest of the march, I thought of Ella, or rather, I felt her presence within me, and felt keenly how I'd let her down. More than once, I lingered in the drift of tear gas, let it fill my sinuses and blind my eyes, as if to prove to her my own capacity for pain. This was an instinct more than a thought. There were fires everywhere, and shattered glass crunched beneath my feet, and the symbols of anarchy and communism were freshly painted on the walls, against which, at one point, I saw a detachment of riot cops huddled behind their shields, which were being pelted with glass bottles and cobblestones the size of fists. Approaching boulevard du Montparnasse I frequently heard the abrupt crack of tear-gas cannons launching canisters that left contrails hanging in the air around us and clattered on the pavement at our feet, and, less frequently, the earthshaking blasts of Molotov cocktails that protesters were hurling into the closed ranks of the police, who scattered to avoid the flames. Standing with the photographers in the no-man's-land between the anarchists and the state, I straightened my spine as an M80 landed close enough to hear the hiss of the fuse, and to see its tiny shower of sparks. The extraordinary volume of the explosion knocked me off my feet, and that was how I came face-to-face with my dim reflection in a half-melted shard of glass.

■

My ears rang for an hour or more. Beneath the ringing, almost too faintly to make out, I heard the sound of Ella's voice. You stupid, was one of the things it said. Later, on the bus home, I ran into Clarisse, and I found myself describing, in better French than I'd ever heard myself speak, everything I'd seen. I was thunderstruck, foudroyé, I told her, when, hours into the march, a large, hostile crowd stood chanting and pounding their chests, apparently at the occupants of a public children's hospital housed in a great glass building that soon came under a barrage of stones and bottles and broken pieces of pipe. Only then, I said to Clarisse—as once again snot began pouring from my nose and I searched my pockets for the least disgusting of the soiled tissues I was still carrying—only then, standing there watching a young woman take a ballpeen hammer out of her pants, did it occur to me to wonder what sort of world these people hoped would replace the one they were trying to burn down.

A world without hospitals, Clarisse said, passing me a Kleenex from her purse. For a few stops we rode in silence, as I tried to recompose myself. We were seated facing each other, against the window, and I stole a glance at her face as we crossed Pont de Tolbiac and she gazed east up the river, where barges marked LAFARGE were being loaded with dirt and sand and rock. I wondered what Ella had said to her about how things between us had broken down—I wanted to ask her (because I knew submitting myself to arbitrary danger and bodily harm wasn't it): What could I do to make things right? Still, she said eventually, returning to our conversation, even if it was true that the French Black Bloc was mostly disenchanted children of privilege, they were nevertheless fighting to correct injustices that didn't directly touch their lives and that would be very easy for them to ignore. She took her glasses off and massaged the bridge of her nose. Maybe they were bored or vain or just wanted to impress girls. But it was possible they were motivated by a sense of human solidarity as well, she said, whereas it would be difficult to mobilize the labor movement on behalf of any cause but its own, the cause of defending against even the slightest encroachment upon the privileges and protections they've enjoyed since '68—which, she said finally, handing me another Kleenex, although it seemed progressive when its antagonist was Hollande, would quickly reveal its nature if even a handful of the millions of migrants in Europe were granted the right to work in France.

■

At the greengrocer when we got off the bus, I waited while Clarisse, in a posture of skepticism she and Ella shared, picked out some lemons and shallots and a bouquet of cilantro, as well as a little vial of eucalyptus extract and a box of sliced pineapple, both of which turned out to be for me. She'd bought tickets to a dance performance in Montreuil for the following evening, she told me as we climbed the stairs, but it turned out she couldn't go, so if Ella and I wanted them, she said, the tickets were ours.

Arriving early, we ended up with seats in the front row, which is to say, on the floor that was also the stage, at the other side of which a gigantic figure in a black suit stood in the shadows with its face hidden by dark sunglasses—a figure of not quite human proportions whose skin was a shiny white plastic and that, when it suddenly started into motion and sank heavily to its knees, caused a shock to run through me from which I didn't recover for the length of the show. The performance proved to entail a series of stunning manipulations of plastic and air, and the first of these began when the kneeling figure produced a translucent pink grocery bag, along with a pair of scissors and a roll of tape; after a few painstaking incisions and transplantations, the plastic bag was transformed into a vaguely human form. A number of industrial fans were arranged cheek to cheek around the stage in a circle, and when they came on, the miniature human was inflated, became lifelike, and as if from joy leapt, pirouetting high into the air toward the lights, more gracefully and weightlessly than a real dancer could ever hope to do, before gently descending and then leaping high into the air again, and so on, in obvious contrast to the heaviness of the monstrous figure in black, who watched its creation twirl in the air in an attitude of abject longing. And then, as if it couldn't help itself, it pulled another dancer, premade, from the hip pocket of its suit, and now these two dancers moved together through the air in such perfect synchronization with the Debussy that had begun to play that it was almost impossible not to credit them with some of the lovelier aspects of sentience—if not quite consciousness, I thought, then a kind of somatic joy. Soon the air was full of these dancers, dozens of them in different colors, and the magic they performed was no less a source of wonder to their ungainly creator than it was a source of torment; before long, in a sudden fit of violence, as the Debussy gave way to something far more sinister, it began to snatch them out of the air and tear them, so to speak, limb from limb, forming from their remains a great mass in the center of the floor, to which it added its clothes as well as its white plastic skin, which it peeled off in a kind of spasm; the figure that stood before us now was itself a sort of plastic bag, an immense black kind of swamp creature that began to perform a grotesque parody of the colorful grocery bags it had just destroyed. Shortly this layer, too, was shed and reanimated by the wind exactly as the grocery bags had been; it became a nine-foot dancing partner for the skulking, tightly wrapped figure that was revealed beneath it, which likewise soon dissolved in a fit of frustration and rage. Over the course of the next forty-five minutes, this cycle of whimsy and fury continued layer by layer—at one point more than two hundred meters of plastic was churning in the air above the stage like a cyclone—until finally the recognizably human form of a pregnant woman emerged, and delivered herself, by way of a simulated birth canal, of a thin sheet of plastic that she then carefully arranged around herself in a circle on the floor, so that, when the fans began to turn once again, the circle began to close around her, until she was sealed within it like a womb.

I was intrigued to discover in the program that the performer, Phia Ménard, a trans woman in her mid-forties, had begun her career as a juggler, a practice that, when she first encountered it as a confused adolescent, provided her first inkling of the joyous purposes to which her body could be turned. I mentioned this to Ella as we walked to the train, who so far had said nothing about what we'd seen. I'm not like you, she said. I want to sit with this, I'm not ready just like that to transform it into talk. It was nearly ten o'clock, and the sun had only just set. In this late daylight, the public square that the theater shared with Montreuil's city hall was full of life. And the air, too, which for weeks had seemed so thick, was light and fresh on the surface of our skin. The terrace of a shabby little café was less than half full, and when I suggested on a whim that we sit for a drink, Ella surprised me by agreeing it would be nice. The waiter went off with our order, and we sat watching the modest little scenes unfold in the various existences being conducted side by side here in the square. Our drinks arrived, and mechanically we touched glasses, then for a few minutes we drank in silence. Against the sky, which was only just beginning to fade, the darting shadows of martins and swifts made invisible patterns, which I tried to visualize and preserve in my mind. The performance had moved me profoundly, and I wanted to find a way to express the mark it had made without claiming to identify with the pain and alienation it described. Without *admitting* that I did. But, setting her glass down on the tabletop, it was Ella who broke the silence, as I continued to watch the birds and the gathering dusk. It had only just occurred to her, she said, how strange her days had been since she'd begun work on her latest project. All day she stalked through public spaces in search of young women who, in their most superficial features—height, body type, hairstyle, skin tone—described a version of herself that belonged six or seven years in the past, before we'd met, a version of herself to which she no longer felt any connection. What did it mean about the life you were living, she wanted to know, that from one year to the next you felt no sense of continuity with the selves you left behind you? It had become an unconscious mental habit of hers, she said, to search the faces of strangers for signs of these former selves of hers, as if there were some concrete reality she might discover in the past of which her life now was only a shadow.

That morning, for the second time that week, she'd risen before dawn in order to be near the front of the line at the maternity hospital for a series of blood tests and ultrasounds that were required for participation in a fertility study that had the potential to dramatically increase her chances of carrying a pregnancy to term. The clinic wouldn't open until eight thirty, but the waiting room was full by seven; unlike other times of day, however, when it was dominated by couples, who tended to erect an invisible boundary between themselves and the world, in the early morning there were only women present. Naturally the atmosphere was thick with their anxiety and their anguish, Ella said, but on the other hand, a certain tenderness was palpable in the air as well, a solidarity that underpinned every utterance and gesture and exchange of glances. The usual barriers to communication that you found in public spaces were absent here; the most intimate conversations developed easily, without preamble, and were open for public participation. Almost anywhere else in the world, even in countries with excellent socialized health care, advanced fertility treatment was a privilege enjoyed only by the wealthy. But in a public clinic in France, as though it could be a matter of public policy that the future belonged to us all, women who otherwise would rarely have occasion to interact shared with each other the most intimate particulars— about their bodies, about their sex lives, about the pain they'd endured and the heartbreak—frankly and on equal footing: for example this morning she'd listened as a Muslim woman in a headscarf, a stern-faced white woman in black jeans, and a thuggish black girl in sweatpants discussed in exhaustive detail their partners' sexual idiosyncrasies, the volume of sperm they produced for collection, and the emotional toll the long process of assisted conception appeared to exact upon them over time—a conversation to which women around the room, fitting every description, contributed as they saw fit. She didn't like to think of herself as particularly susceptible to saccharine images of social harmony, Ella said, but, as Phia Ménard had put it in brief remarks during the curtain call, the world felt increasingly riven by constructed differences, and it was satisfying to be part of a community that arose spontaneously on the strength of a shared experience that rendered those differences moot. Only tonight, she said, as we were filing out of the theater and she'd begun to turn the performance over in her mind, did she perceive how disappointed she'd been that morning when finally her number was called, and how eager she was now to go to sleep, the sooner to wake and reclaim her place in the crowded, windowless room where, more than anywhere else of late, she felt like a three-dimensional human.

It's taken a distance of four years, and the whole rest of civilization grinding to a halt, for me to see how this was a deliberate act of generosity on her part, to invite me like that into her inner life. She was teaching me how to love her—she was telling me what she needed, and it wasn't even all that much. At the time, though, my gratitude was more instinctive. We talked for a long time, nursing our drinks, and though I don't think we added any further insight to her initial remarks, I was overwhelmed by a sense of well-being; and I wondered whether we hadn't finally achieved between us the détente we'd pursued without success during the long day of our walk along the Seine. Our waiter was a dark-haired boy of about eighteen or nine-teen, whose serious expression, as well as an unnatural deepness he let into his voice, betrayed a satisfaction I remembered from the early days of my own career in the service industry—the thrill of being in contact, through my work, with the ways of the adult world. Ella caught his eye, and when he came hustling over with the check, she gave him a bill from her wallet and said good night.

By this time the Euro Final had begun, matches were scheduled all day, and exactly as I'd been warned there were slavering fans everywhere you looked—a group of them boarded the train at Porte de Montreuil and sat across from us, shirtless, wrapped in their respective banners, lost, maybe, on their way home from a visit to what was called Le Fan Zone: in the center of the city, beneath the Eiffel Tower, authorities had staked out space where each day, between noon and midnight, as many as ninety-two thou-sand people could, after a long queue at the security checkpoint at which they'd be frisked and made to pass through a metal detector, be admitted on a standing-room-only basis to watch hours-long matches live on a screen the size of a basketball court. Imagine having one life to live, I said to Ella as we were walking home from our stop, and spending even a minute of it in Le Fan Zone. A new restaurant had opened around the corner from our house, a wine bar called La Chouette de Minerve, and the barman had just stepped outside to smoke, running his hands through his wavy red hair. Printed on his t-shirt, in enormous letters, were the words GANDHI SAYS RELAX. Ella and I read this message at the same time as we walked past, and a moment later when our eyes met, she made a face that's very typical of

French people, whose approximate meaning, in this case, was that we had just shared the experience of looking at an asshole. This gave me an excellent feeling, because, I decided later, once we were home in bed and Ella was fast asleep, it gave me reason to believe that, in her private ranking of the world's most fatuous men, which I suspected she kept fairly up to date, for the moment there was at least this one guy ahead of me.

■

The day after the performance in Montreuil, I received a call from a company whose name sounded like nothing so much as the name of an escort agency, and was given an appointment to interview for a position not as an escort but as an English instructor to what the voice on the other end of the line kept calling *high-powered international financiers*. This voice, it turned out, belonged to the founder, director, and sole employee of Full Service VIP, who was wearing a pantsuit when I met her that afternoon in a café near Montparnasse, where glass was still scattered in the street and the bombed-out husk of the same overturned Citroën had yet to be towed away. During the interview I wasn't required to speak at all, but rather to absorb—along with a fair amount of condescension about the companies I'd listed on my résumé, with respect to a lack of distinction she seemed to assume based on the absence from their names of the terms *Full Service* and *VIP*—various nonsensical permutations of the same few words: *high-powered, executive, international, multinational, global network, global resources, global philosophy, high-finance, high-end, high-pressure, upscale, upmarket, business marketplace, business environment,* and *market opportunity,* this last of which in apparent connection with the preternatural business acumen she herself had demonstrated by launching a Business English company in Paris. The phrase *Full Service,* she went on to explain, was more than a clever *branding strategy*; a crucial part of the what she provided was not only to teach her clients proper American Business English, which was considered more *prestigious* than British Business English in the *global business marketplace,* and not only to teach them proper American manners, which were more prestigious than French manners, but also to impart to them something of the ruthless spirit of American capitalism, for which even high-end French people lacked a natural instinct. She had enjoyed chatting with me, she said when the waiter brought the check, and although my résumé didn't meet her usual standards she was going to give me a shot, because of our shared background in hospitality, to express my gratitude for which magnanimity I was given my first chance to speak. She didn't have any work for me now, she said once I'd thanked her to her satisfaction, but in the event that something came up in the future, she wanted to know if I had a different tie.

■

In the evenings, Ella and I watched films like *La pointe courte* and *Chronique d'un été*, and then when they ended, leaving the TV on so that she wouldn't wake to find herself alone in total darkness, I'd slip on my shoes and trot out into the nighttime air. After some initial apprehension about intruding on territory the neighborhood's teenagers had claimed for themselves, I made it my habit to scramble up the wall on our street and walk south along the Petite Ceinture, which runs along the city's outer edge, where the buildings on either side of the tracks formed a kind of defile of rear windows at which I caught tantalizing glimpses into the private lives of people I'd previously only ever seen in the street. When maybe an hour had passed I'd double back and climb the stairs to our apartment, where I'd crawl into bed and begin the long process of trying to fall asleep; most nights, however, our new neighbors on the top floor of the new condo building, whose charming roof terrace was directly level with the skylight above our bed, were hosting parties that tended to reach their loudest phase just as my eyelids began to sink, so that I was left with the option of either closing the windows and steaming us alive, or lying awake until the party died down, always marveling at the convention according to which, late in the evening at parties given by the spawn of the French bourgeoisie, everyone in attendance was to sing along at the top of their lungs to a selection of favorite rock standards they all seemed to share, so that the whole night felt like a wedding where Journey had just come on, which was not only my least favorite part of weddings, but also my least favorite part of being alive. Was it possible, I'd always end up asking myself, to make a Molotov cocktail from materials I had in the house? On the summer solstice, as France celebrated La Fête de la Musique and as Ella and I celebrated the fifth anniversary of our wedding, the sun didn't set until after ten, and it was another hour still until it was fully dark. Having failed to make any plans that suited our budget, we simply spent an hour or so following the sounds of music in the street—of drum circles and house music and an extraordinarily poor, ska-inflected Nirvana cover band that was playing outside a bar—and then we picked up bo bun on our way home, where we watched *Le fond de l'air est rouge* in two installments: part one on the projector downstairs, and part two on the TV in bed. Back on the train tracks that night, rather than walk south, as was my habit, I walked north, past the back of our own building toward the tunnel. I hadn't gotten far, however, before I saw that on the rooftop of the building next to ours another soiree was getting started; I stood for a moment craning my neck to watch the silhouettes assembled at the railings, inscrutable figures who chatted in the amiable, hushed way of people who are not yet drunk. And then, as I turned to go, it was curious to see that on the ground floor, in the large, yet-to-be-rented retail space, a cluster of stout little halogen work lamps were casting twisted shadows around the room, and that the unfinished floor was lined with mattresses, thirty of them or more, in the spaces between which were strewn the various appurtenances of the men who were lying there with their hands over their eyes, or moving carefully about the room on little personal errands, barefoot or in flip-flops, carrying toiletries under their arms and baguettes, or leaning against the unpainted walls and cracking large cans of beer, the total meaning of which scene it took me a minute to compute. Or in fact I was somewhat stunned. Although I understood safeguarding the right to private property to be one of the rudimentary functions of civilization, I was pleased to see that the building had once again been claimed by squatters. But more than that, I was chastened to learn that the world of migrants and refugees, a world whose cruelty I spent so much time reading about and watching movies about and contemplating, but which even in Place de Stalingrad seemed so far away, in fact shared a party wall with my own world, in which I went around everywhere with my pockets full of soggy Kleenex, looking at things and writing things down. I was turning to leave when all in unison the men in the room came to attention, as unexpectedly someone entered from the street; I was surprised to discover that this person was Clarisse, with bare shoulders and her hair tied in a long plait, doubtless returning from a party at which she'd danced and drank and smoked a staggering amount of pot, and now bearing a handcart from which she produced a case of drinking water, three or four pairs of shoes my father-in-law had left in her house, a box of oranges, and two casseroles wrapped in foil, all of which she presented without once interrupting what seemed, based on her audience's rapt attention, to be an engrossing lecture, during which she looked up now and then with a wry expression to address them individually with familiar little jokes, wagging her finger or covering her face as if to admonish them for the state of their health, causing wide grins to appear on their faces and sending up occasional eruptions of affectionate laughter; I was surprised, as I say, to see that it was Clarisse who had come into the room in the middle of the night, but on the other hand I wasn't surprised in the least, because I knew that she believed, as Walter Benjamin did, that to subscribe to a messianic view of time was pointless if it didn't bear heavily on your behavior in the present, from one moment to the intolerable next.

■

It was only a few days later that by a narrow margin the United Kingdom voted to leave the European Union, a result that truly shook me to the point that I spent most of the following day staggering around Le Fan Zone, looking for English speakers to shed some light on the entire debacle, a hope in which, though I spoke to a great many people, and heard the same joke about converting pounds sterling a great many times, I was sorely disappointed. On the Pont Neuf, I found a pair of sunburned Welshmen drinking rosé from the bottle, one of whom had voted remain while the other had voted leave, who were happy enough to answer questions but soon grew tired of having to repeat themselves and who, when I asked them whether the referendum wasn't such an existentially divisive matter that it would be impossible for them to remain friends, agreed without hesitation that as long as they rooted for the same soccer team they'd be fine.

Later that night in the pocket of a jacket Ella hadn't worn for years, I found a fistful of euros, which I took to the café on Place de la Réunion, where I ordered a half-pint of beer and sat watching dusk settle over the square. I liked to watch the little kids on their kick scooters and plastic skateboards, and on this occasion there was a little girl of about eight or ten, in pink rollerblades and an ankle-length tunic, who raced inexpertly but at terrific speed around the glowing fountain, narrowly averting one disaster and the next, with her features knitted in such fierce concentration that it didn't seem possible that she was enjoying herself at all, until, in the moment after she'd come unscathed through a particularly treacherous passage among various animate and inanimate obstacles, her face opened into an enormous, electrifying smile, as if no greater pleasure were possible in this world than relief. Across the square, unwrapping his customary dessert in the shadows of a vacant shopfront, the boy with the ears was watching this little kid as well, in an attitude of inward recognition that seemed, more than his size or the strength of his voice, to explain the power he had over his peers—his ability to stand outside of them, looking in somehow, even as they crowded around him and tugged at his sleeves. Her smile had an infectious effect on him—he went away smiling, twirling the stem of a leaf. Later, I was waiting for the check, when the girl threw herself down on the edge of the fountain and wrestled out of her pink skates, which she then helped a smaller girl, who must have been her younger sister, buckle into, before she came running barefoot across the square exactly to where I sat; it had escaped my notice that at the table beside mine, in a tunic cut from the same patterned cloth and with her hair wrapped in a brilliant scarf, her mother sat reading a magazine. Had the little girl enjoyed herself, the mother wanted to know, pulling her daughter up onto her lap; she had indeed, the daughter answered. And did she want a glass of orange juice, or a soda, the mother asked. She wanted neither, the daughter said, though she suddenly felt like an ice cream sandwich would hit the spot.

Partly because my mind was clouded by beer, these two figures, the teen-age boy and the little girl, and the quiet, private intensity with which they met the world, as well as an invisible field of energy that seemed to exist between them, formed in my mind the basis of an obscure, metaphysical counterpoint not only to Brexit but to our entire political sphere, the entire culture that had arisen over millennia around the questions of who gets what and how we decide, which suddenly seemed so petty, or, at any rate, seemed powerless to imagine the world as these two children did. That week and the next I wandered around in a bit of a daze, though my hay fever was improving, making notes that were more frenzied and illegible every day. My friend Michael, who ran the company I'd previously worked for, called me to fill in for a tutor who was out of town: at the appointed hour, I addressed myself to the intercom of a fancy but nondescript building on a broad boulevard in the west of Paris, and was admitted to the sprawling, lavishly furnished penthouse occupied by a family of the royal House of Saud, where for several hours, as Chinese housekeepers padded around in their socks, keeping us in steady supply of bottled water and chilled grapes, the princess and I sat at a dining table large enough for a game of half-court basketball and read long columns of text on such topics as women's suffrage, ice melt in Greenland, space mining as the new gold rush, slavery and abolitionism, the evolution of avian flight, colony collapse disorder, the Congress of Vienna, internet comment sections and the practice of trolling, the decline of journalism, as well as selections from Tocqueville's *Democracy in America*, Edmund Burke's *Reflections on the Revolution in France*, Thomas Paine's *Rights of Man*, and Virginia Woolf's *Three Guineas*, a book-length essay that was salvaged from a failed attempt to blend the forms of fiction and nonfiction into a single work—all of which were to be found in the practice versions of the newly reformatted SAT, which the princess was preparing to take in the fall. It was clear to me that in this room any decorative object my eyes might fall upon would be worth more money than I could hope to earn in my lifetime, and so while she worked I stood by the window, watching an airplane carve a long, pale stripe in the distant sky. Some of this material—the princess remarked eventually, tapping the stack of pages before her like a news editor in an old movie—was actually rather interesting. I had her read aloud, to what pedagogic end I can't say, from a passage on the V-shaped flock pattern common to so many species of bird; and listening to her elegant, faintly accented voice, I suddenly remembered the folk ballad of the Ottoman Empire Ella had described in her long email from Macedonia, in which the sight of geese sailing over the mountains reminds a wretched, beleaguered daughter in the Vardar lowlands of the pale girls in heels who conduct their enchanted lives at heights she'll never reach.

Soon another heatwave began, and that afternoon as I covered the windows, Ella observed, as if to herself, that our life had begun to seem like a feverish series of recurring dreams. And I thought to an extent it was true that the siege mentality that had taken hold the previous summer had never really released us. Lying in the dark one night on the mattress we'd dragged downstairs, we realized that neither of us could remember the last time we'd brushed our teeth before bed. We couldn't remember the last time we'd eaten at our kitchen table. No longer did we even discuss buying a vacuum, and we were both sporting more pubic hair than at any time since we'd met. But it didn't occur to me until later that she was referring not so much to the privations of the heat as to the new course of hormone injections she was to undergo that week. Administering these shots once again became a ceremony we observed together with a certain solemnness, and the opportunity this ceremony provided me to be of use was in a way as much a relief to Ella as it was to me—despite the distress the needles caused her—in that it assuaged a peculiar guilt I knew she felt about the impossibility of my sharing in her pain. But each night when the ritual was complete, a sense of dread reclaimed its place in our hearts, and the ensuing silence between us became more and more intolerable—in bed we watched Wiseman films, and I waited in a state of tremendous agitation for her to fall asleep; as soon as she had I pulled my shoes on and went back outside, not so much to clear my head as just to fill my lungs with air. During the previous summer's heatwave I'd left the house as little as possible, and so I hadn't seen how much of the neighborhood assembled each night in the streets, waiting for the heat to vacate their apartments—the loose circles the elderly had formed with their folding chairs; the adolescents in rows on the steps, the faces and shapes of them indistinct in the darkness; and the sum of their overlapping voices creating a murmur that was general in the air. Whether they'd have run air conditioners in their houses all day and night if they'd been able, I couldn't say, but it suddenly became clear to me that to enter into a spirit of community on the basis of momentary discomfort was a fundamental human experience from which it had become the project of modern life to insulate ourselves at whatever cost.

■

In the long stretch of the days that ensued, the silence between Ella and me, which at first seemed to signal a new equilibrium we'd found, became thick with our respective resentments, which were mutually reinforcing and, in a strange way, faintly pleasurable, I think for us both, an effect of that mounting dread. The heatwave ended after only a few days, but neither of us made any move to restore order to the apartment: we left the windows covered, and left our sweated-through clothes spread out to dry across the backs of all our chairs. Into Ella's movements, which were usually so jaunty, there came a certain feline languor, and indeed she directed at me something like the contemptuous indifference that I often intuited in cats. She avoided looking my way whenever our paths crossed, and when by chance her eyes fell on me a chilling blankness came into them, and then after a moment she'd fix me with a perfunctory smile that froze the blood in my veins. She made a point of hauling the mattress back up to the mezzanine without asking for my help, and I made a point of tittering as I watched her struggle from where I lay on the couch. At night when the alarm sounded on her phone, by mutual agreement we executed the ritual of the injections without looking at or speaking to each other, then retreated to our separate corners of the room. I'm not sure how any of this could have been helped. That week Alton Sterling, who was selling CDs outside a grocery store, was detained by two officers of the Baton Rouge Police Department, who tasered him, pinned him to the ground, and shot him six times in the chest and back. The following day, Portugal advanced to the championship by defeating Wales two goals to none in the Parc Olympique in Lyon, and meanwhile, in Falcon Heights, Minnesota, Officer Jeronimo Yanez fired seven shots into a car he'd pulled over for a broken taillight, striking Philando Castile five times, including twice in the heart, whereupon he and his partner, waiting for backup, ordered Castile's girlfriend to the ground to be handcuffed, took her and her four-year-old daughter into custody, and held Castile at gunpoint while he bled to death. The video recording that the girlfriend, Diamond Reynolds, made of these events had already been viewed millions of times by the following evening—as France defeated Germany in Marseille and for hours the explosions of fireworks could be heard echoing off the walls in the public housing complex across the street—when Ella watched it on her laptop; and the expression of abject, uncomprehending horror that became fixed on her face dissolved all the bitterness that I'd been carrying in my gut, so that before I knew it we had gathered each other up in our arms and were having a nice long cry that was unrelated to events in the outside world.

Putting the apartment back in order wasn't a merely symbolic exercise; as a practical matter, the shared sense of purpose it gave us made it possible to reconcile without any discussion of the original, wordless conflict, and the actual work of folding the blankets, hanging the laundry, remaking the bed, and so on gave us numerous occasions to be generous with each other, and to be grateful to each other in small, unimportant ways that in sum served as an approximate apology. Some instinct we shared dictated that we take this process as far as we could. Ella went across the hall to borrow Clarisse's vacuum, and I went out and bought a new mop head and a package of rubber gloves. She vacuumed the floors, the baseboards, the windowsills, behind and under the couch. We dragged the dressers into the middle of the room to get at the dust bunnies hiding beneath. I scrubbed the shower with vinegar and the floors upstairs and down with Monsieur Propre. We dusted behind the TV, behind the books, we emptied the shelves in the kitchen to remove a layer of grime. Every single bottle of oil and vinegar we owned was sticky to the touch; Ella wiped them all down with a warm, damp rag. A thirty-liter trash bag was barely large enough for the disgusting things we found in the fridge. I was long overdue for a new toothbrush, so I used my present toothbrush to scour the grout. From the shower drain, using a coat hanger, I dislodged a scummy tangle of hair the size of a guinea pig. We slept on clean sheets, which seemed to keep us cool all night long, and spent the next morning drinking fresh orange juice and making each other crepes. That night as the clouds became shadows in the deepening sky we climbed through our skylight and ducked under the railing onto the roof terrace next door, from which perspective our block looked brand-new. The days were getting shorter now, but it still wasn't fully dark until well after ten. Wrapping my arms around her waist, I buried my face in Ella's neck, and the smell of her freshly washed hair gave me an extraordinary feeling of peace, embedded in which, I can see only now, was the wish for nothing ever to change.

That was the night of July 9. In the empty Stade de France the grounds crew left the stadium lights on until morning, for reasons that aren't entirely clear. The following evening the Euro Final was to be decided between France and Portugal, and within the same few minutes that afternoon, Michael texted me and Anaïs texted Ella, both asking if we planned to watch. Because the bar Michael proposed was a Portuguese bar and Anaïs was a Portuguese person, I let myself be convinced to arrange for all four of us to watch the match together. In truth I'd have sooner stayed home. And might things not have worked out differently if I had? The inevitable snarling, earth-shaking fight we had that afternoon began when, getting ready to leave for the bar, I discovered that the drain was once again clogged with hair; a dark rage came over me, as I perceived with peerless clarity that by any impartial accounting of all the cleaning we'd done, I'd had the lion's share of the work and hadn't gotten the recognition I deserved. In fact, that was the least of many grievances not to air which I felt would be a serious disservice to us both. I sat down on the edge of the couch, and Ella understood at once what was happening. An expression of sadness crossed her face. Like all French people, I began, she had a special genius for passive aggression, for the nonverbal transmission of contempt, which in her case applied to a long list of failings that included my inability to find work, my as-yet-unrealized ambition to become a writer, my poor prospects for supporting an eventual family even in part; it was clear that she blamed me, I said, in a rising voice, not only for our difficulties conceiving, not only for being absent during her miscarriage, not only for the miscarriage itself, but also and above all for the impossibility of my experiencing any of these things as intimately and immediately as she did, which is to say, for the impossibility of my experiencing these things not as abstractions but rather as events *inside my own body*, a body that maybe it would surprise her to know I'd never asked for and didn't much like.

Ella paused for a moment, as if gathering her strength, and when she started speaking it was in as severe, as spiteful a tone of voice as you might expect, though I was unprepared for it, and it caused me to recoil. Maybe it would surprise *me* to know that she didn't want her body any more than I wanted mine, she said. She stood up and walked across the room to the kitchen and, continuing, turned to face me. It seemed to her that what I understood as contempt could be more accurately described as confusion; there was an unmistakable fear, she said, that came into my eyes whenever I looked at her, and she had never understood what that fear referred to. She was astonished to have heard me even mention the miscarriage, because for all she could see I'd never given it another thought. She couldn't blame me for not sharing a body with her; and she didn't blame me for my abstracted cast of mind. Never had she expected me to suffer to the extent that she did, she said; but the decent, human thing to do would have been to show that

I was moved in some small way, that the loss of her pregnancy continued to hurt me personally and not just on her behalf. Or, failing that, to have shown the least interest in fathoming, even in the abstract, the extent of the pain she was in. It would have been a small comfort, she said, and one she'd needed badly, if I could have found a way to make her feel less alone. Maybe it would surprise me to hear that she didn't want her pain any more than I did; that was something we might have shared. Instead, I'd made it clear that I considered her pain, if I considered it at all, an inconvenience to be avoided at all costs. This was the source of her confusion, she said, which was only just now crystalizing into contempt, as it became perfectly obvious that the fear she saw in my eyes didn't refer to anything outside of me; rather, the fear *was* me: I was a pathetic and desperate little man.

As Ella had spoken, I'd gotten up and followed her into the kitchen, breathing heavily and tearing my hair, and she'd crossed the apartment back to the couch. Now by way of reply to the speech she'd made, I stood in the middle of the kitchen floor. The nearest thing at hand, the coffeepot, was too expensive to replace, whereas in fact we already had an extra electric teakettle at the back of a kitchen drawer. I spiked our original teakettle on the floorboards at my feet, and it smashed into more pieces than I would have thought it possible for plastic to smash, scattered to every corner of the room. The sound it made, an abrupt little pop, also seemed to express my sentiments rather well. But after a long moment during which neither of us said anything, Ella's only response was to cackle, as I'd never heard her do before, a sharp, abrading sound that caused my vision to tunnel out and my ears to ring. From that point things began to happen more quickly. There was a long, rapid exchange of epithets, which ended when I told Ella that she was a cunt. Then, instantly it seemed, we were standing face-to-face. With the heel of one palm or the other, she struck me with staggering force in the temple, the ear, and the jaw. With the heel of her foot she stomped on my toes. In a swift, backhanded motion, she karate-chopped my windpipe. She tore bright red stripes into my chest and biceps, and headbutted me in the cheek. All of this and a great deal more took place in the rough format of a tornado, and might have continued even to this very day if I'd not managed to wrap her in a bear hug with her arms pinned to her sides, and to drag us both to the ground in a sweaty heap, where I planned to remain until her rage was exhausted. There, on the floor, she sank her teeth into my neck, and clamped down with all the strength of her jaws; to extricate myself, in a sincere, blind fury now, I worked both hands around her throat, peeled myself away, and held her pinned to the ground, until in a horrifying moment our eyes met, and I realized she couldn't breathe. Upstairs on my desk, my phone buzzed, and I knew it would be Michael, texting to say that he and Anaïs had found each other and had saved us seats.

■

Drawn by the stadium lights that had been left on the night before, thousands upon thousands of owlet moths, borne on winds from the southwest on their way to Great Britain, had bedded down for the night in the turf. Now as the players took the field, the moths rose up in great swarming whorls, like the cinders of an enormous fire, a dense, smudgy cloud of them, at which the players, coaches, and referees swatted helplessly. We found Michael and Anaïs near the front of the crowd, and stood at the back of the room for a moment, trying to find a point of entry.

A bedraggled troupe of musicians was sitting in front of the enormous TV, pleading with the crowd to let them continue playing until the match began; when the crowd began to boo, the band broke into a medley of disco favorites, such as Gloria Gaynor's "I Will Survive," a strategy that bore immediate results: the crowd, as if magically transformed, immediately began to clap and sing along, and the matter was settled. After a stretch of cloudy days, the sun had come out, and everywhere around us there were sunburned knees, over and around which we would have to step in order to reach our seats. For Ella and I the evening had become a game of chicken, whose object was to enter the convivial atmosphere of the occasion without ever once looking at or speaking to each other and without showing any signs of strain. In the spirit of this game, I endeavored to get us both drinks, and stood for a while at the bar, watching the drinkers lined up there try to get the attention of the barman, a stooped Portuguese octogenarian in a khaki vest who did all his bartending with his left hand, while in his right fist he kept a loose ball of bills and coins from which he made his customers' change, and to which he added the payments he received. This was Adel, the man sitting on the last stool said to me suddenly once I'd ordered, believing it to be his role, evidently, to explain Adel to unsuspecting strangers: Adel had been in business here for thirty years, he went on, and had lost his family in a fire—a pair of facts he presented with a radioactive trace of envy, as if by these facts alone Adel had achieved a special sort of aliveness or authenticity. This neighborhood, east of the canal, was the same that Matthew and Taylor, as part of the vanguard of professional Instagrammers, had visited the previous fall, the neighborhood where so many people had been killed during the attacks, and one I often heard praised for its resemblance to Brooklyn; and I understood that, the way Polish bars did in Greenpoint, holdovers like Chez Adel played a special role in the culture of the neighborhood's new population, to which the man on the stool obviously belonged. I thanked him for speaking to me and found my way to our seats, setting a glass of white wine down on the table in front of Ella, where it sat untouched for the length of the match.

In the first ten minutes of play, Cristiano Ronaldo was injured, and within the first half hour he came off the field; for the remainder of regulation time, nothing happened at all, though somehow our conversation never faltered—Michael and Anaïs got along well, and were both less interested in the match than in the drama of the kitchen door, which when it was open seemed to interfere with the aerial, so that every time the little cook came out with a plate of fries or meatballs, there would be a great uproar as the image on the screen turned to dust, until he returned to his post and shut the door behind him—so that for long stretches at a time it was possible to forget the awful fight we'd had, Ella and I, or to ascribe it to the distant past. Our friends Pauls and Azra, who cared even less about soccer than Michael and Anaïs, joined us for the second half, and for a long time we talked of nothing but the trip to Turkey they would take the following week. Earlier we'd been discussing the tension in Paris this summer, and while Azra was at the bar, I asked Pauls whether, after the bombing in June, the atmosphere in Istanbul wasn't similarly fraught. For a moment he seemed to be trying to get a better look at the teeth marks beneath the collar of my shirt. Turks were used to this kind of thing, he said. What was more troubling, if anything, he added, as if offering a concession to allay some disappointment on my part, was the steady erosion of the nation's democracy, which he predicted would soon be complete. I saw that Ella had overheard this exchange, and that it made an impression upon her. This is when it occurred to me that the paroxysms of our marriage may have reached an end that day, and that the aftermath might well be worse.

Across the street through the open door, I could see a city works employee in a bright yellow safety vest with a propane tank strapped to his back, connected by a rubber hose to a wand that emitted a modest tongue of flame, with which he was burning obsolete markings from the road, soon to be replaced, presumably, by something new. While the rest of us sank into bored silence, Ella and Azra chatted warmly, about what I never learned, for the rest of the match, which ended in extra time when Portugal's Éderzito António Macedo Lopes, well outside the box, shook two defenders and laced a low, hard shot into the back of the net, causing a groan to go up in the crowd, and twisting Monsieur Adel's mouth, behind the bar, into a shy, crooked grin. Outside, Ella and I kissed everyone's cheeks and alluded vaguely to some future occasion when we'd all meet again, and then, along with the rest of the city, we began to file home, still without acknowledging each other, but invisibly tethered to each other nevertheless.

In the streets there was a feeling of disappointment that was a close cousin of humiliation: everyone's faces were still smeared with tricolored grease, their French flags were still knotted over their shoulders like capes, and they didn't quite hang their heads, but nor would they look each other in the eye—as if, I thought, the entire population of Paris had just been stood up for the prom, and now had to slink home in a rayon dress or a rented tux. Elsewhere in the city that night, and notably in Le Fan Zone, there were fairly serious outbursts of soccer-related violence, and in fact, on our way home as well, on the busy platform at République, a group of large British men in their twenties came into confrontation with a group of large Frenchmen in their twenties, over what had been perceived as a gesture of disrespect by the smallest of the Brits, who, for the moment, was being restrained by the largest of the Brits, as meanwhile the Frenchmen, who were substantially outnumbered, held up their palms to show their disinclination to fight. I was standing against the wall, and this was happening right in front of me, with the Frenchmen to my right and the British to my left. I turned to be sure that Ella was nearby and found her, from a distance of about ten feet, staring directly into my face. Don't worry, my love, she said in a neutral tone when our eyes met, and I instantly understood she was referring not to the present crisis between strangers, but to the ongoing crisis between the two of us: Don't worry, my love, soon enough you'll be back in Virginia all by your precious self. Hearing her speak English, the Brits all turned toward her for a moment in confusion. I was confused as well, as to why she'd chosen this moment to make such a remark. The Frenchmen took the opportunity to escape down the steps in the direction of metro lines three and four. Our train arrived, the nine, and there was a general shuffling on the platform. When the Frenchmen reached the narrow tunnel at the bottom of the stairs, the large Brit released the small Brit, and said to him that now they could go, by which he meant that his peacemaking had been a ruse meant to move the inevitable fight away from the crowd. A look of undeniably carnal anticipation flashed in both their eyes, and together with their muscly little horde they hurried down the steps and caught the Frenchmen just inside the tunnel; I went and stood at the top of the stairs, where the sounds of the ensuing beating reached me with sickening clarity, and from where I could see the entangled shadows the combatants cast on the tiled walls. Behind me, the doors to our train slid shut, and when I turned around, Ella was gone.

8
Not Afraid

Even in pre-Christian Europe, places of healing and places of worship were inextricably linked. In the pre-Constantinian Greek East of the Roman Empire, the sick and injured often slept on the floors of shrines to various gods and spirits of healing—such as the Greco-Egyptian goddess Isis, who demanded a sacrifice of two geese, and her consort, Sarapis, who was consulted in the illness that killed Alexander the Great—in the hope these figures would appear to them in their dreams and instruct them in remedies for the mysterious ailments of their bodies, as when, one winter in the second century, the Hellenic god Asclepius appeared to a sickly aristocrat, whom he advised to bathe in the distant Caicus River, and not to wear shoes. Later, as Christianity spread throughout Europe, the concept of Christian hospitlitas, based on Matthew's six works of mercy, became the organizing principle of institutional care not only for the sick but also for the poor, the criminal, and the mentally ill, and hospitals became symbols of a pious, charitable society in which undesirable populations were benevolently secreted away. In the Anatolian city of Edessa, which at the end of the fifth century was overwhelmed by an influx of refugees from the countryside—driven from their lands by swarms of locusts and left now to hopelessly wander the streets, eating leaves from the gutter and falling dead in the porticoes—the Church played a vital role in providing for the care of the sick and the indigent, not only in order to ease their suffering and reduce the rate of their deaths, and not only in order to reduce the spread of pestilence in the general population, but also, by isolating them behind the closed doors of Christian shelters, in order to restore the civic morale of the middle class. In seventeenth-century France, this principle was formalized in a decree issued by Louis XIV—an edict that created the Hôpital Général de Paris on the basis that idleness and beggary were the root cause of all disorder, and that the smooth functioning of society depended upon severely curtailing freedom of movement for the poor—and by the eighteenth century had been implemented to such an extent that most of the nearly two thousand hospitals throughout the kingdom were operating far beyond capacity, and none more so than Paris's Hotel-Dieu, situated across the Seine from Notre-Dame, which in its functions as an almshouse, infirmary, hospice, mental asylum, and prison housed as many as 3,500 people in roughly 1,200 beds when it caught fire in 1772. Jacques Necker, Louis XVI's finance minister, made it his special mission not only to improve conditions in Parisian hospitals, but to fundamentally reform the philosophy of their administration and their role in civic life, a model for which philosophy, the Hôpital Necker, was soon to be established in a former Benedictine monastery by his wife, Suzanne. It was Necker's dismissal from the king's ministry at the end of that century that incited the storming of the Bastille, and it became a platform of the revolution that medicine was the province of science and progress, and that the socioeconomic basis of the family unit, the reciprocal promise of care, applied equally to society as a whole, from which it followed that health care was a human right—one value of the First Republic that in the Fifth has endured the least abuse.

■

It was only a few days after the soccer match that we arrived home in an Uber, and that with her arm hooked over my shoulders Ella made a long, faltering ascent to our apartment, where, breathing raggedly from the tenderness in her gut, she took her computer into bed with her, reasoning that even if the procedure came to nothing, she'd get some work done so the day wouldn't be entirely lost. At eight o'clock that morning we'd presented ourselves at les Vertus, and after we'd signed some papers at the front desk Ella was handed a gown and assigned to an empty bed in a staging area, where we spoke in nervous whispers and held hands. Since our blowout, we'd been constructing an uneasy truce in preparation for this day, with the understanding that whatever our marriage was to become depended on the outcome of an ordeal that was now at hand.

The window by Ella's bed gave onto a rear view of the vast, labyrinthine hospital complex of which Vertus was only a small part, and I spent what felt like a very long time watching an orderly wrestle trash bags into a dumpster, one by one, from a pile that was leaching dark fluid into the concrete, until eventually a pair of nurses came in and wheeled Ella away in her bed down the corridor, where a doctor, in order to reach her ovarian follicles, would pierce her vaginal wall with a double-lumen needle about twelve inches in length, with which he'd then aspirate the follicle's entire contents, including, it was hoped, a healthy number of viable ova; in the meantime another nurse, who spoke with a strong Russian accent, conducted me to a room on a lower floor and left me there to do my humble part.

Now, home in bed, Ella said that in a way she welcomed the practical, material distractions of recovery, such as the cramping, the bloating, the nausea; it was when these ended, she told me through gritted teeth, that the intolerable waiting would begin. But I think by then we both sensed there was something amiss. Because she'd suffered an inordinate amount of pain during her previous oocyte retrieval, having been merely sedated, Ella decided on this occasion to be fully anesthetized, with the result that when she'd returned to the recovery room, where I was waiting for her, it had been difficult for us both to distinguish whatever discomfort she was experiencing from the general confusion of waking up—she couldn't quite tell, she'd told the doctor who came by to check in, whether what she felt was real, or whether it was some sort of neural hallucination, and she couldn't remember her previous procedure well enough to compare. The doctor, having relayed the news that the retrieval had yielded a mere four ova, assured her that aching, stabbing, and shooting pains were all to be expected, and would abate before very long, and so now, though in fact after a few hours home in bed her pain had intensified to the point that she could no longer stand up, she insisted on waiting until morning to see if things improved. I went out to fill her prescriptions, and when I returned, she'd given up on getting any work done and was lying very still on her back, quaking slightly as if from cold. Sitting at the kitchen table, I could hear her breath occasionally escape as a whimper, and finally I went upstairs to insist that we at least try to get a doctor on the phone. Ella dismissed this idea immediately. It's difficult to explain how I felt at that moment—I felt almost angry. Or rather, I wanted to believe her when she told me she was okay. In hindsight, it's obvious her thinking was guided, on the one hand, by the harrowing prospect of descending the stairs in her present state and, on the other, by a reluctance to be confronted with complications that might involve abandoning a process for which she'd already suffered so much. The trouble, she explained, was that the only publicly listed number for Vertus was the emergency room, and they were certain to advise us that if we wanted to speak to a doctor we'd have to come back in. As a compromise she agreed to write an email, which would be answered by the end of the day; because she could no longer sit up, and since she didn't trust me to accurately transcribe a dictated message in French, she called her mom, which turned out to entail a fair amount of squabbling as well, because by the time Clarisse arrived only moments later, Ella wasn't making much sense.

Only once the email was finished did it become clear what a useless exercise it had been. Clarisse proposed calling an ambulance in order to get Ella down the stairs. Though she'd made it down from the mezzanine only with tremendous difficulty, Ella flatly refused this suggestion and insisted instead that we order another Uber. In the kitchen, I could see that some sort of survival instinct had taken hold of her, which she wasn't sure how to direct but which made it impossible for her to sit still; I was preparing a bag to take to the hospital, and she kept getting up from her seat to look for things she wanted to add, or straightening and tidying the countertop, or gathering papers related to her work, hobbling bent fully double around the apartment until I led her back to her seat and told her not to move. The car was due to arrive in just a few minutes when she decided she couldn't leave the apartment in her sweats: once again she struggled to her feet, and started back up the steps toward her dresser on the mezzanine to change into some new clothes, though she couldn't lift her arms over her head. I think now that this was a test she'd put to herself, by which she hoped to prove that things weren't really so bad; in fact I, too, would have preferred to see her wrestle back into her street clothes, in defiance of Clarisse's and my strident objections, and it sincerely shook me to see how readily she abandoned the undertaking instead and let herself be guided, one agonizing step at a time, down the four flights of stairs.

■

As a specialized research hospital, the ER waiting room at Vertus, though technically open to the public, was available principally to patients already in the hospital's care. It was empty when we arrived. It took us a minute to understand that we were to ring a doorbell to signal our presence, and a short while elapsed before a nurse came out to take down an account of Ella's condition. Under the fluorescent lights, it became clear how completely the color had drained from her face. Waves of nausea and spasms of pain shone in her eyes, as did a general, crushing horror that I don't think I'll ever forget. There was no longer any doubt that her present symptoms represented a substantial departure from her routine oocyte retrieval in January. Her chief concern now, and mine, too, though neither of us said so aloud, was whether we'd nevertheless be able to proceed to the second stage of the procedure; at that point, we could conceive of no worse outcome than a further month of waiting, and a repetition of the weeks-long regimen of blood tests and ultrasounds and hormone injections whose myriad side effects made Ella, in her phrase, the enemy of her own self.

Now that we were in the hospital, now that a professional opinion was imminent and it was no longer necessary to convince Ella to leave the house, Clarisse floated various optimistic theories of Ella's pain that all turned on the premise that, although nothing had gone wrong per se, it was perhaps the case that because she'd been under general anesthesia, the doctor who'd performed the retrieval, without the benefit of Ella's reactions to guide him, had done so less delicately than he might have had she been awake, a hazard—she said, giving a little sideways nod of her head—that was likewise common to drunken sex. Ella's mouth formed a thin, pallid smile. She and I both attached a great deal of importance to Clarisse's voice, which had a philosophical register that gave the impression that what she had to say was the result of a great deal of reflection and general expertise. If she made a tasteless joke, that meant things weren't so bad. The waiting room looked into an atrium that, though the sky remained clear and blue overhead, was just then in the midst, it seemed to me, of being swallowed by the unnatural darkness of its own shadow. As Clarisse continued to speak, I became aware of something humming inside me I couldn't yet understand, which anyway I forgot about the moment the nurse returned and led Ella and me to an examination room at the end of a long hall, where the doctor, a woman in her forties who hummed softly as she fitted the transducer wand with a condom and lubed it up, said that she didn't see anything obviously wrong, but that there was a slight chance, based on the ultrasound, that Ella's right ovary was twisted, though without performing a laparoscopy it would be impossible to know for sure. The decision was Ella's to make, the doctor said; we could, if we chose, return home and wait the night to see if things improved. But she warned us that—although it was almost certain that the procedure would merely confirm that nothing was wrong—if it was the case that her ovary was twisted, its blood supply was likely blocked; assuming it wasn't already too late, it would have to be repaired immediately, or it would soon wither and rot and need to be removed.

The possibility that the pain Ella was experiencing was a symptom of irreversible damage to her reproductive capacity had not, up to that moment, entered our minds. I could see in Ella's eyes that she was weighing this possibility against the more likely scenario that she'd undergo an operation that would scuttle a draining, months-long fertility process only to learn she'd misread the signs of her own body. Looking back now, it's difficult to understand how the doctor could have calculated such overwhelming odds that all was well. Perhaps, had we decided against the surgery, she would have played a stronger hand. Or maybe she couldn't imagine that, given the case she'd made, we would even consider taking such a chance. At any rate, after a brief discussion, Ella did finally agree that there was only one possible choice. Ella looked at me and I took her hand, as the doctor sprang into action, proclaiming, with one hand on the phone, that there wasn't a moment to lose: an operating theater was prepared immediately, and the anesthetist was summoned for a compulsory preoperative interview, and meanwhile a nurse showed Ella to a bathroom in a discreet corner of the ward, where she was to shower and change into a gown. At Ella's insistence, I waited in the hall with our belongings, including her clothes, bundled against my chest, listening to the sound of water falling off her body and hitting the floor in sheets, and reading and rereading the same few notices posted on the wall, which illustrated a variety of hygienic practices, listed common symptoms of a rare menstrual disorder, and advocated preemptive screening for hereditary diseases of the heart, bones, and blood.

When Ella emerged, it was clear at once that the exertion of standing had depleted whatever energy she'd had left: her face turned a sickly greenish color, and she could scarcely speak, except to repeat, over and over with mounting distress, that she felt unwell. I don't feel good, she kept muttering, j'ai du mal. She leaned on the wall as I unwrapped the gown and helped her into it, and then, overcome by a sudden urge to vomit, she threw herself on the floor in front of the toilet, where after an episode of violent retching she rolled onto her side and began to quietly moan. By the nurses' station I found a wheelchair, which with the nurse's permission I raced back down the hall; but no sooner had I raised Ella into it than she was overcome once again by a feeling like vertigo, to remedy which she threw herself once again on the tiled floor.

The hallway was long enough that I had time to notice that, despite the circumstances, I wasn't completely insensible to the grade-school thrill of running indoors. It made me feel decisive and assured. Arriving at the desk this time—whereas the first time, in order to secure use of the wheelchair,

I'd told her that Ella couldn't walk—I told the nurse breathlessly that she'd fallen to the ground, bringing a look of alarm to her face, and causing an entire team of nurses to follow me at a sprint back down the hall to the bathroom, where we found Ella on her back, half conscious, still softly moaning and clutching her stomach. In the flurry of activity that followed, two nurses and a doctor hoisted her onto a stretcher, an improvised maneuver they executed with the utmost professionalism and calm, despite the close quarters of the bathroom and the narrowness of the hall. An urgent volley of orders and inquiries continued all around, most of which too rapid for me to understand, and seeing that I'd left our things in a heap on the floor where they now were blocking the way, I bent to gather them up in my arms; rising again, I met Ella's half-closed eyes as the stretcher went past, only just for a moment, long enough to see how frightened she was but not long enough to have said anything I might have wanted to say—there was so much I wanted to say—before another moment arrived and she'd reached the end of the hall, where a set double doors flew open to let her through, and then settled shut again, leaving a silence behind them in which I was alone with her empty clothes.

■

All this time, the force that I'd discovered humming inside me had been growing stronger, which I realized only once I'd stepped back into the waiting room, where I was astonished to discover that hours had passed, that it was after nine o'clock and the sky was beginning to fade. I told Clarisse only that her daughter had been transferred to the surgical ward as planned, leaving out the specifics not so much to spare her the worry as to spare myself having to revisit the scene in my mind, and to spare myself trying to convey in French the turmoil it had produced in me to see Ella's body in such devastated collapse.

Originally, the doctor had told us that in the event everything was in order, as she hoped, the operation would take roughly forty-five minutes, whereas if some sort of surgical intervention was required—to uncoil or remove a torsed ovary, for example—it could take as much as an hour and a half. In the waiting room, expectant mothers came and went, alone and with their partners, or with their own mothers, each of whom when they arrived showed the same hesitancy and confusion about ringing the bell by the door in order to summon the nurse. When a woman who was maybe seven months pregnant came in with a little girl of about five, she unfolded a paper fan she produced from her purse, and although it wasn't especially hot, she deployed it for the benefit of her daughter, a benefit that, because the little girl was sitting directly beside me, I enjoyed as well. Otherwise it was only the silent elevators that moved—a pair of them housed in glass whose ceaseless but irregular rising and falling, which was reflected by the windows across the atrium on the opposite wall, tormented me in a way I struggled to understand. Occasionally the door swung open and we all turned our heads in unison, though more often than not it turned out to be a janitor, or this guy in his socks who kept coming out to visit the coffee machine by the restroom, pumping the hand sanitizer mounted on the wall when he was finished with the self-conscious pride of a man whose wife is in labor, though that occurred to me only much later, deep in the night.

All this time, during that early period of our waiting together, Clarisse and I didn't speak, and we sat in separate corners of the room, though a current of anxiety ran between us—as forty-five minutes, as ninety minutes, came and went—by which we developed a powerful sympathetic bond, something beyond the anxiety you'd expect to attend a loved one's emergency surgery, having to do with the fear that after everything she'd faced so bravely, the loss of an ovary would be more than Ella could bear. Two hours had passed when a nurse came out with intake papers for the last of the patients in the waiting room—that is, for the woman with the fan, who in a heavy Arabic accent described her symptoms at some length. And when the nurse turned to go, Clarisse, leaping to her feet, chased her back through the doors; I sat up to listen as the nurse explained that, although she wasn't assigned to the case, she knew Ella was still in surgery, and that she would confer with her colleagues and bring us an update as soon as she had anything to report.

■

Dusk had fallen, the summer days were growing shorter; soon it was night, and the anxious current between Clarisse and me grew more and more intense. After a short while the nurse returned to summon the pregnant woman, who left her daughter in her seat, instructing her to behave; the little girl sat across from me now, swinging her legs, inexpertly waving the fan at herself and, for a while, seeming to think I needed it, waving it at me as well, a small, poignant act of kindness that, although it soothed the surface of my skin, somehow only increased the humming fear inside my brain.

Because turning the nurse's every word and gesture over in my mind, and comparing the time that had already passed with the doctor's original estimate, I was suddenly powerless to ignore the possibility that the stakes of Ella's surgery were life and death. In my imagination, a number of wrenching scenarios, which I realized now had been gnawing at me for hours, became impossible to keep at bay. I imagined, or rather my brain did, a vivid scene in which I received the worst possible news. That scene played repeatedly in my mind, and it felt real the way dreams do, though even as I sit here now I can't even bring myself to describe it.

Distracting myself was hopeless. I tried to read the book I was carrying, *Minima Moralia*, which I'd grabbed more or less at random upon leaving the house, but I couldn't focus, I kept reading the same underlined sentence again and again—*the unwatchful trust of shared life, is transformed into a malignant poison*—the meaning of which was so far beyond my understanding that after only a few minutes I gave up and turned instead to the news. The Euro Final having concluded without incident, President Hollande was expected to announce an end to the nationwide state of emergency that had been in force since fall. At a campaign event in Illinois, speaking from the same podium at which Abraham Lincoln delivered his "house divided" speech 158 years before, Hillary Clinton enumerated the divisions upon which American politics hinged, cautioned against the existential threat Donald Trump posed to American democracy, cited the Broadway musical *Hamilton* to the effect that the eyes of history were watching to see what we'd do next, and, quoting words Lincoln had spoken during the Civil War, invoked America as *the last best hope of earth*. And while I had no problem following the literal sense of these and other news items, their total effect made me feel only more wretched, more pessimistic, and before long I'd have to stop reading, at which point I'd stare into space until I was once more overwhelmed by horrible thoughts, and then I'd return to the Adorno, and the whole cycle would begin again, until another two hours had passed, midnight had come and gone, and the nurse finally came back to tell us what she'd learned.

■

Ella was still in the surgical block, she said, but she was in stable condition, and although she had no information pertaining to the results of the operation, it was likely close to finished, and we could expect a doctor to come speak to us soon. By now the sky was fully dark, but on the other hand the tree in the atrium, whose waxy leaves reflected the light from the windows that surrounded it on all sides, seemed all the more vivid and frozen in time.

It's maybe an index of how distraught Clarisse and I had become that even such a modest use of the word *stable* left us both awash in relief. By this time the woman had returned for her daughter, and we once again had the waiting room to ourselves. And whereas in the preceding hours we'd said scarcely a word, in the hour that followed we spoke at least as much as we had in the whole of our acquaintance up to that point. Clarisse stood up and stretched—made a lap of the room and returned to her seat. In a long procession of carefully made sentences that seemed to run one into the next without any clear division between them, she said that Ella and I had become so engrossed in the pursuit of a certain kind of future that we'd forgotten how to have fun in the here and now. I tell Ella all the time, she said: Your body is a temple, bien sûr, but it's a playground, too. She told me how as a young single woman in Paris in the sixties, though she'd been a dedicated student, she rarely refused an invitation to a party, to which she brought strong white rum and fell into conversations that lasted until dawn; and how, even during exam periods, she made time to go out danc- ing every weekend, never with potential suitors or groups of friends, which inevitably entailed a host of non-dancing obligations, such as trips to the bathroom or the bar, but rather always alone, with a flask of rum she carried on her hip, in order to spend uninterrupted hours at a time on the dance floor, a practice she continued even after she'd met and married Ella's father, she said; even after she'd given birth to her son, and even during the year they'd lived in Cameroon. It's fine to be serious, she told me; it's a very fine thing to hold the future in mind, but you have to remember that the future isn't as long as it seems.

On the walls in Clarisse's apartment hung ample photographic evidence of this approach to living, which I'd studied compulsively each time I went across the hall, exactly as I'd once studied the photo albums my own par- ents kept of their feckless early and mid-twenties, in the first years after my brothers and I were born, always with the feeling that photographs of my own life would never appear to anyone so enchanting as these ones appeared to me. I thought I knew what she meant, I told Clarisse, and I hoped that we were merely in a phase that when it passed would give way to a lighter kind of life. In New York we'd lived that way, I told her; in New York, our life had been *too* light, and we'd had about as much fun as we could stand: we threw parties and broke things and gathered our friends around us in bars; we ate out and ordered in and, with Marco and my brother and Noah, cooked elaborate, fabulous meals we ate by candlelight as a family, sitting for hours at the dirty table and leaving the dishes in the sink for days. We peed at the end of subway platforms, waiting for late-night trains, and rode to Coney Island to swim in the dirty surf. We made friends with everyone and let drunk people cut our hair. We picked food off strangers' plates in restau- rants, and at work, after hours, we lowered the gates, raided the freezer, and ate ice cream until our stomachs ached, and then to feel better we drank grappa, so we could strip to our underwear and dance on the bar. One night, as some sort of protest against our manager, we smashed an entire rack of glassware against the floor. Another we bought beer for skulking teenagers and followed them into an abandoned building to help them tear down the walls. We walked along the cobbles on Joralemon Street and shattered the curbside mirrors on an entire block of cars. But then, toward dawn, I said, when the two of us would go up to our roof to watch the dawn, I understood that all of this amounted to a kind of stockpiling, a kind of hedge— an investment that wouldn't mature until I could speak about it the way that I was speaking about it now, in broad, sentimental strokes by which I could assure myself that we'd lived well. I'd perfected a description of our idiosyncratic, improvised wedding party as an example of our gameness and our spontaneity—that we had texted my parents a photo from city hall in the morning, and that back at the apartment, as Marco hung quinceañera balloons, the only white decorations he could find in the dollar store across the street, we cooked all afternoon, and served a large salad and two massive trays of mac and cheese to the only thirty or forty people we knew who with just a few hours' notice could come out and get drunk on a Tuesday night. But in fact the party had been prescribed by the immigration lawyer we'd hired, I told Clarisse, who'd said the photos would form an important part of our file, and just the other day, flipping through the stack of photos we'd put together for that purpose, I was dismayed to find that whatever filters we applied to them, they never achieved the elegiac, twilight quality that photos of Clarisse's or my parents' early adulthood did—the testimony they gave to time's relentless melt, which inscribed the lives they depicted with an authenticity that in my own life was always out of reach.

Écoute, Clarisse said, grinning, ça suffit, you think too much. It was after one o'clock now, and the rising and falling of the elevators had become so sporadic as to be almost soothing. Clarisse heaved out of her chair, crossed the room to the water cooler, and brought back a cup of water for us each. Anyway, she said, one day you'll see: in parenthood the world becomes more immediate, as a parent you live your entire life suspended between a state of awestruck wonder and abject fear. The moment you become a parent, you cease to live fully inside your body, and the heart that beats in your chest ceases to be only yours. She drained her water and addressed the remarks that followed to the bottom of her empty cup.

Even when she was a girl, Clarisse said, there was a fierceness behind Ella's eyes that terrified me and amazed me equally, a determination to satisfy this powerful hunger she carried, which applied itself in lovely, unpredictable ways but which made her vulnerable to the world in a way her brother was not. I remember, at six years-old, she watched a handful of Bruce Lee films on TV and became obsessed with learning kung fu—when I pressed her on it, she said in her tiny voice that she wanted to become the *master of herself*. We enrolled her in classes at a karate studio in the nineteenth. Never had I seen her take so much satisfaction in anything as she did in the rapid prog-ress she made in the months that followed, devoting herself with fearsome concentration to perfecting the myriad postures, defenses, and strikes she'd learned before the mirror at home, and wearing throughout each of her belt ceremonies a smile whose shyness and inwardness never failed to break my heart, until somehow after nearly a year had passed it got into her head that if she was to continue it was necessary to go barefoot in the streets on her way to and from the studio; when I explained that if the authorities saw her out walking around without shoes they'd lock me up, her response was to break off her practice of karate entirely, without ever looking back, and to take up dance instead, which although it was a source of misery she kept up for years. Gently, I tried to steer her back toward martial arts, but she refused to even consider it. In a strange way it made me proud, maybe in the way it suggested the sort of psychic independence I'd always craved for myself. And the problem of this independence was foremost in my mind when, maybe three years later, I found most of her clothes packed into a duffel she'd hid-den at the back of a closet in the hall, where she'd moved them, I discovered, not because she planned to run away but in order to make room in her own closet for a kitten she'd bought in secret from a Romani woman down the street, which at that point she'd kept in hiding for over a week, feeding it the leftovers from her own meals, and cradling it in her arms at night when she went to sleep. It would have been monstrous, as I saw it, to have separated her from that cat, and so I agreed that the cat could stay only so long as she took sole responsibility for his care, which she did for about a month, until one day she put mascara in his lashes and with nail polish tried to paint his claws, with the natural result that he savagely attacked her face. After that, she never lifted a finger for that cat again. Pate Blanche is twenty-one years old now, Clarisse said, and still lives with Ella's father, and although he's a repulsive creature, I feel a powerful fondness for him, just as I feel a certain pang whenever I see anything to do with Bruce Lee—as if, she said, the place these figures briefly held in that little girl's heart became permanently fixed in mine.

At some point Clarisse had risen to throw out her empty cup, and as she spoke she paced the floor; listening, I'd invented little errands for myself as well, to refill my own cup, to charge my phone, returning each time to a different seat, so that in the course of our conversation we'd made use of the entire room. Now, Clarisse settled into still another seat, beneath which she found the little girl's paper fan: she picked it up and for a moment examined it carefully, as though she were struggling to make sense of the intricate floral pattern printed in its folds. Then, as if a spell had broken, she looked up at me, putting the fan into service as she went on. More than the inevitable bad chapters in her childhood, she said, more than whatever trouble she caused or injuries she sustained, it's these minor episodes I return to when I can't sleep. As a parent you're confronted daily with decisions of that sort— whether to plant your heels or whether to get out of the way—the invisible marks of each of which you know will accrete in your child's psyche to be carried into the future for years to come, so that after each, no matter what you decide, you're consumed by doubt, your faith in your own instincts shrivels, or mine did, at any rate, until I perceived that in the smelter of all these failures, Ella had been forging formidable instincts of her own. It was following a period of aimlessness, as well as a series of minor and major disappointments that included eviction from her apartment, a cataclysmic breakup of a long-term relationship, and the imprisonment of a dear friend, that she announced she was moving to New York. The prospect so terrified me that I started selling old jewelry that very day, in order to have some cash on hand for any of the million contingencies of New York life that kept me up at night for weeks before she left—none of which, I should add, Clarisse said, laughing aloud, involved her marrying an American man and becoming desperate to have his child, though in fact, she added, it was the romance of such a possibility, and her devoted, generous openness to such possibilities, that, even though it made me sick with worry, also made my heart swell with pride.

At that moment the elevator opened and another pregnant woman came in, followed by a man who, while she calmly crossed the room to ring the bell, selected a pair of seats in the corner and unburdened himself of several heavy bags that the two of them, I quickly understood, had likely packed weeks earlier in anticipation of this moment, the moment her water broke and her contractions began. There was something ostentatious and self-satisfied about their levelheadedness that immediately annoyed me, which was connected, in my mind, to their outdoorsy style of dress. Or maybe it was simply that I resented the interruption; upon their arrival, Clarisse and I once again fell silent, and after the nurse came out and submitted them to her customary whispered interview, I checked the time and saw that it was now close to two o'clock. You should head home, I told Clarisse, I'll call you as soon as I have any news, and you can come back in the morning after you've gotten some sleep. There wasn't any sense in us both waiting up through the night, I argued; once Ella came out of surgery there was no question of leaving her by herself, and if we alternated watches we would be able to count on each other for relief. After some resistance, Clarisse agreed, and then at length the nurse came to summon the couple to a delivery room that had been prepared for them, and I was left in the waiting room alone.

∎

If you'd asked me then, I'd have said hours passed before I saw another living soul. I held my face in my hands, and the events and sensations of the day swirled in my mind in the form of indistinct images, phrases, and sounds—the little girl waving her fan at me to soothe my distress; a grainy, inscrutable ultrasonic photograph of Ella's uterus; the glass we'd once left shattered on the floor of the bar where we worked; Clarisse at her kitchen table, rolling a joint and tying her hair in preparation for a night out dancing by herself; *the unwatchful trust of shared life* and *the last best hope of earth*; and my barefoot little wife, reckoning with her six-year-old body in a full-length mirror, her belt cinched tight, drawing steady, even breaths, convinced that by force of will she could make herself invulnerable to pain—that I could isolate from one another only by setting them down as a series of bulleted sentence fragments in my notes, one of several measures I took against the humming that had resumed in my chest, which now that I was alone I realized was nothing more than the knowledge that in a room not far from where I sat, Ella, unconscious and helpless, was laid out on a table, while a group of strangers cut holes in her and explored her insides. The strong possibility that she'd lose an ovary remained; and even in the best case, the dramatic failure of the procedure was certain to leave her more shattered and alienated than she'd already been. And if you'd asked, I'd have said that hours had passed since Clarisse had left, but in fact, the email announcing that her Uber driver had arrived was time-stamped at 2:08, and the note I tapped into my phone, as the doctor gave me the details of Ella's transfer to another hospital, was created only twenty-three minutes later, at 2:31.

∎

I'm being entirely literal when I say that I felt the room spin around me even before the doctor opened his mouth; his approach, and the grave expression on his face, so neatly matched the horrifying opening frames of the scene I'd spent hours trying to put out of my mind. And because I expected him to deliver one of only three kinds of news—the good news that her ovary had been successfully repaired, the bad news that her ovary had been lost, and the unspeakable news of my imagination—I was prepared for neither the deferral of resolution nor the escalation of stakes the news he gave me represented. There'd been no ovarian torsion, he explained. Rather, since the retrieval procedure that morning, Ella had been internally bleeding, and had required a transfusion of more than two liters of blood; and while they'd corrected the primary source of blood loss, there was a second, smaller source that, even after they'd made several additional incisions for further laparoscopic reconnaissance, they hadn't been able to find. To do so here at Vertus, they'd have to open her stomach from her navel to her sternum, a course of action that had ramifications of its own, whereas at Hôpital de la Pitié-Salpêtrière, he said, located about four kilometers away, just across the river in the thirteenth, they had imaging equipment with which, by dyeing her blood with an iodinated radiocontrast agent, they'd be able to detect the source of this second hemorrhage with ease. She'd be kept under general anesthesia, he said, and transported in an ambulance that would soon arrive—I was to go there and ask for the salle de réveil; that was where she'd be.

According to my call log, I phoned Clarisse at 2:58 to explain what he'd said. An ambulance crew would arrive to retrieve Ella within fifteen or twenty minutes, the doctor had told me, and rather than let Clarisse come to les Vertus, I said I'd text her once we were en route to Pitié-Salpêtrière. In the 118 minutes that followed, I variously stood at the window, paced the floor, locked myself in the restroom, and googled a series of phrases describing the tree in the atrium, which is how I determined that it was a magnolia, *Magnolia grandiflora*, as I wrote down in my notes shortly before 3:56, when I texted Clarisse to say that the medical transport crew had finally arrived: a uniformed team of four who rang the bell and disappeared into the emergency ward with their cart, where they remained until 4:35, according to the text I sent Clarisse from the lobby, having rushed downstairs to catch a glimpse of Ella on her way out the door—her face half masked in tape to hold the tube in her throat—which from an emotional standpoint turned out to be a mistake. My Uber ride began at 4:51. The driver was listening to bossa nova. In my misery, I'd asked the medical crew if I could ride with them, and citing insurance concerns, they'd refused, though as a consolation they'd offered to let me hop up and give Ella a little kiss before they left, a kindness I declined. A bouquet of cut flowers in the cup holder filled the car with its smell; I lowered the window and put my face into the passing air. On the Pont de Bercy, party people were making their way to an after-hours club on the far bank of the Seine, where it seemed some kind of luau was under way. The GPS brought us to a rear entrance of the hospital complex, which, because it was closed and forbiddingly dark, caused a new wave of desperation to come over me. But there were a number of girls in grass skirts ducking through a gap in the fence, a shortcut, evidently, on their way home from the club. I thanked the driver and, though it gave the girls a fright, jumped out of the car and ducked through the fence behind them, and ran off into the shadows, following signs to the welcome desk in a building that was open but in which I encountered only locked offices and empty, half-lit halls. Back outside, another group of party people, headed in the other direction, was also making use of the shortcut, among whose ranks was a tall man dressed as a palm tree, who, as I looked around for the correct building, asked me to take a photo of him and his friends.

Salpêtrière was established in 1656, while a recurrence of the black death was decimating the populations of Naples and Rome, as the women's branch of the newly formed Hôpital Général de Paris, with the exclusive mandate to isolate the city's female lunatics, beggars, prostitutes, and petty thieves from the population at large, in conditions that were monstrous even by the standards of the time; and it was on these same grounds that, over the course of three days in September 1792, during the so-called September Massacres, a gang of armed men raped an unknown number of the hospital's prisoners, and executed thirty-five, ranging in age from seventeen to seventy-one—or so I remembered reading as I continued to cast desperately among its darkened outbuildings, at least a few of which must have been original to the gunpowder factory from which the hospital took its name. Finally, in the only other building with its lights on, I caught sight of the ambulance crew wheeling their empty stretcher back outside. The salle de réveil, the woman at the front desk told me, was on a basement level, above the morgue. In the elevator, at 5:09, I received an email from Uber, asking me to rate my ride with Djamel. When I told the nurse who answered the bell that I'd come about my wife who'd just arrived in an ambulance, I was relieved to find that I was in the right place. This relief was short-lived, however: he asked me to wait while he fetched the doctor, an intern with a serious voice who invited me into an empty break room, and asked me to take a seat.

What does a doctor say to someone after leading him to a private room and asking him to take a seat? During the long moments before he began speaking again, this question rang in my mind. He didn't know, he began, how much I knew about Ella's condition, but it was perhaps best for him to assume that I knew nothing and simply explain everything he'd gleaned from her file. The previous morning, she'd undergone an ova retrieval at les Vertus, he said, where late that afternoon she had returned with complaints of severe, unilateral pain in her lower abdomen. The results of her examination having been inconclusive, the doctor on duty had recommended an exploratory surgery to determine whether Ella's right ovary was torsed, and to correct it or remove it as need be. After a fainting spell that resulted from some combination of low blood pressure, severe pain, and stress, she was rushed into surgery, during which she received a two-thousand-milliliter transfusion when it was discovered that she was hemorrhaging blood from an ovarian artery, an injury the surgical team managed to locate and contain, though at that point it became apparent that there was a second hemorrhage, the site of which the team was unable to find. It was for this reason that after eight hours of surgery she'd been transferred here, to Pitié-Salpêtrière, he said, where, however, by the time she'd arrived, the second hemorrhage seemed to have stopped all on its own.

All that the intern had said I'd listened to with my full attention; and yet, in a small corner of my mind as he spoke, the same horrible scene reappeared, in which I not only received the unspeakable news, but also became responsible for passing it along in the proper order—to Clarisse, to Ella's father and her brother, my own parents and siblings over the phone, certain of her closest friends, and so on—and so the tentative diagnosis that the bleeding had stopped didn't affect me in the way one might expect. Did I have any questions, the intern wanted to know, and after a stunned moment I asked whether I'd understood correctly that, for the time being at least, he felt confident that Ella was out of danger; the intern blinked once and, choosing his words carefully, explained that he could not say definitively that she was out of danger, that too many factors remained unknown, but that no hospital in Europe was better equipped to care for her in whatever crisis might arise.

At some level, I realized that this was his way of saying, within the parameters of his training, that the worst was behind her and that she was safe. But I seemed to have a bodily need to hear him say the actual words. Crises of the most unlikely sort had become routine that day, so in my mind, even the merest possibility that there were more to come took on the proportions of inevitable catastrophe. I think now that the term *stable*, in its medical sense, was coined for use in scenarios of this precise kind, and had the intern employed it in the case of Ella, I might have been spared the dizziness that overcame me, and the ringing in my ears. How long had I been awake, I wondered. For a moment I closed my eyes, and then for a moment when I opened them I seemed to be back in the waiting room at les Vertus. So much of life, I remember thinking in my confusion, you relive even as you live it, or anyway, I said to myself, so much of mine—and this insight felt crucial when Clarisse arrived a moment later, and, rising to greet her, I found that I couldn't keep myself over my feet, so that while the intern repeated his entire performance as they stood in the doorway, I sat at the wobbly table with my head between my knees, from where I noticed, in a discreet corner of the unmopped floor, a trampled white-and-purple lei.

■

All of this, as fucking weird as it may sound, is in my notes. Ella spent the next four days and nights recovering at les Vertus. There was something soothing about our routine there, an afterglow of the intensity of that first night. As hospitals go, there was something pleasant and homey about the place. For an extra charge of eighty-five euros per night, which was covered by Ella's mutuelle, she was assigned a private room. Each morning, I installed myself in the armchair beside her bed, where I sat for long, calm hours all day and well into the night, nibbling at the croissants and cookies I picked up for her each morning but for which she had no appetite, with my notebook open in my lap, reviewing the scribbles I'd made that night, that week, all throughout the preceding year, as Ella, with morphine seeping into her veins, drifted in and out of consciousness. At two a.m., after the night nurse came by on her rounds, I'd change out of my sweats and pack my things in order to catch the last bus home, less than a ten-minute ride on the 64, and in the morning after a dreamless sleep I'd fill my thermos with coffee and be back in my chair by nine.

Now I've been reviewing those notes again—and of course everything is different, everything, every week for four years a new calamity, every week and every hour, every sleepless night consumed in violent, helpless rage. And each day I'm astonished at how little I've ever understood, how much I've ignored, all of which, like a wave rolling over the sea when there's been an earthquake in the distance, has crashed at our feet. The entire floor where Ella spent that week at Vertus has been repurposed as a refuge for victims of domestic abuse. Perfume factories are making hand sanitizer, everyone who knows how to sew is making masks, trucks containing respirators crisscross the continent on empty highways, escorted by armed guards. And this is to speak only of France, which is managing relatively well. Pitié-Salpêtrière and hospitals all over the country are well past capacity, after decades of austerity, nurses and doctors and hospital administrators appear each night on the news with exhausted, desperate eyes, and each night to steel our nerves we gather at our windows to applaud. And meantime I've been reading about the Salpêtrière of the seventeenth, eighteenth, and nineteenth centuries, when patients slept two or three to a bed, and pregnant women in some cases delivered children lying head to toe. The so-called lunatics were kept chained to walls, to be gnawed on ceaselessly by lice, scabies, and rats. And if you'd told me that morning—the morning Ella finally came out of surgery, as the twenty-fourth hour passed that I'd been awake—that the waiting room for the salle de réveil had been designed in homage to this ignominious past, I wouldn't have batted an eye.

But that's only to say it was a small, airless room with uncomfortable chairs and a faintly

disagreeable smell. They planned to keep Ella under anesthesia just a few hours longer, for observation, I'd heard the intern tell Clarisse, in order to be certain she was no longer losing blood. In the meantime, with my cap pulled down over my eyes, I'd sat listening to a woman in her forties make a series of tearful phone calls in each of which she repeated the same essential information, using the same essential words each time: there'd been a car accident, her husband was in a coma, there was nothing anyone could do but wait and see. The anguish in her voice made a strong impression on me. Nearly two hours had passed since our conversation with the intern, and still I felt unsteady and somewhat frayed. With the thought that it would help to get some sugar in my blood, I went upstairs to the main lobby in search of a vending machine. And when I came back with an orange Fanta and a package of gluey madeleines, I found Clarisse in the hallway, talking to a nurse with long braids, who was saying that Ella was emerging from the anesthesia, and would soon be awake.

Before I met Ella, I don't think I'd cried since puberty, whereas I have the distinct feeling that in these pages I've reported more instances of my crying than I can count—each of which, I'm quite certain, and numerous others I've left out, provoked by the sight of Ella's face after a period of distress. And throughout the entire ordeal of her surgery, I knew I'd hold myself together exactly that long as well. The salle de réveil turned out to be what in American hospitals is known, less poetically, as a post-anesthesia care unit: a long narrow hall, in this case, with a low ceiling, in which dozens of hospital beds were arranged in two uneven, haphazard rows, and which at that early hour—just after seven o'clock—was kept in darkness, as if to heighten a nightmarish atmosphere whose chief feature was a disembodied chorus of lowing, frightened voices that rose from all around, in competition with the numerous monitors whose beeping corresponded to the rhythms of as many hearts.

But right here in the front of the room, point being, adjacent to the nurses' station, Ella was drowsing comfortably in her bed; her eyes, when Clarisse and I took our places to either side of her and both reached out instinctively to take her hands, opened heavily, whereupon, needless to say, I was reduced to a soppy mess, and then reduced further still by the wide-eyed, open-mouthed expression that appeared on her face as she learned that it was morning and that she was now in Pitié-Salpêtrière. After eleven hours of intubation, her lips were cracked and dry and gray, and while I moistened them with cool, damp pads of gauze, which the nurse had brought as much in kindness to me as to Ella, I could see that she was studying my face for signs of what she'd endured since she'd collapsed on the bathroom floor. How strange, she said later that day, during the ambulance ride back across the river to the hospital where this all began, that she would need to rely on me to make known to her the experiences of her own body, which had undergone so much during a period that for her brain had passed in the blink of an eye—a gulf that, as she pondered it somewhat less than lucidly from her hospital bed in the following days, seemed to give her a certain distance from which to reflect upon the events of not only that night, not only that long, fraught summer or the long, strange year, but upon the entire course of her life, which seemed to her, like a river that bursts its banks over a low plain—she said drowsily one afternoon at Vertus—to have spread far and wide before her with the stillness of a lake.

To visitors she kept saying she couldn't wait to get home. Her boss called about a pair of exciting projects starting soon, a miniseries and a feature film, and Ella promised to be back in the office by the end of the week. She could already feel her strength returning to her, she told me at one point, and she was eager for life to resume. That was the same day that the doctor who'd performed the ova retrieval came by and revealed, as if in confidence, that he'd only just reached her ovarian follicle and begun to harvest eggs when, perhaps as an adverse reaction to the anesthesia, she went into a seizure the violence and duration of which he'd never before witnessed, and which was almost certainly the cause of the internal injuries she'd suffered. Needless to say this revelation alarmed the both of us, and mystified us as well. But on the other hand—Ella added, as she was dozing off, to her earlier comment about life resuming—a small part of her wouldn't mind living like this for all time.

■

Which was how I felt as well: the heatwave, the blizzard, those long days in the hospital, now the quarantine, crises of any magnitude that suspended the mounting anxieties of the everyday. The first night after the surgery, not having slept for thirty-six hours, I left Ella with her mom (who'd gone home to rest in the morning) and returned to the apartment around six o'clock, where I slept for three hours, until I was awoken by the sound of fireworks that a group of kids was setting off from the tracks, which were exploding against the sky directly over our building, where I could see them from the bed, a bracing reminder that Bastille Day had arrived. On the nightstand, a flash of silver caught my eye. That bangle, a fine, closed loop. I didn't know exactly what that object signified in Ella's psychic landscape, but I put it in the bag I'd packed her, and then not an hour later she was twisting it on her wrist when we discovered that in Nice, the festivities had ended with a trail of eighty-six bodies on the Promenade des Anglais. From the bus on my way home again, I saw the barman at La Chouette de Minerve, and he was wearing the same shirt: GANDHI SAYS RELAX. The following night, tanks rolled in the streets of Ankara, and three hundred people were killed when an attempted coup against the government of Recep Tayyip Erdoğan was put down. And point being that the state of emergency, which Hollande promised was near an end, seemed instead to have reached cataclysmic proportions worldwide, whereas there in the stillness of the hospital, the private animus between Ella and me seemed either to have become suspended or to have entirely dissolved, and to such an extent that the larger part of me, and not only some small part, couldn't bear to leave.

And yet, conversely, I have to confess that each night when I did leave, another small part of me resisted the thought of coming back. I remember walking into the empty apartment that night, the night of the fireworks and the first after Ella's surgery: I found the same chaos we'd left behind us, and before I went to sleep, despite my exhaustion, I spent some time putting things back in order. Now each time I returned there to sleep, I found that order intact. Alone in the middle of the night, the apartment seemed so vast. Likewise the bed—drifting off to sleep as my thoughts became harder to direct, I found myself envisioning another, frictionless sort of life. The afternoon of the fifteenth, while Ella had visitors, I took the train to République, where the altar that had been established, beneath the monument at the feet of the lion, in commemoration of terror incidents in Paris, Nigeria, Cairo, and Beirut, among others, had already been expanded to include the victims of the attack in Nice the night before, new flowers piled upon old flowers, new spray paint, new votives pressed into the melted wax of the old, a palimpsest of tragedy before which the growing crowd observed a reverent hush.

At the very base of the statue was a shallow fountain that had been drained, which rose a few feet above the general ground and served now as a sort of chancel. There I spoke with a young woman whom I found sitting against the pedestal, far to one side in the shade, with a book spread in her lap, who said her name was Emilie and that she was a desk agent at Charles de Gaulle. The book was *Sentimental Education*, and she told me that reading it here had a special, anachronic effect, in the way that the contemporary sensory data in the air around her intermingled in her consciousness with the nineteenth-century descriptions in the book. She was excited to talk to me, she was eager to share her thoughts, and I could tell she liked showing off her English, which was quite good. We watched together as, to one side of the monument, near the lion's tail, an old woman with a large bottle of Evian was patiently watering the potted flowers that had been left there, and meanwhile, directly beside her, a street drunk poured a modest amount of beer on the ground, raised his fist, and closed his eyes, swaying for a long moment over his unsteady feet. Emilie giggled and touched my arm. Was this how she planned to spend the rest of the day, I asked her. Her apartment wasn't far away, she said; she'd probably go home soon and pour herself a glass of wine, put on a record and lie flat on her back.

Perfect, I said. Why not?

Why not join me? she asked. I'll read you some Flaubert.

Comme tu veux, she said when I declined, and turned back to her book. As if it were no big deal. That sort of thing never happened to me, and I wasn't exactly tempted, but the simplicity of it, the cheap intimacy contained in that *tu*, in contrast with my attachment to Ella, presented a vision of freedom that shook me to the core. As if all the intense feelings I'd collected in my notes, real fear, real sorrow, amounted to only that. Breathing hard, I wandered off, stealing glances into the faces around me, wondering how they articulated, in their own minds, the instinct they'd followed to this place—was it really as simple as grief, or was it to give vent to something else? And at just that moment, a British news crew put the same question to a young man who'd hung a French flag from the pedestal, on which he'd scrawled the words VIVRE ET MOURIR ENSEMBLE: What personal reasons, the newswoman asked him in English, did he have for coming here? Stooping slightly to speak into the microphone, he gave a long and thoughtful reply, in an almost cartoonishly elegant French accent. As he spoke the newswoman nodded sympathetically, and then when he finished, she asked the same question again: Was he *personally* affected by the attacks? He paused for a moment, as if uncertain whether to answer in the more truthful sense that yes, as he'd just finished explaining, the entire nation had been personally affected by the attacks, which was why they were here; instead, he answered, his whole body growing tense, in the sense the question intended— that no, he wasn't personally acquainted with anyone among the dead.

A short man in tinted glasses and an angler's vest was circulating among us with an armful of individually wrapped roses, which he handed out for free, to be laid at the base of the shrine. He gave me a rose as well. When I asked what brought him here, he said that embedded in the concepts of citizenship and nationhood was the presumption of allegiance, which flowers gave people a way to express. He interrupted himself to turn and watch a small melodrama that was unfolding behind him as he spoke: the newswoman was trying to interview the drunk in English, touching off a torrent of abuse in French, to the effect that she was a parasite, exploiting the death and grief of strangers for the benefit of her career; and as the Englishwoman turned to go, the drunk, drawing upon the strength of his whole body, expectorated in her hair. You move somewhere, you have to adjust, the man with the flowers went on, you have to assimilate, life in France is beautiful if you go at it in the French style, and what kind of person would refuse? You see men in the streets in djellabas, you see women in hijab, you say to yourself, mais non, c'est pas possible, ici c'est la France. I said that a lot of the people he was describing were born in France, and his eyes got wide, as if in agreement: Ingrates, he said, clucking his tongue. Thanking him for his time, I collected some biographical details to finish up: his name was Eddie, he said; he was from Iran, and he'd lived in Paris for forty years. And your profession? I asked him, and he grinned, hoisting his bundle of roses to emphasize his reply. Well, I'm a florist, he said.

■

Maybe it was with Emilie in mind that I offered to read aloud to Ella, less as a diversion, as it turned out, than to lull her to sleep; often I read numerous sections of *Minima Moralia*, or entire chapters of *Aftermath*, only to find she'd drifted off after a single page. Though maybe it's not too fanciful to think these pages penetrated her consciousness in some way, and helped frame the thoughts that came to her when she woke. One morning, I arrived to find Docteur LeFebvre standing by the bed, examining a new page in Ella's file. She was sorry for everything Ella had been through, she said; surely Ella preferred not to think about it for the moment, but there was some provisionally good news. Of the four ova that the retrieval procedure had produced, three had developed into healthy embryos by the third day; and of these three, by the fifth day one had continued to develop into a blastocyst of exceptional quality, which the lab had frozen for future use. The chances that a three-day embryo—such as the one that produced Ella's previous, spontaneously abortive pregnancy—would successfully implant were roughly one in five, and then the chances that a successfully implanted three-day embryo would progress to a live birth were one in three. Whereas, she said, half of all blastocysts that rated as highly as ours led to clinical pregnancies, and of those clinical pregnancies that survived to the thirteenth day from the date of the transfer, 95 percent were born at full term. Recent evidence, furthermore, she explained, suggested that, rather than damaging these odds, the process of vitrification by which blastocysts were now preserved may actually have improved the probability of their success. For now, Ella was to focus on her recovery, which by all appearances was going well; in as little as six weeks, Docteur LeFebvre said, we could expect to defrost the blastocyst, in order to complete the procedure that had gone so catastrophically awry.

Ella received this news in silent contemplation, and when the doctor left, she made no comment, but instead asked me to read to her. But no sooner had we found the last paragraph she could remember hearing than she'd given herself back over to sleep. In the afternoon, though, she asked me to raise the blinds and inclined her bed to a sitting position. She'd been thinking, she said, of the trope in film of the bereaved mother who, although it torments her, can't bear to disturb the bedroom of the child she's lost. It was a convention she felt she understood, one that struck her as authentic, having to do, she said, with a need to define one's grief in terms of physical space. And while she didn't want to compare the end of her pregnancy with the death of a child, it struck her as a particular cruelty of miscarriage that one's own body became the site of a terrible loss. I know, my love, she said, I can't expect you to understand how suffocating it is to exist inside such a body. The dark line on her belly, for example, which when it first appeared in the winter had been a source of unfathomable joy: now she found herself tracing it with her fingertip, standing before the mirror. And it was true that as the physical signs of her lost pregnancy faded, she'd experienced some psychic relief, but then in the past month, the various hormone treatments she'd undergone had caused those physical signs to reappear: her appetite, the weight she'd gained, the pain in her lower back, the occasional hopeful flutter in her gut. These sensations, she said, which in fact referred to the future, had the intolerable effect of casting her endlessly into the past. But now, my love, she said, although I almost dare not say so aloud, this healthy embryo makes it possible to imagine a future in which everything I've suffered will be redeemed.

Then she fell silent, her eyes fell shut and her breathing slowed, and for a long time I watched her sleep. In my mind I replayed the scene of that moment in the salle de réveil when she first blinked awake. Later, in the hall with Clarisse, I tried to describe that feeling in French, but the best I could do was to say that I felt large. And now, watching Ella twitch in her dreams, I renewed the resolution I'd made then, to somehow keep that feeling at the center of my life. For a long time I sat in my hospital chair and watched the sky. And then hours had passed, night had fallen, and I was scratching some of these thoughts into my notes, when I found her watching me, Ella, her eyes shining in the dark. Are you going to write about this, my love? she said in her nighttime voice, and then before I could answer, she said, You have to promise me you won't.

9
States of Emergency

To think of that summer, to think of the entire year, makes me mildly nauseous—if you'll forgive the borrowed phrase. To have felt so certain about all that upheaval near and far, that it was only the cost of a better world that was in store. And what has it come to? That first miscarriage: that baby would by now have learned to walk, to speak, to spell her name. Our apartment, the top-floor studio where Ella and I once lived, now it's home to someone else. At night I walk the silent streets, I listen to the sirens in the distance, I take photos of the wildflowers growing up through the cobblestones, and the brush that's grown waist-high in the park, and the long, obscene trails of sloughed-off rubber gloves. And back home, until nearly dawn each night, I read and reread those notes, where, despite everything they record, there remains this faint, radioactive trace of optimism, almost whimsy, to detect which now makes my ears ring with shame. And never more so than in the pages accounting for the days and weeks after Ella came home from the hospital and, despite some soreness, returned to work. In Syria, government forces laid siege to Aleppo. In Macedonia, where the so-called Balkan route had been closed since March, hundreds of men, women, and children were crowded into a camp with a tin roof and no walls. WikiLeaks released a massive trove of stolen emails. In the northern hemisphere, scientists observed the highest average temperature ever recorded. In a suburb north of Paris, on the hottest day of the year, a twenty-four-year-old man named Adama Traoré died in handcuffs in the courtyard of the local gendarmerie, and his last recorded words were *I can't breathe*. I set all this down in my notebook, but nonetheless, in the wash of relief and gratitude that Ella was home and safe, the whole world seemed to vibrate with a possibility of goodness that only I could see.

■

The week that began with Melania Trump's breathtaking observation that a country should be judged by how it treats its citizens also began with an email from my mother's sister, announcing that she and her husband were in Paris, and would love to see me if I had time. She suggested it would be easiest to meet at Shakespeare and Company; the plan we arranged was to have a coffee at the first picturesque place we found and then to spend the afternoon wandering aimlessly. I rode the train to Saint-Michel, and from the bookstore, we set out south, into the Latin Quarter; immediately upon turning the corner we came to an elegant terrace café on a wedge of sidewalk, which was entirely empty apart from, unmistakably, sitting alone with a stack of notebooks in the shade, the author Zadie Smith.

Chuck and Susie didn't seem to recognize her. They ordered a half bottle of wine, and I ordered an espresso, and as our conversation got stalled in the phase of pleasantries, Ms. Smith sat no more than three meters away, doubtless overhearing every word we spoke; it wasn't long before I was absolutely beside myself with self-awareness, being unable, for my own part, to help overhearing every word we spoke through her ears, a kind of double-consciousness that gave our conversation the feeling of trying to run underwater, or of being chased in an anxious dream. All that was to be expected. But I wouldn't have guessed how satisfying it would be, nonetheless, to sit there in her presence, and to maybe even enter the landscape of her imagination—a landscape I'd spent so much time exploring in the pages of her books.

We spent the rest of that day wandering, as planned. And on the move our conversation became more natural: we talked about the RNC, we talked about my grandfather's career in advertising, the flooding of a few weeks prior, and the soldiers in fatigues who patrolled the streets no longer in teams of three but rather, since the attack in Nice less than a week before, in teams of four now. And we discussed my uncle's work as a test prep tutor in an anti-poverty organization in South Boston, the aim of which was to help disadvantaged students, mostly black and Latino, surmount obstacles to their advancement, as compared with my own part-time work as a tutor preparing the children of wealthy Parisians for the same tests, the effect of which work being, in essence, a deliberate reinforcement of those same obstacles—wasn't it interesting, my uncle said, lacing his fingers over his gut, that essentially we were nemeses? And though I agreed it was interesting, I had no interest in discussing it with him, though on the other hand I'd have liked very much to discuss it at length with Zadie Smith, who of course by that time was long gone.

In the narrow, crowded lanes of Île de la Cité, we walked round and round, and Chuck and Susie's tireless, well-intended questions about my life circled nearer and nearer to the heart of a matter I was unwilling to raise even with myself. How was Ella, they wanted to know. It was a question for which I had no answer, and I'd perfected the skill of burying it in the deepest recesses of my mind. Since she'd been home from the hospital she'd been acting like nothing had happened, but I couldn't tell whether she was avoiding me or herself, and I was worried about leaving for Virginia again before I found out. None of which could I convey to my aunt and uncle, except to say she was busy, that her career was taking off and for fear of losing momentum she was running herself off her feet. I'm proud of her, I said. But it's a shame. I've been here six weeks, and the only time I get to see her is when she's asleep. Before long I leave again, and then I won't even have that.

In sympathy with this predicament, they both invoked long-distance relationships of their own—not, they clarified, in their very successful marriage to each other, but in their catastrophic first marriages, though they hastened to clarify further that it hadn't been the distance that had led to the ends of those marriages, or at any rate, that it had been a combination of things. We strolled along the river on the Left Bank and on the Right Bank, and on either bank of Île Saint-Louis, and when we finally stopped to rest, it was less than fifty meters from the bookshop where we'd begun, on a bench in the shade, in the courtyard of the Église Saint-Julien-le-Pauvre, the oldest church in Paris, which was built on the ruins of a still older church where Gregory of Tours, Chuck told me, stayed in the sixth century. When, during the formation of the Third Republic, Chuck went on, the church was reassigned to the diocese of the Melkites, which is to say the Arabized Catholic Church of Turkey and the Levant, many commentators regarded it as a betrayal of the neighborhood's essential Roman Catholic character, which was how the neighborhood came to be known as Latin in the first place. In the courtyard of the church, now in service as a public park, there was a small glass memorial to French Jewish children who were transported to death camps—and in particular, French Jewish children of the fifth arrondissement, thirteen of whose names visitors were encouraged to take a moment to read.

As Chuck spoke, Susie was looking through a collection of vintage postcards she'd discovered in a little shop, and passed one to me that featured the Pont Saint-Michel, just downstream, during the famous flooding of the river in 1910. Had the flooding of a few weeks previous, she wanted to know, gotten quite so high? It hadn't quite, I said, thinking of Ella, though it had still been something to see.

■

In the days that followed, I kept inventing reasons to return to the Latin Quarter, not so much hoping to run into Ms. Smith again as taking comfort in the idea that there were traces of her nearby. Alone in the apartment, I was suspended in my distress, but out in the streets I felt lighter than myself, the city was this reservoir of potentiality where I could bob along, with my head full of high-flown thoughts I addressed to her, an act of imagination I thought she'd understand. Without being able to say quite why—thought it occurs to me now that I wasn't retracing my long riverside walk with my aunt and uncle so much as retracing my long riverside conversation with Ella the month before—I was sure no other writer could have made Paris so incandescent to me, simply by appearing before my eyes. I'd once crossed paths with Deborah Eisenberg in the Jardin du Luxembourg and come face-to-face with Richard Ford in a doorway in Montparnasse, and in neither case did I feel anything beyond the uncanny sensation of recognizing them from the jackets of their books. At an exhibit in the Pompidou, I once saw Agnès Varda, a sincere idol of mine, but for whatever reason, I was unmoved. As I walked through the gallery of Saint-Andre, I turned all this over in my mind, watching the tourists pick over the postcard shops, and settle into their chairs at the very cafés their postcards featured, and take photographs of themselves in those cafés, as if their photos would become postcards as well; and it was inconceivable to me that this idyll they'd created in their minds included patrols of soldiers in teams of four, or even three, or even that the presence of such patrols served as an assurance, as it was purportedly intended to do, that we were safe here, rather than as an insidious reminder of just the opposite: that we were vulnerable everywhere to attack by an invisible enemy, and that we required protection that only a powerful government could provide. On the internet, I discovered that Ms. Smith had in fact recently given a talk at Shakespeare and Company, where she'd remarked that it had become necessary of late for literature to intervene in the culture of our day. Whether she was thinking, when she spoke those words, of Don DeLillo, who's said about his own work that it concerns the problem of living in dangerous times, I couldn't say. But I was thinking of DeLillo now, still only a week since a man in Nice had driven his truck through more than a mile of crowd beside the beach, the aftermath of which had been documented in a horrific video Ella and I had watched almost by accident in her dark room at les Vertus within minutes of its being filmed, because it was DeLillo who'd also said that in our culture of blur and glut, the only meaningful act is the act of terror; and it was DeLillo who long before that had been hired as a junior copywriter, or so my aunt claimed within Zadie Smith's hearing, at Ogilvy, Benson & Mather, by my grandfather, a young creative director at the time with a reputation for spotting talent. Which I regretted not knowing years before, because now I remembered that I'd run into DeLillo once as well, not in Paris but in New York: not long after Ella and I were married, I dragged her to a reading at Barnes & Noble, and since we were running late and she hadn't eaten, I was carrying takeout from a budget sushi place called Sumo, where in those days we ate twice a week because it was across the street from our apartment and it was cheap and rarely made us sick. We arrived with enough time for her to eat, but it had rained briefly while we rode the train under the river, and in Union Square there was nowhere dry to sit. So I spread the shitty little smiley-face bag out on a bench, and stood over Ella as she ate her sushi with her fingers from her lap. DeLillo was on the bench across from hers, also sitting on a plastic bag. Another writer of his stature might have made some winning or salacious comment, but DeLillo only stared at us with the same naked bewilderment that appeared on every page he'd ever written, each word of which I'd read. Inside, to a packed house, he read a story called "Human Moments in World III," answered three questions from the audience, and then shyly asked the moderator if he could go home, and all the while Ella's stomach made swampy, Sumo-related noises that could be heard in every corner of the store.

■

In other words my thoughts were all in tangles. Or to put it another way, the result of my encounter with Ms. Smith was a kind of sensory and cognitive intensification, a feeling I associated with New York, with the first year of my marriage, with emerging from a movie theater into the bright day, with emerging from the subway to fresh rainfall, or with looking out the window of an airplane as it descends toward its destination—a feeling I've never been quite sure whether to call lucidity or its opposite, though it occurs to me now it might be better described as a state of psychic leisure. Maybe I just needed a chat. Maybe I was papering over my very particular distress with a gentle melancholy that made me feel sort of grand. Like I say, since she'd been home from the hospital, Ella had resumed her work with her usual consuming vigor, but between us I wasn't sure where things stood; it was soothing somehow, this spell that came over me as I drifted through her native city, where a vast matrix of invisible phenomena and relations seemed to amount to a single, total social fact. On one of those days, on the Pont Saint-Michel, I listened to a pair of children in heated debate over whether the water in the river they were looking out at flowed into the sea, or in from it, each invoking his respective teacher as the final authority, so that, although one of them was right and the other was wrong, there was no hope of the question ever being settled. Both boys appeared to be of North African descent. Not far from where they stood, I'd have liked the opportunity to point out to Ms. Smith, there was a plaque commemorating the 1961 murder of some two hundred supporters of the Front de Libération Nationale, who had taken to the streets in peaceful protest of the curfew applied to *all Algerian Muslim workers, French Muslims, and French Muslims of Algeria* by the then prefect of police, Maurice Papon. The population of Algerian Muslims then living in Paris lived in fact not in Paris but overwhelmingly in the shantytowns that surrounded it, which the government had erected in the period between World Wars to accommodate an influx of African men, whom it had funneled there to augment the diminished labor force, with the expectation that when the work of rebuilding the country was complete these men would return from whence they came, instead of sending for their wives and kids. For the Algerians who marched in three giant columns from the systemically enforced obscurity of these banlieues toward the center of the city that night in 1961, it must have felt like something of a triumph to discover they were tens of thousands strong; contained in any exchange of glances would have been the hope that they, French citizens, after all, would finally become impossible to ignore. Papon, who'd recently been awarded the Legion of Honor, would later be convicted of crimes against humanity for his cooperation in administering the transport of Jews to death camps, but never in his lifetime was he held to account for his instructions that protesters in violation of his eight thirty curfew be beaten, tortured, and shot, and then summarily dumped into the Seine, either alive with their hands tied to ensure their drowning, or already dead and stripped of any papers or belongings that could be used to identify their bodies when they washed up on the banks, as they inevitably continued to do for weeks, all of which, the entire affair, proved to be a matter of such indifference in the general public conscience that the government's massive and clumsy attempt to cover it up went unchallenged for forty years. The plaque, installed in 2001, reads in full, *À LA MÉMOIRE DES NOMBREUX ALGÉRIENS TUÉS LORS DE LA SANGLANTE RÉPRESSION DE LA MANIFESTATION PACIFIQUE DU 17 OCTOBRE 1961*, and is the closest the French government has ever come to acknowledging its role in the massacre, which, though it doesn't acknowledge the French government's role in the massacre at all, nonetheless enraged many commentators and politicians at the time, because in their eyes it supported terrorism, promoted civil unrest, and above all encouraged disrespect for the police.

The teachers of the boys who were arguing which way the river flowed weren't likely to give conflicting accounts of these events; the massacre isn't taught in schools. I'd learned about it from Ella's dad, an Algerian Jew who moved to France after the war and who, the week of the massacre, celebrated his thirteenth birthday in the Parisian suburb of Créteil. Even now, he'd once told me, when he brought the events of that week up in certain company, he often found himself met with blank, dismissive stares, and this was because, he explained, it's so difficult for anyone as extensively educated in French history as most French people are to imagine there's anything of importance they don't already know. On the bridge, tourists gave a wide berth to the two boys, who'd worked themselves by this point into a chuffing rage. It seemed like only a matter of time before they'd come to blows. Everywhere you look, I remembered my uncle saying at the café—his mustache damp with wine, his fanny pack riding up past his belly button, and whether within Ms. Smith's hearing or after she'd left I couldn't recall—everywhere you look and see an unbridgeable chasm of difference you'll find a misunderstanding that can be traced back to everyone's earliest days in school. To which I'd added, either because Ms. Smith was still there to hear or because I was already locked into a habit of imagining she was there to hear, that for example the introduction of religious teachings into a secular system of education, for the purpose of consolidating the support of the rural poor, a pillar of GOP strategy since Nixon that had finally yielded Donald Trump, was also crucial to Erdogan's ascendancy in Turkey, where, I said, since the attempted coup d'état a week before, nearly forty thousand teachers had been fired or placed on leave. Whether the boys came to blows I never found out: their voices faded into the background, and the noise of the rest of the world faded away as well. An image of Ella had appeared in my mind, at the moment she awoke in the hospital, before she knew where she was or what had happened, and her eyes searched the room until they found mine; I went down to the river and stood staring at the dull surface for a long while, imagining the silence beneath it, and waiting to see a reflection of the world that never appeared.

■

That night, I had drinks with Azra and Pauls, and I described the scene to them much as I've described it here. Where was Ella, they wanted to know, why was it they never saw her anymore? She was working, I said, my eyes getting damp; she was always working, or doing things related to her work, or related to securing future work, or going to the theater alone. And when would she be joining me in Virginia? Maybe never, I said, but seeing the alarm in their eyes I explained that she kept getting calls for jobs, and wouldn't be spending August and September with me as planned; I hoped she'd visit me in October, but if she was hired onto another production, she'd have to stay, she wasn't established enough yet to be turning anything down, so that when I left the following week, it wouldn't be certain when we'd see each other again. And also there was the problem of her green card status to clear up, I added, and I went on like this for who knows how long, explaining the external circumstances that made Ella's return to the US uncertain. But the longer I went on, the more obvious it became that it wasn't really external circumstances I was really worried about—obvious to me and, I could see now, obvious to Pauls and Azra as well, I could see it was making them uncomfortable, and I changed the subject to an essay Azra was writing about the disappearance of an asylum seeker at whose hearings she'd served as an interpreter.

We were in a place called Les Grands Voisins, the site of a defunct hospital, Hôpital Saint-Vincent-de-Paul, the vacant grounds of which had been overrun by a gang of industrious hippies who, over the past year, had put every wing of every building to use in hippie enterprises, none of which smelled quite the way you'd expect. There were campsites available for twenty-two euros per night, which included a tent, access to a shower and toilet, wi-fi, a pedal-operated washing machine, and a coffee and croissant per camper each morning. There was a thrift store, a bar, a restaurant, a canteen, numerous studio galleries, workshops, office space for monthly rent, another restaurant, another bar, various plots for urban farming, urban beekeeping, urban husbandry, beer that could be won by answering trivia questions that cost a euro to hear, a Russian steam bath, open-air barbering, yoga of all sorts, craft, dance, music, and language lessons of all sorts, parking for caravans, an ice cream truck that had been converted into a Balkan history center, hundreds of places to sit, and all of which leaving plenty of room for, in the whole of the two main buildings, actual squatters, which is to say people squatting of necessity, many of whom were asylum seekers from Syria, Iraq, Afghanistan, Libya, Nigeria, the upkeep of whose quarters all this hippie stuff was meant to support, and who themselves led many of the more popular workshops, which were subscribed through the end of the year. That day in fact there was a Syrian culture festival, organized and run by the hospital's Syrian residents, and a Syrian DJ was making beats for a series of men, presumably also Syrian, as well as a few women; it gave me a terrific feeling to observe how well the sound of Arabic in all its natural percussiveness lent itself to the form. All of this, the entire scene, I thought that Zadie Smith, whose brothers are rappers in English, would appreciate for the way it transformed the white-savior industrial complex into an actual complex where to partake of an idea of oneself as a white savior, it was unavoidable not only to do so in the context of undeniably privileged material consumption, and not only to sincerely interact with and learn about foreign cultures, but also to submit to a hierarchy in which the members of those cultures held all the cards.

What's more, I found myself saying aloud to Pauls and Azra—and here I did actually find myself looking around the courtyard half expecting to find her—Ms. Smith was bound to appreciate the entire scene for the fact that many of the people who were here spending money, a lot of whom, it bears mentioning, weren't white, had quite possibly been born in this very hospital. To make up for having interrupted Azra—who'd been saying that since the failed coup the week before, she'd been having a hard time focusing on her essay, or on really much of anything at all, beyond reading the news and fretting over her emails to and from her father, an academic many of whose closest friends and colleagues had been indefinitely suspended from teaching and barred from leaving the country—I launched into a lengthy account of the fascination with Ms. Smith that had resulted from my having crossed paths with her a few days before. How to explain, I asked, the importance I'd attached to this encounter? The two of them, exchanging glances, looked at me with open pity. They didn't know me that well, but they could see that I was flailing and felt an obligation to be supportive. I'd been worrying at the bite mark on my neck, which had turned a jaundiced color. Something about the look in Pauls's and Azra's eyes made it plain to me that in fact I badly needed support, that I had a lot on my mind I wanted to talk about and I didn't really know how, that even if I did know how it would be impossible to do so without violating Ella's privacy and even my own, that I badly wanted people to know that I was in pain, that Ella was in pain, but that I didn't want to disclose the source of that pain, it was just too raw. Wasn't it possible, suggested Azra, that my fixation on Zadie Smith was related to certain details of her biography that she shared with my own wife, an experience of the world that was beyond my reach, such as the fact of their both being descended from Caribbean slaves on their mothers' sides, their both harboring an abiding fondness for the working-class immigrant districts in which they'd been raised, their both having expended considerable energy in understanding and articulating the internal pressures that afflict mixed-race children in mixed-race homes, their both having weathered this pressure, throughout their lives, with grace and equanimity? No, I said, I didn't think that was it at all. Pauls's and Azra's glasses had been empty for some time, and I wondered if I should give them an opening to call it a night. A large line was forming for merguez, and when the smell of it reached us I realized I couldn't think of the last time I'd had anything to eat. A small flock of sheep went past, it was hard to tell who was leading them. Azra began a story about her landlady being Islamophobic: Of course I don't mean *you*, she'd always say. I lapsed into silence, thinking now not of where Zadie Smith might be, but where Ella might be, and why we never saw her anymore—after everything she'd been through, how could I bear to be away from her for months on end? A young man walked by in a t-shirt that bore the image of Donald Trump, which the three of us each saw at the same time. He must have been Spanish, or maybe Italian, and whether he was aware of the disconnect between whatever levels of irony he intended by wearing such a shirt in this place and the palpable effect his wearing the shirt was having on people around him wasn't clear. He was grotesquely pimpled, wedging his merguez sandwich into his mouth and tearing it apart with his teeth. Islamophobia, Pauls was saying, is as French as pomme chaussée. On the beaches in places like Nice, I'd read somewhere, women had been banned from wearing what were called burquinis, on the extremely French premise that this protected women's rights, when of course what was really being protected was the right of non-Muslim beachgoers not to be confronted with expressions of Islamic faith. All week in Cleveland, Trump had been rising in the polls on the strength of his continued assurance that he'd keep his constituents safe, by which he meant roughly that he'd enact a sort of vengeance on their behalf. Brexit was a wake-up call, Pauls was saying in his patient, professorial way when my attention returned to the present moment, for the following reasons, America isn't going to make the same mistake. But I didn't catch the reasons, I was thinking again about the moment Ella awoke: I was thinking that I'd lived that awful night inside the fear of losing her, without realizing that if she survived I might lose her nonetheless. Pauls and Azra, their glasses still empty, stole occasional glances at my own glass, which, if they were in a pessimistic frame of mind, they probably saw as half full. I wondered what would become of the kid in the Trump shirt, in a cosmic sense, and for that matter what would become of the sheep, also in that sense. If it's true we're living in dangerous times, I said to myself then, because I still believed that Zadie Smith could hear my thoughts, it's worth asking: Dangerous for whom? When I got home Ella was already asleep, and because I knew in the morning she'd rise and go before I woke, I sat by the edge of the bed and watched her for a time, and wondered about her dreams. The lightness of her breathing, the openness of her face, the warmth of her body, crowded everything else inside me out. In her sleep, as I settled into bed, she registered my presence, and threw her arm around me, held me close, would not let go, and so for a long time I lay awake, watching clouds move past our skylight in silhouette, and listening to pigeons rustle their wings.

■

Was it that day or the next that I packed my bags? Because I couldn't stand to be alone in the house with them, I went out one last time to wander, taking the train into the center of the city, walking along the river, past the bookshop, and coming finally into the wedge of park that adjoined the Église Saint-Julien-le-Pauvre, from which the wedge of sidewalk where I'd sat in the presence of Zadie Smith could be seen. Among other Juliens, the church is named for Julien l'Hospitalier, the former nobleman who features in the second of Flaubert's *Three Tales*, whose good works included the ferrying of sick and indigent wanderers across the river, putting them up in the hospice he'd set up on the far side, as he is pictured doing in a thirteenth-century bas-relief that can still be found above the doorway of a cabaret theater around the corner from the church that bears his name. Beside the decrepit church, I found a tourist taking a photograph of a sign; as I stood reading the sign she'd photographed, which turned out to forbid urination on the church walls, I heard the sound, from an open window, of voices joined in singing the familiar spiritual "Down by the Riverside," which in its baptismal imagery connects sleep, and dreams of peace, with the crossing of the river Jordan to the Promised Land. This was the first number in a performance by a Congolese gospel choir, the Legend Singers, which had just gotten under way, and though I didn't recognize the songs that followed, they were without exception slower than the one they'd started with, and exceedingly beautiful—expressions of the same profound sorrow that became the basis for the blues. I stood listening there beneath the window for a long time, watching a little boy no more than three years old kicking a rubber ball around the courtyard, while a woman I assumed was his mother sat nearby reading a translation of *Song of Solomon*. This boy and his ball became the small element of chaos that connected the various strangers seated on benches and in the grass all around, who were all eventually called upon to return it whenever it came their way. A pressure was mounting in my chest, and I realized I was in danger of bursting into tears, and a moment returned to me from an interview Zadie Smith had given on the *Charlie Rose* show more than a decade before, in which her voice brimmed over with emotion in expressing her belief that the writing and reading of fiction were, as she put it, a great good in the world, a premise I despaired of having grown to mistrust.

The next morning, after another sleepless night, I rose, well before dawn, and ordered a cab to the airport. I didn't know if Ella would want to be woken, her first day on still another job would begin a few hours later, but I couldn't help pressing my lips to her forehead, to her cheeks, very lightly to the lids of her eyes. Only once the cab was waiting for me in the street, and I'd hoisted my bags onto my shoulders and left my key by the door, did I hear her footfall behind me. My love? she said, and I turned, and she sprinkled me with water from the tap—a farewell ritual that came to her, by way of her grandmother, from Algeria. My love, she said again, and I turned to her, to be sprinkled with water once more. We repeated this sequence a third and final time, and then, finally, we said that we loved each other, and I went down.

And then in the window seat at the rear of my plane, where I'd spent most of my flight with my notes, at last I put my pencil down to look out over the landscape of Quebec and New Brunswick, where, between me and the Saint Lawrence Estuary, a seemingly endless series of lakes and the network of rivers and streams that connect them were at times difficult to distinguish from the shadows the clouds cast on the earth. And of course the clouds themselves fascinated me, in the way they hung motionless in empty space—one in particular, a long, straight, and seemingly endless stripe, which at a certain moment passed within wing distance of my plane, the contrail, I realized, of another plane, which must have passed that way not too long before—how startling it was to see such a vivid demonstration of the traces of other lives I so often suspected my own course through the world of intersecting. At length my thoughts returned to the flood my aunt had asked me about, when the Seine had swelled its banks and risen higher than it had since 1910—it had been a passing reference to this recent flood that had been the cause of the disagreement between the two boys on the bridge: Where had all that water gone, where had it come from in the first place? It was true that it was dizzying to think of it that way: to think that all the water on the planet formed a single, zero-sum system that with the application of enough brainpower could be kept track of. As the water rose, the prime minister admitted that it would be a long time before things returned to normal. The president visited the Louvre for a photo op with the art handlers who'd begun preemptively to move things to higher floors. Together, that same week, they announced the extension of the emergency suspension of civil liberties that had been in effect since the attacks of November. As the water reached its highest point, Ella and I walked along beside it, and I watched her smile at how ordinary life had become suspended, how a hush pervaded even in the densest crowds, how the gray sky brought the world close. She peered into each of the quiet faces that passed her, and when I saw how each one renewed an expression on her own face that hung between delight and mischief, I knew that without her to crowd the things inside me out, I would be lost. I watched her turn, on the Pont Saint-Michel, where an old man, though he couldn't himself have remembered, was pointing out to her how much higher the water had risen a century before; she turned to me, and waved, and then a month passed, the water receded, no one knew to where, and I began my descent.

Acknowledgments

Thank you first of all to the many people who ushered this thing into existence: especially my agent, Jackie Ko, who took the project on when it was still just a chapter and some loose talk, and stuck with it for many more years than most sensible people would; and my editor, Brandon Taylor, whose intellect and sensitivity gave the book new textures and dimensions, on the page and in my own mind; and the entire team at Unnamed, with special thanks to Allison Miriam Woodnutt, who's done so much to find the book a place in the wider world.

I'm enormously grateful to the many wonderful teachers I've had over the years, and without guidance from Rob Cohen, Jeff Allen, and Jane Alison I would be no kind of writer at all. I'd also like to thank Dinaw Mengestu for his thoughtful feedback on an early chapter of the book, and for his general encouragement and kindness.

Thanks are due, as well, to The Paris Review for publishing an excerpt of the book long before it was finished.

The volume in your hands would be a great deal slimmer and duller without the numerous scholars, journalists, and critics whose work I consulted. To name only a few, they include: Joshua Cole, Robin Banton, Seth Graebner, Jim House and Neil MacMaster on French colonialism and the Algerian War of Independence; Adam Shatz on Frantz Fanon; W.G. Beasley, Jilly Traganou, and Donald Keene on Edo and Meiji Japan; Dorothy E. Roberts on both child welfare and *Loving v. Virginia*; Christopher R. Leslie and Jennifer Ware *et al* on *Loving v. Virginia*; Chamyl Boutaleb and Richard Boyd on Alexis de Toqueville; David Soll on the New

York water system; Earl Swift's excellent *Chesapeake Requiem: A Year with the Watermen of Vanishing Tangier Island*. Quotations from the book on dreams in the fourth chapter are from the extraordinarily weird *Dream Life: An Experimental Memoir*, by J. Allan Hobson; the character in this book to whom those quotations are attributed is otherwise completely fictional. A full bibliography is available by email.

I owe a huge debt to Emina Ćerimović, a complete stranger who was exceedingly generous with her time and expertise, and who entrusted to me a story I'd never have dared try to tell without her help. To the character who shares her first name, the real Emina lent authorship of a scathing report on the detention center in Macedonia, along with her moral seriousness and other obvious virtues; the character's vices, routines, habits, and social persona, on the other hand, are hers alone.

The narrator of this book alludes liberally, by way of approximate quotation, to the works of Susan Sontag, John Berger, Theodor Adorno, and Walter Benjamin, among others; these allusions generally appear in proximity to mention of their authors; a list of citations is available by email.

Thank you to Ben Samuel and Annie Hylton quite simply for their friendship.

My favorite people in the whole process of writing this book are my early readers: Helen Chandler, Adam Roux, and Piers Gelly provided especially helpful feedback, as did Zach Fox, Will Hunt, and Pwaangulongii Dauod. Thanks also to Ayşegül Savaş and Andrew Martin for the warmth and generosity of their insight and counsel.

Un immense merci à Victoryah Lupapa, l'une de mes personnes préférées au monde, qui a pris les seules photos de moi que j'ai jamais appréciées, dont celle qui apparaît sur la jaquette de ce livre.

And of course, my family: Mom, Dad, Mike, Pete, and Emma, for decade upon decade of support and faith.

And most of all: Lola, my love. You are magnificent. It's a poor reward for everything you put up with, but this book is for you.